# RUNAWAY TRAIN

### *A NOVEL*

## S. W. CAPPS

D. X. VAROS

Book cover design and layout by, Ellie Bockert
Augsburger of Creative Digital Studios.
www.CreativeDigitalStudios.com
Cover design features:
Home Video Camera by BillionPhotos.com / Adobe
Stock; Rear view of walking businessman, isolated by
denisismagilov / Adobe Stock; High resolution fire
collection isolated on black background By Jag_cz /
Adobe Stock; White van isolated on white. Rear view.
Delivery and carrying transportation concept. By
Maksym Yemelyanov / Adobe Stock; Black microphone
with blank box on the blue background. News concept.
3 By Foxstudio / Adobe Stock; Territory of abandoned
industrial area waiting for demolition. Broken and burnt
buildings. Former Voronezh excavator factory By Mulder
photo / Adobe Stock; Building fire among fields and
huge black smoke cloud by leszekglasner / Adobe Stock.

ISBN
978-1-955065-04-7 (paperback)
978-1-955065-05-4 (ebook)

**THE FAIRNESS DOCTRINE**

*All radio and television stations must present controversial issues of public importance in an honest, equitable, and balanced manner.*

Established by FCC, 1949

Abolished by FCC, 1987

# CHAPTER 1

*August 1987*

*(NEWSWIRE): PRES. REAGAN PROPOSES CEASE-FIRE BETWEEN SANDINISTA GOVERNMENT AND CONTRA REBELS ... DOW JONES INDUSTRIAL AVERAGE REACHES ALL-TIME HIGH OF 2,722 ... BROADCASTERS BEGIN AIRING NEWS WITHOUT 'FAIRNESS DOCTRINE' RESTRICTIONS*

August in Oklahoma. Hell couldn't be much hotter.

As he pulled into the gas station, sweat dripped from his forehead to his chin. He wiped it with the back of his hand. It was a big day, one he'd dreamed of—and feared—for as long as he could remember. The day Stacy Zwardowski would finally become a man.

"Fill 'er up?"

"Please." He stared through the grimy windshield. In the distance, a marquee flashed 90 degrees, but the humidity made it feel like 120. Stacy adjusted his tie, glancing at the suitcase on the floor, the maps in the backseat, the wind-blown banners above. *How had he gotten here?* It was a bit of a blur.

He'd been working two jobs in Portland, the kind a kid gets to fill the gap between college and career—one in a fast-food restaurant, the other in a used bookstore —the paychecks giving him just enough money to help his mom with groceries and buy beer. When he wasn't working, he was writing, reading a book, or shooting hoops.

The last summer of childhood.

The call came on a Monday morning. "This is Terrance Meeks," the man said. Half asleep, Stacy struggled to make sense of his words. "I had a chance to review your tape. You're a little rough around the edges, but I think you show promise." The news director broke into a memorized spiel about the TV station and the requirements of the job. His philosophy was simple. "We give viewers 'News They Can Use'." Stacy had no idea what that meant, but an interview was set for the following Monday, enough time for him to buy a cheap suit and make the three-day drive over two mountain ranges and seven states. He'd pulled into Avalon late last night, tired, hungry, and nearly out of money. If things didn't go well, he wasn't sure he could get back home.

The nozzle clicked, the hammer of a gun. Stacy rolled down the window, taking in the endless horizon. Not a mountain in sight. Not even a molehill. Then again, no self-respecting mole would ever put up with this heat.

"Twelve even," the attendant drawled.

Stacy handed him a twenty. "Channel Eight's up the road?"

"You on TV?"

"Just an interview." He grabbed the change and steered past the pumps.

On the radio, Exposé sang *Point of No Return*. "Good morning, Avalon!" a voice rattled the speakers. "Time for a KAVN news update. I'm Nate Shefler. On this final day of August, a Dexter County jury..."

Stacy killed the radio as a row of satellite dishes came into view. He squinted to read the sign—*KEGT-TV CHANNEL 8*.

*This was it.*

After letting a truck full of chickens pass, he turned into the lot, glancing at his watch—eleven on the nose. He grabbed his coat and hurried up the walk.

\*\*\*

The doors wheezed open as 'Stormy' Raines stepped on the mat. His mother had nicknamed him 'Stormy', a reference to his cloudy gray eyes. His real name was Vernon. After a beat, he moved inside, the cold air embracing him like a dead relative. He looked left, right, then pulled a cart from the waiting arsenal. The air smelled of fresh-baked bread, Boston's *Peace of Mind* playing over the Muzak.

As he moved to the Produce section, he passed a balding store manager and bagger. Gripping the cart's steel handle, he made his way to a fruit display, the enclosure housing colorful rows of oranges, lemons, grapefruit. "How ya'll doin'?" a man in a blue smock asked over a hill of bananas.

Raines ignored him, moving from Produce to Meat & Poultry. As he grabbed a bloody pork shoulder, his image danced off the chrome. The supermarket was quiet this morning. Only four customers. A woman and her child. An old man with a walker. And 'Stormy' Raines.

He moved up one aisle and down the next, collecting items. A jar of pickled okra. A tin of smoked sardines. His feet ached in his stiff leather shoes. He'd worn them just twice before. Once at his wife's funeral. Again on his silver anniversary at the Uniroyal plant, a job he'd hated for twenty-five years.

"Clean-up on aisle six," a loudspeaker crackled. He heard nothing. There was a buzz in his head, a tingling in his flesh. As he made his way down the last aisle, sweat pooled in his concave chest. He'd always been a frail man. A weak man. But not today.

He tossed one more article in the basket, a jar of gefilte fish in liquid broth. The floating tissue looked like chunks of human brain.

"I can help ya," an attractive checker spoke up. He pushed the cart to her register. "Shoppin' for the missus today?" She smiled, her lips parting to reveal a wad of gum. She had big brown eyes—deer's eyes.

He reached in his coat and pulled out a .44 Magnum. As the woman gasped, he squeezed the trigger and watched her fall.

\*\*\*

"You must be Stacy."

Stacy nodded and stood, all six-foot-three inches of him. The man coming toward him was forty-something and crimson-cheeked. He wore loose slacks and a tie that looked like a gift.

"Terrance Meeks. We spoke on the phone. You're a tall one."

"Pleasure to meet you, sir." Stacy studied his expression. The interviewer looked more nervous than the interviewee.

"Come with me." He tore out for the hall, Stacy hurrying after him. "Sorry to rush you, but we've got a situation."

"Oh, that's..." The man stopped at a door marked *ENGINEERS*.

4

"Wait here." He stepped inside, Stacy peering through the crack. "Unit eight ready?" A slovenly tech pointed to a camera in the corner. "Ever use an Ikegami 730?" Before Stacy could answer, Meeks shot past him, camera in tow. "Pretty simple," he called over his shoulder, disappearing in a closet at the end of the hall. By the time Stacy caught up, the man had stuffed a bag to capacity. "Shouldn't need more than two camera batteries. Gave you an extra for the deck, too."

"But..." Stacy's face grew hot. "...I'm here for an *interview*."

"Congratulations, kid. You got the job. Now where's your car?"

"My car?"

He grabbed a tripod and deck, pushing his way past. "Yeah. I apologize, but I've got two reporters sick and everyone else out on assignment." He lowered his shoulder against the door, sunlight beckoning. "Nearest crew's in Tishomingo, a good half-hour from here." Stacy followed him outside. "All our news cars are gone. You'll have to use your own today."

As they reached the lot, Stacy scraped to a halt. "Sir." The news director turned, a look of impatience replacing the one of worry. "I've never...I mean, this is my first—"

"I know, kid, but that's the nature of the beast." Despite the heat, the first-time reporter shivered. "Which one's yours?" Stacy pointed to his '76 Celica. As they loaded equipment, the man spewed instructions. "When you get there, set up the tripod and mount the camera. Deck's ready to go. Camera needs a battery." He slammed the trunk. "When you're ready to roll, just hit the black button."

"But..." It was all happening too fast. "...what about a monitor?"

5

"We don't use monitors. And your deck only records. There's no playback, rewind, or fast-forward."

"Then how do I check footage?"

"You don't." He opened the door and shoved Stacy inside. "Take a right out of the lot. It's a mile down on your left side."

"*What* is?"

Meeks looked more nervous than ever. "A shooting. At the Super-K Market." Stacy gulped. "And don't forget to white balance."

\*\*\*

The manager's glazed eyes stared at nothing. He was dead before he hit the floor.

'Stormy' Raines moved from the checkout stand to the Produce section, proud of his efficiency. Two bullets. Two bodies. His gait was smooth, his senses heightened. He could smell every vegetable—onions, asparagus. He could taste them—eggplant, tomatoes, butternut squash.

A sudden move caught his attention, the Produce manager darting from one display to another. The frightened employee took refuge behind a mountain of potatoes, the Lord's Prayer on his lips.

Raines moved left, gun drawn. He'd never killed anyone before today, never even struck a man in anger. He was making up for lost time.

The man in the blue smock bolted for the door, catching the gunman by surprise. Raines fired but missed, shattering a jar of salad dressing. He thought about going after him, but there was more prey nearby. Easier prey.

As the Muzak droned on, he heard the faint sound of whimpering. The noise grew louder as he approached the Dairy section. Behind a refrigerator, a woman and her child cowered, praying the gunman would miss them.

6

He didn't.

Raines drew down on the pair, his eyes two stagnant pools. "Run, Breanna..." The woman shoved her four-year-old daughter away. "*Run, dammit!*" Darting off, the girl heard the sound of a gunshot behind her. And no further instructions from her mother.

\*\*\*

The sky over Super-K Market was the perfect blue of a Hollywood backdrop.

But this was no movie.

Stacy's hands shook as he steered the Celica into the lot. Screeching to a stop, he dashed to the trunk. Adrenaline was in charge now. He could feel his arteries expanding, hear blood rushing through his ears. A shot rang out as he raised the lid.

"Are you fuckin' nuts?" Stacy turned to find a cop heading straight for him. "Move the hell back! You wanna get yourself killed?"

"No, sir." He dropped back twenty yards and began assembling his gear. The tripod was easy enough. He spread the legs and dropped it. The camera came next. *How the hell did it fit on the tripod?* After three attempts, he locked it in place.

Another shot rang out as he reached for the deck, his skin turning to gooseflesh. To the left, cops hunkered down, guns drawn. To the right, officials set up a makeshift control center. Every few seconds, a new vehicle sped into the lot, sirens screaming. Stacy looked around as he attached the camera cable.

*He was the first journalist to arrive!*

"This is Sergeant David Eckles of the Avalon Police Department," a bullhorn sounded. Stacy slammed a tape in the deck. "Give yourself up." He hit the camera's power

7

switch. Nothing. "Come out with your hands in the air."
He hit it again. Still nothing. *What the hell was wrong?*
As he moved for a closer look, he kicked the bag at his
feet—*ouch*—a battery! He grabbed the brick and locked it
in place, the viewfinder leaping to life. *Yes!*

Aiming the camera at the gun-toting officers, he hit
the black button, the deck clicking, then humming. He
stared through the little window. *Tape was rolling!*
Panning the camera, he captured a wide shot of the store.
He rolled on the sign, the man with the bullhorn, a young
bagger fleeing from an exit. How he maintained his
composure, he didn't know. But one thing was certain—
Stacy Zwardowski, *TV reporter*, was doing his job.

\*\*\*

When the old man heard the first shot, he knew he was in
trouble. He couldn't move quickly, not with a walker. As
he inched forward, he heard a second shot, then a third.

A fourth shot sounded as he reached the checkout
stand, ten feet from freedom. But his walker snagged the
leg of a candy rack. 'Stormy' Raines fired, blood spraying
the register, walker collapsing under the weight of the
body. Admiring his deed, he heard the commotion
outside—the sirens, the screeching tires, the cop on the
bullhorn. None of it stopped him. He still had work to do.

Making his way up the center aisle, he listened for
little feet. As he reached the turnaround, he spied the
overhead mirror. The circular glass held the image of the
little girl, her body reduced to a fetal ball. Raines stepped
around the corner, stopping in front of her. She'd lost a
shoe somewhere. And she held a fuzzy gold duck to her
chest, plucked from the stuffed animal rack behind her.

As he took aim, the pair locked eyes. He wanted her to look away—needed her to—but she refused. "Why?" she uttered.

He held the gun till it shook. "Stop looking at me!" he screamed. The girl held her stare. "Stop it, *goddammit!*"

"Come out with your hands in the air!" a voice echoed around him. "I repeat. Drop your weapon and come outside. Hands where we can see them." He stared at the little girl, wanting desperately to hold her now, to tell her how sorry he was for taking her mother. But what good would that do? He raised the gun and fired the rest of his bullets at the ceiling, offering a primordial scream that released the last few ounces of pain he was holding onto.

With nothing left, he headed for the door.

\*\*\*

Stacy winced at the bone-chilling scream. He wasn't alone. Even to the casehardened eyes of the law enforcement community, the unfolding scene was a disturbing one.

As the standoff continued, more media began to arrive. A reporter from the *Avalon Herald*. Nate Shefler from KAVN. A maroon van with the words *KPXZ-TV* on the side. "Channel 8 first on scene?" the driver sniped. "Now, *that's* a story!"

Stacy ignored him, pretending to focus. But as he stared at the viewfinder, he saw a man emerge from the market. He wore a rumpled coat and shiny shoes, hands hanging loosely at his sides. One was empty. The other held a .44 Mag.

"Hold it right there!" the bullhorn sounded. Stacy's heart leaped to his throat. "Drop your weapon!" Cops took aim. The suspect didn't move. "I repeat. Drop your weapon and put your hands in the air!" Still no movement. To the left, an officer crouched behind a shield. To the right, a sniper stared through paper-thin crosshairs. "You're completely surr—"

The perp raised his gun, shots exploding on all sides. The first bullet struck him in the chest, the next in the head. In all, they'd find nine slugs in 'Stormy' Raines' body, but eight were unnecessary. The sniper was lightning quick. And deadly.

The gunman sagged to the ground, blood pouring like tomato juice down the curb. Stacy's eyes locked on the image. *Could this really be happening?* It was the stuff of nightmares, but it *was* happening. And he had the video—he checked to make sure he was still rolling—*yes*, he had the video to prove it.

As police swarmed the body, Stacy forced himself to zoom, then pulled back for crowd shots. Heart pounding, he unlatched the camera and moved left for a better angle. But as he dropped to a knee, he felt a tap on his shoulder. Looking into the sun, he saw the glowing face of a female reporter. She had dazzling green eyes and near-perfect teeth, her chestnut hair holding firm against the wind. "Katie Powers," she introduced herself. "We got here fast as we could, but the road from Tishomingo's a two-lane." An obese camera op came up behind her, breathing hard and eating an Eskimo Pie. "This is Bub. He'll take over for you."

"But I don't..." Stacy climbed to his feet.

The woman smiled, an efficient smile that told the world she was going places. "Terrance sent us." He still looked confused. "Terrance Meeks. Our news director." He glanced at the pin on her chest—a gold *8*. "He needs you back at the station to go live at noon."

*Live? On day one?*

He handed her the camera and turned for the car.

10

"Aren't you forgetting something?" He looked back, having no idea what she was talking about. She smiled again. "Your tape."

"Oh…" Stacy felt like an idiot. "…right."

He punched the *EJECT* button. When the cassette unspooled, he pulled it out and walked away. "You might want to hustle, sweetie. You're on in half-an-hour."

\*\*\*

Meeks shoved the tape in a machine. "Okay…" He glanced at the clock, a cigarette dangling from his lip. "…we've got fifteen minutes to air, and you're the lead. I'll have Randy slam this together while you write the script."

Stacy felt his heart race again. He'd come here for a simple interview, and now, an hour later, was about to walk onto a set and tell thousands of people about the most horrific thing he'd ever seen. *Could he really do this?*

If he expected to make it in this business, he'd better do it.

"Here." Meeks grabbed a Steno and ripped away the top page. "I phoned Avalon P.D. and got some more details."

Stacy stared at the scribbled notes. *Shooting began at eleven. Motive unknown. 4 bodies.* It wasn't much to go on, but he'd seen enough in person to fill in the gaps.

"Shit!" Stacy looked up to see Meeks adjust the monitors, both a dull dark blue. Deep within the azure sea, he saw silhouettes—police officers, the front of a market, the Super-K sign.

"What's wrong with the TVs?"

As Randy the editor sneered, Meeks took a drag. "What did you white balance on?"

Stacy's palms grew moist. In college, he'd shot all his stories on VHS. The tapes were inexpensive, the cameras

11

simple. Just focus and shoot. He had no idea what a white balance was. "I...uh..."

"Randy..." Meeks' brain kicked into high gear. "...we shot a feature at Super-K last month. Throw some exteriors together and we'll run with it." As the man darted off, Stacy swallowed hard, his boss offering a conciliatory smile. "No worries, kid. I'll take the fall for you on this one. Just don't let it happen again." He flicked ash, cutting his eyes to the clock. "You better get busy."

Stacy nodded, heading to a typewriter. As he fed the machine, he stared at the page, mind blank. "No," he whispered. *Not writer's block.* "Not now." Sweat beaded on his forehead, the clock ticking unmercifully. Ten minutes to twelve. Nine-and-a-half. "Come on, think." He'd written hundreds of stories in school, thousands maybe. If there was one thing in the world he felt comfortable doing, it was writing. He glanced at the notes. *4 bodies.* A sentence bloomed. *FOUR PEOPLE ARE DEAD, THEIR ONLY CRIME—BEING IN THE WRONG PLACE AT THE WRONG TIME.*

The rest of the story flowed easily. As he typed the last word, someone strode into the room. "Where's my lead?" Stacy yanked the script. The man had blonde hair and orange skin, Kleenex protruding from his collar like the peels of an onion. "Raul Guttierez." *Funny, he didn't look Hispanic.* "I anchor at noon and six. You ready?" Stacy nodded, grabbing his coat. "What about makeup?"

"Makeup?"

Raul reached in his pocket and pulled out a compact. "You can use mine today, but you'll need to get your own." Stacy took it—reluctantly. "Bathroom's up the hall. Make it quick." He headed for the set, Stacy staring at the thin pink canister in his hand.

*This would be a first.*

To his relief, the restroom was empty. He looked in the mirror, applying makeup to his forehead and cheeks, then rolled his eyes. His face had an orange tint to it. He could've passed for Raul's brother. As he ran a comb through his hair, the door flew open, a skittish floor director leaning in. "Two minutes."

\*\*\*

Stacy trembled as he took his seat at the anchor desk. It would've been easy to blame the air conditioning, but he couldn't lie to himself. *He was scared to death!*

"You'll do fine," Raul spoke up. "Just wait for my cue." Stacy nodded, looking around the room. The set was small and sterile, the flimsy walls painted with italicized 8s. To the left, a green screen dwarfed everything in front of it. To the right, a separate set featured two chairs and a plant. There were three cameras in the room, one for the establishing shot, two for close-ups.

"Minute-thirty," the floor director announced.

"You want to run through this once?" the anchor asked.

"You read my mind!" Meeks butted in, snuffing out a cigarette on his way to the set. "First time out, never hurts to do a run-through."

"I'll say it doesn't." The three of them turned, a hawkish man in an expensive suit approaching from the left. He had an air about him that said, 'I'm better than you, and don't forget it.' "Thad Barker. Meteorologist." He smiled, one eyebrow arched. "Why, I'll never forget my first—"

"I'm sure it's a great story, Thad," Meeks humored him, "but we're fighting the clock here." The man shrugged and walked off. "Okay, let's try it."

13

Raul read the lead-in with mock enthusiasm. As he finished, he turned to Stacy. "I'm sorry, what was your name again?"

"Stacy Zwardowski."

"Stacy...Zu—?"

"That's not going to work," Meeks intervened. "First name's too effeminate. Last name's too...*Polish*. What's your middle name?"

"My what?"

"One minute," the floor director barked.

"Your middle name. What is it?"

"It's..." Stacy hesitated. "...William."

"Okay, you're Bill Stacy."

"What?" Stacy was aghast. William was his father's name, and he had no desire to share it—or anything else—with the man. "Hold on—"

"Gotta give 'em the name upstairs." Meeks bolted for the door. "Trust me, the C.G. op'll love you."

Stacy turned to Raul, shaking his head. "I like it," the anchor offered. "My real name's Paul Goldberg."

"Thirty seconds. Mic check, please."

Stacy clipped a mic to his tie, then shoved an IFB listening device in his ear. When the others finished speaking, he recited a line of script.

"Fifteen seconds," the floor director cut him off. Stacy drew an icy breath. *He could do this*, he told himself. "Ten." The lights grew hotter, the air thicker.

"Hey, Stacy," Barker hollered at the last possible moment. "Don't pull a 'Cindy Brady' on us." He laughed at his own joke, then composed himself.

"Five...four...three..."

"Ready camera one," the director called from the booth. "And roll intro."

Stacy heard music in his ear, followed by the words, "This is the Channel 8 Noon Report. With Anchor Raul

Guttierez. Meteorologist Thad Barker. And Chett Starr with Sports."

The music built to a crescendo, then faded. "Take one. Cue talent."

Raul smiled. "From the Oklahoma oilfields to the Texas plains, a good day." His expression grew ominous. "Texomaland is in shock at this hour..."

Stacy glanced at his script, a backup in case the teleprompter crashed. His hands were two blocks of ice. His stomach roared like the Red River. *Just look at the camera and read the prompter*, he told himself. No different than the newscasts he'd practiced in school. *Like hell!* No classroom held *this* many people!

"...Reporter Bill Stacy joins us, back from the tragic scene. Bill." Stacy nodded, ready to utter his first words on TV.

"Thank you, Raul." Not exactly *Masterpiece Theater*, but at least he didn't stutter. "Four people are dead..."

In the booth, Meeks held his breath. "Roll tape," the director whispered, careful not to throw his young reporter off. As the T.D. nailed his cue, the producer crossed her fingers. But Stacy's delivery was flawless. True, he looked a bit nervous, but that was to be expected. After all, this was his one and only television debut.

"...we'll have more details as they become available. Raul." Stacy turned to the man on his right, relieved—overjoyed actually—that he made it through without fainting.

"Thanks, Bill." The anchor smiled, pivoting back to camera. "In other news..."

Stacy sat quietly till the segment ended. When he heard, "Clear," he gathered his script and made a beeline for the restroom. Racing into the stall, he grabbed both sides of the bowl, revisiting his ninety-nine-cent ham-

and-egg breakfast. Coughing and spitting, he didn't hear the door wheeze open, Thad strolling in to check his hair.

When Stacy emerged, they stared at one another, the weatherman fighting a turgid smirk. "Welcome to Channel 8, *Bill.*"

# CHAPTER 2
## September 1987

*(NEWSWIRE): AMERICA CELEBRATES 200TH ANNIVERSARY OF CONSTITUTION ... SEN. JOSEPH BIDEN DROPS OUT OF PRESIDENTIAL RACE WHEN PRESS UNCOVERS PLAGIARISM IN SPEECHES ... NASA CONFIRMS DEPLETION OF OZONE, BLAMING MAN-MADE CHEMICALS*

"First off, let me apologize for yesterday." Terrance Meeks pulled a Salem from the pack on his desk, searching his pockets for a match. "I never send a green reporter into the field without a thorough review of the gear." He paused, out of pockets. "You don't have a light, do you?" Stacy shook his head. "Good. Nasty habit." He shoved the cig behind his ear. "But if I've learned one thing in my twenty years in the business, it's never say never."

Stacy nodded, sitting uneasily in his boss' office. "Well..." He wasn't quite sure what to say. "...at least it can't get any worse."

"I've learned never to say *that* either." Meeks walked to the Mr. Coffee behind his desk and filled a mug.

Paperwork cluttered the credenza, along with a photo of his unattractive wife and equally unattractive kids. "We work in a strange market here. Half our coverage area's in Oklahoma. The other half's in Texas." He pointed to a map on the wall. "Welcome to Texomaland. Three hundred thousand viewers sprinkled over an area ten times the size of Long Island. Half pissed off when we do a Texas story, the other half mad when we report from Oklahoma." He sipped coffee as he walked back to the desk. "Every inch of land is devoted to farming or oil. The economy stinks. That's why I believe in useful news. Employment outlooks. Economic reports. That's what our viewers need." He peered into Stacy's eyes. "These are good people. Hardworking people. They just need some help, that's all."

They needed more than help. They needed hope. And Terrance Meeks was doing his best to give it to them, even if it meant bumping splashier stories and bigger headlines for what he deemed *useful* news. When he said he cared about these people, he meant it.

Stacy, on the other hand, cared little for people. As a kid, he'd mostly kept to himself, making few friends in high school, even fewer at Portland State where he graduated Summa Cum Laude with a Journalism degree. "Did you grow up here?"

"Born and raised. Got a job at KAVN out of college. Came to work here a few years later. If I have my way, I'll never leave."

"Never say never."

The news director smiled. "You're a quick study. Any questions?"

"Well...I would like to know what I'm making."

"Oh, Christ, Stacy, I'm sorry." He set his mug down. "First thing I should've told you. We start all our reporters at $5.75 an hour."

18

*$5.75?* That was a quarter less than he made at Burger Town, and a dollar less than Howell's Books. "Is that negotiable?"

"'Fraid not." He pointed to a pillar of tapes. "If you won't work for that, one of them will."

Stacy stared at the leaning tower. He had high hopes when he began sending out tapes three months ago. His plan was simple. He'd land a reporter's job in a top-100 market and work his way up. But things soon unraveled. When top-100 markets said no, he turned to top-150 markets, then top-200, receiving nothing for his efforts but form letters and shipping bills. When he got the call from Meeks, he ran straight to the library. The Nielsen index listed Avalon as the 170th largest market in the country. That put him at least three stops from respectability—and real money.

"Are there any benefits?"

"Just one. The opportunity to hone your craft and move on." Stacy planned to. And quickly. "Come with me."

He followed his boss into the newsroom, hearing the last few words of a conversation between Thad Barker and Randy the editor. "...biggest fuck-up since Igor took the wrong brain!" The two men burst into laughter, composing themselves as they looked up. "Oh...hey, Bill, how are you today?"

"My name's Stacy."

The pompous weatherman shrugged. "Okay, Stacy it is. Most of us use our TV names, but whatever floats your boat." He left the room, snickering.

"All right, everyone. Listen up." Meeks spoke with his back to a grease board. "We've got a busy day ahead, but first I want to introduce the newest member of the Channel 8 team." Stacy faced the crowd. All but two of them were smoking, and even they appeared to be looking

19

for cigarettes. "This is Stacy Zwardowski. Bill Stacy when you address him on air." As Meeks rattled off names to his new hire, "Phil Twitchell, Connie Callaway, Jennifer Riggs," Stacy's eyes moved to a cabinet in the corner. There were dozens of ¾" tapes inside. He wondered if anyone kept inventory. "Our camera ops, Terry Perkins, Darryl Rogers, Bub DeSpain." Stacy glanced back with indifference. He wasn't here to make friends. "Amy Chow, our producer, and last but not least, Texomaland's favorite reporter, Katie Powers." As the crowd feigned applause, the attractive journalist shot them the bird, winking at Stacy. He looked away.

"Settle down, folks." Meeks turned to the board. "Katie, I want you to handle the follow-up on yesterday's shooting. Jennifer, you and Darryl..." For the next few minutes, he doled out assignments, pairing reporters with cameramen, sending others out alone. As the crowd thinned, he turned to his new employee. "Stacy, we'll go easy on you today. You'll be with Phil and Terry. I want you to do a feature on leasing a new vehicle. I've already lined up your interviews. Both sponsors. Nice guys."

Stacy nodded. Not exactly demo tape material, but Meeks was the boss.

"Remember gang..." He raised his voice as they filed out of the room. "'News You Can Use'. That's what we're here for. We must never lose sight of that."

***

"I've been here two years, but I've got tapes all over the country." Trapped in the back of the Ford Escort, Stacy stared at the man in the passenger seat. Phil Twitchell was older than his on-air mates, and there was a distinct sadness about him, an almost pathetic aura that said dreams—his dreams—were merely that. "First offer I get,

I'm gone!" He hummed the *Movin' On Up* theme from *The Jeffersons*, then guffawed.

Stacy looked to the horizon, remembering what a college professor once said, "A reporter's average stay in a beginning market is fifteen months." If that was true, Twitchell had overstayed his welcome. Stacy had no desire to do the same.

"How about you, Terry?" Twitchell asked. "You ready to move on?"

Terry Perkins stared through the bug-caked windshield. He wore a denim jacket despite the heat, his hair styled in a mullet. "Nyi don't know."

Twitchell guffawed again. "Case you haven't noticed, Terry doesn't say much." The man had his reasons. Born with a harelip, he'd faced more than his share of ridicule. "'Course, we can't say that for everyone at Channel 8." Twitchell turned. "Watch what you say to Jennifer. She sleeps with Raul, and Raul tells Meeks everything! Connie and Randy have been known to mess around. And we think Amy Chow's a lesbian."

Stacy nodded, studying his car lease notes. "What about you, Phil?"

Twitchell's cheeks reddened. "Well...I've never had much luck with the ladies." *Shocking.* "But I do sorta have my eye on Katie Powers." Stacy looked up. "Oh, don't get me wrong. We're not seeing each other or anything. But we come from the same little town in Texas."

"How long's Katie been here?"

"About six months. Long enough to realize that she, like the rest of us, is getting screwed." Stacy raised an eyebrow. "No health insurance. No overtime pay. And the story assignments...Jesus!" He moved closer. "Take it from me, start building a file for slow days."

Stacy made a note in his Steno as they passed a city limit sign.

"Durant, Oklahoma," Twitchell announced. "Pronounced *Doo*-rant by the locals. Not as big as Avalon, but it's the Bryan County seat. There's a college. A movie theater. Make a right at the light, Terry." The cameraman set his blinker. "Your first interview's with the Chevy dealer. But be careful. He's good friends with Wilhelm."

"Wilhelm?"

"Dick Wilhelm. He owns Channel 8. Owns three other stations in Texas, too. Unfortunately, he lives near Avalon, so we get the 'pleasure' of his full-time company. You'll meet him the first time you screw up."

"I already screwed up." It pained Stacy to admit it. "Came back to the station with blue video yesterday. Lost a close-up of the Super-K gunman getting shot."

"That's a shame, but Meeks wouldn't have used it anyway. He doesn't go for all that blood and gore stuff. 'Course, the competition doesn't exactly agree with him. And between you and me, neither does Wilhelm."

The Escort shuddered to a stop at the courthouse. "Well..." Twitchell climbed out. "...good luck."

*\*\*\**

"Just one more shot, Mr. Hatchet."

"Take yer time, boys," the gregarious car dealer bellowed, a crowd of salespeople behind him. "Long as ya make me look good, ya can take all day!"

The insincere laugh that followed made him sound like...well...a used car dealer.

"Ready, Terry?" Having finished the interview and two-shot, the quiet camera op aimed his lens at Stacy. "We use this shot for editing. If you can just spell your name."

"It's Lamont Hatchet. L—A—M..." The reporter took fake notes, looking serious for the camera. When the man

22

finished, Stacy thanked him. "Who else y'all interviewin' today?"

"Mort Taylor..." Stacy unhooked the mic. "...at the Ford dealership in Avalon."

"Mort Taylor?" He sounded indignant. "Y'all be careful. Them Ford dealers'll lie to ya." He laughed again, looking to see if anyone heard. No one did. "Ah, well, just make sure I get more airtime than ol' Morty!"

Stacy turned to go, stopping at a row of new Cavaliers. "Mind if we get some footage in your lot, customers looking around, cars lined up, that sort of thing?"

"Shoot all ya want, fellas. This is free advertisin'!"

Stacy frowned. This was supposed to be news, not free airtime for local sponsors, at least that's what he was taught in Journalism school. Still, no matter how he spun the story, it came off sounding like a commercial. He thought for a moment, then turned to his cameraman. "Phil said there was a college in town?"

The man's eyes were vacant.

"You know, a university?"

Still vacant. He apparently needed subtitles.

"Okay...get me some B-roll. I'll be right back."

As Terry manned the camera, Stacy headed for a payphone.

"Hello, this is Stac—" He checked himself. "Bill Stacy from Channel 8 News." He hated his cheesy TV moniker. "I was wondering if I could speak with someone in the economics department."

\*\*\*

Stacy watched from the back of the studio as the Channel 8 News Team signed off. His was the last story to air, following Thad Barker's weather forecast, Chett Starr's

23

sports report, and Raul Guttierez's feature on lawn bowling. When the floor director yelled, "Clear," they left in three different directions.

"Stacy." The reporter turned to find an anxious Meeks in the doorway. "Mr. Wilhelm wants to see you...immediately."

"Wants to see *me*?"

"Yeah, and it's best not to make him wait."

The reporter followed his boss, buttoning his collar and re-tightening his tie. As they made their way up the hall, Stacy wondered what he'd done.

"Okay, listen..." Meeks stopped in front of the man's office. "...don't interrupt him, act humble, and tell him it'll never happen again."

"*What*'ll never happen again?"

"It doesn't matter. Just nod and show remorse." He tried to smile, but it looked like a gas pain. "No worries, kid."

Stacy watched him leave, the air turning cold. After a pause, he cleared his throat and knocked. "*Come in!*" The voice was loud and brash, the hair on Stacy's neck standing. He stepped inside.

The man behind the desk matched the voice, forehead protruding like a bill over colorless eyes, hair and mustache black. "I understand that, Mort," he spoke into the phone, glaring at the man who'd just entered his office. "Of course not." Although wrinkles invaded his face, he refused to acknowledge them. That would be a weakness. And if there was one thing Dick Wilhelm hated, it was weakness. He pumped his finger at a chair. Stacy sat. "I couldn't agree with you more."

As the man groveled, Stacy took a deep breath—Johnson's Wax—his nervous eyes scanning the room. It was impeccably neat. Matted photos, spaced and aligned, covered the walls. One of Wilhelm with Oklahoma

Governor Henry Bellmon. Another with ex-President Lyndon Johnson, a station owner himself. A polished bookcase held fake plants, all recently dusted, and an 8 X 10 of two men holding a *Wilhelm & Son: General Contractors* sign.

"Count on it, Mort." The G.M. nodded, tapping his flawlessly-arranged desk. As he hung up the phone, he leaned back in his chair. "Well, son, you're off to a rip-roaring start. Just what the hell were you trying to prove today?" He didn't wait for an answer. "We sent you out on a fluff piece. 'A Good Time to Lease a New Car'. Does that sound like something for *60-Minutes*?"

"Sir...I'm not—"

Wilhelm stood, walking to an open cabinet. The files inside were color-coded, labeled, and arranged in alphabetical order. He removed one. "This is what pays my salary. It's what pays *your* salary. If we have pissed off advertisers, we have cancelled contracts. Cancelled contracts mean people lose their jobs. Capiche?" Stacy nodded, the man shoving the file back in place. "What in the world made you put that goddamn economics teacher in your package?"

"Well...I just thought the piece was a little one-sided without—"

"One-sided?" Wilhelm chuffed. "Son, the Fairness Doctrine is dead, or didn't you get the memo?" He walked back to his desk. "I just spent the last ten minutes kissing Mort Taylor's ass, and while I was on the phone with him, Lamont Hatchet called and left a nasty message." Stacy cut his eyes to the desktop, the first he'd seen without an ashtray and pile of butts. "If I can't figure out how to appease them, what do you think'll happen?" Stacy shrugged. "They'll take their money elsewhere!"

He stomped to the bookcase, picking up a canister of fish food. "There are three stations in this market. KPXZ

Channel 2. KYTF Channel 7. And us." He sprinkled food into three separate bowls, each with a Siamese Fighting Fish inside. If kept in the same tank, the innocent looking creatures would tear each other to shreds. "For the past two years, our newscasts—the six and the ten—have finished dead last in the ratings. That means fewer advertisers, less revenue, and smaller paychecks for you and me." He wiped his hands with a handkerchief and walked back to the desk. "But that's all going to change."

Wilhelm sat, leaning forward. The anger in his face was gone now, replaced by something else. "What's the most important ingredient in TV news?"

"Well...I'd have to say good writing."

"Twenty years ago, I might've agreed. But not today." He pulled a remote from the drawer and powered up a monitor, Mary Hart spewing box-office drivel. "Today, our job isn't to inform." The screen changed from a close-up of the anchor to a Victoria's Secret photo shoot. "It's to entertain. TV's a visual medium. And pictures are everything! That's why viewers go ape-shit over fires, police chases, murders. The more visual, the more graphic—the better. People eat this crap up!"

"But..." Stacy was confused. "...I thought our motto was 'News You Can Use'."

"News is what *I* say it is!" His tone was impassioned, his stare razor sharp. Stacy looked more bewildered than ever. "Look..." The man's eyes softened as he powered down the TV. "...the news business is changing. If we don't change with it, we're as dead as the dinosaurs. There's a whole new breed of programming out there. *Donahue. Geraldo. A Current Affair*. Watch them. Learn from them. They're the future of television in this country."

The man stood, his lecture winding down.

"I realize you're new here and have a lot to learn." Stacy stood, too, legs wobbly. "But if you remember one

26

thing from our little discussion—just one—let it be this. Don't ever make one of my sponsors look bad, even in the interest of 'fairness'."

Stacy nodded, trying to look humble. "It'll never happen again, sir."

"You're right. It won't." As Wilhelm sat again, Stacy turned to go. "Oh, by the way..." The shell-shocked reporter looked over his shoulder. "...I watched your piece tonight. You're a damn good writer."

***

Stacy scanned the empty street. He'd been waiting outside the Ferndale Apartments for an hour. He was sure the woman on the phone said eight o'clock. All around him, crickets chirped at the moon, silencing themselves when a killdeer shrieked.

The bird was as agitated as he was. He'd never rented an apartment before. In college, he'd lived at home with his mother. And though he knew this was all part of growing up—the apartment, the job, the life away from her—it was a tough transition.

He slipped on his coat, the nighttime air beginning to chill. Two weeks had passed since his arrival in Avalon. It felt like a year. During that time, he'd botched his first assignment, looked like a fool in front of coworkers, and been reprimanded by the owner.

On the positive side, he'd logged ten stories, appeared twice on set, and cashed his first paycheck, using the money to settle his motel bill and reserve the apartment. The bland complex featured four units attached like boxcars, a vacant lot on either side. The place was by no means attractive, but the price was right— $350 a month, all bills paid—and it was furnished.

A pair of high beams split the night, moving past the Super-K and veering to the curb. Stacy watched an elderly woman step from the car. "Sorry, I'm late. The old man needed a bottle." She trudged up the walkway, head down. "Got first and last month's?"

Stacy froze. "They told me all I needed was a twenty-five-dollar—"

"Well, they told ya wrong," she snapped, turning to face him for the first time. "Hey, you're that news guy!" She was the first person to recognize him.

"Yeah...I work for Channel 8, but I don't get paid again—"

"Don't sweat it, darlin'." She smiled, her dentures slipping a bit.

*This celebrity stuff wasn't bad!*

She fished a ring of keys from her housecoat, shoving one in the lock. As they moved inside, Stacy looked around. The living room featured a sofa, end table, and chair, the kitchen cozier than most closets. There was a small bathroom. And the place smelled like rotting hamburger. "Where's the bedroom?" The woman reached down and pulled a sleeper from the divan. With a sigh, he finished surveying the room. It had a TV. A kitchen table that could double as a desk. And a phone—he could finally call home without saving up coins. "I'll take it."

He signed the lease, committing to three months in this shit-hole, not one day more. He was sure he'd be gone by then. She handed him a key. "Well, if ya paid the cleanin' deposit, you're good to go." He showed her out, grabbing his suitcase and heading back inside.

As the door slammed, the room went quiet. The smell was definitely getting worse. He made a note to buy some air freshener. "Home," he uttered. In the distance, a lonesome train chugged deep into the night.

28

*** 

Stacy glanced at the clock—5:45. He had fifteen minutes to put his story to bed.

"Sorry to bother you, Bill." He looked up to see Norma Howard, the portly receptionist with the gray beehive. "The UPS man left some packages for you. I had him stack them next to my desk."

"Thanks." He went back to work, shuttling tape. As he hit *PLAY*, he heard the familiar countdown. "In three...two...one..."

"By the way," she prated on, "you're doing an excellent job. Maybe we could have dinner sometime."

"I'm sorry." He hit the *AUTO-EDIT* key. "Did you say something?"

She flushed red. "We'll talk later. Ciao."

*Ciao?* Stacy watched himself on the monitors. He stood in a windswept field, oilrig pumping behind him. "...produced 137 million gallons last year, the lowest totals since 1940. Bill Stacy. Eight News." Finished—and with ten minutes to spare.

*Plenty of time to make a copy.*

He walked to the cabinet and grabbed a tape. His oil package was by no means an Emmy candidate, but all he needed was a few good stories. He envisioned his next stop—Colorado Springs, Salt Lake City, Las Vegas maybe.

When the dupe finished, he went back to work, cutting his package down to a VO/SOT for the ten o'clock report. The shortened version was designed to give the late news a different look than the early. He wondered how many people watched one newscast, let alone two.

As the news wound to a close, he grabbed his coat and hurried to the lobby. The boxes were huge, but in his mother's defense, she'd warned him. He picked one up, straining all the way to the car.

29

"Y'all need some help?" Chip Hale, Channel 8's technical director, was enjoying a post-news smoke—and from the smell of things, it wasn't a Marlboro.

"Uh...sure." Stacy popped the trunk, the man tossing his joint.

"What're ya, robbin' the place?" He looked to be in his mid-thirties with a ragged ponytail and permanent smirk. "How many ya got?"

"Just four."

"Oh, is '*at* all?" he joked, his accent screaming Oklahoma. The pair walked back to the lobby, grabbing the other boxes. "What *is* this stuff anyhow?"

"Some things from home." They made their way back to the car, filling the trunk.

"There's a party tonight. Everythin' ya could ask for—*wine, women, and weed!*"

That was Chip's mantra.

"Oh...no thanks." Stacy could count the parties he'd been to in life on one hand, with several fingers to spare. "I've...got a lot to sort through."

"Suit yourself. If ya change your mind, it's at Connie's place. B.Y.O. whatever!"

Stacy climbed in the car and rolled out of the lot. A few minutes later, he pulled up to his apartment, the sky beginning to rumble. He wasn't used to thunder. Despite all the rain in Portland, electrical storms were rare. Luckily, he got all four boxes inside before the first raindrops fell.

As he opened the packages, it felt like Christmas in September! Clothes. *His* clothes. For a month, he'd gotten by on the meager collection in his bag. Now he stared at a clean pressed mountain of options. Along with his things, his mother had sent him a new suit. Stacy's eyes grew moist. He knew she couldn't afford it. He also knew she'd never let him pay her back. As he mined the remaining treasures, he found shoes, a basketball, and two 5 X 7 frames. The first held a black-and-white photo of Stacy and his father, the child in the picture no more than a year old, the next a photo of him and his mom. There was a note attached—*FOLLOW YOUR HEART*.

It was her favorite saying, one she took every opportunity to repeat.

He set the frames down and attacked the final box, having a pretty good idea what was inside. As rain hammered the roof, he tore back the tape, revealing the item he'd longed for—the Underwood No. 5.

He'd written every story in school on the old typewriter. Crafted his cover letters. Even addressed his demo tapes. He checked the levers and clamps. Despite his best maintenance efforts, the thing was in sad shape, the *H* and *Y* keys missing completely. He'd searched every antique shop in Portland for replacements but never found a match. Setting the machine down, he reached for the final item. His mother had included a fresh ream of paper, along with another note—*WORK HARD*.

It was her *second* favorite saying.

Smiling, he glanced at the clock, then fed a sheet in the typewriter. After a pause, he began to type, rewriting his oil story with subtle improvements. His mother was right. If he was going to make it in this business, he'd *have* to 'work hard'. His coworkers at Channel 8 might have more experience, might even be better skilled.

But they could never outwork him.

"Thanks, Mom," he whispered. "For everything."

# CHAPTER 3

## *October 1987*

*(NEWSWIRE):  VICE PRES. BUSH ANNOUNCES
PRESIDENTIAL CANDIDACY ... STOCK MARKET
DROPS 500 POINTS ON 'BLACK MONDAY' ...
U.S. AND CANADA SIGN PACT TO ELIMINATE
TARIFFS BY YEAR 2000*

"Drug bust, Stacy," Meeks announced in a restive voice.

Stacy hurried to his desk, the assignment an upgrade
from the chamber luncheon he was scheduled to cover—
and a serious candidate for his demo tape. "Where?"

"East of town." Meeks lit a cigarette. "I talked to the
undersheriff this morning. They arrested two people and
nabbed a pretty good sum."

"Of what?"

"Marijuana." The news director took a hit. "Darryl's
already packed."

Stacy headed for the door. "You want me back by
twelve?"

Meeks looked at the board. "Radio in. We'll cover it with a reader at noon, then do a set piece at six and ten." He flicked ash. "And remember, 'News You Can Use'."

Rushing outside, Stacy glanced at his watch—8:45. He'd already learned that arriving early paid dividends. First, if a story was breaking, you got dibs. Second, in a profession wrought with deadlines, every minute counted.

He hopped in the Escort, Darryl Rogers pulling out of the lot. The man sat low in the driver's seat as if ducking a punch, his posture the residue of an overbearing mother. Ironically, he'd chosen a mate just like her. "Think I'll have time to call my wife before we start shooting?" Stacy shrugged. "She keeps pretty close tabs on me."

After stopping at a payphone, Darryl veered off Highway 199 into a pasture, six sheriff's vehicles and two news vans marking the turnoff.

Once again, Channel 8 was last on scene.

Stacy grabbed his Steno and climbed out of the car. A reporter from KYTF was interviewing one of the deputies, a cameraman from KPXZ shooting the old farmhouse. "Well, if it ain't the boys from Channel 8!" Stacy turned, spying a pole-thin officer in a bur-covered uniform.

"How do you do, sir?" The reporter offered his hand. "I'm Bill Stac—"

"Hell, I know who ya are. I watch ya ever' night." The man grinned, putting Stacy at ease. Despite the badge, he had a friendly face. And his eyes, the same metallic color of his gun, held Stacy like they'd done so before. "Marvin T. Bridges. Dexter County Undersheriff. You can call me Marv."

"Nice to meet you, Marv." Stacy watched as Darryl hooked up the deck. "Can you tell me what happened?"

"Few weeks back, we got us a tip these folks was growin' more'n alfalfa. One a' our undercover guys made a buy, so last night we got us a warrant an' popped 'em both."

"Can you give me names?"

"Harold Albert Griggs an' Edna Maxine Griggs. Man an' wife."

Darryl handed Stacy the microphone. "Can we interview *you* or would you prefer we talk to one of your deputies?"

"Interview away."

Stacy raised the mic. "What time did the bust go down?"

"At 0-200 hours," the undersheriff swapped English for 'police lingo', "we issued a warrant on the alleged perps and conducted a thorough search of the grounds. At 0-300, two deputies located an extensive growth of marijuana. That's when officers read the suspects their Mirandas."

"How much marijuana did you find?"

"We've yet to make an exact determination, but it appears to be a hundred pounds or more." He picked a foxtail from his sleeve. "We've also confiscated cash, ultraviolet lights, and scales commonly used for weighing and selling."

"What are the charges?"

"That's a question for the D.A.'s office, but I'd assume with an amount this large, they'll be charged with possession and possession with intent to distribute."

Stacy asked three more questions, then wrapped up the interview. "I appreciate your time, sir."

"No pro'lem." The undersheriff had apparently reverted to English—though not exactly the Queen's. "I'll take ya out ta the harvest site. We got most a' the plants dug up. Feel free ta shoot what ya want."

35

As they walked together, Stacy skimmed his notes. "Is this a sizable bust?"

"Not bad, but for every one we catch, another ten go free. Marijuana's the number three cash crop in this state, behind cattle an' wheat." He stepped through a wall of reeds. "Too much land ta cover's the pro'lem. An' the way they're protectin' their crops nowadays—"

"What do you mean?"

They came upon ten bundles of freshly-reaped pot, Darryl zooming in. "Bear traps. Pit bulls. An' that's just the pot growers. The meth labbers're worse."

"Seems like an awful lot of trouble to go to."

His expression turned tempered-steel serious. "Be surprised what people'll do when money's on the line."

Stacy nodded, writing as fast as he could.

"Well, I best get back ta the office. You boys watch out for ticks." He ran a hand through his graying crewcut. "Any more questions, talk ta one a' m'deputies."

\*\*\*

The high-pitched whistle sounded like a scream, steam rising to the ceiling in billowy clouds. Kaye Bridges stared at the wall, her husband grabbing the teakettle.

"Don't mind if I do," he uttered in the same happy tone he used on everyone else. Unlike everyone else, she knew it was bullshit. "How was your day, darlin'?"

"Same as every other, I'm afraid."

He smiled, grabbing a mug and filling it with water. After filling hers, he dropped a teabag in each. "Got us a couple more bad guys today."

Her face—once a beautiful face with clear blue eyes and the softest lips he'd ever kissed—offered no expression. This was his war. Not hers.

36

"Figger they'll do some time, too." Still no expression. As much as he loved her, he didn't know what to say anymore. After a burning sip, he turned on the TV. The black-and-white image was grainy—a twist of the antenna helped. From the electronic snow, a face emerged. He turned up the volume.

"...couple could face up to thirty years behind bars. Bill Stacy. Eight News." The man on the tube disappeared, replaced by a glib anchor and weatherman.

Marv Bridges looked at his wife. Her eyes had moved to the set, her stare one of profound sorrow. They'd never discussed Bill Stacy's resemblance to their son. They didn't discuss anything these days. But both had noticed it, feeling the icy knot it produced every time he appeared on screen. At times, it was too much to take. At others, strangely comforting.

"I'm gonna..." Bridges stood, searching the room for an exit. After a beat, he headed for the room at the end of the hall.

"Why do you torture yourself?" she cried.

"It ain't torture," he responded, disappearing inside. As the door fell shut, the images began to soothe him. The football trophies on the dresser. The fishing poles. The bed, still unmade from the last time Jake slept in it. Neither Bridges nor his wife had the courage to change things. Sure, there was talk, at least in front of friends and family. But it was just talk. As long as Jake's room stayed as it was—pennants on the walls, desk buried under clutter—maybe, just maybe, they'd awake from the nightmare.

Bridges walked to the bed, turning on the lamp. Jake's letterman's jacket hung from the footboard, the leather sleeves beginning to crack. The kid had earned his first letter as a sophomore, a wide receiver with a boundless future. He'd wanted to go to OU, the dream of every kid in Oklahoma. He had the talent. The grades. The whole package.

Then he discovered cocaine.

His father raised the coat to his cheek. He could still smell his son in the fabric. Feel his skin. He closed his eyes, hearing his infectious laugh, the jokes he used to tell, the excuses for why his room was always a mess.

What Bridges wouldn't give to take back the arguments. To do things differently.

He lowered himself to the bed, hugging the jacket to his chest. He'd never forget the call, the one every parent dreads. "Jake's dead, Marv. I'm sorry." The words were forever in his ear, the feelings they produced never far away. The only way to quell them, at least for *this* grieving father, was to dedicate himself to the job. Going to work every day and ridding the world of useless trash like Harold and Edna Griggs seemed like the best way—the only way—to honor his son.

He killed the lamp and fell back on the bed. When his thoughts grew muddled, he let sleep take him, escaping to a wonderful world of summer days and soaring footballs.

And of laughter. Sweet infectious laughter.

\*\*\*

"What time's your next interview?"

Stacy looked up from his notes, staring at Katie in the front seat. She really was beautiful, he thought—almost perfect—and no one seemed to care that she couldn't write a lick. "One-thirty...with a rancher up in—"

"Ever seen the Arbuckle Mountains?" Bub interrupted. Stacy glanced out the window at the passing foothills—in Oregon, they wouldn't even merit a name. "A few million years ago, they looked like the Rockies."

Stacy found that hard to believe.

"There's a lot more beauty here than meets the eye," Katie added. *Oh, really?* he thought. "There's even a gorgeous waterfall about a mile from here."

"Yeah," Bub confirmed, slowing down in Sulphur, "and the rock formations are incredible. Like layers on a devil's food cake." The salivating cameraman often referred to food. "Hey...it's 'Okra Tuesday'!" He skidded to a stop in front of Pearl's, the trio making their way inside.

"That's Katie Powers," someone whispered. "And Bill Stacy." It was the first time a viewer had used his name— *even if it wasn't the one God gave him.*

Stacy felt ten feet tall.

They made their way to a booth, a skeletal waitress with a badge that read *DORIS* bringing menus and iced teas. "Cobb Salad, no dressing," Katie ordered. Stacy chose the Monte Cristo, Bub the chicken-fried steak. As Doris brought rolls, Bub shoved two in his mouth, the scent of warm bread filling the room.

Stacy stared through the plate-glass window. "Seems like a...nice little town."

Katie smiled. "Lots of cattle money here. Turner Falls, too." Doris returned with their lunches, the diner known for its lightning-quick service—a journalist's dream. "Did you know our G.M. grew up here?"

Stacy grabbed a knife, spreading jam on his sandwich. Another Dick Wilhelm reference. These people sure loved to talk about their boss.

"His grandfather moved to Sulphur in the 1920s and started raising cattle." She sprinkled pepper on her salad. "Wasn't long before he saw the huge potential for real estate development. He figured with the oil industry pumping out cash and the Arbuckles attracting tourists, Texomaland would be a gold mine for construction."

Stacy looked outside—Main Street wasn't exactly bustling. "I take it things didn't work out."

"They did for him. With the money they earned from cattle, Wilhelm & Son parlayed a modest little construction business into a multi-million-dollar empire."

"So why didn't our G.M. follow in their footsteps?"

"No interest," Bub cut in, 'chewing cud'. "When he graduated from OU, his dad bought him a radio station here. It was losing money hand over fist, but Wilhelm turned it around. Turned three TV stations around, too. In fact, the only venture he's ever lost money at is Channel 8."

"What happened to the construction business?"

"Closed in '81 when old man Wilhelm died. Junior died two years later. And that's when things really got interesting."

"Yeah," Katie took over, "the money—and I'm talking millions—went to foundations all over Texomaland. And Dick Wilhelm didn't see a penny." She paused. "Well, that's not entirely true. He did inherit a thousand head of cattle. And the family ranch. That's where we're shooting your livestock B-roll."

Stacy looked from one to the other. "How do you know all this?"

"People talk. And in our business, it pays to listen." She smiled, then glanced at the clock. "We better *stop* talking—"

"—and start eating!" Bub finished her thought, mouth stuffed to capacity. With his plate nearly clean, he flagged Doris down. "Can I get an order of okra to go?"

***

40

"Fire!" A thousand images filled Stacy's brain. *Billowing smoke. Curling flames. Someone running.* He swallowed hard, hoping saliva would douse the fire in his gut.

"Where?" was all he could muster.

"At the Uniroyal plant!" Amy Chow shoved a camera at him.

"Do I...get a cameraman?"

"Sure, Bill." She pointed to the empty room. "Take your pick." It was the first Sunday he'd been asked to work. Meeks had changed the schedule to provide better weekend coverage—and hopefully better ratings. On-air talent now worked one of two shifts, Tuesday through Saturday or Sunday through Thursday, Sundays featuring a skeleton crew. He turned for the door. "And don't forget to white balance!"

It was a running joke at Channel 8, one he found little humor in.

Speeding out of the lot, he could see a dark plume in the distance, a spiraling coil that, in truth, wasn't very impressive. Still, it didn't take much to elicit memories.

He rolled down the window, needing air. It had turned cold in recent days, the fall colors blazing—golds, oranges, reds—all in sharp contrast to the black cloud ahead.

As he arrived, he could see just one fire unit on hand, a single hose dousing the flames. He circled the plant, parking next to the KPXZ news van. "'Bout time, Bill!" the now-familiar cameraman quipped.

"Hey, there..." Stacy flinched as a man ducked under the *CAUTION* tape. To his relief, it was Marv Bridges. "...we meet again, Bill Stacy."

"How are you, Mr. Bridges?" He powered up the camera.

"I thought we agreed on Marv." The undersheriff spit in a cup. "An' I'd be a whole lot better if I's still sittin' in

41

church. Then again, I *was* cravin' a chew. Not sure if 'at's a sin'r not."

"It's a sin, all right." Both men turned to the voice. It came from a short sturdy fireman, his forearms cut from granite. "But with all the sins you've amassed, I wouldn't worry." He took a drag on his cigarette and tossed the butt, staring at the undersheriff with the most trenchant eyes Stacy had ever seen.

"Comin' from you," Bridges shot back, the hint of a smile on his tobacco-stained lips, "I'll take that as a compliment."

"It'd be the first." Roy Maghee strolled to his friend's side, badge reflecting the sun. He looked younger than his fellow lawman, but both graduated from Avalon High in '59. They played football together there, Bridges an all-state receiver, Maghee a nose guard. Bought their first car together, too, a '56 Chevy with three wheels and one bumper. Even shared a girlfriend. And in the end, both chose public service careers, Bridges with the sheriff's office, Maghee with the fire department. "How's Kaye?"

"'Bout the same." Bridges spit again. "Ya'll met Channel 8's newest ambulance chaser?"

Maghee turned, stopping cold. "Nice to meet you," he finally offered. "I'm Roy Maghee." He didn't extend a hand—reporters had burned him before.

"How do you do, sir?" Stacy aimed his camera at the building, the flames all but out. Unless it was arson, this wasn't much of a story. "Do you know who I can talk to about the fire?"

The man sparked another cigarette. "Best bet's the chief investigator." He shook the match. "And that'd be me."

"An' you're in for a real treat," Bridges added. "He's quite the public speaker. Maybe he can tell ya 'bout his val'dictorian speech. Eighteen seconds, start ta finish. Still a school record."

"Yup."

"See there?" Bridges ducked back under the tape. "An' that's just a taste a' things ta come." He scraped tobacco from his lip and dropped it. "Well, I best get home. Got me a six-pack a' Hamms an' the Game a' the Week awaitin'."

As the undersheriff left, Channel 2's camera op shoved a mic at Maghee. The fireman ignored him, waiting for Stacy to begin.

"Sir, was anyone hurt in the fire?" It was an odd first question.

"No."

"Have you determined a cause?"

"We have." Maghee was living up to his 'man of few words' reputation.

"Well, what *is* it?" the KPXZ cameraman butted in.

The investigator glared at him, turning back to Stacy. "We've determined the fire to be accidental in nature. Caused by a maintenance man burning leaves, the investigation a Uniroyal matter."

"Jesus Christ!" The irate camera op stomped back to the van. "I can't believe I wasted an hour on this shit!"

Stacy stared at Maghee, face red. Although he'd done nothing wrong, he felt the overwhelming urge to apologize. "I'm sorry, sir."

The man tossed his cigarette and walked away.

\*\*\*

Stacy rushed into the building, tying his tie. He'd stayed up late again, rewriting his scripts on the Underwood. When his alarm went off, he'd slept right through it.

"You must be Bill."

43

He looked up to see a busty redhead at the front desk. "Where's Norma?"

"She resigned. I'm Cindy." He eyed the lobby. Gone were the nail polish bottles and glass trinkets. The desk was stark now, but for a lone photo of an angry Chihuahua. "You've got a nine o'clock meeting."

"Oh...thanks." The place seemed quieter than usual. When he reached the newsroom, he found out why. Practically everyone was gathered inside, with a few notable exceptions. Raul Guttierez was missing. So were Phil Twitchell and Connie Calloway. Stacy scanned the flock. Katie stood next to the water cooler, a look of uncertainty in her beautiful eyes. "What's going on?" he asked.

"D-Day," she whispered. "Wilhelm pulled the plug."

"What are you talking about?"

"He's been threatening to clean house for months. He finally did."

Stacy looked around. "Where's Terrance?"

"Don't know."

A hush fell over the crowd as Dick Wilhelm entered. His forehead looked larger than usual, his mustache blacker. As he moved to an empty desk—Twitchell's—several people lit cigarettes, smoke filling the room. "I have in my hand the last eight ratings results, people." He surveyed the faces. "And they're not good. I can't say that any *one person* was responsible for these numbers. But some of you were more responsible than others. Those people are no longer with us."

Stacy took note of the multiple casualties. Meeks was definitely gone. So was Terry Perkins and half the sales department. Unfortunately, Thad Barker had survived the blitzkrieg, as had Amy Chow. But thirteen had not.

With one sweeping brushstroke, Wilhelm had created a whole host of enemies.

"Over the next few weeks, you'll begin to see their replacements arrive. Until then, every one of you will be asked to do more. That's going to mean some long days and nights, people. But rest assured, we'll all benefit." He raised his hand and waved off smoke. "Now to some important business. I'd like to introduce our first new hire, and believe me, we're lucky to have him." A rawboned man with a larger-than-life head entered the room, shirt starched to a saber's edge. "I'd like you to welcome Larry Toole, Channel 8's new anchor and news director."

Stacy and Katie looked at each other, then back at their new boss. He had the face of a ferret, eyes too close, mouth too small. And there was something else about him, a sense of perennial movement, of refusing to rest for even a moment.

"Larry's a hometown boy. Went to Avalon High, then to the University of Texas. But we won't hold that against him." Wilhelm's joke fell on deaf ears, the assemblage in shock. "After graduating from UT, he came back and joined Channel 8 as a reporter. But he was too good to hang onto. Joplin snatched him up after a few months, then Tulsa, Oklahoma City, and Dallas. For the last three years, Larry's been working as a reporter in Big D. But thanks to a little coaxing—and a lot of money—he's come home." The man rolled up his sleeves as if preparing to sift through sludge. Wilhelm took his hand, a sign of open solidarity. "Welcome home, Larry."

As the new chief faced his tribe, Stacy shuddered, not sure why. "Good morning, folks. As Dick told you, and I hope he didn't lay it on too thick..." He smiled at the G.M., Wilhelm smiling back. "...I've spent the last ten years climbing the television news ladder. During that time, I've seen it all. I've covered presidential elections, natural disasters, high-profile trials. I know the news business,

45

inside and out. And I know what it takes to build a winner. That's why I accepted this challenge." He walked to the cooler and filled a Dixie cup, Stacy noting an obvious hairpiece.

"We're going to turn Texomaland on its ear! People don't watch the news to be informed. They watch it to be entertained. Wowed. And that's what we're going to do. *Wow* them!" He downed the water like a shot of whiskey, crumpling the cup.

"What about 'News You Can Use'?" a brave soul asked.

"Fuck 'News You Can Use'!" Toole barked, Wilhelm smiling like an alley cat. "We want our viewers glued to their sets. Rushing home to catch the six. Staying up to watch the ten." He looked around the room. "Who here can name the best-selling newspaper in the country?" Two people responded with the *New York Times*, another *USA Today*. The brazen news director shook his head. "It's the *National Enquirer*, folks." Stacy's stomach gurgled. "Say what you want, but that little rag is changing the face of newsgathering in this country. And so are its television counterparts." He took the ratings sheets from Wilhelm. "These reports tell us something. They tell us we've been doing it wrong. Well, it's time we start doing it right."

"Bravo!" Wilhelm trumpeted, Toole lighting a cigarette.

"But Rome wasn't built in a day. Righting a sinking ship, especially one that's spent years in the shitter, takes time. But I promise, in two short months, you won't recognize this place." Smoke rose like a pestilent cloud, several people coughing. He walked to the grease board and grabbed a pen. "As you all know, November is ratings month."

"Don't worry, boss," Thad interrupted. "I've got some great weather planned." A few people laughed, none harder than the pompous meteorologist.

Toole ignored him.

"As much as I'd like to implement *all* my plans, it isn't possible given the time frame we're up against. But that doesn't mean we can't start skewing the numbers." He penned his first bullet point—*MOSs*. "I'm a big fan of Man on the Street interviews. Not because I give a shit about what people have to say. But because it's a great way to make them tune in." He smiled, smoke escaping his lips. "Think about it. Who doesn't want to see themselves on TV? The yokels we interview at the mall will tell their friends, their neighbors, their relatives." He paused to flick ash. "They'll all be watching. And one of them just might have a Nielsen box."

He scribbled his next bullet—*TOWN HISTORIES*. "Now I know this sounds like bullshit but hear me out. There are hundreds of towns in our coverage area. And everyone has a story. A story and a potential Nielsen family." He looked to the wall calendar. "There are thirty days in November. That's sixty newscasts, folks, not counting the noon. We're going to highlight sixty towns." Bub DeSpain grinned, thinking of all the dining possibilities.

Toole snuffed out his cig, adding a final point— *BREAKING NEWS*. "And now for the big one. One of the reasons this station continually sucks the hind tit is its lack of attention to breaking stories. Shit happens, folks. And it's our job to make sure we don't miss it." He looked at Stacy with eyes the reporter had seen before—the eyes of a bully. "Reporters and cameramen, I'm going to ask you to eat, drink, breathe, sleep, and shit the news. From now on, you're like firemen, ready to perform when needed, sunup or sundown. You'll carry a camera in your personal vehicle. Take home tapes, batteries, everything you need to file a story. And most importantly..." He walked to a stack of boxes. "...everyone gets one of these. Your own personal scanner. I want it plugged in next to your bed—volume on high!" *It seemed a lot to ask of people making $5.75 an hour.* "News doesn't keep a nine-to-five schedule, folks. We can't afford to either."

Toole moved to the center of the room. "I'm excited to be here. This is a great opportunity for all of us, but we've got work to do. Look around." He smiled, but the expression in his eyes didn't change. "The people you see are here because they deserve to be. But no one's safe. Reporters, you're only as good as your last story. Producers, your last newscast. Camera ops, your last close-up. If you're not cutting it, someone else will." More cigarettes blazed, the room a toxic cell.

"That's all for now. I'll be choosing a co-anchor soon. Consider the next few weeks an audition." He turned the board over, exposing the day's assignments. "Now get to work."

# CHAPTER 4

*November 1987*

*(NEWSWIRE): SUPREME COURT NOMINEE DOUGLAS GINSBURG WITHDRAWS AFTER ADMITTING HE SMOKED POT ... ARAB LEADERS BACK IRAQ IN PERSIAN GULF WAR ... LT. GENERAL COLIN POWELL NAMED NAT'L. SECURITY ADVISOR; FIRST BLACK TO HOLD POSITION*

The question of the day was, "Should Oklahoma have a state lottery?" Stacy spoke to ten people at the mall, four outside Taco Bueno, six more at the Chickasaw Motor Inn. The answers ranged from "Hell, yes!" to "Over my dead body!" But none of it mattered. Channel 8 wouldn't be airing the footage.

Larry Toole knew from experience how to 'boil a frog'. You couldn't just toss it in hot water—the damn thing would jump out! No, you had to ease it in, then slowly and meticulously turn up the heat. That's what he was doing. Introducing his techniques in small doses.

Getting employees comfortable with the new direction at Channel 8 before he asked for more. Much more.

Stacy thought he was already asking a lot. The news director wanted twenty MOSs a day from every reporter, two stories, and a host of unplanned scanner runs, which meant chasing down breaking action to see if it was newsworthy. More often than not, it wasn't. As a result, Stacy was working twelve-hour days. And his nightly writing ritual had become a thing of the past.

"Jesus!" A scissor-tailed flycatcher swooped past the hood. As the news car sped on, Stacy shook the cobwebs. It was the third time he'd nodded off today. He clicked on the stereo, Tiffany's *I Think We're Alone Now* afflicting the airwaves.

He'd spent the morning interviewing teachers at a rural high school. Voters were deciding the fate of a bond issue that would pay for a new gymnasium. Educators were confident the measure would pass, but Stacy wasn't so sure. Yes, local residents wanted better education, but over the past five years, fifty thousand oil jobs had dried up, many in Dexter County. For families struggling to put food on the table, a new gym seemed like a luxury.

"Good morning, Avalon! I'm Nate Shefler with a KAVN news update." Stacy hiked the volume. "Channel 8's longtime news director, Terrance Meeks, was given the axe..." He shut it off, shaking his head. Apparently, twenty years in the news business didn't buy any professional courtesy.

The Escort rattled to a stop, Stacy spying an antique shop. The little store was the only one open in a deserted town square, the window featuring an old sewing machine, two washboards—and an Underwood No. 5!

A bell tolled as he rushed inside, the shop filled with old clocks and Victrolas. "Help ya?" A man emerged from the back, his face a graph of wrinkles.

"Can I see the typewriter?"

"Sure can." He moved with the speed of a tightrope walker, Stacy wondering if he used every item in the store when it was new. "This ol' girl belonged to m' brother." He struggled to carry it, the room smelling of dust and mold. "Bet he typed a thousand letters on 'er."

Stacy stared at the timeworn machine. Several keys were missing, including the *H* and *Y*. Even for spare parts, it wasn't worth forty dollars. "Thanks anyway."

"Base to Mobil 3!"

Stacy rushed back to the car, grabbing the handset. "Mobil 3 here."

"Stacy. Larry Toole. Someone just robbed the Hardee's in Kingston."

Stacy was already late for his next interview. He had more B-roll to shoot. And Chett needed a bite from the football coach. He had about as much chance making it home before ten as the old man in the antique shop winning a footrace. "On my way."

\*\*\*

Stacy pulled the almanac from the stacks. He loved libraries. As a kid, he'd spent most of his time in one. "How's it going, Darryl?"

The henpecked camera op swapped one photo for another. "Couple more."

Stacy's first town history assignment was Avalon, the information bountiful. Originally part of Chickasaw Indian land, the unnamed outpost became a vital, albeit bland, stop on the Santa Fe Railroad. Agents, perhaps as a joke, named the community after the Avalon of Celtic legend, the island paradise where King Arthur and his court went after death. Stacy couldn't help wondering what the ex-monarch and his pals would think of Avalon, Oklahoma.

Scanning the book, he jotted down notes. In 1889, the first business was established. In 1925, a tornado destroyed half the buildings in town. A Sulphur firm won the contract to replace them. Wilhelm & Son—*there was that name again*—erected twelve in all, among them the courthouse, hospital, elementary school, and library.

"Did you know Wilhelm's grandfather built the building we're standing in?"

"Yup..." Darryl zoomed. "...and just about every other in Texoma."

Something beeped, Darryl reaching in his pocket. "Is that a—?"

"Sure is." He held up a pager. "Now when my wife wants me, she just dials a number and hits two zeros, our secret code."

"But Darryl..." Stacy ignored the 'two zeros' comment. "...the only people who carry those are doctors."

"My wife wants a mobile phone, too...you know, the ones built into a briefcase." Stacy shook his head. "Not sure if they'll catch on though. I mean, why would anyone carry a phone around when there's one on every corner?"

*He had a point.*

After ten minutes at a payphone, they were back on the road. In addition to the town history, Toole wanted a follow-up on the failed bond issue, two pick-up shots for an AIDS piece, and, of course, the twenty MOSs.

"Pull over!" Stacy barked, his startled camera op cutting the wheel. They lurched to a stop in front of Calvary Church. Someone had spray-painted the word *SATIN*—an illiterate attempt at honoring the Archdemon —on the huge double-doors. Stacy's mind raced back to his childhood, to the house on 78th Street. He came home from the library to find *POLACK* carved in the door. He'd spent the next two hours sanding it off before his mother got home.

"Get me a shot of that, would you?" He was sure Toole would approve.

As Darryl set up gear, Stacy found the minister. The man, who wore the last surviving leisure suit, agreed to speak on-camera. "Friends," he declared in his most anguished lilt, "despite your inequities, I forgive you. This congregation forgives you. God forgives you." Not exactly what Stacy was looking for, but he thanked him anyway.

As Darryl packed up, Stacy asked the preacher if he knew who was responsible. "One of the ignorant little fucks in the neighborhood, I reckon!"

Stacy stared, at a complete loss for words. If he'd learned one thing in his short time in Avalon, it was this— things weren't always what they seemed. And neither were people. Not even in a town named for an island paradise.

*\*\*\**

He grabbed the tapes and headed for the door. Stacy had waited for the newsroom to empty before making copies— ten in all—each with his best three stories at Channel 8. By tomorrow, they'd be stamped and on their way.

As he moved up the hall, he heard his own voice coming from the lobby—Cindy had failed to kill the television again. Stopping at the sofa, he watched his ten o'clock package, a report on cemetery vandalism. As usual, the writing was crisp, but he worried about his delivery. He needed more inflection. More modulation. *More something.* "...residents are asked to contact local police. Bill Stacy. Eight News."

"Good thing it was a cemetery piece. I looked like a damn corpse!"

"Don't be so hard on yourself." He wheeled to see Katie in the hallway. "It takes time to feel comfortable on camera."

"Even for 'Texomaland's favorite reporter'?" he groused.

"I was only trying to help."

He stared at her, tasting the heel of his shoe. "Sorry."

"You might try glancing away from the camera once in a while. It sorta breaks the monotony of a long standup. Makes you look more natural."

"Thanks." He thought about adding something but left it at that.

Her eyes shifted to the tapes. "Looks like someone's ready to leave."

He glanced down self-consciously. "I...guess."

"So you've learned everything there is to learn?"

"I...uh..." He wasn't sure what to say.

"You really don't like it here, do you?"

"No...I mean..." He glanced up the empty hall. "...I just..." *Why was he stammering?* "That's what we're supposed to do, right? 'Hone our craft and move on'?"

She powered down the TV, then made her way to the door. Without turning, she spoke to his reflection in the glass. "You're off tomorrow, right?" He nodded, wondering what that had to do with anything. "Meet me here at eleven."

Before he could respond, she slipped into the night.

*\*\*\**

"Wow." He stopped at the brink of a limestone pool. Fifty feet away, the waters of Honey Creek spilled over age-old rocks to form a picturesque waterfall. "This *is* beautiful."

Katie smiled, enjoying his reaction. He'd arrived at the station as told, only to be whisked away in her red Mustang. Twenty minutes later, they rolled up to Turner Falls, picnic supplies in tow. "I told you there was more beauty here than meets the eye." She led him down a dubious path. "You want to spread the quilt?"

He looked at her and sighed. If he wanted to leave Avalon, a relationship—any relationship—would only complicate things. *Stay focused*, he told himself, unfurling the blanket.

"You should see it in springtime. The falls are much fuller. And the Judas trees bloom. Little pink blossoms everywhere." She lowered herself to the quilt, her chestnut hair catching the breeze.

After a pause, he joined her. "What made you think of a picnic? I mean, it was forty degrees yesterday."

"There's an old saying, 'if you don't like the weather in Oklahoma, wait till tomorrow!'" He nodded, trying to look comfortable. "Besides, we work with the best meteorologist in Texomaland. When in doubt, ask Thad Barker."

"Yeah, well..." Stacy's eyes narrowed. "...I'm not too big on Thad."

"Oh, he's not so bad. A little vain maybe, but everyone in the industry is." He couldn't argue. "I suggest you make friends with him though. Come tornado season, you'll need to keep pretty close tabs on the weather."

"I'll keep that in mind." He shifted in his seat, searching for another subject. "So...what do you think of our new boss?"

"I don't know what to think," she responded. "I'm still numb from all the firings. I talked to Phil on the phone this morning. He's a complete basket case."

Stacy shrugged. He felt bad for the others, but he was far more concerned with himself. "I guess we *are* lucky to still have jobs."

"Don't ever forget that, Stacy."

It was a strange thing to say, but he nodded anyway, reaching for the basket. "What did you make us?"

"I didn't *make* anything," she giggled. "I don't exactly cook, so I went to the deli and picked up two of everything." He raised the lid, revealing subs, grapes, brownies, and sodas. "I didn't want you to go hungry. You're a big boy."

Stacy's face grew hot. "How did you...get the day off?"

"I switched with Jennifer. She's anchoring tonight. I'm anchoring Sunday. It's what I really want to do, become the full-time co-anchor at Channel 8, then work my way up to network." He nodded, suspecting as much. "What about you, Stacy?"

"I want to report. That's all I've ever wanted to do."

"Well, you're good at it, sweetie." She picked a grape and placed it in her mouth. "But we didn't come here to talk about work. Tell me about yourself."

It was the one question he dreaded. *Who was Stacy Zwardowski?* In his twenty-two years, he'd yet to find a suitable answer. Was he a dedicated honor student? A hopeless loner? They were apt descriptions, but they didn't define him, did they? No more than high school basketball player or *POLACK*. Truth is, he knew little about the Zwardowski name, even less about its history, his mother unable to enlighten him.

"Not much to tell really."

"Sure, there is. I want to hear about your childhood. Your parents. Friends."

Stacy peered at the blue-green water, wishing he was back in his apartment. "I... was born in Oregon," he finally began. "Little town called Newport." She popped a soda and handed it to him. "Don't remember much about it really. Mom and I moved to Portland when I was two. Lived in six different rental houses, some decent, some not so decent." A memory flashed. He suppressed it. "She was always there for me. Even home schooled me for a while."

*God, he sounded pathetic!*

"What happened to your father?"

Stacy watched a blue heron take flight. He'd never forget the day his mother told him. She took him out for ice cream, then, with tears in her eyes, whispered, "Daddy's flying with the angels now." Stacy was so young. The two scoops of Rocky Road took most of the sting away. But he never forgot the words.

"He died."

"I'm sorry. Do you miss him?"

"No." He could've elaborated. Could've told her how his father left when Stacy was young. How he died in Alaska a few years later. Or how the experience ruined his mother. Instead, he tossed a pebble in the water and watched the expanding rings.

"Well, if you ask me, fathers are overrated anyway." He looked up. "When I was ten, my dad bought me a new bicycle, a bright yellow Schwinn with streamers and everything. When I was sixteen, he handed me the keys to a new car. And for high school graduation, I got a string of pearls."

"If you're trying to make me feel better, you're doing a lousy job."

She flashed a bittersweet smile. "I had everything a kid could want, Stacy. But what I really wanted—what I *needed*—I never got." The smile faded. "My father never hugged me, never told me he loved me, never even said, 'Good job.'" Tears welled in her beautiful eyes. "And when he divorced my mom, he went months without bothering to tell me why."

"That's..." Stacy felt uncomfortable. He appreciated Katie's candor, but it came too easy—and too soon. "...rough."

She wiped her eyes. "Listen to me, carrying on like this on a first date."

*First date?* He hadn't asked her out, didn't even know what she wanted when he showed up this morning. And with his demo tapes mailed, he had no intention of—

She moved closer, her skin flawless, her mouth inviting. Stacy's pulse quickened. Before he could say another word, she leaned in and kissed him, every nerve in his body on overload. When they parted, both were out of breath.

"So..." He exhaled. "...what are we going to do on our *second* date?"

***

He killed the camera and thanked the principal. As she left, Stacy packed his gear, glad to be working alone today—*he couldn't wipe the smile off his face!* His date with Katie was all he could think about. He liked the woman. Liked her a lot. And he was sure she felt the same.

A bell sounded, kids gushing from the building like water through a busted levee. Within seconds, he was surrounded. "Bill Stacy!" one of them screamed. "From Channel 8!" another added. "Bill Stacy, Eight News!" Guarding the camera, he made his way through the mob—it felt like a scene cut from *The Wizard of Oz*, the one where Munchkins discover speed.

As he reached the car, someone shoved a Pee-Chee at him. "Will you sign this?" The kid was serious. "Mine, too!" another begged. He tossed his equipment in the trunk, signing autographs for twenty minutes. The experience was surreal. He couldn't wait to tell his mother.

"Base to Mobil 4."

He grabbed the handset, still smiling. "Mobil 4 here."

"Stacy. Larry Toole. What's your 10-20?"

He started the engine. "Leaving the school now."

"Get to the interstate. We've got a Signal 82. And a bad one."

"But..." Stacy was confused. "...I didn't think we covered accidents, at least that's what Meeks said."

"I'm not Meeks."

He pulled out of the lot, punching the accelerator. "Which exit?"

"Lake Murray Drive. Now haul ass."

He hopped on I-35, arriving at the scene minutes later. He could see a jackknifed truck up ahead, a smoldering trailer behind it. Four OHP units blocked traffic, along with three fire engines, two paramedics, and an ambulance.

It was a bad one, all right.

He grabbed the camera, a trooper stopping him just shy of the carnage. That was fine with Stacy. He could shoot more than enough from here. "What happened?"

"Fatality. Twelve-year-old girl." Stacy took a breath, the air thick with fuel and burning flesh. "Guy was pullin' a ski boat, his daughter in back." The trooper waved someone by. "A semi clipped the trailer. Boat flipped over and exploded."

Stacy swapped tapes, shooting the snarled traffic, the rescue vehicles, the mangled steel. He zoomed in on the yellow tarp. *Just shoot it and leave.* But as he focused, a gust of wind revealed the body. Without thinking, he moved from behind the viewfinder.

It was a mistake.

The thing on the ground no longer resembled a little girl. It looked more like a manikin, the torso black, the clothes burned away. Moments ago, this charred corpse was a human being, with dreams, hopes—a life. Now her fingers were curled claws. And white smoke billowed from the hole that was once her mouth.

Stacy stepped back, mind spinning out of control. *What a horrible turn of events!* Before he got the call from Toole, he was signing autographs at the elementary school. Now he was staring at the blackened remains of a twelve-year-old girl.

He wondered what it would take to wipe the smile off his face.

Now he knew.

\*\*\*

"'Morning, Mom." Stacy held the phone to his ear, wiping sleep from his eyes. It was seven in the morning in Oklahoma, five in Oregon.

"'Morning, sunshine." It felt good to hear her voice. Since moving to Avalon, he'd called her twice a week, knowing she missed her boy as much as he missed his mother. But finding time lately had been difficult. "What's wrong?"

"Nothing's wrong." He offered a half-chuckle but knew it didn't fool her. His mother had a sixth sense about such things. Like the time Dexter Monroe took Stacy's book. Without a word, she marched out the door and found the neighborhood bully, shaking him down till he handed it over. She had no idea who she was messing with, nor did she care. She was there for her boy without reservation. Stacy, after all, was her life. "How's the nightshift working out?"

"I don't mind it. Fewer doctors. And less work."

"Since when is 'less work' a good thing?" It was a valid question. Helen Zwardowski's work ethic was second to none. Over the course of Stacy's lifetime, she'd juggled dozens of jobs and cared for a child, all while putting herself through nursing school. True, they'd never had much money. But they always managed to get by.

"There's more to life than work, Stacy."

He'd never heard her say *that* before. "Mom, are you all right?"

Sons had a sixth sense, too.

"I'm fine, honey..." There was a pause, Stacy moving the phone to his other ear. "...I've made some mistakes, that's all. I just don't want to see you repeat them."

"What mistakes?"

"Never mind. How's the job coming?"

He glanced at the clock. "Okay, I guess." He rubbed his forehead, the bedside scanner beginning to chirp. For the past few weeks, he'd had trouble sleeping. At first, he blamed the workload, then the horrible accident. But it was more than that. "The guy I've been telling you about...my new boss..." He ran a hand through his untamed curls. "...I'm just not sure we see eye to eye."

"They hired him for a reason, Stacy. Maybe you can learn from him."

"Maybe."

"And besides, you won't be there long, right?"

The scanner sounded again, something about a missing cat. "Already mailed the tapes. Should hear something in a week or two."

"Things always seem to work themselves out. In the meantime...are you making friends?"

He looped the cord over his finger. *Should he or shouldn't he?* "Well...I...did meet a girl." He hesitated, waiting for a response. None came. "She's a reporter, too.

We sort of...went out the other day." He waited again. More silence. "Are you going to say anything or not?"

"Follow your heart, Stacy."

# CHAPTER 5

## December 1987

*(NEWSWIRE): PRES. REAGAN AND SOVIET LEADER MIKHAIL GORBACHEV AGREE TO ELIMINATE MEDIUM-RANGE NUCLEAR MISSILES ... SMOKING BANNED ON ALL FLIGHTS UNDER 2 HOURS ... U.S. DOLLAR CLOSES YEAR AT RECORD LOWS VS. YEN AND MARK*

"So what do you think?"

He stared at the sign, the words *KEGT: THE GREAT 8* emblazoned in red. Stacy turned to Katie, adorable in her matching scarf and mittens. It was thirty degrees outside, with freezing rain in the forecast and winds out of the north.

"I think I know where my next raise went."

She grabbed his arm and led him to work, the sound of banging filling their ears. "What *is* that?"

"No idea." He held the door and followed her inside, tracking the noise to the studio. Most of their slack-jawed coworkers were gathered near the set, at least what was left of it. A twelve-man construction crew was busy gutting the thing.

"Never liked the old set anyway," Thad shouted over the din. "Always thought it clashed with Chett's yellow teeth." The sportscaster responded with his trademark finger pistols—replacing index with middle.

Stacy searched the room for more victims of the new regime. By now, he and his coworkers were gun-shy. When changes happened at Channel 8, they looked for missing employees. No one appeared to be gone, but there were two new faces in the crowd. A man in a pinstripe suit stood next to the rubble, hair enormous. Stacy couldn't stop staring. He'd never seen a mane so thick. Behind him was a bespectacled black man. He knelt in the corner, examining the switches of the Ikegami. Long and lean, he looked like an Olympic sprinter, or at least someone who'd been running for a while. Stacy watched him peer through the lens, a sudden realization striking him— KEGT had no black employees.

"Good morning, people." Everyone turned, Larry Toole entering the studio with a surgically-enhanced blonde. Stacy, along with everyone else, found himself staring at her breasts—the low-cut blouse helped. "I see you've found your way to ground zero." Someone laughed uncomfortably, the crew hammering away. "Out with the old, in with the new, I always say. The new set'll be ready by six. And it's going to kick serious ass! Rotating backdrops. Levitating monitors. The competition won't know what hit them!"

Stacy's eyes moved from breasts to boss, Toole's follicles, both real and synthetic, fused in symbiotic harmony. "Today marks the beginning of greatness, folks. You saw the sign out front. *The Great 8*. It's got a nice ring to it, doesn't it?" Several people nodded, Katie among them. "From now on, when we tag our stories, it's

'Jennifer Riggs, Great 8 News'. 'Katie Powers, Great 8 News'." He turned to Stacy. "'Bill Stacy, Great 8 News'." *We get it.* "In order to be great, we have to *believe* we're great. When we believe it, the viewers will, too." He paused to light a cigarette.

The ratings results were in, Channel 8 finishing last again. But Toole expected as much. He expected something else, too—a slight spike in the numbers—which is exactly what he got. Under his direction, KEGT was showing signs of life. "We're going to give our viewers more. We're going to entertain them, dazzle them, shock the hell out of them if we have to. Starting today, we're going to inject this little market with the big-city glitz of *Entertainment Tonight* and the in-your-face punch of *A Current Affair*."

Toole stepped to the base of the disappearing set. "Before I send you out on your assignments, I want to introduce three new people." He pointed to the man with the healthy tresses—perhaps he'd hired him out of 'hair envy'. "Reg McNair joins us from Lawton." The new reporter smiled. "Manning the camera is photog extraordinaire Julius Candelle." The young man ignored his intro, examining more switches.

Thad leaned in and whispered to Randy, "Amazing what they can teach chimps to do nowadays." Stacy couldn't believe his ears. In shock, he watched him walk over and greet the new hire, patting him on the back and smiling.

Stacy hated him now more than ever.

"And last but not least..." Toole turned to the buxom blonde. "...I'd like you all to meet my new co-anchor, Lisa Lynn." The woman smiled, teeth whiter than her pearl necklace. She had a 140 I.Q. but acting dumb had gotten her much further than acting smart. "Lisa's just starting out in the news business. But she did win the Miss Texas pageant last year."

Stacy looked at Katie.

She was seething.

***

"That was my job, Stacy. *Mine!* Wilhelm and I had an understanding." He handed her a gin and tonic—three parts gin, one part tonic. She killed it in one gulp. "I've done everything they asked! I've paid my dues!"

He'd never seen Katie like this before. He'd also never seen her apartment, a far cry from his own. Nagel prints lined the walls. And the furniture was new. She even had a real bedroom and bath. "Why don't you go talk to him?"

"I *did* talk to him!" She grabbed the remote. "You know what he said?" Stacy shook his head, opening a beer. "He said my writing wasn't good enough. As if that's why they hired 'little Miss Texas'!"

He had no idea why she hated Lisa so much. In truth, they were a lot alike. Both had won beauty contests. And both wanted to anchor. Katie's first shot at reading the news came in third grade. She and her friends produced a weekly newscast on 8mm film—private school had its benefits. At the end of the year, the little journalists showed their reel on 'Family Night'. Katie's mother was there, her father away on business.

"*Goddammit!*" She hit the power button, the TV hissing to life.

"Are you sure you want to do this?"

"I'm sure."

"I'll put another log on the fire." As he stoked the flames, he watched his old pal, Lamont Hatchett, grace

66

the screen, the man, saddled to a longhorn steer, promising 'easy terms' and 'year-end clearance sales'.

Stacy walked back to the sofa, the TV going black. Out of the void came the ear-piercing whoosh of a rocket blast, accompanied by detailed graphics of Texas and Oklahoma. The flying states came together at the Red River, a synthesized beat lauding their union. "Get ready, Texoma!" a narrator growled. "This is the Great 8 ten o'clock report." A sizzling comet zipped around the map, the states dividing to reveal a giant *8*. "With the Great 8 News Team, led by award-winning anchors Larry Toole and Lisa Lynn." Stacy and Katie looked at each other. *What awards?* The giant *8* exploded, electronic fragments raining down to form a wide shot of the new set. "Prepare yourself. The news starts *now!*"

As the camera moved in for close-ups, Larry Toole smiled, an aerial shot of Avalon sparkling behind him. "Good evening, Texomaland." A smooth hydraulic lift hoisted a monitor over his shoulder, the on-screen graphic—*FLU SCARE*. "Health officials say it has all the makings of an epidemic..."

Stacy sat bolt upright. "That's not my lead-in!" Toole's speech didn't exactly breech the truth, but it stretched it. When the anchor finished, the director rolled Stacy's package, a routine advisory on the need for annual flu shots. The words 'scare' and 'epidemic' were not only unnecessary but downright misleading. "Jesus, the guy's here one month and he's already—"

"*Shhhhhhh!*" Katie raised her hand as Stacy's package dissolved to a close-up of Lisa Lynn. The woman wore ruby-red lipstick, her cleavage in frame.

"In a related story..." Her voice was high-pitched and shaky—a Minnie Mouse knock-off—nothing like the one she used in real life. "...two elderly Sherman residents were hospitalized—"

Katie bludgeoned the *ON-OFF* switch. "Un-*fucking*-believable!" Stacy started to say something, but she wasn't done. "Did you see that bimbo? It sounded like she sucked helium! God knows what else she sucked to get my job! We're going to be the laughingstock of this market, Stacy. Did you see that skimpy blouse? She might as well have worn nothing! Maybe next time she'll just sit there with her thirty-eight double-Ds flapping in the *goddamn wind!*" She wheeled and fired her empty glass at the fireplace, shards flying everywhere.

"Katie..." He stood, taking her by the arms. "...you're right, she's awful. But that just means she won't be here long. I mean, people aren't stupid. They know when they're being manipulated. A fancy set and fake boobs won't change the ratings. When Wilhelm figures that out—"

"You don't understand, Stacy." She stared at him, eyes welling with tears. "It's always the same. I'm not good enough. I'm *never* good enough!"

He didn't know what to say, so he pulled her close and held her. Finally, "*I* think you're good enough. I think you're perfect."

She leaned back and looked at him. "You do?"

"Yeah..." He brushed a tear from her cheek. "...and if Wilhelm thinks your writing needs work, then we'll work on it, together."

A fragile smile effaced her pain. "You'd do that for me?" He nodded. After a pause, she moved forward, kissing him on the mouth. He tasted salt, then felt her tongue. Heart pounding, he pulled her closer, moving his hands over her body. As the fire roared, she took his arm and led him to the bedroom.

\*\*\*

Making love to Katie Powers was like running a marathon. It started slow and steady, then turned to an all-out sprint for the finish line, a test of physical and emotional wills. At times, she looked deep into his eyes, at others past him. But her touch was undeniably electric, her movements catlike and deliberate.

"Where to now, dude?"

Stacy flinched at the sound of his new cameraman's voice, a thin falsetto with an Oklahoma twang. Julius Candelle stared at him, eyes magnified through thick glasses. "Sorry. Make a left at the light."

Stacy was daydreaming again, the image of him and Katie raiding his addled brain. He hadn't been looking for a relationship—now he was knee-deep in one. *How much sleep had he gotten the night before? One hour? Two?* Hard to say, but as the afternoon wore on, it was getting harder and harder to concentrate.

"Seem a little out of it, dude."

Stacy stared at the man. The lanky camera op looked older than his twenty-three years, his expression one of wisdom. "Just tired is all."

"Too much partyin' last night?" A silver cross dangled from his left ear, catching the December sun.

"Something like that." He had no intention of elaborating—his mother had raised a gentleman. "You can pull over any time."

Julius veered to the curb. "What you got in mind?"

They stared at Banks Park, several kids climbing the jungle gym, a few others gliding down slides. "I just need some B-roll to go with the stats."

State officials had released a study showing slight increases in Oklahoma child abuse cases. Toole saw it as an attention-grabbing six o'clock kicker. "A deadly trend," he called it, "one linked to the spiraling Texomaland economy."

He'd already written the lead-in.

"It's a child abuse piece," Stacy explained, "so make sure you shoot from a distance. No faces. We don't want any false light lawsuits."

The new camera op climbed from the car, his expression dark. He was more than familiar with today's topic, having grown up in one of the poorest sections of Oklahoma City. Grabbing the gear, he dropped to one knee and aimed his lens at the sun.

"What are you doing?" Stacy leaped from the car. "You'll burn the tubes!"

The man turned. "We're still usin' *tube* cameras?" Stacy nodded. "Dude, that ain't gonna work. That ain't gonna work at all!"

"It's going to have to work. It's all we've got."

He climbed to his feet, clearly irritated. "How am I s'posed to give you anything creative with this old door stop?"

"Not my problem." Stacy was getting irritated as well—he still had a standup and three interviews to shoot. He thought for a moment. "You want creative?" He walked to the sandbox and picked up a ball, placing it in front of the camera. "Frame your shot with the ball in the foreground, the kids in the distance." The man didn't move. "Now what's wrong?"

"I ain't gonna shoot that."

"Why not?"

"It's a trumped-up shot. This is news. We're s'posed to shoot what we see, not what we want to see."

"Oh, for God's sake! This isn't Journalism school." Stacy tossed his Steno and took over. "Do you know how much work we have today?" The cameraman shrugged. "A *lot*, that's how much."

Stacy had never been prone to outbursts. But deadline pressure did things to people, lack of sleep only

70

adding to the problem. He zoomed in and hit *RECORD*. Perhaps the biggest surprise wasn't the outburst itself but the realization that things were changing—*he* was changing.

And not necessarily for the better.

*** 

"You know what to do, a shot of the defendants, a few cutaways." Bub DeSpain nodded, Stacy heading for the courtroom. As he pushed through the door, he ran into Marv Bridges.

"Watch it, young man." The undersheriff offered his bigger-than-life grin. "Ya wanna be arrested for assault on an officer?"

"No, sir."

"Don't call me sir. An' ya *shoulda* been arrested for that Thanksgivin' piece ya did. 'The Dangers a' Overcookin' a Turkey'? That was a crime burnin' a bird like that!"

Stacy smiled. "It wasn't *my* idea."

"Didn't think it was. Told the wife ya had more sense."

"You watch Channel 8 every night?"

"Figger since the fourth estate's watchin' me, I best be doin' the same with them. 'Sides..." He winked. "...I like that Katie Powers."

Stacy flushed red—*did Bridges know something?* "You don't have a Nielsen box, do you?"

"Only box I got near the TV's a box a' Cheese Nips. An' it gets plenty a' use."

"All rise."

Both turned to see Judge Harold Brinkman enter, wearing a tattered robe and a scowl. After a nod, Bridges moved to the back wall, Stacy sitting.

As the bailiff riffled through information, reporters took notes, Bub shooting through the window. Cameras weren't allowed in Judge Brinkman's courtroom. He felt they impeded the judicial process.

"Harold Albert Griggs and Edna Maxine Griggs, you've been charged by the state of Oklahoma with possession of marijuana and possession with intent to distribute." Stacy recognized the couple from their unflattering mug shots. They shared a public defender. "You wish to make a plea?"

"We do, your honor," the lawyer spoke up. "My clients would like to plead guilty to the first count. Not guilty to the second count."

The judge reviewed his notes, then turned to Harold Griggs. "Sir, according to these charges, ten bundles of marijuana were harvested from your property. Do you expect this court to believe you grew a hundred-and-fifty pounds of marijuana and had no intent to distribute it?"

"Hell, yeah..." His attorney elbowed him. "...I mean...yes, yer honor."

The magistrate peered down through half-moon spectacles. "Just what were you planning to do with it then?"

Harold Griggs looked at his lawyer, then back at the judge. "I's gonna smoke it."

Several onlookers chuckled, the Assistant D.A. and court stenographer among them. As Stacy glanced around the room, everyone seemed to be smiling—everyone but Bridges. For the first time Stacy could remember, his friendly expression was gone, replaced by one of hatred. Apparently, the man found no humor in what this, or any other, drug pusher had to say.

\*\*\*

The phone rang six times before he found the handset. "H-h-hello."

"Stacy. Larry Toole." Half-asleep, Stacy stared at the clock—3:00 a.m. "I just got off the phone with Julius. He'll meet you there." The man sounded wired, Stacy still in a fog. "The fire's at the old mill." *Fire?* His senses racked into focus. "According to the scanner, it's a three bagger."

Stacy stared at the device next to his bed. He'd killed it around midnight, unable to sleep.

"You dressed?"

"Yeah..." He climbed to his feet. "...I'll be out of here soon."

"Sooner the better." *Click.* Stacy moved to the bathroom, splashing water against his face. A minute later, he was dressed and headed for the car.

Climbing in the Celica was like stepping into a meat locker. It took five minutes to defrost the windshield, another ten to make it across town. As he turned on Martin Luther King—formerly 3rd Avenue—he saw the yellow-orange glow, the building fully engulfed. He wondered how the fire started. The place hadn't been used in years. That meant no electricity and no vindictive employees. He looked to the cloudless sky. Lightning hadn't started it, that was for sure.

He rolled to a stop, taken aback by the sheer size of the blaze. Flames leaped fifty feet in the air, smoke replacing stars. He'd never seen a fire of this magnitude. He was struck by its formidableness—its power.

"What's up, dude?" Julius waved, mounting a Sony DXC-3000 to the tripod.

"Where did *that* come from?"

The cameraman grinned, teeth showing over a ratty scarf. "Don't worry 'bout where it came from. Just be glad we got it." He hooked the camera to the deck and began shooting, first a wide shot, then a series of close-ups. His gloved hands worked quickly, panning, zooming, then hoisting the new toy to his shoulder. "Now for the good shit!" He headed straight for the fire, ducking under the caution tape when no one was looking. Stacy thought he was crazy. He was also damn glad to have him. By now, Darryl would've called home twice and Bub would be looking for marshmallows.

The fire roared for two-and-a-half hours, the unbearable heat making Stacy forget the winter. In many ways, it seemed a living thing, angry and unconquerable. But three fire units eventually tamed the beast. By six in the morning, flames were a memory.

Channel 2 showed up at 6:15, Channel 7 an hour later. Julius, sweat-soaked and soot-covered, had already captured three twenty-minute loads, Stacy having interviewed Roy Maghee, two witnesses, and an ex-mill foreman.

It didn't happen often, but Channel 8 had scooped the competition.

Stacy and Julius returned to the station, conquering heroes. Toole was ecstatic. Amy Chow blocked time for her new lead story. After drinking half the water cooler, Julius headed to the edit booth, Stacy sitting down to type.

An hour later, he got the call from Maghee. "The mill fire was suspicious."

Stacy leaned forward, still covered in ash. "Meaning?"

There was a long pause. "Meaning the actual cause hasn't been determined. But all accidental causes have been ruled out."

When Stacy told Toole, the man rejoiced. Now in addition to exclusive footage, he had a legitimate lead!

At 12:01, Toole leaned into camera, trying his best to look humble. "Good day, Texomaland. Investigators are calling it arson..."

***

Roy Maghee pressed the buzzer, juggling presents as he reached for a cigarette. His wife's stare said, 'Don't even think about it.' After twelve years of marriage, the pair could speak volumes without uttering a word.

Marv Bridges opened the door. "Well, if it ain't the 'Princess an' the Pauper'." Tanya Maghee smiled. Her husband didn't. "Kaye's in the kitchen, havin' a go at the goose. Make sure she don't overcook it this year." The woman hugged him on her way past, the place unkempt as ever.

"Merry Christmas, Ebenezer."

"Ya work all day on that one?"

Maghee handed him the gifts. "Don't say I never gave you anything."

Bridges stared at the presents. Had it really been two years since the Maghees gave Jake that tackle box? The kid's smile had lit the room. "Lemme guess…fruitcake an' Cold Duck." His guest nodded. "Not exactly Waterford crystal, but thanks."

Maghee walked to the fireplace, trying to get warm. There was no Christmas tree. No carols being played on the console. It was downright depressing—same as last year. "You going to break into *Jingle Bells* or are we going to crack that Duck?"

"Kaye…" The undersheriff hollered. "…we're goin' outside ta inspect that deck I been meanin' ta put in." As usual, there was no response. Grabbing a hat, he led his friend through the back door.

"That's a fire hazard, you know." Maghee pointed to a wad of extension cords, each leading to a dust-covered power tool.

75

"Ah, well..." Bridges half-smiled. "...ain't like we got much ta lose." He looked to the dirt in the backyard. "I was gonna put in one a' them fancy gazebos. Plant some trees maybe." He turned back to his friend. "Can't never seem ta find the time."

"You'll get to it."

Bridges shrugged, popping the plastic cork. "Guess I shoulda grabbed a glass. We'll have ta make like the old days." He raised the bottle and chugged, then passed it to Maghee.

The man sipped, lighting a cigarette. "You remember the time we caught those bass at Muxie's pond?"

Bridges looked indignant. "You mean, *I* caught 'em. You just snagged logs."

"That's not how I remember it."

He grabbed the bottle back.

"We filled three ice chests with fish," Maghee continued, "then took them to the high school in the back of that old Chevy I bought."

"*We* bought. An', yeah, I 'member. It was one a' the few times it ran."

The investigator took a drag. "It was pitch dark when we got there. Couldn't see the ground beneath us. But somehow we managed to dump all those fish in the pool before hightailing it home."

Bridges chuckled, bumming a cigarette. "Not sure how we *made* it home after all them beers. Circulated a petition the next day, askin' for the day off on account a' the 'Christmas Miracle in the Swimmin' Pool'." Both men laughed. "Said it was bigger'n Mary givin' birth in the stables! Even threatened ta call the papers."

Maghee flicked ash in an empty pot. "Only papers we got were the ones serving us detention. I told you I had a bad feeling." Even then, Maghee was famous for his bad feelings. They were rarely wrong.

"How's I s'posed ta 'member we had three ice chests instead a' two."

"You could've at least grabbed the one with my name on it!"

They laughed again, downing more champagne. But as Maghee took another hit, his expression grew serious.

"I've got another bad feeling, Marv." The lawmen looked at each other, smoke wafting between them. "Whoever set that mill fire knew what he was doing." He stubbed his cigarette out in the dirt. "I'm afraid we haven't seen the last of him."

\*\*\*

Stacy knelt at the doorstep, snow falling in wispy flurries. Three letters and a package blocked his path. He grabbed them on the way in. It was pushing midnight. He'd worked another twelve-hour shift, then gone shopping, anxious to get a frozen pizza in the oven.

But like 'the cat', curiosity was killing him.

He set everything down and opened the package. It held one of his demo tapes, with a note from the CBS affiliate in Boise. *Thanks for submitting your work, but we've hired another candidate.* The letters were much the same, offering words like *however* and *unfortunately*. The last letter wasn't a letter at all, just a copy of Stacy's resume, the words *NO THANKS* scrawled at the top.

He stared at the pile, trying to decide what he was feeling. Strangely enough, it was relief. A lot had happened since he mailed those tapes. *Katie* had happened. And though staying in Avalon wasn't part of his plan...maybe it was the right thing for now.

He reached in the bag and pulled out a Heineken. Stacy didn't treat himself to expensive beer often, but it *was* New Year's Eve—and his birthday! Born at 11:59 p.m.

on December 31, 1964, he was the last 'Baby Boomer'. He opened the beer and drank, setting the bottle next to the Underwood. As he stared at the keys, his mind drifted back to his twelfth birthday. His mother had wrapped a cigar box in newspaper. Inside, a note told him to look in his room. When he did, he found the typewriter sitting on his desk, a huge red ribbon tied to the space bar.

It was the greatest gift he'd ever received.

This year, his mother sent him a pair of galoshes and three new ties. He hadn't made it home for the holidays. He'd spent Christmas alone, Katie having used vacation time to be with her family in Texas. She'd called once or twice but sounded distracted. Chip Hale had invited Stacy to a New Year's Eve party, but, as always, he declined.

He fired up the oven and turned on the radio. As he drank, he stared at the empty room. In the corner, miniature lights blinked on a dying Christmas tree. In the window, a strand of tinsel formed a melancholy smile.

"Happy New Year, Avalon," a voice echoed through the speakers. "This is Nate Shefler, wishing you all the best in the coming year. May your goals be met, your resolutions realized, and your dreams come true."

As *Auld Lang Syne* played again and again, Stacy killed his beer. He'd never felt so alone in his life. So filled with questions about where life was taking him.

The new year would bring answers.

Some he was ready for. Some not.

# CHAPTER 6
## January 1988

*(NEWSWIRE): VICE PRES. BUSH AND CBS NEWS ANCHOR DAN RATHER SPAR ON LIVE TV OVER V.P.'s ROLE IN IRAN-ARMS DEAL ... SCIENTISTS WARN OF 'RADON GAS' DANGERS TO AMERICAN HOMES ... REDSKINS DEFEAT BRONCOS 42–10 IN SUPER BOWL XXII*

Stacy stared at his desk calendar. 1988. The number looked strange. Futuristic. In the year to come, a black man would make a serious run at the White House. The space shuttle would soar again. And GM would proclaim, "This is not your father's Oldsmobile." On TV, Geraldo would break his nose in a brawl with white supremacists, Donahue would wear a dress, and Oprah would shed sixty pounds. Is Elvis alive? It's a question people would be asking. And those same people would elect the country's 41st president, George Herbert Walker Bush, who promised, "A kinder, gentler nation."

"Quiet down, people!" A hush fell over the newsroom as Dick Wilhelm entered, smiling. It wasn't the smile he used on advertisers. The G.M. actually looked happy—jubilant in fact. "I trust you all had a pleasant holiday." Stacy surveyed the room. Everyone was there but Katie. She'd driven back late last night and had probably overslept. He hoped Wilhelm wouldn't notice. "I have a surprise for you. Follow me."

They moved down the hall in a nervous procession, Thad making arm motions to mimic a freight train. When they passed Toole's office, the news director spoke into the phone—pacing, smoking.

Cold fire greeted them as they filed outside, the January sun obscuring their view. "This way, people." Like a well-dressed Moses, Wilhelm led his followers around the corner, not to the 'Land of Promise', but to the next best thing—at least in his eyes. "There it is. Our chariot to glory!"

The crew looked puzzled, Stacy stepping past Reg McNair—no one could see over that pompadour. On the patchy snow sat an Econoline van, equipped with all-terrain tires and a telescoping microwave. The back doors were open, a man with wild hair and a *Great 8* parka polishing the console. "What is it?" someone asked.

Wilhelm faced the crowd. "This, my little friends, is what separates us from the competition." As he moved forward, Katie tiptoed in from the rear. She wore a pretty new dress—a Christmas gift, no doubt—so formfitting it made her breasts look two sizes larger. Stacy couldn't stop staring.

"You're looking at Texomaland's first—and only—live truck. And tomorrow, it's going to have the *Great 8* logo emblazoned on both sides!" Several people pushed forward, Julius leading the way. "As you can see, I've spared no expense. There's an edit bay, an audio suite, and enough generator power to light Avalon for a month." Stacy peered into the van. The accommodations were

80

indeed plush, the impressive control panel blinking red, white, and blue—a silent tribute to the U.S. of A.

"I've done my job, people. Now it's your turn." He pointed to the man in the parka. "I want you to keep Brannuck here hopping." The G.M. had emancipated Don Brannuck from the *ENGINEERS* room. And with an extra dime an hour in his pocket, he had no intention of going back. "This is the best system money can buy, and you can bet your life we're going to use it. I want to go live at noon, six, and ten. I want to knock Channels 2 and 7 on their unsuspecting asses!"

"You won't have to wait long." Toole appeared from nowhere, smile rivaling his boss'. "I just talked to Avalon P.D." He glanced at a note, Wilhelm looking hopeful. "Nineteen-year-old girl was working the nightshift at McDermott's. Somebody robbed the place, then led her away at knifepoint. No one's heard from her since." He looked to the sparkling van. "Button her up, Don, and get the hell out of here." He turned to Katie. "And Miss Powers, now that you've decided to 'grace us' with your presence, you and Bub can join him. You'll be the lead at noon—live from the fucking scene!" He handed her the note. "The rest of you have wasted enough time. Go get your assignments."

Stacy smiled at Katie, then made his way inside with the others. From the corner of his eye, he saw Wilhelm and Toole high-five.

*** 

"You've been here four months now?"

Stacy sat, watching his boss move back and forth through the tiny office. Other than when he anchored, Toole never sat—he had too much energy. "Yes, sir."

"It's Larry. *Sir* makes me feel old." He smiled. Stacy didn't.

The news director went back to the file, his close-set eyes scanning the text. He was conducting reviews of every employee, and Stacy's number was up. The reporter surveyed the room. Toole's desk was as neat as Wilhelm's, notes divided into piles, files an exercise in symmetry. Hard to believe this was once Terrance Meeks' office.

"My predecessor had some nice things to say about you." Stacy squirmed in his seat, Toole taking a hit of his KOOL. "I'll read it to you. 'Good instincts. Strong voice. Excellent writer.'" He looked up, smoke clouding his yellow-green eyes. "I agree with every comment but the last."

Stacy moved forward. "What's wrong with my writing?" The question came out more challenge than query.

Toole raised a hand, smoke trailing like the remnants of a candle. "Nothing, *per se*. Especially when compared to your coworkers'. But you can do better." He reached for a script. "This is your lead-in from last night. 'The winter weather has led to a blood shortage in Texoma. As Bill Stacy reports, health officials are asking area residents for help.'"

"Yeah..." Stacy's skin prickled. "...so what?"

"My point exactly." The news director snuffed out his cig. "If I'm one of the poor bastards in our coverage area, sitting in my Barcalounger, thinking about my shitty job, my wife's affinity for other men, why should I give a fuck about your story?" Stacy had no answer, Toole setting the script down. "This lead-in's gutless. It gives the viewer no reason to stay tuned. To care about the information you spent the better part of a day collecting for him." He grabbed a pen and scribbled something down. "Read this."

82

Stacy cleared his throat. "'Better not have a serious accident in Texomaland. As Bill Stacy reports, there may not be enough blood to save your life.'" He handed the script back, gut twisting with indecision. "So..." He chose his words carefully. "...you want us to scare our viewers into paying attention?"

Toole shoved the page back in the folder, grabbing another KOOL. "What do you think of me?" Stacy didn't answer. "I'll tell you what you think. You think I'm brash, vain, pompous, and egotistical." He struck a match, inhaling smoke. "And you're right. Those qualities put me on the fast track as a reporter. They got me out of this hellhole in six months, out of Joplin in eight. They took me all the way to the big time as a reporter. And they'll do the same for me as a news director." He blew an asp-like trail. "Now you can buy into the program and come along for the ride, end up in New York, L.A., Chicago, wherever you want. Or you can keep doing it *your* way and spend the next ten years in Avalon, Oklahoma."

Stacy had no intention of staying here that long. "I... want to get better, sir."

"*Larry.*" Smoke curled from his nose. "Then I'm going to ask you to do things. Get involved with your stories. Become part of what you're covering. If there's a flood, put on waders and stand chest-deep in water. If there's a fire, get close enough to singe your eyebrows. If someone spurns an interview, ambush him. And if that doesn't work, set up your camera and pound on the door. You might get the footage of a lifetime." He paused for another hit. "And one more thing—never trust a cop. His job is to keep information from you. Your job is to get it in spite of him."

Stacy sighed. *Grandstanding? Ambush interviews?* This wasn't what he signed up for. Then again, Toole's record spoke for itself. And if he wanted to keep his job—

at least for now—he'd better comply. He knew one thing. There was no way *his* future included ten years in Avalon, Oklahoma. "I'll do my best."

"I know you will. And as a sign of faith, I'm giving you the primo assignment today." He snatched an article from the corkboard. "One of the local yokels petitioned the city to change his street name back to 3rd Avenue. Doesn't like writing Martin Luther King, Jr. on his envelopes, he says." Stacy had seen the article in the *Herald*. "He's tired of getting the runaround, so he called in some friends."

"Friends?"

"The KKK. They're holding a rally outside the courthouse at five. Sheets. Hoods. The whole nine yards. I want you and Julius to interview the old man, the city manager, some people in the black community. Then we'll go live at six..." His smile widened. "...from the heart of the fucking rally!"

Stacy hesitated. "Sir...I mean, *Larry*...I hope you don't mind me asking this, but why are we covering this story?" Toole looked puzzled. "I mean, aren't we just playing into their hands, you know, giving them a forum for their...views?"

Toole flicked ash. "I've covered nine Ku Klux Klan rallies over the years. From little towns in Missouri to the steps of the Texas capitol. You know the best thing about the Klan?" Stacy shook his head. "You never know what they're going to do. Suppose this little gathering turns ugly. Maybe a fight breaks out. Or the 'sheets' square off with Avalon's finest. Is it a story then?"

Stacy nodded, albeit reluctantly. But he had one more question. "You said *Julius* and I...is that really a smart idea?"

Toole blew a smoke ring. "I think it's brilliant."

\*\*\*

84

"Martin Luther King, Jr. was a damn Communist!" The man in the snow-white robe screamed into a bullhorn, trying his best to insight the crowd. It wasn't working—the eight people on hand looked bored. "It's time the white man stood up to the establishment. Time we say no to our minority-ruled leaders. Time we take back what's rightfully ours!"

His face grew redder with each statement. Behind him, twenty Klansmen stood in a half-circle, robes starched, hats resembling dunce caps. They'd driven up from Alabama, their confederate-flagged pickups parked in the alley behind City Hall. To the left, a line of stern-faced policemen held batons. To the right, a row of potbellied sheriff's deputies watched and listened. News crews from Channels 2, 7, and 8 jockeyed for position on the frozen lawn, along with Nate Shefler from KAVN and Billy Nemetz of the *Avalon Herald*.

Stacy sat in the live truck, shuttling tape for his six o'clock package. He'd gotten the bites Toole requested, plus an extra from Judge Brinkman on the right to assemble. "Ready to send, Don?" Brannuck nodded, swapping out patch cords at record speed. In the deep catacombs of the *ENGINEERS* room, he'd seldom experienced stress. Now it weighed on him like a steel overcoat.

Stacy climbed from the van, summoning Julius. They moved to the courthouse, Brannuck setting up lights. Toole would introduce the piece, then bring Stacy on live for a follow-up with the Klan leader. The man had agreed to the live-TV format, a perfect way to advance 'the cause' without expunction.

"Two minutes," Brannuck warned, handing Stacy a microphone. The reporter inserted his IFB, Julius framing the shot with Stacy in the foreground, Klansmen in the distance.

"Mic check, Bill," he heard the director in his ear. Stacy recited a line of text. "Thank you." Nodding, he waved the Klan rep over, the man yielding the bullhorn to a short fat Kluxer with three missing teeth. The pair had ridden from Huntsville to Avalon together, the eight-hour trip giving them time to discuss 'the revolution'.

"How do you do, sir?" The man removed his hat. Without the hood, he wasn't very imposing. Ethan 'Butch' Stark was 5' 8" with sad eyes and a creampuff nose, his flesh the color of a newborn piglet's. Stacy clipped a mic to his robe. "When they toss it from the studio, I'll introduce you, then ask a few questions. Half-a-minute's all we get." The man nodded, putting his hat back on.

"Ten seconds," Brannuck hollered, checking his signal for the umpteenth time. As Julius zoomed, Stacy held his breath. *Rocket blast. Narrator.* Then Toole, reciting the lead-in with the passion of a preacher.

"Roll video," the director whispered. The piece ran for ninety seconds, the out-cue, "...still underway at this hour." When Stacy heard it, he lowered his notes.

"Joining us now live from the Dexter County Courthouse is Great 8 reporter Bill Stacy. Bill, I understand things are a bit tense."

*That wasn't the toss Stacy'd written!* "I'm not sure *tense* is the right word, Larry. But there *are* a number of law enforcement agents here to make sure things don't get out of hand." He turned to the man on his right. "Ku Klux Klan leader 'Butch' Stark is with us tonight. Mr. Stark, are you disappointed in the turnout?"

"No, I am not!" He looked into camera. "We have hundreds of brothers in Dexter County, thousands across Texomaland. Unfortunately, not everyone—"

"Why are you here?" Stacy cut him off. "We know about the alleged street name dispute, but why are you *really* here?"

The man narrowed his gaze. "We're here to educate the people of Avalon. To open their eyes to the atrocities bein' perpetrated on the white man in America."

"What exactly are those atrocities, sir?"

"The coloreds are takin' our jobs, our tax money, even our women. And the politicians are lettin' 'em. We're tired of bein' ignored. Tired of bein'—"

"Thank you, Mr. Stark. I'm afraid we're out of time."

"What do you mean?"

Stacy turned. "The rally is scheduled to end at seven. Attendees are asked to leave the square in an orderly manner. Larry."

Stacy stared, Julius holding his shot. After a pause, Brannuck yelled, "Clear!"

"What kinda shit was that?" the Klansman carped.

Stacy looked at him, gut twisting. Another bully, this one—like so many others—finding strength in numbers. "We do a half-hour newscast, Mr. Stark. I think we gave you ample time."

"Ample time, my ass!"

Julius took Stacy's microphone, then reached for the Klansman's.

"Don't touch me, *nigger*!"

Stacy instinctively stepped forward. "You better watch your mouth!"

The little man sized up the hulking reporter, then summoned his followers. They moved in like flies on dung, reaching beneath their robes to produce tire irons and chains. "Think ya can take on twenty of us?"

"He won't have ta." Stacy wheeled to see Marv Bridges pointing a shotgun, deputies and police officers

87

closing in behind him. "Ya make one wrong move an' them pretty little white sheets're gonna get awful red."

The man stared up both barrels, then looked back at Stacy, his mouth twisting in an ugly knot. "You an' me ain't *really* so different, are we?" They stared at one another, a million thoughts swirling through Stacy's brain.

"That's enough, Stark," Bridges intervened. "This meetin's over."

"Permit says we got 'til seven, *chief.*"

"I don't give two shits what your permit says." Bridges cut his eyes to the street. "I suggest you an' your skirt-wearin' pals go find the rock ya'll climbed out from under. 'Less, a' course, ya'd like ta stick around an' visit our friendly little jail."

"On what grounds?"

"Well…" Bridges spat tobacco. "…I'm sure we can come up with somethin'."

Stark glared at him, then turned to his friends and nodded. One by one, they shuffled off to the alley, floating like ghosts on an ebony sea. Stark looked over his shoulder one last time. "'Member what I said, boy. An' 'member somethin' else. We ain't done, you an' me."

"*Move!*" Bridges barked.

Grinning like a possum, he slunk into the night.

\*\*\*

Stacy watched the ten o'clock news in disbelief, his exchange with 'Butch' Stark airing in its entirety. Although the on-air feed was killed immediately after the interview, Julius' camera continued to roll. Brannuck discovered the tape when he returned to the station, handing it off to Toole.

"Eureka!" he yelled as if striking oil. After clearing four minutes at the top of the newscast, Toole introduced the 'exclusive' video. The scene was indeed riveting. Even Stacy found himself glued to his set, the footage making him bristle all over again. Especially the part where Stark claimed they were somehow alike.

*Ridiculous!* Stacy didn't hate black people. Didn't judge anyone on the color of his skin. He stared at the TV, eyes moving to his own reflection in the glass. *Was it ridiculous?* If forced to admit it, he didn't necessarily trust blacks. Was even a little scared of them. He took a drink, the beer going down hard. It *was* true, at least partially. He did have those feelings. But only because the kids who picked on him when he was young were black. *He had reason to be afraid...didn't he?*

Someone knocked at the door.

He started to get up but changed his mind, in no mood for visitors. The knock came again, harder this time. "All right." He walked over and peered through the eyehole. "Julius?"

"We need to talk!" Stacy opened the door, the cameraman barging in.

"Okay...let's talk."

"I don't need you or anybody else stickin' up for me." His voice was higher than usual, his glasses fogged with sweat.

"Sticking up for you?" Stacy killed the television. "What are you talking about?"

"You know what I'm talkin' 'bout. I don't need you comin' to my rescue. I can fight my own battles."

Stacy watched his expression turn from anger to hurt. "I know you can...it's just, I didn't like what the guy was saying—"

"You think *I* like what he was sayin'?" The anger was back—at new levels. "Think I like bein' treated like a second-class citizen? Nobody does. But that's what it's like. Blacks on one side of town, whites on the other. I know. I lived my whole life in this state. And I'll tell you somethin' else." His stare was buck-knife-sharp. "It doesn't take a knight from the Ku Klux Klan to use the word *nigger* either!"

Stacy wasn't sure what to say, but he had to say something. "Look, Julius...I may not have grown up black, but I did grow up poor—"

"That ain't the same! Nobody ever made their mind up 'bout you before you even met. And the shit dude was spewin', that's what white people think, isn't it?" Stacy shook his head. "Well, I got news for you. I never asked for special treatment. Don't believe in it! Don't want it!" He paused for a breath. "But I'll tell you somethin' else I don't want. I don't want people bein' nice to my face and talkin' shit behind my back."

"Julius, I never—"

"I'm not talkin' 'bout you. But I hear things. And I got eyes. I know I'm the only brother at Channel 8. I also know I've been here a month and not *one person* has asked me over to his house...or to a party...or to grab a beer after work." He paused again. "Bet *you* didn't have to wait that long." Stacy stared at his coworker, then down at the floor. "Doesn't always take a Klansman to make you feel worthless, does it?"

Without warning, the window exploded, glass flying everywhere.

"*What the—?*"

Julius scrambled to the door, Stacy on his heels. Throwing it open, they stared in horror at the despicable thing in front of them—a wooden cross engulfed in flames.

Stacy turned to Julius, light dancing in the hollows of his cheeks. The man's eyes refused to blink, refused to stray even one degree from the vile tempest before him.

He looked harder than he had moments ago—older—the unbearable heat doing little to vanquish the chill. Finally, he walked to the planter and grabbed a hose.

It took more than a minute to extinguish the blaze. When the last flame flickered out, he stared at the smoking crucifix. Stacy, unable to look at the thing a second longer, stepped forward and kicked it over, the cross breaking into pieces. "I'll call the police."

"They ain't comin' back." Julius coiled up the hose. "Besides...how do you think they got your address in the first place?"

Stacy stared at the smoldering wood. 'Bill Stacy' wasn't in the phonebook. Stacy Zwardowski was. And only his coworkers and a few city officials knew his real name.

"Say what you want 'bout Larry Toole, but he's right when it comes to cops—never trust anyone with a badge." Julius moved up the walk, stopping in the halo of a streetlamp. "Better yet, never trust anyone."

\*\*\*

"You're the talk of the town, Stacy!" Darryl steered through the darkness. It was four in the morning, no one up but cops, drug dealers, and journalists—they were all about to meet. "My wife had her Bunco group over, and that's all they talked about. You and that KKK guy!"

The cameraman droned on, Stacy trying to ignore him. His clash with 'Butch' Stark had indeed brought attention. Billy Nemetz had interviewed him for the paper. Nate Shefler offered a guest DJ spot. And Channel 8 ran endless promos— "The Great 8 News Team. Fighting for a Better Texomaland!" Stacy couldn't wait for things to return to normal—even if normal did include the occasional 3:00 a.m. wakeup call.

Toole had rousted him from sleep again, this time for a methamphetamine bust. Sheriff's deputies had raided a compound near Ratliff City, finding two wired suspects and a lab rivaling Dr. Frankenstein's. Stacy's assignment was to get as much footage as possible and wait for the live truck.

Toole wanted to break into *Good Morning, America*.

"We're close." Stacy drew an ice-cold breath, the air reeking. "There!" He pointed to a sheriff's vehicle, one of eight lining the frozen driveway. Darryl pulled over, passing an Oklahoma Bureau of Narcotics van.

As they walked up the drive, they passed several deputies, some nodding, others ignoring them. Stacy couldn't help wondering which one tipped off the Klan.

"Bill Stacy!" a voice came from the shadows. "We gotta stop meetin' like this!" Marv Bridges stepped through the weeds, a windbreaker his only shield against the cold. "Figgered y'all'd be the first ta arrive, 'least nowadays."

"How are you, Marv?"

"Fair ta middlin'."

Stacy cut his eyes to the ground. "By the way..." He looked up. "...thanks for your help the other night."

"Don't mention it." He tromped down a path. "This way, fellas. An' don't go strayin' off on your own. This here's one dangerous crime scene." Stacy grabbed the tripod, Darryl gulping. "Came upon these boys at two in the mornin'. Had ta be quiet as church mice, too. Listenin' devices everywhere."

Stacy stopped at a long-dead hedge. The scene before him was surreal. Portable lights enveloped a crumbling shack, the roof sagging like a mattress. Chickens—most still alive—filled a makeshift coop. And two chained Rottweilers guarded the door. Stacy covered his nose. "What *is* that?"

"Phenylacitic acid," the undersheriff answered. "Used in the cookin' process. Bad stuff, too, but we in the law enforcement community love it. Gives 'em away ever' time."

Stacy took notes, Darryl zooming. "How did they survive in these conditions?"

"This ain't even the worst I've seen. Meth labbers don't need but a little food an' a lotta dope ta get by. These fellas ate eggs cooked on a propane grill. An' crapped on the floor when they couldn't make it ta the outhouse."

"How did you find them?"

"UPS man tipped us off. Ain't nobody untouchable. No matter how cut off from the outside world he *thinks* he is."

Stacy had a thought. "Any chance we could shoot inside?"

Bridges started to answer, but an OBN agent intervened. "I don't see why not. As long as we can get a copy of the tape."

Bridges glanced at Stacy, then pulled the bureau man aside. "Jim, these boys're friends a' mine. Not sure I want 'em goin' in there."

"Come on, Marv," the man argued. "You and I both know we're fighting a losing battle in this state. People need to see what we're up against."

Bridges thought for a minute. "Okay. But only the cameraman."

The agent turned to Stacy. "'Fraid you're a little tall for the HAZMAT suit."

"HAZMAT suit?" Darryl spoke up.

"An' a gas mask," Bridges added. "Chemicals'll knock ya for a loop otherwise. An' there's always the chance a' explosion." Darryl's face turned cocaine white. "For the record, my vote's still no, but if Jim's givin' his blessin'."

All eyes were on Darryl. A tick had developed in his left cheek, his pupils big as aggies. He wasn't used to making decisions. "I'd like to call my wife."

"Darryl," Stacy fumed, "these guys crap on the floor, for God's sake! They're not going to have a phone."

"I can radio her from the car. We have a CB at home!"

The lawmen smirked, Stacy frowning.

"All right, but make it fast. The competition'll be here any—"

"You must be psychic, Bill." Everyone turned as a muscular cameraman stomped through the grass. "Psychic powers *and* diplomatic grace with the KKK? You're a man of many talents." Stacy sent Darryl on his way, the Channel 2 camera op slipping on a plastic suit. The next few minutes passed like hours, an icy breeze stirring the dogwoods. As a rooster crowed, Darryl squeezed through the boscage.

"Sorry, my wife said no."

Stacy nodded, disappointed but sympathetic. He wasn't sure he'd have gone in either, not with the info Bridges supplied. If Stacy didn't know better, he'd swear the undersheriff was looking out for him. "Okay. More exteriors then."

As Darryl manned the camera, Stacy's gut twisted. He hoped Toole—and more importantly Wilhelm—wouldn't be watching Channel 2 tonight.

\*\*\*

"It must be eighty degrees in here." Katie fanned herself with a copy of her script, Stacy lowering the thermostat. He'd worked all day to clean his apartment, even found the source of the 'mystery stench'—a dead rat behind the fridge.

94

"I just can't shake this cold." He carried her plate to the sink, having prepared his mother's Irish Pot Roast. As always, she'd eaten next to nothing. "I'm not complaining. At least I'm still employed." Darryl Rogers was not. Turns out Wilhelm *did* watch Channel 2, firing the cameraman the minute he saw him.

Katie plucked her lead-in from the Underwood. "How many live shots are you up to?"

"Counting yesterday..." The scanner chirped behind him. "...ten."

Things had indeed been hectic. If *he* wasn't going live at noon, six, or ten, it was Katie or one of the others. The new live truck had taken over everyone's life. In the last month, he and Katie had worked on her writing twice, met for dinner once—and had sex less than that.

She handed him her script, then walked to the refrigerator. "Did I tell you I talked to Phil?" He shook his head, reading the new lead-in. Helping Katie with *her* writing had replaced working on his own. "He didn't sound good. He's living at home and working at Dairy Queen to pay for the tapes he's sending out." Stacy glanced at the closet—he'd shoved his demos inside before Katie arrived—then back at the script. "And he was crushed when Raul got that reporter's job in Springfield."

"This is much stronger, Katie. It gets right to the point, even frightens the viewer a little. I think Toole would love it."

"You do?" She opened a beer, voice quivering with schoolgirl hope.

"I do." She sat down next to him, offering a sip. Stacy shook his head. "I'd hate to pass this cold on to you."

"I'll take my chances." Their lips met with the fire of long-parted lovers. He'd failed to realize how much he missed her touch, her incredible skin. Dropping the script, he swept his hands over her body. She unbuttoned

95

his shirt. He pulled at her top. In no time, they were aroused to the point of eruption.

"Make love to me!" she demanded.

As he unhooked her bra, something stopped him. "What did you do?"

She pulled back, then looked to the floor. "Nothing, Stacy..." He continued to stare. "...I just...had a little surgery, that's all...when I went home for the holidays." She waited for a response. None came. "It's no big deal."

He'd suspected it for weeks. His suspicions were now confirmed.

Her new breasts were huge, as large—if not larger—than Lisa's.

"This doesn't have anything to do with our new co-anchor, does it?"

"Of course not!" she fired back. "How could you even think that?"

"Well..." He hesitated. "...it just seems odd that a month after we hire—"

"I don't want to talk about it." She pulled away, re-fastening her bra.

"How could you afford something like that?"

"Not that it's any of your business, but my father paid for it."

"Your father? But I thought—"

"It was a *gift*, okay? He asked me what I wanted for Christmas. And that's what I told him. Jesus, Stacy, most men would be happy!"

"I want *you* to be happy."

"I am." Her expression said otherwise.

He thought about leaving it at that—but didn't. "Because it's a hell of a price to pay if you're doing it for the wrong reasons...and I just think...well...I liked you better when you were all real."

It was a horrible choice of words, but editing was impossible.

"*All real?*" She shot to her feet, re-buttoning her blouse. "And just how *real* are you, 'Bill Stacy'?" He tried to calm her, but she wouldn't have it. "We've been seeing each other for months. How much have you told me about yourself?" She stuffed a foot in her pump. "I don't know any more about you today than I did at Turner Falls. You're a closed book. Too damn perfect to let anyone in." She stepped into her other shoe. "Well, some of us *aren't* perfect. Some of us have to do whatever it takes to make it in this business. And some of us have feelings. But you wouldn't know anything about that, would you?"

"Katie, listen—"

"No, *you* listen!" Tears streamed down her cheeks. "You don't know what I've been through! You have *no idea* what it's like to have a father who looks at you the way my father looks at me!" She stomped to the door and turned. "And until you do, don't judge me! Don't *ever* judge me!" She flung it open and stormed away, rattling the new window.

*Jesus, so much for honesty!* But deep down, he knew she was right. He hadn't shared his feelings with her, hadn't opened up about anything. As the scanner blipped, he looked to the framed photos on the table. She was right about something else, too.

He had no idea what it was like to have a father like Katie's.

He had no idea what it was like to have a father at all.

# CHAPTER 7
## *February 1988*

*(NEWSWIRE): FLORIDA GRAND JURY INDICTS GEN. MANUEL NORIEGA ON DRUG CHARGES ... TELEVANGELIST JIMMY SWAGGART BEGS CONGREGATION'S FORGIVENESS FOR 'UN-SPECIFIED SIN' ... CHRISTIANS AND MOSLEMS CLASH IN SOVIET REPUBLIC, LEAVING 31 DEAD*

Larry Toole was born on April Fool's Day. But his arrival was no joke. His parents had tried for years to have children. When they stopped trying, Larry Albert Toole II 'reported live' on the scene. Tipping the scales at just two-and-a-half pounds, the scrawny preemie was offered little hope. But the Tooles had money, Larry, Sr. an oil man, Evelyn an attorney. Ignoring their doctor's advice, they chartered a plane to Europe, walking out of a clinic five weeks later with a healthy baby boy. It wasn't theirs, of course. But a young nurse was able to retire early on what the Tooles paid her to make the switch. And the baby's real parents, a blue-collar couple from Sweden, buried 'their child' a week later.

Little Larry grew up on the right side of the tracks. Went to the best schools. Wore the nicest clothes. As a result, money meant nothing to him. Fame was what he wanted. And power.

In high school, he landed a job as a DJ. His shift ran from midnight to four, but he had no trouble staying up— sleep was less important to him than money. His late-night program got so popular, the station moved him to primetime, clearing the wee hours for his other passion— terrorizing the local community. He and his friends trespassed, 'borrowed' cars, and used drugs, all with regularity.

By the time he graduated high school, Toole had a rap sheet longer than the Cimarron. To avoid prosecution, his parents struck a deal with the D.A. Their son would go to college out of state, returning home only after he received a degree—a Broadcast Journalism degree, as it turned out. With delinquency behind him, he could focus on becoming the best reporter UT ever turned out. He spoke like his network heroes, even dressed like them, amassing a wardrobe that rivaled Cronkite's. And when he graduated top of his class, he knew just where he wanted to go—KEGT in Avalon. A month after hiring on, Toole aired an exposé on the D.A.'s office, causing three people to lose their jobs, the prosecutor who'd banished him landing in prison.

Revenge was sweet. And so was the TV news business.

"Katie, Stacy." He waved them into his office. "You two are working together today." They glanced at each other, not having spoken in days. Stacy knew the quarrel was his fault but was too stubborn to admit it. "Just got a call on the hotline." Toole had instituted a 'Great 8 Tip

Number' to elicit story ideas, running flashy bumpers at the end of every news promo. It was starting to pay off. "Guy from the Rowdywear plant."

"The pants manufacturer?" Katie asked.

Toole nodded. "Seems the owner's bouncing checks. Workers haven't been paid in weeks. The ones who haven't walked are ready to revolt. Tipster says if they don't get paid by closing time, they're going to demonstrate in front of the plant. And here's the best part. He only called one station."

"You think the owner'll talk to us?"

"Who gives a fuck?" Toole lit a cig. "What's he going to say? 'Times are hard?' 'We're doing what we can?' It's all bullshit anyway. Besides, why create sympathy for the man? This story's about the little guy. It's big business versus the non-unionized laborer. I want you there at five sharp. Shoot the demonstration. Talk to employees. Get someone—anyone—to go on camera and condemn the front office. And when it comes to the owner...well...we'll just say he's unavailable for comment."

Stacy shifted in his seat. "Is that really fair?"

"No less fair than failing to pay your employees."

"I couldn't agree more, Larry," Katie offered, chest out.

Stacy shot her a glance. "One more question...why both of us?"

He raised the KOOL to his lips. "New concept I'm testing out. Team coverage. 'Reporter A' covers one angle, 'Reporter B' another. Then we use the truck for back-to-back live shots." He paused to blow smoke. "Stacy, you're on the main story—the payroll problems, the disgruntled workers. Katie, you do the related piece— 'What Would a Plant Closing Mean to the Local Economy?'" He smiled, smoke encircling his head like a riot helmet.

"It's ratings month again. I want our friends at Channels 2 and 7 to know they're in for a dogfight. Any questions?" They shook their heads. "Good..." He pointed to the door. "...as in *good*-bye!"

*\*\**

The drive to Rowdywear, Inc. that afternoon was a long one. A freak storm had dumped six inches of snow on Avalon, painting the landscape a shimmery white. The competition would lead their newscasts with weather stories. Channel 8 had other ideas.

"So," Stacy broke the week-long silence, "did you get the bites you needed?"

"Oh, you're talking to me now?"

"Look, Katie...about the other night..." He turned on Main, passing a snowplow. "...I didn't mean what I said...I was in shock! I mean, you have to admit, that was some surprise."

The hurt in her eyes faded. "I know it was. And I meant to tell you. It's just..." She smiled. "...how do you bring something like that up? 'Sorry about your chest cold, Stacy. And speaking of chests, I had my boobs done.'"

They laughed awkwardly, Stacy taking her hand. "I'm sorry. I didn't mean to judge you. I just didn't want you to think you had to change." He hesitated. "I like you the way you are."

She leaned in to kiss him, but the scene outside stopped her. "My goodness!"

Across the way, three hundred people filled the parking lot, some carrying signs, others chanting. The demonstration was larger than expected. When Toole saw the video, he'd be giddier than a dog in heat. "There's

Brannuck." The engineer stood next to the live truck, ankle-deep in powder.

"Y'all ready to edit?" he shouted as the Escort swerved to a stop.

"*She* is." Stacy reached in the backseat, handing Katie her tape.

"Need any help, sweetie?"

"No..." He glanced at his watch. "...I've got a *whole hour* before we go live!"

She smiled again. "Thanks for the apology, Stacy."

"Sorry it took so long."

She moved to the truck, Stacy facing the mob—it looked like 'double-coupon day' at the Piggly-Wiggly! Camera rolling, he went to work. There was plenty of B-roll to be had, but only two people agreed to speak on-camera, neither offering much insight.

Then he met Ernest Farmer.

The company bookkeeper was nervous. He handed Stacy a stack of ledgers that included high-dollar payments to the owner's wife and sons. "He's paying off gambling debts with our money. Has been for months. Pays his family out of the coffers, then they pay the bookies."

Stacy couldn't believe his ears. "Let me get the tripod."

"No cameras. Damn things give me the shakes. But I'd swear to it in court." He lit a cigarette. "I'll probably have to."

Stacy begged him to reconsider, then bolted for the car. "Mobil 1 to Base!" He kept Farmer in his sights, Toole answering. "Larry, I've got a situation." He paused to catch his breath, the news director jumping in.

"Enlighten me."

Stacy recapped the bookkeeper's claims. "What do you think?"

103

"I think we just hit the jackpot!"

"But I can't verify his story." He glanced at his watch again. "Not in the next twenty minutes anyway. And he won't go on camera."

"You let me worry about that. Just get me your piece by 5:50."

*5:50?* That gave him ten minutes to write, edit, and send. "Mobil 1 out!" He scratched out a script and sprinted for the truck. It took a new personal record, but Stacy pulled it off, Brannuck microwaving his package at 5:49.

"Stand by," the engineer hollered. As Stacy hit his mark, Katie manned the camera. Watching his piece on the live truck monitor, he fought hard to control his pulse. But it soared at the end of his package—a man appeared in silhouette, a rather obese man, his voice electronically garbled. The C.G. read *Unnamed Source, Rowdywear, Inc.* But the man on-screen was unmistakably Bub DeSpain, reciting the gambling allegations like a company insider.

Stacy knew Toole was capable of stretching the truth. *But faking an interview?* This was too much.

"Bill Stacy joins us live with the first of two Great 8 team coverage reports. Bill, this has all the makings of a scandal."

*It sure as hell does!*

After a shaky breath, Stacy somehow managed to respond.

\*\*\*

He pulled to a stop and checked the address—*406 Wewoka Street.* This was it. Grabbing the twelve-pack, Stacy climbed out of the car and headed for the house. The street was black, but for the soft glow of lamplight on the melting snow.

104

As he reached the step, he paused, wondering if he was doing the right thing. He rang the bell anyway. A minute later, the door opened.

"What do *you* want?" Julius yipped like a terrier.

"I was...in the neighborhood..." Stacy stepped back, pointing to the basketball court up the street. "Can a guy get a game down there?"

"Black guy can. *You* can't."

"What's that supposed to mean?"

"Welcome to Oklahoma."

Stacy looked down, remembering their conversation —the one that forced him to see himself differently. He looked back up. "Thought you might want to share a twelver."

Julius glared at the cans. "Schlitz Malt Liquor? Let me guess, that's what all the *brothers* drink!"

Stacy felt more uncomfortable than ever. Yes, he'd seen a commercial with black partygoers enjoying Schlitz, but that wasn't why he bought it. *Okay...that was part of it.* More importantly, "They were on sale."

Julius stared, light framing him like a stained-glass saint. "I'll say one thing. You got balls comin' here at night."

"You think this is bad? You should see the neighborhoods *I* grew up in." No reaction. "Look, I didn't come here to compare upbringings, but I'm not going to have *any* balls if I stand out in this cold much longer. Are you going to let me in or not?"

Julius eased the door back, Stacy stepping inside. The room was surprisingly warm, a row of candles burning on the mantel. In the corner, a thirty-five-inch TV offered nothing but static, an overstuffed couch pushed against the wall. Stacy took it all in, having no idea what to do next. He'd only thought of dropping by, not what the hell he was going to say.

105

"Nice place," he managed, clutching the twelve-pack to his chest.

Julius killed the TV, Stacy noticing a signed 8 X 10 of Jacques Cousteau.

"Cousteau, huh?" No response—this was much harder than expected. No wonder he'd never bothered to cultivate a friendship.

"We gonna drink that beer or not?"

"Absolutely!" Stacy pulled two cans from the box, handing one to Julius. As they drank, they looked at each other, Stacy mustering another, "Nice place."

"You said that."

"Well, I'm saying it again." He walked to the couch and sat, hearing for the first time music playing—Robert Cray's *Strong Persuader*. "You like jazz?"

"It's blues, man. And why would I listen if I didn't like it?"

Stacy looked to the turntable, wires leading to a nice stereo and speakers. From the looks of things, Julius—bad neighborhood or not—had money. He also had a guitar. "You play?"

Julius stared, Stacy seeing the first hint of a smile on his lips. "Not as good as my man, Robert, but I play a little. You?"

"No, I'm not musical at all." He paused to drink. "My mom signed me up for accordion lessons once."

"*Accordion?*"

"I'm half-Polish!" he defended himself. "She thought it would help me get in touch with my roots." Stacy shook his head in disgust. "Never could figure out how to play the keys with one hand and those damn little buttons with the other. I don't know how Lawrence Welk does it?"

"Lawrence Welk? Dude, you *are* white!"

"Well, what about you? A black man listening to blues? Not exactly a stretch!"

106

They stared at each other, then laughed. "Anyway..." Stacy took another drink. "...after the accordion, I gave up all hope of a music career."

"Looks like you made the right choice." Julius grabbed the paper. "You see the article in the *Herald*? 'Rowdywear Chief Caught With His Pants Down'. Even gave you credit for breakin' the story."

"Yeah, well..." Stacy stared at the headline. "...I'm not exactly proud. The guy skipped town and now three hundred people are out of work. Besides, did you see the interview with Bub at the end of my package? If anyone finds out—"

"They won't. Toole's good at coverin' his tracks."

"Maybe. I just wish he'd keep *his* tracks off *my* stories."

Julius nodded, taking another drink.

"So..." Stacy stood, making his way to the guitar. "...you going to play this thing or not?" Julius picked it up, grinding out an impressive riff that rivaled the Persuader's. As Cray sang *More Than I Can Stand*, Stacy shook his head. "You're a lot better than you say you are." The cameraman smiled, breaking into the first few notes of *Foul Play*. "But I don't know why that surprises me. Anyone who can come up with his own chip camera—"

"Hey..." He stopped playing. "...I didn't steal that camera!"

"I didn't say you stole it," Stacy backpedaled. "And besides, even if you did, you think I'd tell the cops...the same guys who turned the KKK onto me?"

"Don't matter if you do. I didn't take none of those things."

"Things?" Stacy raised an eyebrow. "You got more than a chip camera in here?"

Julius downed his beer. "I got a *lot* more!" He put the guitar down and walked to the bedroom, Stacy grabbing two more cold ones. Inside the closet, Julius removed a piece of drywall, revealing an entire 'electronics store'. The DXC-3000 was surrounded by lights, batteries, an underwater 35MM, and the piece de resistance—an infrared video camera. "An 'associate' of mine calls when he finds somethin' up my alley." He picked up the infrared. "Like this baby—*military* issue, years ahead of the consumer stuff. You should see what I've shot."

Stacy grinned, the beer taking affect. "What are we waiting for?"

Julius grabbed a tape marked *NIGHTTIME FUN* and walked back to the living room. As Stacy sat, he hit *PLAY*.

A green image filled the screen. "Is that Banks Park?"

"Just keep watchin'." Strange shapes began to identify themselves. A pair of slides. A park bench. Two people.

"Hey, they're screwing!"

"You ain't seen nothin' yet." As they drained the twelver, they watched six couples use the bench for everything from oral sex to S & M. One man came alone, climbing to the top of a slide and masturbating. The camera zoomed.

"My God, that's Raul!"

"You *know* the dude?"

"He worked at Channel 8!" Stacy shook his head. "Seemed so normal. A little arrogant maybe..." The man on TV was flapping his free arm and howling at the moon.

"Guess you never really know anyone."

The screen changed to a close-up of a cow. "What's this?" Before Julius could answer, two teens knocked the heifer on its backside. "Is that cow tipping?" Julius nodded. "I always thought it was bullshit...no pun intended."

"Ain't bullshit, dude. Just hard as hell to find one in the dark." As Julius tossed his empty, Stacy stared at him, grin widening. "What are you thinkin'?"

\*\*\*

They crouched in the snowy field, Julius holding the infrared, Stacy drinking Seagram's. They'd picked up a bottle on their way to the ranch. Both were drunk.

"Dude, I can't believe you talked me into this."

"*Shhhhhh*," Stacy warned, shoving the pint in his pocket. "You're gonna scare 'em away."

"Scare *what* away?" Julius lowered the camera. "We been here half-an-hour and I ain't seen one cow."

"Truss me...they're here." The drive to Sulphur took more than an hour—they hadn't exactly traveled in a straight line. "I shot a story in this field. Wilhelm's got a thousand head. We juss gotta find 'em, thass all." Stacy stood. "*Here, bossie, bossie!*"

Julius yanked him back down. "Are you crazy? If Wilhelm catches us on his property..." He shook his head. "You'll just get fired. *I'll* go to jail!"

"Oh...sorry..." Stacy cupped both hands over his mouth. "Here, bossie, bossie!" he whispered, both men giggling till their sides hurt.

"Dude, we're gonna freeze to death out here!" Julius snatched the bottle, polishing it off. "Cow tippin' don't work 'less you got a *cow*..." The drunken fools started laughing again. "...and right now, I wouldn't know one if it bit me on the ass!"

"Lemme see that thing." Stacy grabbed the camera, sweeping the lens from left to right. Wilhelm's ranch was the only one for miles. Nestled between rocky bluffs and the Washita River, it was completely hidden from the outside world. "Hey, thass it!" Stacy pointed—in the

109

distance, a line of trees marked the end of the field. "If I was a cow, thass where I'd go. Wilhelm's got five hundred acres, only *half* cleared. Cows are bound to take cover at night. I mean, they don't wanna get hit by lightning or something!" He jumped to his feet. "Thass where they're at. Right back in those woods!"

"Dude, you're crazy if—"

*Mooooo.* Both men jerked to the sound. It came from the left, a hundred yards off in the direction of the house. They looked at each other, teeth chattering. "*Less doooo this!*" The punchy dolts took out in a sprint, screaming like maniacs.

Even a deaf cow would've heard them coming!

"*There!*" Stacy hollered, pointing to a wide-awake calf near the barn.

As they drew a bead on it, the porch light blazed, both men skidding to a stop. In one fluid motion, Wilhelm stepped onto the porch, raising his shotgun. "Less get outta here!" Stacy rasped.

"Took the words right outta my—" An explosion lit the night, both men diving for cover. As the shooter reloaded, they leaped to their feet.

"*Show yourselves, you sons of bitches!*" Wilhelm roared.

He scanned the night, firing again and again.

But the terrified intruders were long gone.

***

Stacy knocked on the door, head pounding. He couldn't believe his bloodshot eyes when he read the note—*Mr. Wilhelm wants to see you.* He knocked again, the sound hammering his eardrums.

"Come in!" Holding his breath, he turned the knob. This was it. The end of a promising news career. Six

110

months of hard work, four years of Journalism school—all ruined by one drunken evening. *His mother was going to kill him!* With the confidence of a lamb at slaughter, he stepped into the office. "Have a seat." The G.M. sprinkled food in a fishbowl, his expression unreadable.

Stacy skulked to a chair, the air so thick he needed a machete. A tone sounded, "Mr. Wilhelm, Mort Taylor from—"

"I'll call back." Stacy gulped—*this wasn't good.* The man placed the food on the shelf, label out. "And Cindy, hold my calls."

"Yes, sir."

Wilhelm sat. "I'm sure you're wondering what this is about."

Stacy had a pretty good idea.

"When I hired Larry, I hoped his philosophy—our philosophy—would germinate quickly. But I must confess, I didn't expect *you* to lead the way." Stacy looked like he'd fielded a question on live TV, a question he wasn't prepared for.

"First, your little skirmish with the Klan. Brilliant idea, goading them into an on-air confrontation." The dazed reporter thought about interrupting but didn't. "And now this whole Rowdywear mess. Hell, I've known Ike Rowdy for twenty years and never suspected a thing. But you nailed his ass to the wall!" As Stacy's stomach turned, Wilhelm stood, circling the desk. "I've been watching you, Zwardowski. And so has Larry. You've got the potential, not only to make it in this business, but to be great."

"I..." Stacy was in shock. "...thank you, sir."

"No, thank *you*." He crossed his arms, eyes still black but glowing. "And to show we mean business, starting next week I'm raising your pay to $6.25 an hour."

Stacy knew he was dreaming now. Fifty-cent raises didn't happen at Channel 8. He reached down to pinch himself, but nothing happened. "Wow...I mean...thank you very much."

"Don't mention it." The G.M. uncrossed his arms, moving to the file cabinet. "I've got a good feeling about you, young man. Keep doing what you're doing, and there'll be more rewards to come." He cut his eyes to the door. "You can go now."

\*\*\*

"If it pleases the court, we'd like to call Viola Dern."

Stacy and Katie sat in the courtroom. They didn't come up to Clarion often. For one thing, it was an hour-and-a-half away. For another, it was KPXZ country, home of the rival station's headquarters.

As the accused, a woman of eighty, shuffled to the stand, District Attorney Ross Barton salivated. His reputation as a vicious prosecutor was legendary. "If *you* get charged with a crime," he once said, "*I'll* exact the payment!"

Dern was accused of killing her husband, but her lawyer argued suicide. Toole expected a verdict today. That's why he sent both reporters, Stacy to cover the trial, Katie the related spousal abuse angle. It was Channel 8's tenth 'team coverage' report.

Their boss had promised a dogfight. The competition was getting one.

"Congratulations on your raise," Katie whispered.

"But how—?"

"It's all over the station." The accused killer fielded questions from her lawyer, both reporters waiting for the cross-examination. "'Course, I would've preferred hearing it from my boyfriend."

112

She'd never used *that* term before. He wondered why she hadn't brought it up earlier. They'd just spent an hour together, sharing ribs at the café next door. "Katie—"

"*Cross*," the judge growled, Barton walking to the podium. All eyes—the reporters' included—turned to the D.A. He wore a black tie and suspenders, his expression grim.

"Mrs. Dern, do you know how a bolt-action .22 works?"

"No, sir." She was a frail little thing, hair thin, voice shaky.

"As our weapons expert pointed out, with a bolt-action rifle, you have to expel the cartridge manually." He turned to the gallery. "And we've heard testimony that when investigators discovered the body, they found a casing on the rug."

"M'husband fiddled with guns all the time. They's prob'ly bullets everywhere."

"According to investigators..." He strolled to the jury box. "...the chamber of the gun was empty."

"'Course it was empty. Jimmy Lee'd just shot himself."

The courtroom door wheezed open, Bub rushing in. "Katie," he whispered, "we gotta go!" She glanced at her watch. "Toole just radioed. They found a body near Cottonwood. They think it's that convenience store clerk."

She grabbed her things. "Bye, sweetie."

Stacy nodded, still focused on the testimony.

"If your husband shot himself, how did the casing get from the chamber to the floor?" Barton stroked his mustache. "In all my years, I've never known a suicide victim to eject a cartridge. *After* he's pulled the trigger."

"Your honor..." The court-appointed attorney shot to his feet—he should've seen it coming, but public defenders rarely did. "...I'd like a recess!"

Stacy scribbled notes, one thought filling his head—
*God help him if he was ever on the wrong end of a Ross
Barton prosecution!*

Outside the courtroom, Katie waved Bub on,
stepping into the restroom. After securing the door, she
stuck two fingers down her throat and vomited. With a
thousand 'extra calories' in the bowl, she flushed the toilet
and hurried off to meet her cameraman.

***

A dark figure moved up the tracks. If one listened, he
could hear the sound of crunching gravel. But no one
listened. The people of Avalon were sleeping.

Navigating the grade, he made his way to the
warehouse, a pole in one hand, a paper bag in the other.
Stopping at a long-forgotten delivery door, he set the bag
down and produced a Kelly Tool. He slipped the blade
between the lock and jam, splintering the wood.

There was no movement. No alarm. He'd expected as
much. The place had been empty for a decade. Grabbing
the bag, he pushed his way inside. The structure was still
largely intact. It featured two massive floors. He was
interested in neither.

Entering a stairwell, he climbed to the attic, using the
pole to separate cobwebs. With one swift kick, he broke
down the door, the room mineshaft-black. He clicked a
switch on his glasses, two rays of light illuminating the
darkness. As long-trapped dust danced in the beams,
rodents fled for cover.

It wasn't a full-size attic, more like a sectioned
cockloft. Dropping to his knees, he crept over the floor,
setting the pole down and opening the bag. Inside was a
Styrofoam cup filled with gasoline, a sheet of Saran Wrap
securing it.

114

The simplest tools caused the greatest devastation.

He reached in his pocket, pulling out packing peanuts, a cigarette, and match. After pouring the gas out, he placed the peanuts in the cup, then grabbed the pole and rammed it through the floor. Six holes, six more in the wall.

More than enough to help the fire to spread.

Striking the match, he lit the cigarette, smoke filling his lungs. He expelled it. With great care, he wedged the cigarette down in the peanuts, its tip in position to ignite the contents, the gasoline—the whole damn warehouse!

As smoke wafted past his nose, he grabbed the pole and clicked off his glasses. In the darkness, a rat scurried over the floor—or maybe it was the fleeing arsonist.

Moments later, there was only silence.

And the red glowing tip of the fuse.

***

Stacy stepped down from the truck, clothes covered in soot. Channel 8 had done it again, arriving on scene before the competition. As usual, Toole had rousted Stacy from slumber—*did the man ever sleep?* —and Julius, surprisingly energetic himself at four in the morning, had delivered more amazing footage.

Neglected for years, the old warehouse went up like kindling, the foundation all that remained. Stacy walked to the *CAUTION* tape, motioning to Roy Maghee. He'd already sent his package for noon, Julius slamming it together before leaving with new reporter Mike Bartell.

"Five minutes!" Brannuck yelled.

"Where's my new—?"

"Right here!" A man in red Sansabelts hurried up the street, hair plastered with gel. "Sorry, I got turned around in the traffic circle."

Stacy stared at him—he looked like *Bob* of *Big Boy* fame. "What was your name again?" With all the employees coming and going, it was hard to keep names—on-air or otherwise—straight.

"Rrrrrich Martin." He spoke as if auditioning for a radio spot.

"Why do you say your name like that?"

"I took this job 'cause I need the money. What I really want is a career in sports. And every sports guy's got his own schtick, right? I mean, Chett's got the finger pistols. I'm gonna say my name like a rrrreving engine."

Maghee cleared his throat, both men turning. "Still not sure about this." But he *was* sure—the man never did anything without careful consideration.

Stacy led him to his mark. "We're the lead, so a little Q and A after the story is all." He'd warned Toole about Maghee's brevity, but his boss insisted on the chief investigator. Stacy handed him an earpiece, Rich staring at the camera. "Arson again?"

"Too early to tell." Maghee shoved the IFB in his ear, then lit a cigarette.

"Must be tough when things are a total loss."

"Every fire tells a story."

"Two minutes."

"If it *is* arson, what then?"

"In extreme cases, we call in the ATF." He blew smoke. "But we're a long way from there. So I caution you and your staff to report this story professionally."

"How the heck do I zoom this thing?" Rich was totally lost.

Stacy excused himself, walking over to focus.

"Stand by," Brannuck hollered. As Stacy rejoined his guest, a promo aired on the live truck monitor—Bill Stacy at the Rowdywear plant. "Don't Gamble With Your Future. Watch the Great 8 News Team at Six and Ten."

Maghee stomped out his cigarette.

"Is the Texomaland Torch on a rampage?" Stacy tugged at his collar, his lead-in rewritten again. "I'm Larry Toole."

Maghee watched the ensuing package, eyes glued to the screen. When the story ended, Toole tossed it to Stacy.

"Roy Maghee of the Avalon Fire Department joins us. Investigator, is this incident connected to the mill fire in December?"

"I can't answer that."

Toole jumped in. "Would you at least concede it's a *possibility*?"

Maghee turned to the monitor. "It's possible."

"Then are we talking 'serial arsonist' here? And if so, what's the profile?"

The man acted like he didn't want to answer, but Toole wasn't the only one manipulating the interview. "Serial arsonists are responsible for very few fires. But to answer your question, the serial arsonist is typically male. A loner. Employed but with a dismal personal life. He's cunning with a desperate need for control. And sets fires to take revenge on a world that's wronged him. But like any addict, he needs a bigger fix every time. That's why he's so dangerous." He turned back to Stacy. "But remember, we've yet to determine a cause in this fire."

"Thank you, sir." Stacy paused—*so much for brevity!* —reciting Toole's outro, "As new information breaks, the Great 8 News Team will bring it to you. Live from the scene. And faster than anyone else."

"Great stuff, Bill."

"Clear."

Stacy lowered the mic. "Sorry about that."

Maghee sparked another cig. "It behooves us to work together. I'll need a copy of your video. From both fires."

"So you *do* think they're connected?"

"Again, I can't answer. But I'd like to review the tapes."

"I'll see what I can do."

Stacy passed the request onto his boss, Toole offering a curt, "Fuck no!"

"But Larry—"

"Channel 8's footage belongs to Channel 8. If he—or anyone else—wants it, they can get a court order!"

# Chapter 8
## March 1988

*(NEWSWIRE):* *EX-SENATOR GARY HART WITHDRAWS FROM PRESIDENTIAL RACE AFTER 'INFIDELITY' REPORTS ... IRAQI TROOPS ATTACK KURDISH TOWN, KILLING THOUSANDS WITH CHEMICAL WEAPONS ... EXPERTS SAY AIDS VIRUS SPREADS VIA KISSING, DINING OUT, AND TOILET SEATS*

"Beertender, three more frosties!"

Chip Hale slapped Stacy on the back, gyrating to Def Leppard's *Hysteria*. Julius, nursing a twelve-ounce stein, was doing his best to keep a low profile—he was the only black man in the bar. Another ratings month had come and gone, and Chip insisted they go out to celebrate. All three had worked a twelve-hour day, Bud's Fillin' Station the last place Stacy wanted to be.

"I need to make a phone call." He promised Katie he'd meet her at eleven. It was pushing midnight.

"Suit yourself." Chip, who didn't own a watch, raised his glass and drank.

Making his way through the crowd, Stacy passed a line of occupied barstools. Laborers drinking their paychecks. Roughnecks drowning their sorrows. And Terrance Meeks.

"Terrance?"

The ex-news director swiveled, cigarette in hand. He looked ten years older than the last time Stacy had seen him. "Hiya, kid."

Stacy wasn't sure what to say. "Sorry," was what came out.

The man waved him off, smoke following. "Bad things happen sometimes." He lifted his half-empty glass. "Looks like you're doing okay. I've been watching."

Stacy glanced at the clock. "Where are you working now, Terrance?"

"Texoma's got three stations. One fired me. The other two already have news directors." He scratched his whiskered cheek. "I applied for my old job at KAVN. But they never called back."

"What about outside Texoma? I mean, you're an experienced—"

"This is my home, Stacy. We own a house here. My kids go to school here. This is all they know." He paused as the jukebox transitioned to INXS's *Devil Inside*. "It's all *I* know."

The man's expression turned dark, Stacy stepping away. "Well...good luck...and if there's anything I can—"

"There *is* something, Stacy." Meeks seized his arm, breath stinking of liquor and smoke. "Don't sell out!"

They stared at one another, Stacy's arm throbbing. "Okay, Terrance...*okay!*"

Meeks let go. As the music built to a crescendo, he grabbed his coat and walked away. *What the hell was that all about?* Stacy wasn't the one handing out assignments. He was just doing what he was told—same as he did when

120

Meeks was in charge. Maybe the man was just bitter, a little jealous even.

Either way, Stacy couldn't afford to worry about it now.

His girlfriend was waiting.

\*\*\*

"You've got to be kidding," Stacy keyed the handset.

"I'm *not* kidding," Toole answered. "And I suggest you change your tone."

Stacy shook his head, a million responses swirling. He chose one— "Mobil 4 out." Still shaking his head, he climbed out of the car. It was a beautiful day, the sky a brilliant sapphire, the air surprisingly warm. Rich Martin stood in the shade of a redbud tree, camera ready.

Stacy made his way over, State Senator Dale Rigginns waiting. The man wore an expensive suit, his back to the façade of Rigginns & Clarke, Attorneys at Law. "Good morning, Bill."

"'Morning, Senator." Stacy took the microphone from Rich. "I apologize for the delay. I had to check something with my boss."

"Quite all right. I'm always happy to make myself available to the hard-working members of the media. And may I say that Channel 8 does an outstanding job keeping my constituents informed." He paused, adjusting his hundred-dollar tie. "By the way, have you and Rob—"

"Rrrrrrrich," the cameraman interjected.

"—taken time to vote?"

"No, sir."

"Well, make sure you do. And remember, it's Rigginns. Two *g*'s. Two *n*'s." He attempted Chett's famous finger pistols, mistaking Stacy for the sportscaster.

121

"Sir..." Stacy felt queasy. "...I have something to ask...and it's embarrassing." The man smoothed his Ginsu-like lapels. "As you know, it's Super Tuesday and we've got reporters all over Texoma. We've even got salespeople doing interviews today." He paused, wondering how to say this without looking like an idiot. "Our live truck can only be in one place at one time, so our news director...he..." *God, this was humiliating!* "I need to get a reaction from you as if you'd won the election. And another as if you'd lost." Stacy's face matched the man's crimson tie. "Then we'll air the one that makes sense...and pretend it's a live interview."

"You've got to be kidding!"

"That's what I said."

The friendly politician was gone, replaced by the testy lawyer. "Well, let's get on with it then!"

Stacy faced the camera. "Rich, this has to look like nighttime, so you'll need to change filters." Rich twisted a knob, offering an astonished thumbs-up. "Joining us now live is a happy State Senator Dale Rigginns..." Two minutes later, the verbiage changed from "happy" to "disappointed", the politician making a weak attempt at humility—he wasn't much of an actor.

Stacy thanked him for his understanding. As the man walked off, he offered one last comment. "I hope to hell you use the *first* one!"

\*\*\*

He set the jack, his tire having blown when he turned up Main. As Stacy pumped the handle, a car stopped next to him. "Get in."

He turned to see Dick Wilhelm at the wheel of a black Lincoln. "But—"

"I'll call my service." The man leaned over and opened the door, Stacy climbing inside. Gunning the accelerator, Wilhelm reached for his newly-installed phone. "It's at the corner of Oak and Main," he explained. "Fit it for a new set of radials."

Stacy's eyes widened. "But, sir, I can't—"

"It's on me. Just keep up the good work." He turned into the lot. "And do me a favor." Stacy wondered what *he* could do for Dick Wilhelm. "Tell Larry I'll be down in five minutes."

*Uh-oh.* This had all the makings of another meeting. Stacy wondered how many heads would roll this time. Katie's was the first he saw. She was pouring coffee, hands shaking. Across the way, Julius tinkered with a cable, Chip leafing through a magazine.

Toole snapped his fingers to nix the chatter. "I've got some announcements." The room fell silent—even Thad stopped talking. "First off, by now you've noticed that Lisa Lynn is no longer with us." Stacy made eye-contact with Katie, his smile saying, 'I told you so.' "I'm proud to announce that Lisa's hiring on with the ABC affiliate in Denver. That's a hundred-and-fifty-market jump, folks. And it just goes to show what can happen with a little hard work." *Hard work?* The woman spent more time under the knife than at a typewriter!

"Obviously, her departure leaves us with a hole to fill. This time, I've decided to hire within." He walked over to Katie. "Starting tonight, Miss Powers will take over as my six and ten co-anchor." The crowd gasped, Katie's jaw dropping. "And we're not going to miss a beat." Toole put his arm around her, Stacy tensing with jealousy. "We're going to give viewers the same quality newscasts they've been getting since I arrived in October—*better* even—which brings me to my next point of business."

Wilhelm stepped into the room, Toole nodding. "I met with your G.M. yesterday to go over last month's ratings results." He reached in his pocket for a cigarette. "For the first time in almost three years, we finished second in the ratings." A huge cheer rocked the newsroom, accompanied by hugs and high-fives. Everyone was whooping it up.

Everyone but Toole.

"*Quiet, goddammit!*" A nervous hush fell over the troops. "I said, we finished *second.*" He scanned the faces, the newfound silence deafening. "Second place isn't good enough. Second place is for fucking losers!" He walked to the center of the room. "When I agreed to return here, I did so to be *number one* in this market. As long as I'm in charge, we'll *never* settle for second place. Do you understand me?"

Everyone nodded, cigarettes blazing.

Toole lit his own. "From now on, we treat *every* month like ratings month. The road to number one is paved with hard work. And believe me, you're going to work your asses off!" Stacy looked to Katie—*isn't that what we've been doing?* "Come May, there's going to be a new ratings king in Texomaland. The Great Channel 8!" He blew smoke, his red-rimmed eyes sweeping the room. "Your assignments are posted."

As everyone swarmed Katie, a tone sounded. "Bill, you have a call on line two."

Stacy grabbed the phone.

As he listened, his expression changed, Julius watching. When Stacy dropped the receiver, the camera op rushed over. "Dude, what is it?"

A few feet away, the crowd toasted Katie, the new anchor laughing like a high school cheerleader. "My... mother..." Stacy sagged to a chair, Julius steadying him. "...she just...had a stroke."

124

Helen O'Roarke was born on the Oregon coast, at the end of World War II. Her mother suffered two miscarriages before giving birth to a baby girl, her father—4F due to a heart condition—beaming with pride.

Helen grew into a bonny child with eyes that held the depths of the sea. Bright and stubborn, she outperformed her classmates in every subject, holding her own on the athletic field as well—at least till she fell ill in the winter of '53. What started as a nagging cough led to pneumonia, forcing her to spend weeks in the hospital. But her illness was a blessing in disguise. While conducting tests, doctors discovered a congenital heart defect. The disorder was treatable, they explained, but the risk of "future events" would always be there.

Fiercely independent—a trait she'd one day pass on to her son—Helen refused to acknowledge her condition. She went back to school, working even harder to separate herself from the pack, her newfound goal to become a physician.

But a year before high school graduation, an Alaskan crab boat pulled into town, William Zwardowski on board. She was working in the infirmary when he came in for stitches, the injured fisherman the most ruggedly-handsome man she'd ever seen—broad shoulders, piercing eyes, and a crooked smile. The attraction was palpable, but Helen wasn't looking for love. And her father had warned her about dating "men at sea".

Over the next few weeks, William sent eloquent notes. He was different, she told herself. He made her feel special—wonderful—like no one ever had. As time went on, she let her guard down, sleeping with him the night he returned to Alaska. She wasn't coerced. She loved William

125

Zwardowski and was ready to give herself to him—body and soul. He, she was certain, felt the same.

A month later, the family doctor confirmed what she already knew. Helen was pregnant. Her father refused to speak to her. Her mother couldn't stop crying. It took three months to locate William, the news hitting him hard. But he agreed to 'do the right thing'. Two weeks later, the young couple married. Helen quit school. William took a job at the cannery. And they found a shabby apartment near the wharf, where Helen gave birth to an eight-pound baby boy.

It was the happiest day of her life.

Stacy William Zwardowski was a carbon copy of his father—same piercing eyes, same crooked smile. His mother fell in love with him the moment she saw him. So did his father—just not enough to make him stay. William left his wife and son a year-and-a-half later, Stacy becoming the only 'man' in Helen's life. She loved her boy like no other and would do anything to make him happy, even if it meant sacrificing her own dreams for his. She never made it to medical school, but she did work her way through nursing college, graduating at the top of her class. It was the second happiest day of her life, and Stacy, a spray of pink carnations in hand, was there to share it with her.

"Sir?"

Stacy's eyes moved from the window. "I'm sorry...did you—?"

"I asked if you wanted coffee." The flight attendant smiled.

He shook his head, the woman moving on. The last few hours were a blur. When the shock wore off, Stacy phoned the hospital. His mother had suffered a "massive stroke", driving herself to the E.R. before "collapsing in the foyer". She was in intensive care, the rep explained, having lost the "use of her right side" and the "ability to speak".

Stacy closed his eyes, praying it was a dream. But when he opened them, he was still on the plane, barreling toward home. Wilhelm had booked the flight, even picked up the tab, Stacy having just enough time to pack a bag and drive to the airport.

"Tray tables up." The attendant winked as she passed, the aircraft beginning its slow descent into Portland. Stacy looked to the distant lights, wondering what waited for him there. His mother could no longer speak. No longer use her arms to hug him.

Tears pooled in his eyes, but he willed them away. He needed to be strong. Now more than ever. Gathering that strength, he reached down and buckled his seatbelt.

\*\*\*

Room 305. The door was white and daunting. The air smelled like gauze. Stacy hesitated, hands shaking as he clutched the pink carnations. After a breath, he grabbed the knob and pushed his way inside.

The room was empty.

Staring at the fresh-made bed, he reached in his pocket to retrieve the note—*ICU ROOM 305*. He walked back to the door, pulling it open to check the placard.

"Can I help you, sir?" He turned to see a candy-striper in the hallway.

"I'm here for Helen Zwardowski." She glanced at the flowers, then at the distant station, a doctor and nurse huddled in conversation. "I'm her son," Stacy added.

She cut her eyes to the room. "You can wait inside."

Confused, he watched her leave, then headed back in. The room felt warmer than before, light glowing orange in the corner, clock ticking noisily on the wall. He could

127

smell disinfectant, taste his own saliva. The door wheezed open, a young intern stepping in. "Mr. Zwardowski." He waited for the damper to close. "I'm afraid your mother has died."

The words rendered Stacy powerless. As they dug their claws into his brain, the sights, scents, sounds—every sensation in the room—melted away like hot wax, leaving a black tingling nothingness behind.

From the void, an image emerged—his mother, young and alive, hair blowing in the Newport breeze. "These things happen," the doctor explained. But Stacy didn't hear, the sound of the sea filling his ears, his mother's smile illuminating the darkness. "...first event caused paralysis..." She looked down at her son, taking his little hand. "...blood clot from the heart..." They walked together, barefoot in the sand, waves tickling their toes. *'Look what I found, Momma!'* He handed her a seashell. "...second stroke proved fatal." She smiled, humming a forgotten lullaby, her voice drifting off in the wind. "Mr. Zwardowski?"

Stacy blinked, the image gone, gray light from the window replacing it.

"We're sorry for your loss. Stay as long as you need to."

As he turned to go, the candy-striper returned. "These are your mother's things." Stacy stared at the box, still unable to speak. "I'll just set them on the bed for you." She tried to smile, but the effort failed. A moment later, she was gone.

He stood for a long time, not trusting his legs. Finally, he moved to the bed, staring at the items in the box. His mother's coat. Her worn leather purse. And an address book, one of her famous notes acting as a bookmark. He didn't need to read it. He already knew what it said. *WORK HARD. FOLLOW YOUR HEART.*

The words seemed empty now.

As did everything else.

His mother was gone. And he'd never see her. Never hold her. Never hear her voice again. A tear streaked down his cheek, followed by another. As the flowers hit the floor, he grabbed her coat and clutched it to his chest.

"Goodbye, Momma."

*** 

He grabbed the mail, shoving the key in the lock. It felt strange to be back in Oklahoma. Strange to be anywhere, if he was being honest.

There'd been no funeral—his mother didn't want one—just a simple burial at a cemetery he'd never heard of. The funeral home provided a bouquet, Dick Wilhelm a handsome wreath. Stacy had read something once—the ancient Greeks buried their dead with a coin to pay the ferryman. Helen Zwardowski was buried in her nurse's uniform, taking nothing with her but the ring on her finger.

There wasn't much else to take.

Stacy had spent three days cleaning out the little house, adding a handful of things to the box from the hospital. Everything else was sold—the furniture, the car, the rest of his mother's clothes. He wasn't sure why she bothered with a will. The boiler-plate document took seconds to read, the lawyer charging for an hour.

Juggling everything, he pushed his way inside. The place looked the same as it always looked, the air smelling of last week's dinner.

But it wasn't the same. Nor would it ever be.

Setting his things down, he sorted the mail—a few bills, some ads, another rejection. Normally, there'd be disappointment, relief...*something*. Today he felt numb.

As he tossed the letter, a strange thought struck him—*this was home now*.

Stacy moved to the window, forcing it open. A gentle breeze licked his face. A bird sang on the horizon. He moved to the answering machine, hitting *PLAY*. Four messages—one from Katie, one from Toole, two from Julius, each offering condolences.

He hit the *ERASE* button, creating silence. Total silence.

As he surveyed the room, he wondered what to do next. There was no manual for this sort of thing, no handbook on how to go on after losing your best friend. He stared at the box, the Underwood, the framed photos of his parents—they looked like items plucked from a shipwreck.

Something fluttered to his left, a northern cardinal lighting at the windowsill. The bird stood motionless for a time, locking eyes with Stacy. A minute passed, then another. He half-expected the bird to speak.

Instead, she sprang from her perch. And soared to the heavens.

Stacy rushed to the window, scanning the empty sky. Knowing she was gone, he swallowed hard. "Fly with the angels, Mom."

\*\*\*

Marv Bridges stared at the card, reading what he'd written —*Sorry for your loss. Over time things'll get better*. He thought about leaving it at that. *But not much*, he added, signing it at the bottom.

"He's not Jake, you know."

Bridges turned, his wife peering over his shoulder. She wore a faded dress and no makeup. "Never said he was."

130

"Well, you act like it." She walked to the table and dumped a load of laundry.

"The kid just lost his mother, Kaye. I figger the least I can do—"

"Now there's something you're an expert at—the *least* you can do."

He tried to laugh it off. "Look here, woman—"

"What about *my* loss?" she cried, Bridges flinching. "You ever think about that?"

He waited a long time, then, "We *both* lost a son."

"I'm not talking about Jake." The man stood. "I'm talking about *you*, Marv!"

"Me?" She nodded, her eyes racked with pain. "I ain't gonna listen ta this."

"Yes, you are!" She cut him off as he turned for the door. "You're going to listen to every damn word!"

"But we been through this."

"No, we haven't. Not together."

"What's that s'posed ta mean?"

She stared at her husband. "You haven't dealt with Jake's death."

"Oh, really?" His expression changed from angst to outrage. "An' *you* have?"

"No." She filled the void between them. "I haven't dealt with it either. Because I can't do it alone."

"Last I checked, I been here every day, same as you have."

"You haven't been here a *single* day since Jake died!"

"Well, if 'at ain't the biggest buncha—"

"Is it?" Her stare cut to the bone. "Then tell me something. When's the last time you took me out to dinner? Or bought me flowers? Or talked to me about anything other than work?"

"If ya don't wanna hear—"

"It doesn't bring him back! Can't you see that?"

131

They stared at one another, his wife waiting for a response he couldn't give.

"You're a caricature, Marv. You put on the same face, day after day—the happy-go-lucky undersheriff. But you're *dead* inside."

"C'mon, Kaye, ya don't mean that." He raised his beer as a peace offering, trying to elicit a smile.

"I don't want your beer. I want your attention. Your anger once in a while. I want you to *feel* something! Because I need someone to talk to. Someone to make love with." She paused, her face wet with tears. "I need the man I married!"

For a long time, Bridges said nothing. Finally, "I ain't that man anymore."

"But you *could* be," she pleaded. "We just need some help." She reached in her pocket. "I got a number off the TV...a grief counselor...here in Avalon—"

"I ain't goin' ta no shrink!" He moved to the hallway. "What's he gonna say anyhow? 'In order to deal with your loss, Mr. Bridges, you need to talk about your feelings. Starting with what it felt like when you got the phone call. How bad it hurt when you saw the body. And how much you miss him every single day. When you can do *that*, Mr. Bridges...well, then everything'll be A-okay.'" He turned to his wife, skin redder than the blood beneath it. "Well, it ain't okay. It ain't *never* gonna be okay. I lost a son, goddammit! My *only* son. An' I ain't never gonna fish with 'im again. Or watch 'im play football. Or give 'im a damn hug. He's *dead*, Kaye! An' you're right about one thing..." He narrowed his gaze, fighting the emotions he'd worked so hard to bury. "I died right along with 'im."

\*\*\*

132

"Sorry about your mom, Stacy." Toole raised his cigarette and puffed. "Sometimes life can really fuck you."

Stacy nodded, still in a malaise.

"We'll ease you back in today. No live shot. Just an interview with the chief investigator." Toole reached for the folder on his desk. "Not sure if you heard, but we had another fire. The old hospital. Place hadn't been used in years, but there was talk of renovation." He chuckled, handing off the script. "Nothing to renovate now."

Stacy skimmed the text, the story well-written but over the top. "Who did this?"

"Bartell covered the story. *I* wrote the copy." He fished out a newspaper article. "You can pull more details from this. The angle's simple. Just tell the viewers where the investigation stands."

Stacy stared at the newsprint. "Do you think all these fires are connected?"

"I'd bet my life on it." He handed Stacy the folder. "Roy Maghee's meeting you there. Who do you want on camera?"

"Julius." The response came without thought, the reporter turning to leave.

"Oh, and Stacy..." He looked back, still in a funk. "...I really am sorry."

As he left the office, he bumped into Thad. "Glad to see you back from vacation. Most of us had to wait a year till we got a week off!" The man walked away, waving to Randy up the hall.

Stacy turned, seeing Julius for the first time. The cameraman moved toward him, eyes glistening. He didn't say a word. He just extended a hand, Stacy taking it.

The drive to the scene was a quiet one. As Julius steered, Stacy reviewed notes. The fire had started at three in the morning, the building vacant. Based on the script, Channel 8 had captured more amazing video, Toole's

133

words describing the scene in vivid detail—*AS THE ROOF COLLAPSED, A GEYSER OF FLAMES BURST INTO THE SKY.*

"Check it out, dude." Stacy looked up as Julius pulled to the curb.

"Jesus..." They'd passed the old hospital a hundred times. Even empty, it was an impressive structure, the mayor calling it the 'most advanced facility in Texoma' when it opened in '37. Now it looked like a burned casserole. "This is the worst one yet."

The scene reminded Stacy of his own life—an appropriate first story back.

Julius set the brake, both men grabbing gear. As Maghee moved toward them, he finished off a cigarette. He knew the old hospital well. His mother had worked here for twenty years, a supervisor in the burn unit. As a youngster, he'd witnessed firsthand what fire could do to people. He watched nurses scrub wounds. Listened to patients scream. "Heard about your mother. I'm sorry."

Stacy thanked him—word traveled fast in a small town. "This shouldn't take long. Tell you the truth, my heart's not in it."

"Understandable. I lost my mother ten years ago."

He'd lost his father, too. Roy, Sr. was a decorated firefighter, his name appearing in numerous headlines. For pulling a woman out of a burning house. For saving a child from a frozen pond. And finally, for dying in a warehouse fire. A greedy landowner had set the blaze for insurance money. The act claimed the life of a father. And set a son on the dogged path of arson investigation.

The only thing Roy Maghee hated more than fire... was the person behind it.

"You ready?" Stacy looked at Julius.

"Already rollin'."

"Sir..." He turned to Maghee. "...where are we in the investigation?"

"Still interviewing witnesses. Looking at similar cases."

Stacy checked his notes—nothing was flowing today. "What have you found?"

"Burn patterns indicating point of origin in an attic crawl space. We also have evidence of 'non-accidental' cause."

"Can you share that evidence?"

"I cannot."

Stacy didn't feel like pushing. "Last question, this is the third suspicious fire in as many months. Is there a common thread?"

The investigator glanced at the camera. "Can you kill that thing?"

Julius powered it down.

"In the process of researching the properties, I found an interesting denominator." He lit a cigarette. "But I need you to promise me this is off the record." Stacy promised. "All three buildings were raised by the same construction firm."

"Wilhelm & Son?" Maghee looked surprised. "When we did our town history pieces, the name Wilhelm & Son cropped up again and again."

Maghee nodded, having done the same research. "As I mentioned when we spoke last, it behooves us to work together. I think you can help me on this case."

"But how—?"

"It's no coincidence these fires involved Wilhelm & Son buildings. These are revenge crimes. Someone's out to get Dick Wilhelm. Someone who wants to snuff out every legacy of the family name left in Texoma." He paused to flick ash. "Do you know anyone who hates

Wilhelm that much? Anyone who's been wronged, punished, or fired unjustly over the last few months?"

Stacy's eyes moved to Julius, suddenly at war with his own thoughts. Helping a law enforcement agent went against everything Toole preached. He looked to the charred earth, then back at the investigator. In the smoke-tinged breeze, he heard his mother's voice, "Follow your heart."

He smiled, the first in a long time. "How big a list do you want?"

# CHAPTER 9
## *April 1988*

*(NEWSWIRE): REAL ESTATE MOGUL DONALD TRUMP TELLS 'OPRAH' HE'D WIN IF HE RAN FOR PRESIDENT ... EX-DEPUTY PRESS SECRETARY LARRY SPEAKES ADMITS HE MADE UP QUOTES FOR REAGAN ... GUNMEN HIJACK KUWAITI AIRLINER, HOLDING 112 HOSTAGES, KILLING 2*

"Are you thinking about your mom, sweetie?"

Stacy blinked—for the first time in weeks, he wasn't. He looked from the ceiling to the woman beside him. "How well do you know Phil Twitchell?"

Katie sat up in bed. "If you're insinuating that we slept together—"

"No." *He wasn't insinuating that at all.* "It's just..." He hesitated, wondering if he could trust her. "...do you think he's capable of violence?"

"What in the world are you talking about?"

He took a deep breath, then shared Maghee's theory with her. "He thinks it's Wilhelm they're after. And that's why they've targeted the buildings."

"But Wilhelm had nothing to do with the construction business."

"I know that, but Maghee thinks they're after the name." He shoved a pillow under his arm, leaning forward. "I did some research last night. There are sixty-four Wilhelm & Son buildings in Texoma...well, sixty-*one* now."

"And you think the arsonist is picking them off one-by-one to hurt Wilhelm?"

"It's not my theory. It's Maghee's."

Her expression turned cold. "And you think Phil—?"

"I'm not accusing anyone, Katie. But you said yourself, Phil was a 'complete basket case' after Wilhelm fired him."

"Of course, he was a basket case. He just lost his job! That doesn't mean he's capable of burning down buildings. Think about it, Stacy. He doesn't even live here anymore!"

"Well, he owns a car, doesn't he?"

"I'm not going to listen to this!" She hit the remote, a late-night replay of the Great 8 newscast piercing the darkness. "There's no way on earth Phil Twitchell—"

"I didn't say Phil did it. He's just on the list."

She turned, Toole's image flickering in her eyes. "*What* list?"

Stacy hesitated—he hadn't planned to tell her, but there was no turning back now. "When I...interviewed Maghee...he asked for a list of names...you know...people who might have an axe to grind with Wilhelm."

"And you *gave* it to him?" He nodded. "Have you not listened to a single word Larry's said over the past six months?"

Stacy's abashment turned to anger. "Since when does Larry Toole have all the answers? Since you became his precious co-anchor?"

She ripped back the covers and stormed to the bathroom. As the door slammed, he looked to the TV, a two-dimensional Katie looking back. "Joining us with tomorrow's pinpoint forecast is Great 8 Meteorologist Thad Barker."

He stared at the screen, wishing he'd kept his mouth shut. Before tonight, only one person—Julius—knew about the list he'd given Maghee, a list that included such names as Terry Perkins, Darryl Rogers, and Terrance Meeks.

He realized now, the fewer people who knew about it, the better.

"Nothing but clear skies, Texomaland. A great day for some fun in the sun!" As the weatherman and his cohorts swapped pleasantries, Stacy heard coughing in the bathroom, followed by a flushing toilet.

When the door opened, he closed his eyes and pretended to sleep.

\*\*\*

Crisp winds blew out of the north, a moist breeze from the southeast. As dark clouds gathered, Stacy could almost taste the faraway Gulf.

"One last question, Mr. Bitner." Today's story, 'Are Farmers Worried About Drought Conditions?', seemed silly with a storm brewing, but that was the assignment. "What would a drought mean to you personally?"

Clay Bitner looked to the parched earth, his fifty-acre parcel sown for peanuts and cotton. "I got me a wife and three kids," he responded. "Without these crops, I can't feed m'family." A dog barked in the distance—the farmer had tied it to a post when the newsmen arrived. "A drought'd ruin us."

Stacy thanked him, Julius pulling the camera off the tripod. "Mind if we grab some footage in your field?"

"Okay by me. But I wouldn't dillydally. Those clouds don't look good."

"We'll be gone in ten minutes."

As the man headed for the barn, Julius hiked the Sony. "Where to, Stace?" Stacy surveyed the acreage. To the west, red earth rose in a sloping ridge, framed by hundreds of cedars. Bitner's grandfather had planted them. He'd built the house, too—a modest clapboard with a shingle roof and sun porch.

"Just get me a shot of the plants. I can use file footage for the rest."

"Works for me." They moved into the field, Julius dropping to one knee. As he zoomed, he glanced over his shoulder, the clouds black as night. "I don't like this, dude."

Stacy felt a raindrop. "Good thing you didn't grow up in Oregon. Where I come from, a little rain never stops anyone."

"Ain't *rain* I'm worried 'bout."

As Julius triggered the camera, more raindrops fell, Stacy's coat turning dark. A memory flashed, he and his mother splashing through puddles. Stacy smiled. "Just like home, Julius, just like—*ouch!*" The rain suddenly turned to hail, pebbles landing like bird shot.

"Come on!" Julius ran for the cedars, Stacy right behind him. The hail came in sheets now, the sound deafening. With every step, the stones grew larger, hammering their bodies as they dove for cover.

Safe beneath the trees, Julius wheeled to shoot, Stacy taking stock of his wounds. He had a welt on his neck and a cut on his ear. But as he stared at the wall of hail behind him, he wondered how he'd gotten off so lightly.

Then, as quickly as it started, it stopped.

Stacy stood, staring at the changed vista. In less than a minute, the land had been drained of color. He took a breath, the air thirty degrees colder—and hauntingly still. A wave of euphoria swept over him, the joy of a survivor. "Unbe-*liev*-able!" He crunched through the ice, smiling at Julius, the man's expression unsettling. "What?"

"I think we better go."

Julius' voice sounded strange, like he was speaking into a bucket.

Before Stacy could respond, his ears popped, the cedars stirring. "Julius?" Out of nowhere, a massive funnel cloud swooped over the ridge. The black fog of swirling wreckage was enormous, five hundred feet wide and bearing down fast. Stacy couldn't believe his eyes. In the twisting mess, he saw a boat, several trees, and a motor home.

"*Run!*" Julius screamed.

Stacy bolted for the barn a hundred yards away, the roar behind him a hellish freight train's. As debris rained down like fire and brimstone, he checked on Julius.

The cameraman was right behind him, rolling video the entire way!

Clay Bitner staggered from the barn, winds tearing him to shreds. Raising a hand to block the dreck, he searched for the newsmen, but they were nowhere in sight. As he dashed for the house, he heard the dog howl. He didn't have time to untie the thing.

He had to get to his family.

Stacy gasped for breath, he and Julius under siege. The tornado was a thousand feet wide now, its lethal winds raging at three hundred miles an hour. The barn was still fifty yards away. They'd never make it.

141

"*Julius—?*" The cameraman tackled him, the pair tumbling into a ditch. Stacy lay face down in the mud, Julius on top of him. The reporter tried to get up, but his coworker held tight, dirt pelting their bodies like a sandblaster. The roar of the cyclone was unbearable. As it passed over them, Stacy could feel the weight of Julius' body lighten, feel his own body being lifted.

He could think of nothing to do but hold on—*and pray!*

Ellen Bitner had just poured herself a cup of tea when the first hail stone struck. Her twin daughters were playing on the rug, the baby down for a nap. The pounding ice sounded like golf balls against the roof, but that was nothing compared to what came next. Racing to the bedroom, she plucked her daughter from the crib, the child's screams disappearing in the roar. As they ran for the living room, a window shattered behind them. "*Mommy!*" Her daughters covered their ears, the house moaning like a specter.

Clay Bitner grabbed the door of the sun porch. It ripped off and flew away. He fought his way inside, the structure disintegrating around him. He heard trees uprooting, nails being ripped from wood. "*Clay!*" his wife screamed. As if tethered to ropes, he pushed forward, step by painstaking step. When he reached the kitchen door, he saw them, wife clutching the baby, twins latched to their mother's legs.

"*Ellen!*" He grabbed the knob and hung on, his body going horizontal. "*Get the girls in the cellar!*" His fingers were slipping. "*Please—*"

He hung on a second longer, then disappeared.

"*Nooooooo!*" She ran for the door, but a falling hutch blocked her path, the china shattering inside. "*Claaaay!*" she sobbed, her daughters wailing in terror.

142

As shelves gave way, the family parrot squawked in its cage, pictures breaking by the dozen. They'd never make it to the cellar now! In a panic, she headed for the hall, girls in tow. She thought about getting in the bathtub, but instead grabbed every blanket she could find. The roar was mind-numbing now, the house coming apart at the seams. As more windows exploded, they hid beneath the bedding, walls crumbling around them. "*Somebody help uuuuuus!*" she screamed.

When no one did, she braced herself, the house lifting off its foundation.

***

Stacy opened his eyes. His lashes were crusted. And his body ached.

*But he was alive!*

"Julius?" He could no longer feel the cameraman on his back. Struggling to his knees, he tried to focus. The ground was speckled with insulation and hay, utility poles surrounding him like giant matchsticks. "Julius!"

He staggered to his feet, eyes sweeping the alien plain. Every cedar on the ridge was gone. As were the crops, barn—and house!

"Dear God!" He rushed to what was once the Bitner home, limping over debris. "Julius...Mr. Bitner... *anybody!*" He passed broken branches, razor-sharp aluminum. "Can anyone hear?" he yelled. No response, the air reeking of sulfur.

Panic was setting in. What if he couldn't find anyone?

*What if he was the only one to survive?*

*No.* Julius had to be alive. *Had to!*

143

"*Juliuuus!*" he hollered again, scanning the stark horizon. To the left, a pitchfork wobbled. To the right, a tractor balanced on its nose.

"Stacy?" a muffled voice sounded.

The reporter wheeled—*was he hearing things?* "Julius?"

There was a long pause, then, "Over here, dude."

He'd definitely heard it that time, and it was music to his battered ears!

"*Where are you?*"

A mound shifted. "How the hell should I know?"

Stacy shoved a TV out of the way, clawing at the wreckage. "Julius...can you hear me?"

"'Course, I can hear you. Get me outta here." Stacy removed two sheets of siding and a closet door. Beneath them, Julius lay caked with mud—and grinning from ear-to-ear. "Check it out, dude." He climbed to his feet. "I'm still rollin'!"

Amazingly, the Sony was still on his shoulder, still hooked to the deck, and yes, still rolling. "Why, you crazy—"

A child's cry silenced them. They stared at one another, then raced toward it, hurdling a picket fence. Most of the slats were gone, as was the gate, the hitching post, and the dog tied to it.

"*Can you hear us?*"

The cry came again, followed by a woman's voice, "*Heeeelp!*"

They dove on the pile, tossing junk over their shoulders. "*Dude!*" Julius spotted a foot. Fueled with adrenaline, they dug Ellen Bitner out, baby still nestled to her bosom, daughters still clinging to her legs.

*All four were alive!*

"My husband..." She struggled to catch her breath. "...did you find Clay?"

144

Stacy and Julius glanced at each other. "No, ma'am. Not yet."

They helped her to her feet, girls holding on as if the ride wasn't over. With two black eyes, she looked for her house. Everything was gone—the walls, furniture, even the bathtub. Yet strangely, the cup of tea remained on the kitchen table. And the parrot still squawked in its cage—though it was stripped of all feathers.

"*Claaaaay!*" she screamed. "*Where are yooooooou?*"

Stacy and Julius searched for an hour, but they never found Clay Bitner. His wife called for him again and again, as did the children. But he was gone.

"Mobil 1 to Base." Julius had parked the Escort on the south side of the house. When they found it, it was on the north side, seemingly unscathed. "This is Stacy..." Julius cranked the engine. It started on the first try. "...do you copy?"

The radio was dead, or at least non-operational in the aftermath of the storm.

Their only choice was to go for help.

After ensuring the family's safety, they pulled away from the farm, snaking their way through rubble. In a few hours, the area would be crawling with volunteers—Red Cross, FEMA, the Salvation Army—but right now, it was eerily quiet.

Stacy stared through the window. The land around him had been forever altered. Just like the lives the twister had touched. Stacy's and Julius' included.

\*\*\*

"My God, sweetie!" Katie clung to his filthy neck. She'd treated him miserably since the Phil Twitchell incident. It felt good to be hugging again. "Are you—?"

145

"All right," Toole butted in. "No time for that." He advanced down the hall in a goosestep, cigarette blazing. He had his lead story—*boy, did he!* —and thanks to Julius, some award-winning footage to go with it. "We have a newscast to do, people." He turned to Stacy. "You ready?"

Katie—along with everyone else—stared in disbelief. "You can't be serious...look at him!" Stacy's shirt was black at the neck, his coat slashed to ribbons. In addition, his left eye had closed, and his face was covered in mud. "He needs medical attention!"

"And he'll get it. Soon as we finish."

"Tape's ready." Julius limped up the hall, looking worse than his counterpart. His skin was riddled with cuts, and one of his pant-legs was missing, exposing a swollen knee. "Total runnin' time's three minutes. But I can cut it down—"

"We're airing it *as is*." Toole sucked on his KOOL, no longer able to suppress a smile. "This one's going to make us famous, boys. What do you say, Stacy?"

All eyes moved to the reporter. Sensing he had no choice, he nodded agreement. "Let me just change—"

"You're not changing a thing!" All eyes shifted back to Toole. "People wait an entire career for an opportunity like this. Do you know how lucky you are?" *He didn't feel lucky.* "When this hits the feed, every news director in the country's going to shit himself. And they're going to air the footage with a big fat C.G. at the bottom— '*Courtesy KEGT, Avalon, Oklahoma!*'"

"But what about his face?" Katie spoke up. "He can't go on the air like that."

"The hell he can't!"

"One minute," the floor director barked.

"Come on, Stacy. Let's go make history." Stacy stared at his boss, then at Katie. With a shrug, he headed for the set. "*Yes!*" Toole bellowed. One-by-one, they took their seats, Julius rushing the tape upstairs. "After we read the intro, I'll toss it to you. I just want you to recount your experience. Not like a reporter. Like a victim. And don't be afraid to sound shaken." *Shouldn't be a problem.* "I want our viewers to feel what you're feeling. To know what you've been through. And to see that you're here, in spite of it all, to tell them about it."

"Ten seconds." Katie checked her lipstick, Larry adjusting his tie. As the floor director mouthed the countdown, the news intro blared.

"Dismay, destruction, and death." Katie spoke with genuine concern. "Good evening, I'm Katie Powers. Tonight, Texomaland residents are counting their blessings. Or mourning their losses. This after an F-5 tornado ripped through their lives."

"The deadly twister," Larry hopped in, "zigzagged across both states, leaving stunned Texomalanders to sift through the ashes. I'm Larry Toole." The director cut to a wide shot. "Ten people are dead, another fifteen are missing, the loss of property incalculable. Joining us now live is Great 8 reporter—and tornado survivor—Bill Stacy." He turned to his shell-shocked set-mate, placing a hand on his shoulder. "First of all, Bill, let me say how thankful we are to have you here safe." Toole leaned in as if speaking to a child. "Now I know this is difficult, but can you tell us what happened?"

Stacy turned to the camera. "My photog and I were shooting a story on the drought." Chip rolled video from the booth, the images shocking. Everyone in the building watched in amazement, Dick Wilhelm smiling like a raffle winner. Stacy shared his story, at least the parts he could remember. As the video turned to static, he stared at the desk. "Sadly, we weren't able to save Mr. Bitner. Our thoughts and prayers go out to his family this evening..."

147

He almost lost it, unable to get the little girls' faces out of his head. "...they can certainly use some."

Toole beamed, already envisioning the news promos. "Thank you, Bill, for that captivating report. And for ignoring your injuries long enough to share it with the folks at home." He turned, offering a reassuring nod. "We've got an ambulance standing by to take Bill and his cameraman to the hospital." In actuality, Brannuck would drive them, but only if necessary. "And we'll update their conditions at ten." Toole switched gears. "Here to explain how this deadly system moved over Texoma is Great 8 meteorologist Thad Barker." The director cut to a close-up, Stacy waiting for the segment to end. All he wanted was a hot shower and a good night's sleep—if he *could* sleep, that is.

Thad reviewed charts and explained graphics, covering his ass for the bungled forecast. "...so as you can see, Larry, *no one* could've predicted a freak storm like this."

"Thanks, Thad. And you'll have tomorrow's pinpoint forecast for us later?" The weatherman winked, Larry facing the camera. "When we return, Reg McNair reports on disaster relief efforts. And the price of stamps soars to twenty-five cents! Stay with us."

"Clear!"

As Stacy hobbled off the set, a grating voice stopped him. "Hey, Dorothy, glad you and your little dog made it back to Kansas in one piece!"

The emotions of the day—of the last few weeks— came to a sudden boil. Stacy wheeled, grabbing Thad by the throat. "*You son of a bitch!*" In the man's terrified eyes, he saw every kid that ever picked on him. The empty bed at the hospital. The tears of the Bitner girls.

*They had to go through life without a father!*

"Stacy, no!" Katie watched him cock his fist, Larry turning to see the blow. It sent Barker through the green screen, his skull bouncing off the concrete floor. Dazed and whimpering, he covered himself to prevent further attack. None came.

Stacy had already left the studio, an orange smear of makeup on his throbbing right hand.

\*\*\*

"I don't have to tell you how serious this is." Dick Wilhelm crossed his arms, leaning against the desk. Even on days like today, he loved the television business. As a child, he'd spent countless hours studying the black-and-white images, absorbing everything from Lloyd Bridges' *Sea Hunt* to Edward R. Murrow's *See It Now*.

As an adult, he'd used that experience to build a network—the radio station in Sulphur, the TV stations in Texas, and KEGT in Avalon, the station he grew up watching. His goal was to build an empire. And he wasn't about to let a clash between employees get in the way.

"Your altercation with Barker is potentially damaging."

Stacy stared at the floor. He knew it was damaging. And he knew how serious this was. *He was about to lose his job, for God's sake!*

"Do you have anything to say in your defense?"

Stacy drew a long breath. "I know what I did was wrong. And I'm sorry."

"I'm the one who's sorry." Larry Toole tapped on a fishbowl, stirring the creature inside. "I shouldn't have put you in that situation. I know what you've been through..." He turned, trying to look sincere. "...and I didn't help matters by putting you on set."

149

The speech sounded rehearsed, but Stacy nodded anyway.

"Striking a coworker is a serious offense," Wilhelm continued. "There are legal implications. And it puts me, as owner and general manager, in a precarious position."

Stacy continued to look down, waiting for the axe to fall.

"I believe, however, that every dilemma is an opportunity in disguise."

Stacy looked up, his superiors staring down at him.

"We get our asses kicked up north every ratings period." Toole circled the desk. "There are several reasons, but we think our lack of *physical* presence there is the key. Channel 7's studios are in Paul's Valley. Channel 2's are in Clarion." Stacy had no idea what this had to do with him. "Because of your actions yesterday, we've been forced to accelerate our plans. Barker's filed a restraining order. And his attorney—"

"Thad hired a lawyer?"

"I'm afraid so." Wilhelm and Toole looked at each other, their shocked employee shaking his head. "Look, Stacy, everyone at Channel 8 knows Thad's an asshole, but we all put up with him, because the viewers love him. And besides, he's got a contract."

"Yeah, well, contract or not, he's a racist. Do you know what he called Julius?"

Toole raised his hand. "That doesn't make what you did right. Although I must admit, there were more than a few people who enjoyed the hell out of it." The news director fished for a cigarette, the G.M. glowering—smoking was strictly forbidden in his office. "We need to wrap this up."

"As I mentioned, Stacy, we've been presented with an opportunity." Wilhelm stood. "With the restraining order in place, you can no longer work here. It wouldn't be practical to keep you and Thad apart."

"That's where Clarion comes in." Stacy turned to his agitated boss. "We've rented space downtown, a mile from KPXZ headquarters. The office is small, but it'll have everything you need—an edit suite, a camera for live shots, and a microwave. Best of all..." He offered a lecherous smile. "...we'll be erecting a huge *Great 8* sign in the middle of town!"

Both men snickered, Stacy looking from one to the other. "Are you saying—?"

"We're not firing you, Stacy. This is a fucking promotion! How does 'Bill Stacy, Bureau Chief' sound?"

"But...what about the lawsuits?"

"I've got an army of lawyers," Wilhelm responded, "who, between you and me, need to start earning their money. And before *you* ask for money, there's no raise to go with this move. I'm dropping a bundle on this little outpost. It's a huge gamble on my part. But I expect it to pay off." He glanced at Toole, then back at Stacy. "You bring us up in the ratings, and we'll talk money."

Stacy nodded, deep in thought. Clarion was ninety miles away. He couldn't possibly drive there every day. *And what about Katie?* She was the regular co-anchor now. If he moved, they'd barely see one another. *Then again, what were his options?* He turned to Toole. "Am I going to be working the new bureau alone?"

The news director smiled, moving into the hall. "You and a camera op." He lit a KOOL as if coming up for air. "And I've got a pretty good idea who you'll take."

\*\*\*

Julius struggled under the weight of a box. "Damn, dude, what's in this one?"

"Be careful with that. My typewriter's in there."

He glared at his roommate. "Maybe *you* shoulda got the last six boxes then!"

Stacy ignored him, plugging in the stereo. They hadn't planned on moving in together, but Clarion was a college town, and in April rental properties were scarce. Stacy saw the ad in the paper—*Fresh-Air Cottage, 3-Bedroom, Transportation Nearby*. After paying the deposit, they learned that '*Fresh-Air Cottage*' meant no A/C, '*3-Bedroom*' meant two rooms and a closet, and '*Transportation Nearby*' meant train tracks up the street.

"Where do you want it?"

Stacy pointed to the stack in the corner, the boxes holding everything from clothes to demo tapes. He hit the power switch. "Done."

"Already?" Julius sniped, tossing him a cassette. Stacy popped it in the deck, the familiar riffs of Robert Cray filling the room.

"You've got this on LP *and* cassette?"

"Had it on 8-Track, too, till it melted in the car." He moved to the beat, careful not to twist his wounded knee. "Well, I guess it's official," Julius shouted over Cray's *Still Around*. "We're home."

Stacy let his eyes—one still black—wander the room. The walls were covered in faux-mahogany, the bedrooms smaller than jail cells. He'd given Julius the one with the closet to store his 'questionably acquired' gear. Stacy took the one with the view—and scent—of Long John Silver's.

"Where's the hammer?"

"On the windowsill." Julius reached for it, staring through the pane. Across the drive, a man with muttonchops raked grass. When he saw Julius, he looked away.

"I'm still not sure 'bout this. White dude and a brother livin' together's beggin' for trouble."

"You were the one who said Clarion was more liberal."

"It *is* more liberal, but it's still Oklahoma." He closed the curtains and moved to the wall, pounding a nail.

"You going to tell me what that's about?"

Julius hung the Cousteau photo. For a long time, he didn't speak, then, "When I was a kid...Jacques Cousteau kept me alive."

"Kept you alive?" Stacy grabbed a box. "This ought to be good."

"Depends what you mean by 'good'." Stacy peeled back tape, Julius clearing his throat. "I used to watch him on TV. Down in the basement. Just me and Cousteau, cruisin' in the *Calypso*." Beneath his glasses, dark eyes mirrored a distant sea. "Seems so free out there on the ocean. No one tellin' you what to do." He studied Stacy for a reaction. "This one time, he dove right into a pool of sharks. *Sharks*, man! And they were comin' right up to the lens! That's what made me want to be a cameraman."

He stepped forward, eyes glowing like an eel's.

"You know he invented the Aqua-Lung? Watertight goggles, too. And when he was a kid, he cobbled up a box to take pictures underwater. Dude's a genius!" He looked to the dark blue carpet, his mind doing the backstroke. "Got *my* first camera when I was five. Used to shoot bugs, horny-toads, anything I could get close to. When I was eight, I tried to make a waterproof box of my own. Ruined the camera—and got a hell of a beatin' for it—but that didn't stop me. When I got older, I started tapin' all the *Undersea World* episodes. Still got 'em, too. My dream was..." He corrected himself. "...*is*...to work for Jacque Cousteau as an underwater photographer."

"Are you serious?"

"Hell, yes, I'm serious! I collected cans to pay for swimmin' lessons when I was little. Took divin' classes in high school. Got certified in college. I've been sendin' tapes to Cousteau ever since." He glanced at the photo. "All I got to show for it's that picture. But I ain't givin' up."

Stacy wondered how realistic it was for a man who'd never seen the ocean to get a job in one, but he kept his doubts to himself. "You shouldn't give up, Julius." He stared at the photo. "But none of that tells me how Cousteau 'kept you alive'?"

Julius reached for a box, peering inside. "When I was in the basement...I was out of my father's way." Stacy waited for him to elaborate, even considered a follow-up, but decided against it.

As they worked in silence, a train roared up the tracks, rattling the walls. By the time they raised the curtain, it had already passed, a trail of smoke the only evidence it had been there.

\*\*\*

The monitor flickered, then bounced into focus, a huge anaconda filling the screen. "Check it out, Jul. We've got a signal."

"*Wild Kingdom.* I've seen this one a buncha times." Julius pulled up a chair, the clock reading five to midnight. They'd spent the entire day helping Brannuck hook up the microwave. It was the bumbling engineer's third attempt at the job, the previous two ending in failure.

The Clarion bureau was supposed to be operational by mid-April, but on the last day of the month, they still couldn't send video. Instead, Julius was forced to make the hour-and-a-half drive every day, arriving in Avalon with just enough time to edit. That meant a 3:30 deadline for Stacy, who had to finish his scripts before his partner left. The drive was taking a toll on Julius, the early

154

deadlines killing Stacy. None of that mattered to Toole, however. The rabid news director was assigning four, five, even six stories a day—an attempt to establish a noticeable presence in Clarion.

"Wait'll you see what dude does to this snake."

As Marlon Perkins narrated, his sidekick, Jim, followed the anaconda into the water. Slime covering his safari suit, Jim seized an opportunity and dove, reappearing with the beast wrapped around his neck. "The South American Anaconda," Perkins explained, "reaches lengths up to thirty feet. And by the looks of this fella, he's a full-grown male." Jim struggled for a foothold, disappearing again. "They eat birds and small mammals, but the larger snakes have been known to attack cattle." Jim emerged from the depths, face turning blue. "Anacondas kill their prey by suffocation, but they can also deliver a lethal bite." Jim's eyes were bulging now. The end seemed near.

"Watch this, dude."

As Perkins described death by asphyxiation, Jim took charge. Digging his thumbs into the snake's belly, he went under again, emerging moments later with the snake in distress. As a bored llama looked on, Jim gripped the boa like a Gucci handbag, it's head falling limp in his hands.

"I told you, man. There's only one rule in the jungle— don't mess with Jim!"

They cracked up, but their laughter was short-lived. The late-night program gave way to the latest news promo —Stacy running from the tornado. "When Disaster Strikes, the Great 8 News Team is There!" He hit the power button, the image shrinking to a monochromatic dot.

"I'm starting to hate these damn promos!"

The door flew open, an excited Brannuck rushing in. "I done it! I done it!" He was completely out of breath, having just climbed down the twenty-foot extension ladder. "The microwave's up! So's the antenna! Turn on monitor two!" Stacy punched it up, color bars replacing black. "I told ya, fellas! I told ya!"

"You told us, all right," Julius whispered. "'Bout three weeks ago."

The phone rang, Stacy and Julius staring at each other. They'd unplugged the scanner an hour ago, using the outlet to re-charge some batteries. Stacy hit the speaker button. "Clarion bureau—"

"Why the hell are you still there?" Toole roared.

"We've been—"

"Get to Will Rogers Elementary. It's on fucking fire!"

Gut twisting, Stacy reached for a map. "Will Rogers ...that's—?"

"Corner of Fourth and 89er. I suggest you haul ass!"

# Chapter 10
## May 1988

(NEWSWIRE): SOVIET UNION BEGINS WITHDRAWING TROOPS FROM AFGHAN-ISTAN ... POLLS SHOW DUKAKIS AHEAD OF BUSH IN RACE FOR WHITE HOUSE ... SURGEON GENERAL SAYS TOBACCO PRODUCTS ARE 'ADDICTIVE'

By six in the morning, Will Rogers was a smoldering mess. Three fire units worked till dawn to save the historic structure, but the relentless blaze won out. Channel 7 arrived at 6:30. Channel 2 was still missing. KEGT, meanwhile, captured a glut of breathtaking footage, from firemen risking their lives to flames illuminating the Clarion sky.

It was another huge victory for Channel 8.

"Can you tell us what this school meant to you?" Stacy asked.

Mildred Divine took a shaky breath. "I started teaching here in '48..." She glanced at the people on hand—students, parents, teachers—all heartbroken.

"...it's been my home for decades. And these people... they're my family." Her lip began to quiver, Julius zooming. "Everything I'd kept...the notes, the gifts from students...forty years of memories were in that classroom..." Unable to continue, she turned away, melting back into the crowd.

Stacy hated asking questions like that. They were designed to elicit emotion, from interviewees at their most vulnerable. The technique was used by every journalist in the business. *But was it right?* He couldn't help feeling he was invading his subjects' privacy somehow, exposing them unfairly for his own personal gain.

"We've got enough, Jul." He unhooked the mic. They'd talked to three teachers, six parents, and the fire chief, all while Brannuck worked feverishly to establish a signal.

"Five minutes!" he hollered from the truck. As they moved their gear, the sound of screeching tires stopped them.

Channel 2's news van had arrived, its occupants furious.

"Just what kinda shit are you trying to pull?" The burly camera op leaped from the vehicle, veins bulging. "We been on a wild damn goose chase for hours, looking for a 'meth lab bust'. I wonder who left that tip on the hotline!"

"What are you talkin' 'bout, dude?"

"You know *exactly* what I'm talking about!" His eyes moved from Julius to Stacy. "We see what you're doing, with your fancy live truck and your little office. You're trying to come up here and fuck us! Well, dropping a bogus lead mighta worked once, but it'll never work again!"

Stacy had heard enough. "If you think for one—"

158

"Excuse me, gentlemen." The bickering journalists turned. Clarion Fire Chief Gary Schnea stared from beneath a blackened helmet. "I thought you'd like to know. We just discovered a body."

*\*\*\**

The victim was Leonard Catesby, a 63-year-old janitor known for hitting the bottle and falling asleep. This time he never woke up. Toole had a field day with the story— 'Texomaland Torch Turns Cold-Blooded Killer'—Stacy going live three times, twice from the scene, once from the office. By the time he and Julius called it a day, they'd been up for thirty-nine hours.

"How does a beer sound?"

Julius climbed in the Escort. "Sounds great if you're buyin'."

"I'll get the first round. You get the next two."

A minute later, they pulled up to the *Lion's Den*, the marquee flashing five of eight letters. "This the joint Brannuck's been ravin' 'bout?"

Stacy nodded, climbing out of the car—he could already taste the ice-cold beer inside. Julius hesitated. There were three vehicles in the lot, all pickups. He knew by now to keep his guard up at a place like this.

They opened the door and walked inside— cinderblock walls, shadowy booths. "Two Michelobs, please." Stacy handed the bartender a five.

As the man slid them their mugs, Julius stared at the broken jukebox, the empty dance floor. "This *looks* like a place Brannuck'd rave 'bout!"

Stacy snickered, hoisting his glass. "To Don Brannuck, the worst engineer in the history of television."

"I'll drink to that."

They made their way to a booth, passing an elderly couple, a dozing midget, and a man with a guitar, all smoking like wood stoves.

Sliding into their seats, they drank in silence for a time, but there was something Stacy needed to ask. "Have you been thinking what I have?" Julius shrugged, raising his mug. "It just seems strange that our little arsonist friend decides to hit a building in Clarion—another Wilhelm building, by the way—right after we move to town."

Julius adjusted his glasses, the flame of a candle dancing in each lens. "Just a coincidence, dude."

"Is it a coincidence that someone gave Channel 2 a bogus tip this morning? And that today happens to be the first day of ratings?"

Julius stared, the man with the guitar strumming a decent version of *Desperado*. "I'm not big on conspiracy theories. Not even sure I buy Maghee's idea. And besides, I ain't gotta solve 'em. I just gotta shoot 'em."

Stacy nodded, raising his stein. "Maybe you're right."

As the midget snored, the guitarist transitioned to Robert Cray's *I Wonder*. Julius turned. The man had thinning hair and an S-shaped nose, the vibe he emitted one of disquiet. *But, man, could he play!*

As he strummed his steel-string Gibson, he looked up. "Evening, gentlemen. It's an honor to be in the midst of celebrities." His slit of a mouth formed a cryptic smile. "Bill Stacy and Julius Candelle, the Great 8's latest attempt to infiltrate Clarion." The reporter and cameraman exchanged glances. "Don't worry, boys. I'm not clairvoyant. Just highly attuned to the world around me. I read about the move in the paper. And, of course, I watch Channel 8 every night."

"You play a mean guitar, dude."

"Thank you, young man. I hear you do, too." Julius turned to Stacy, the reporter returning his stare. "Let's see if you know this one…" He moved his fingers up the frets, playing a haunting Paul Simon tune. When he broke into song, he stunned them both.

*"Everybody loves the sound of a train in*
*the distance.*
*Everybody thinks it's true."*

He looked up, fingering the refrain. "I love this song, Mr. Zwardowski."

The unexpected reference hit Stacy like a bad note. *Zwardowski?* "How do you know so much about us?"

He changed chords. "I should've properly introduced myself. Trevor Carson, Attorney at Law. Well, at least I used to be. Used to work for Channel 8, too. Until I grew… uncomfortable there."

He paused to reiterate the chorus, Stacy leaning forward. "Uncomfortable?"

"Let's just say we had an ethical discord. Unfortunate part is I haven't been able to find work since." He glanced at the stirring midget. "On the positive side, I've got all night to make music now." With that, he began singing again, his voice smooth as the polished table.

*"What is the point of this story?*
*What information pertains?"*

Julius turned away, ready to end this conversation— 'Trevor Carson, Attorney at Law' was giving him the creeps. "Whatta we got tomorrow, Stace?"

"I believe this song is a metaphor," the man continued. "For finding the truth, no matter the cost."

"What does *that* mean?" Stacy asked.

Before he could answer, Julius stood. "Let's get outta here, dude."

"But the next round's *yours*."

"I'll buy you a case if we can go now!"

161

As they moved for the door, the man sang two more verses, substituting his own lyrics for Simon's.

*"Two disappointed believers.*
*Two people playing the game.*
*Fires raging across Texoma.*
*What's the arsonist's name?"*

Stacy and Julius turned in unison. The strumming sage no longer faced them, his cig glowing red in the pegbox.

*"From time to time, he tips his hand.*
*I'd look within if I were you.*
*Everybody loves the sound of a train in*
*the distance.*
*Everybody thinks it's true."*

\*\*\*

"I'm looking for an Underwood No. 5."

"Underwood?" The clerk scratched his head. "I knew me a Cecil Underwood once. Had one a' them port wine birthmarks. An' bowlegged as—"

"Thanks," Stacy cut him off. As the door slammed behind him, he looked up the street. The nursing home was a few blocks away—he still had ten minutes before his interview with the owner.

"Hey, Jul," he hollered, spying a phone booth. "I'll be right there." The napping camera op waved from the car, still catching up on two weeks' lost sleep.

Stacy stepped in the booth. It was ninety degrees inside and smelled like skunk. He checked his watch— now that Katie anchored the news, she didn't leave for work till two. He fed the machine and dialed.

"Oh...hi, sweetie." She sounded surprised.

"I had some time between interviews, so I thought I'd call."

"I'm glad you did." She didn't sound glad. "So are you and Julius all settled?"

"We've still got some boxes to go through, but at least the microwave's up."

"Yeah, I heard about all the problems."

"Yeah." *Conversation wasn't exactly flowing.* "Listen, I need to ask something. But you've got to promise it stays right here."

"Oh, God, not another crazy arson theory!"

"First off, they're not crazy. Second..." He stopped himself, having no desire to argue again. "Look..." He took a skunk-tinged breath. "...Julius and I ran into someone the other night. At a bar. And he said things, like he knew us or something."

"You're a public figure, Stacy. Our viewers know all sorts of things about us. Why the other night, Larry and I—"

"The guy said he used to work at Channel 8. As a lawyer. And he talked about the fires like—"

"I knew it!"

"Just hear me out, will you?"

There was silence, followed by a dubious sigh. "What was his name?"

"Trevor Carson." More silence.

"Never heard of him. He was probably just yanking your chain."

"I don't think so. When he sang the last—"

"*Sang?* What are you talking about?"

*God, this was going to sound stupid!* "He didn't ...talk about the fires exactly. He sang about them—"

"How much sleep did you get the night before you went to that bar?"

"What's that got to—?"

"And you were drinking, right?"

163

Sweat gathered at the small of his back. "Look, Katie, if you're insinuating—"

"I'm not insinuating anything. I just know when you're tired or drunk—"

"I had one beer!"

"Well, you still might've heard wrong. Or misinterpreted what he said. Even if you didn't, you need to be careful who you go striking up conversations with. There are crackpots all over Texomaland."

"I didn't—"

"Hold on..." He heard a voice beneath hers. "...Larry wants to talk to you."

"Larry? What the hell's *he* doing there?"

"He stopped by with the head-shots for the billboard campaign. You should see them. They look fabulous."

"Stacy. Larry Toole." His voice sounded more strained than usual. "I just got word. The Dexter County Sheriffs made an arrest in the McDermott's case. There's a two o'clock press conference in Cottonwood. I need you to meet Brannuck there."

Stacy scribbled directions, his dementia story a memory. "On our way."

***

"Well, if it ain't the Great 8 twins!" Marv Bridges smiled, happy to see his old friends from Channel 8. He'd been put in charge of today's press conference, about to deliver a bombshell.

"How are you, Marv?" Stacy and Julius climbed out of the Escort.

"Not s'good since m'buddies packed up an' moved ta Clarion." He paused to spit. "But I'm gettin' by."

Stacy and Julius smiled. "Heard you made an arrest in the McDermott's case." Bridges nodded, swapping chew for a Winston. "Can you give us a name?"

"Now, that'd ruin the surprise, wouldn't it?" Bridges lit his cigarette, dropping the match in the creek below. The Clear Boggy Bridge—scene of the crime—was three miles from town but felt like a thousand. Giant oaks lined both sides of the blood-red road, the old bridge a paradigm of rust.

The perfect place for a murder.

Bridges looked at Stacy. It was the first time he'd seen the kid since his blowout with Kaye. He'd spent a lot of time thinking about what she said. And though it pained him to admit it, she'd struck the nail dead center. Part of him *had* died with Jake. And he didn't know if that would ever change. But, like his wife, he was beginning to miss the 'old Marv' something awful. His sincerity. His bad temper. Even his ability to create some good old-fashioned mischief. As smoke filled his lungs, he cut his eyes from Stacy to the bridge. A thought came—a mischievous thought.

"You two ever hear 'bout the legend a' Clear Boggy?"

Like every good fisherman, Bridges held his line, waiting for a nibble.

"What legend?" Julius spoke up.

Bridges set the hook. "Just an ol' yarn. Doubt we got time for it anyhow."

"Sure we do." Stacy glanced up the road. "The other crews aren't even here yet."

The undersheriff's mind flashed back to his son's thirteenth birthday. He and his friends were old enough for a little adventure, Jake insisted. Why couldn't they spend the night at the old Rimshaw place? After all, the abandoned farmhouse was only a half-mile away. Kaye put her husband in charge of talking them out of it, but

Marv opted for a different approach. "Ya'll know 'bout old man Rimshaw?" He waited till they reached the door, sleeping bags in hand. "Sliced his own throat in the upstairs bedroom. Ghost still walks the place, lookin' for his head. Have fun, fellas."

They were home in half-an-hour.

"All right, but we gotta make this quick." Time to reel them in. "It all happened 'round the turn a' the century. Young girl, lived up the road a piece, got herself pregnant. Didn't wanta shame her folks, so she kept the pregnancy a secret."

He blew smoke, the Channel 7 news van cruising to a stop.

"Nine months pass, with nobody knowin' a thing. Then she goes into labor. It was a stormy night, clouds swallowin' the moon, wind blowin' like a hurricane. 'Round midnight, she sneaks out, amind ta have the baby all by herself. Made it far as 'is ol' bridge 'fore she collapsed. Gave birth right over there." He pointed to an ancient oak. "That's when she did somethin' terrible."

Their mouths hung like bass.

"After she had the baby, she kissed it on the forehead..." He drew on his cig, a pronounced glint in his smoke-gray eyes. "...an' tossed it in the river."

"Jesus!" they whispered.

"Terrible's it was, that woulda been that. But as she started home, she heard somethin'. Real faint at first, but it got louder." Stacy and Julius gulped. "It was the sound of a baby cryin'. Way off in the pitch-black night. Longer she listened, louder it got. When they found her the next mornin', she was lyin' under that tree, babblin' like a lunatic. Spent the rest a' her life in an institution's what I hear."

The crew from Channel 2 roared up in a cloud of dust. Time to go for the kill.

"Legend has it, if ya come out here on a stormy night, an' stand in the exact middle a' that ol' bridge, ya can still hear the baby cryin'. Lonesome an' low. A sad little voice lost forever on the water an' wind."

He shrugged, tossing his cigarette.

"Maybe that's what drove our killer ta take the life a' that poor little convenience store clerk. Right here in the very same spot." Stacy and Julius looked at each other. "C'mon fellas. We got us a press conference ta go ta."

As he walked away, he smiled—maybe there was hope for the 'new Marv' yet.

They crossed the bridge, joining the other crews. Billy Nemetz of the *Avalon Herald* was there, too, along with Diana Grimm of the *Clarion Gazette*, and D.A.s from Coal, Dexter, and Quintoc Counties.

Bridges waved to Ross Barton, the prosecutor in the Viola Dern trial, then began. "Thank you for joining us on short notice, folks." The tension in the air was thicker than sorghum. "As you know, in February, we found the body of nineteen-year-old Shelley Plunkett under this bridge. The woman had previously been abducted from McDermott's Convenience Store." His eyes scanned the crowd, offering no hint of what was to come. "The Dexter County Sheriff's Office, in cooperation with Coal and Quintoc Counties, has conducted a thorough investigation, interviewing more than thirty witnesses. The result is today's arrest, our suspect charged with robbery, kidnapping, and first-degree murder."

He paused to make sure everyone was listening.

"The name of the accused is Nate Shefler of Avalon, Oklahoma."

There was a collective gasp. The people on this bridge had worked with the man, covered events just like this one with the unassuming radio jock. Shocked, but never at a

167

loss for words, they fired off questions like guided missiles, Bridges taking them all.

As the event wound down, Brannuck rolled up in the truck. "Ya'll better call Toole. He's champin' at the bit."

Stacy excused himself. "Mobil 6 to Base."

"What have you got?"

"They arrested Nate Shefler, Larry."

"Are you kidding me?" Toole laughed like a madman. "I love this fucking job!"

\*\*\*

As Stacy watched the ten o'clock news, Julius organized VHS tapes. He wasn't kidding when he said he owned every *Undersea World* episode. The compilation rivaled his *NIGHTTIME FUN* collection, which now included footage of campers consorting in front of their tents and couples defiling the fifty-yard line at the local field.

"Toole re-wrote my intro again!" As Stacy popped the tab on his sixth Brown Derby, the scanner blipped, then fell silent.

"Why do you still watch, dude?" Julius shoved the last tape in place. "All it does is gets you riled." He raised a hand, Stacy tossing him a beer. They'd moved past buzzed an hour ago and were well on their way to shit-faced.

"You know what I hate most?" Julius shrugged, grabbing his guitar. "I hate the hype. Everything we cover's so sensationalized by the time it airs, I barely recognize it."

Toole followed the Nate Shefler story with a murder in Wilson and a shooting in Leon. Not to be outdone, Katie detailed an assault in Hugo and a stabbing in Gainesville.

"I hate ratings!" Julius ignored him, tuning his instrument. "If it's not blood and gore, it's sex." Toole

168

returned from the break with a team coverage report on strip clubs.

"From G-strings to T-storms." *Nice segue, Larry!*

Thad stood in front of a new green screen. "There's a storm headed our way, with strong winds and a chance of rain. But don't let that keep you from watching the end of the newscast." He tendered his best porcelain smile. "The Great 8 News Team is giving away another trip to the Arbuckle—"

Stacy killed the TV, guitar replacing prattle. A half-hour passed, the wind getting stronger, the case of beer lighter. The phone rang at 10:50.

"Hello, Stacy." Katie's tone was all business.

"Whass going on?" He tossed another empty on the pile.

"I'm calling to...*are you drunk?*"

He didn't appreciate the accusation—even if it was true. "We've got the day off tomorrow...maybe you could come up?"

"I'll be in Oklahoma City. Larry and I are going live from the capitol."

*Larry and I?* It was starting to sound like a broken record.

"I called to update you on Trevor Carson. I asked Larry—"

"You *what*?" He shot to his feet.

"I asked Larry if he ever—"

"I specifically asked you *not* to say anything."

"I know you did. But I figured—"

"Dammit!" He kicked the pile at his feet, cans flying everywhere.

"I didn't call to argue, Stacy. You wanted to know if Carson worked at Channel 8. I found out for you. Why does it have to be this big secret anyway?"

"I have my reasons."

"And let me guess, you're unwilling to share them." When he didn't answer, she soldiered on. "Larry said a man by that name worked in the legal department, years ago. But he was delusional. That's why Wilhelm fired him. And no one's seen him since."

"I've seen him."

"And heard him, too—*singing* about the fires, right? Think about it, Stacy. He was crazy then. He's crazy now. Forget about him."

Stacy wasn't about to forget.

Despite Toole's best efforts to discredit the man, he'd just confirmed his story.

The reporter hung up, Julius studying him. "What's up with you two anyway?"

Stacy peered out the window. As wind rattled the glass, he turned. "What do you say we go to the bridge?"

\*\*\*

It was a miracle they found the Clear Boggy at all, an even bigger miracle they weren't arrested. Taking the Escort was Stacy's idea— "We can monitor the CB that way!" But as they stumbled from the car, a bottle of whiskey in tow, both realized it was a bad one.

"How'd I let you talk me into this?" Julius seized the bottle, the air electric. "This is ten times worse than cow tippin'!"

"*Shhhhh.*" Stacy lumbered up the road, on edge but doing his best to hide it. He knew the minute he heard Bridges' story, he'd have to check it out, alcohol giving him the extra boost he needed. "We're journaliss, right?"

Julius didn't respond, his head on a swivel.

"If there's anything to this bridge legend, we're gonna find out."

"Ask me, some things are better left unknown."

"Don't be a wuss." Stacy took the bottle, moving past the oak.

"Better a live wuss than a dead duck!" They started to giggle, the laughter ending when they reached the bridge. It was a simple structure. In the shroud of night, it looked like a tunnel. Sinister. Foreboding. "I don't hear nothin'. Let's go home."

Stacy grabbed him by the coattails. "We gotta stand in the exact middle. Thass what Bridges said." He looked to the pit-black center. "You go firss."

"Why the hell should *I* go first?"

"If I take the rear, nothing can sneak up on you."

"That's the dumbest thing—"

"Juss go!" Stacy pushed him, the wind blowing in fitful gusts. Their gaits grew stiffer with every step, their footfalls shorter. When they reached the center, neither knew what to do. A minute passed. They stood in darkness. Listening.

But there was no ghostly voice. No baby's cry.

Julius snatched the bottle, relief washing over him. "Now can we—?"

Stacy shushed him again, still listening. But they heard nothing but the sound of wind, and water fifty feet below. "Well, I guess—"

*Waaaaaaaa.*

They looked at each other, hearts in their throats. "Dude—" The sound came again—*could this really be happening?* As they pondered the question, it came again, louder and longer.

*Waaaaaaaaaaaaaaaaaaaa.*

Julius bolted first, followed by Stacy a millisecond later, the bottle dropped in haste. *They'd never been so scared in their lives!* As Julius ran, Stacy passed him like a white Carl Lewis. But he tripped near the oak, Julius

171

landing on top of him. The last time they found themselves like this, Dick Wilhelm was shooting at them.

But this was worse.

"Get off me!" Julius screamed, caught in a tangled web of arms and legs.

"You get off me!" Stacy fired back.

The cry came again—*Waaaaaaaaaaaaaa*—the 'ghost baby' right on top of them!

That's when Stacy noticed the branches. High up in the tree.

"Let's go, dude..." Julius wiggled free. "...we gotta—" He paused to see what Stacy was looking at. Directly above, two limbs rubbed together when the wind hit just right, the wood-on-wood friction creating a perfect crying sound.

*Goddammit, Marv!*

They laughed for ten minutes, each claiming the other was more frightened than *he* was. Unfortunately, the adrenaline stole their buzz. But they still had half a bottle of whiskey, if they could just find it. Stacy walked back to the bridge, Julius joining him. In the absence of light, searching was difficult. But Julius—used to seeing the world through a black-and-white viewfinder—made short work of it.

"There, dude."

Stacy picked it up, unscrewing the cap. The wind had died some. They heard water chuckling below. "Well..." He offered Julius a drink. "...now we know."

"Not sure knowin' was worth it." The cameraman sipped.

"It's always worth it." Stacy leaned against the rail, eyes far away. Hundreds of questions swirled, one pressing. "What do you think Carson was trying to tell us?"

Julius shrugged, handing the bottle back. "Who knows? Dude was crazy."

"I don't think so, Jul." He took a swig. "I think he knows who the Torch is."

"Come on, Stace. You sayin' some drunk in a two-bit shitkicker bar knows more than your buddy, Maghee?"

"I think he knows *something*." Julius reclaimed the bottle. "Maghee thinks the Torch could be an ex-employee, right?" As the man drank, Stacy searched the darkness. He'd considered this axiom before, but he'd always talked himself out of it. "What if it's a *current* employee?"

Julius nearly choked. "Are you nuts?"

"Carson said, 'Look within.' Remember?"

"Dude said lotsa things...or *sang* 'em anyway. That don't make 'em true." He looked away, shaking his head, then floated an idea of his own. "Fine...you want theories? What if *Carson's* the Torch?" Stacy had thought of that. "I mean, dude fits the profile. Male. Loner. Feels like the world—or at least Channel 8—screwed him."

"He fits the profile. But he didn't do it."

Julius frowned. "If you ask me, we ain't gettin' paid enough to worry 'bout it."

Stacy couldn't argue, but he had another question. The one that kept him up at night. The one he'd been afraid to ask—until now. "What if Larry Toole's the Torch?"

Julius did choke this time. "Toole?" he coughed. "What the—?"

"Think about it, Jul." He moved closer, thunder rumbling. "When was the first fire?" Julius couldn't answer, still coughing up whiskey. "A month after Toole hired on. And how about this? There've been four fires since he got here."

173

"There've been four fires since *I* got here, but I don't see you accusin' me. Why would Toole set those fires?"

Stacy looked him in the eye. "For ratings."

"You're outta your—"

"Am I?" He took the bottle and capped it. "Then I've got three questions. How come it always happens at night? How come we always get a call from Toole? And how come Channel 8's always the first to arrive?"

"'Cause we're the only ones livin' with scanners!"

"That's one explanation. Here's another—suppose Toole calls before word ever hits the scanner?" Julius dismissed him. "It's not that big a stretch, Jul. He's hyped every story we've ever done. Faked interviews. Why couldn't he start a few fires?"

Rain began to fall, stinging their skin. "It doesn't add up, Stace. Maghee says the Torch is after Wilhelm. Toole's got no beef with him."

"Maybe Maghee's wrong, at least on motive. Maybe the Torch isn't doing this for revenge, but for greed—or power." He paused, the rain falling harder. "Toole sure fits *that* profile, doesn't he?"

Julius didn't know what to say. But he knew one thing—if they stayed out here much longer, they'd have to swim home. Heading for the car, he stopped under the oak. "You know what you're sayin', right? We got a man dead!" Stacy nodded, lightning flashing. "Right or wrong, you best keep your theories between us."

\*\*\*

He pinned the Polaroid to the corkboard, the photo featuring Bill Stacy and Dan Rather, the keynote speaker at today's OU graduation. Julius had taken it moments after commencement, the new camera his latest acquisition. Stacy grabbed a pen, applying the perfect caption—*OPPOSITE ENDS OF THE TV NEWS PAY SCALE*.

"Oh, crap!" He lunged, yanking his script from the new fax machine. "I hate this damn thing. I could call in my scripts and clean the entire office in half the time it takes to send one page!"

"Newest technology, dude."

"I liked the *old* technology." He picked up the phone and dialed. "Can you take my scripts, Amy?"

"Why don't you fax them?"

"If you let me dictate, we'll be done in three minutes."

"I don't have three minutes." She handed the phone to an intern. When the coed finished typing, it was five till six.

"Mr. Toole wants to speak to you."

"Mr.—?"

"Stacy. Larry Toole." *Why did he always introduce himself?* "I need you and Julius at the Eagle Feather Motel, pronto."

Stacy pinched the bridge of his nose. He'd been up since five, driving to Norman for the ceremony, then making stops in Moore, Shawnee, and Holdenville on the way back. "Can this wait till tomorrow, Larry?"

"If it could wait till tomorrow, would we be talking tonight?" Stacy sighed, Julius pulling the last tape from the feed. "Take one of your personal vehicles and park outside room seven. Don't say anything. Don't do anything. Just wait till someone comes out. And shoot them."

"But who are we shooting? You've gotta be—"

"I don't '*gotta be*' anything. This is the lead at ten."

Toole hung up, Stacy turning to Julius. "Hope you're not hungry."

The man yawned, reaching for his camera. "Where to, dude?"

175

They drove in silence, crossing the railroad tracks and heading east. At the turn of the century, four families lived in Clarion. Today, the Quintoc County seat boasted a college, two glass factories, and a hearty pecan crop. And though the oil slump of the '80s had taken its toll, city leaders were committed to downtown revitalization.

The Eagle Feather Motel wasn't part of the plan. The dilapidated inn was a hovel for the seedy and a burden for police. But the rent was cheap, twenty bucks a night or $7.50 an hour—*YOUR CHOISE*, the sign read.

Julius parked the Subaru, fishing his camera from the backseat. He'd prepped it at the office. Now all they had to do was wait—*for what, they had no idea!* Stacy rolled down the window, a breeze delivering the scent of dumpsters.

An hour passed.

Two hours.

Three.

At 9:35, the door opened, a couple emerging. Julius leaped from the car, already rolling, Stacy flooding the subjects with light.

The man tried to shield his face, his companion, a middle-aged woman in stiletto heels, mugging for the camera. "You bastards!" he screamed, leaping in a Cadillac. As Julius zoomed on the plate, the car squealed out of the lot, reporter and cameraman having no idea what they'd captured.

Ten minutes later, they were back at the office, feeding it to Avalon. "Whatta you s'pose that was all about?"

Stacy shrugged, powering up the monitor. As Mort Taylor mounted a Clydesdale, offering "huge savings on Mustangs", Julius pulled up a chair for the news intro.

"Scandal rocks a Texoma town." A monitor rose over Toole's shoulder, the graphic—*TOWN DICK CAUGHT*.

"Clarion Assistant Police Chief Trey Allenbaugh found himself in a compromising position tonight."

Stacy looked to Julius, the director rolling video.

"In this exclusive Great 8 footage, Allenbaugh's seen in the company of a known prostitute." The man repeated his shocked response for all Texoma to hear, then darted for the Cadillac, his license filling the screen. Below, a C.G. read *VIDEO COURTESY CLARION BUREAU*.

"Dude, we're dead!" The pair watched the rest of the story in horror, the video repeating itself three times. "The cops ain't *never* gonna forget this!"

Toole's story was a Pearl Harbor attack on the Clarion Police force, Stacy and Julius his naïve kamikazes. And like World War II, there'd be huge payback for a story with more holes than Swiss cheese. For one, Toole failed to mention that he, not Allenbaugh, had hired the streetwalker, paying her to lure the off-duty cop back to the motel. Second, the hooker waited till after the sex act to reveal her profession, threatening to call the press if she wasn't paid. The officer, who'd lost his wife to ALS a year earlier, complied as planned. *But why the attack in the first place?* The answer lied in another unreported fact— Trey Allenbaugh was a minority stockholder in KPXZ, one who'd taken a public stand against Channel 8 moving to Clarion.

"Payback's a bitch!" Toole would later boast.

*It sure was.*

"We'd like to recognize Clarion bureau chief Bill Stacy and videographer Julius Candelle for their contributions to this report. In other news..."

As Julius stared at the monitor, Stacy fired his notepad at the wall.

177

# CHAPTER 11
## *June 1988*

*(NEWSWIRE): U.S. FARMERS SEEK DISASTER RELIEF FOR WORST DROUGHT IN 50 YEARS ... 'WORLD HEALTH ORGANIZATION' SAYS 5 MILLION PEOPLE HAVE AIDS ... NBA'S LAKERS WIN FIFTH TITLE IN 1980s*

They expected retribution. But not this swiftly.

Stacy was interviewing a local farmer when Amy Chow radioed— "The police want to see you at one o'clock." Before he could respond, she added, "And don't think this gets you out of your crop damage piece. If nothing good happens"—and by 'good' she meant tragic— "it'll be the lead at six."

Julius drove as if hauling nitroglycerin. "Don't worry, Jul. It's going to be fine." But Stacy wasn't convinced either. He'd written the same sentence three times.

"I don't like cops."

"We interview cops all the time."

"This ain't no interview."

They pulled to a stop at the *CLARION POLICE* sign. Stacy swallowed, throat dry as the field they'd just left. "Stay cool, Julius. We were just following orders."

They walked up the path, the air smelling of dead marigolds. As they reached the door, a man in a black Stetson greeted them. "Leonard Allenbaugh, Jr.," he introduced himself. "I'm the chief of police—and Trey's father." Their guts rumbled in unison. "This is Sergeant Dumars. Detective Sanders. And Fire Chief Schnea." Stacy recognized the man from the elementary school blaze. "Mr. *Stacy*, you come with us. Mr. *Candelle*..." He spoke the names as if they tasted like zinc. "...you go with them."

As the cops led Julius away, his expression was a condemned man's. Stacy's was no better—the blood had left his face, too.

The chief escorted his guest to a tiny room. Inside were two chairs and a table. "Sit yer ass down," he ordered, all pretense of etiquette gone.

"Are you comfortable?" the fire chief asked. "Can I get you something to drink?" Apparently Schnea would be playing the role of 'good cop' today.

"May I ask what this is about?"

"We'll ask the fuckin' questions!" Allenbaugh threw his hat on the table, a crease marking the equator of his brow.

Schnea shot him a cautionary glance. "Would you like an attorney present?"

"An attorney?" Stacy looked from chief to chief. "Why would—?"

"Not saying you do or don't. But we're required to ask."

"I don't think—"

"Where were ya the night a' April 30th?" Allenbaugh charged.

180

Stacy stiffened. "I'm not...sure. That was more than a month ago."

"Maybe this'll jog your memory." The chief leaned in. "Will Rogers Elementary burned down that night."

"Will Rogers?" Stacy was taken aback. "You're not suggesting—?"

"We ain't suggestin' nothin'. Just answer the damn question!"

Stacy's mind spun like a top. He'd prepared himself for several scenarios—but not this one. "We were at the scene..." The man grinned like a jackal. "...with the *other* news crews!"

"An' I bet Channel 8 beat 'em all there, didn't they?" He moved forward, gun anchored to an arthritic hip. "Where were ya *before* the fire?"

Stacy thought hard, an image surfacing—Jim from *Wild Kingdom*, battling a giant snake. "We were working. At the new office."

"Just you and Candelle?"

"No...Don Brannuck was there...our engineer. He was with us the entire night."

Allenbaugh glared at Schnea, the man getting up and leaving. Stacy suddenly felt vulnerable, like being in the alley with Dexter Monroe, the bully from 78th Street.

"Maybe it's just me..." The chief moved closer, breath stinking of Lucky Strikes. "...but I find it real interestin' we get us a suspicious fire, right after you *fucks* from Channel 8 roll into town."

"Sir," Stacy rasped, "I can assure you, we had nothing to do with that fire."

"Maybe not." He held his ground. "But I'm gonna do everythin' in my power to dig up some evidence. An' when I do, you and your little nigger friend are goin' down." He offered a repellant smile. "Tit for tat."

Stacy stared in disbelief. "Are you threatening me?"

181

"Call it what ya want."

Stacy stood, anger replacing fear. "Am I a suspect in this case?"

Allenbaugh reached for his Stetson. "You're a 'person of interest'—for now."

"Well, then—*for now*—we're through talking."

The man slithered to the door. "Ya best 'member somethin', boy. I got lotsa eyes in this town."

***

Roy Maghee lit a cigarette, poring over the 'Torch' files. His unflagging attention to detail is what separated him from ordinary investigators. And he knew from experience that one little 'crumb' could reveal the whole 'cake'. The phone rang. "Maghee."

"'Morning, sir, it's Bill Stacy."

"How are you, Bill?"

"Not bad. Considering the Clarion P.D. just interrogated me."

Maghee flicked ash. He'd heard about the incident, having already talked to Gary Schnea. But he wanted the reporter's account. "What happened?"

Stacy recounted the story, filling in details from the Trey Allenbaugh scandal.

Maghee took a drag. "I wouldn't worry. Schnea's a good man"

"Schnea's not the one I'm worried about."

"You're innocent, Bill. And contrary to popular belief, we in the law enforcement community aren't out to convict innocent people."

There was a long pause. "We've had four fires, right?"

Maghee paused himself. "That's right."

"All non-accidental? All Wilhelm buildings?"

182

"Correct." He sparked a new cigarette with the old, snuffing out the butt.

"And you still believe the person doing this is out to get Wilhelm?"

"I do."

"Well, what if you're wrong? I mean, there's no shortage of Wilhelm buildings, right?" Maghee's eyes moved from the ashtray to the photo on his desk—he and his wife on South Padre Island. "What if a fifth fire destroyed a non-Wilhelm building? Would that force you to rethink things?"

The investigator leaned back, smoke filling the room. Could he trust Bill Stacy? Reporters had lied to him more times than he could count. "Of course, we'll keep that confidential," they assured him. "This is all off the record." That's why friends were dumfounded when he married Tanya Sheldon, the pretty young anchor from Channel 8. She'd moved to Avalon from Ft. Lauderdale in the mid '70s, looking for experience and a chance to move on. What she found was Roy Maghee, a handsome young firefighter with poor communication skills and a chip on his shoulder. She hated interviewing the man, his sound bites shorter than a list of Oklahoma Presidents. But she couldn't deny the way he made her feel. He felt the same, though no one could've guessed it. That's why she fell out of her chair when he arrived on set, diamond ring in hand, the night she announced her departure for Sioux City. It wasn't easy, opening himself up like that. But he had no choice. He loved her. And twelve years later, he continued to wonder what might've happened if he didn't take that chance.

"Is this line safe?"

"I assume so. I'm calling from home."

Maghee lowered his voice. "We've already had a fifth fire, Bill. Or at least a fifth attempt."

183

"What do you—?"

"When we conduct an arson investigation, we keep certain details from the public, details only we and the arsonist know." He tapped his cigarette against the desk. "You've already helped me by providing a list of suspects. Now I'm going to help you. But if you broadcast this information, we'll never speak again."

"You have my word."

"Two weeks ago, a night watchman at the Avalon Library called. He'd found something in the attic, a cup full of foam peanuts with a cigarette inside. Fortunately, the thing burned itself out before it had a chance to ignite the gas beneath it." Maghee took another hit. "We found holes in the walls and ceiling, too. Ventilation holes, probably punched with a pike pole."

"Do you think all the fires were started this way?"

"We have evidence to suggest that."

"Can you tell me what brand of cigarette you found?"

The question caught Maghee off guard. He'd planned to keep that info to himself, along with the fact they'd discovered a still-unidentified print on the filter. "I'm not—"

"Please, sir. It's important."

He looked to the pack of Marlboros on his desk. If the reporter burned him, the investigation would be seriously compromised. He shifted his gaze to the photo. "It was a KOOL."

After a beat, Stacy responded, his voice clear and decisive. "I want to add another name to the list. Larry Toole."

\*\*\*

184

Julius reached in his pocket—two quarters and a wad of lint. "Dude, can you spot me today?" Stacy glanced up from his notes. "For the dogs."

He looked past Julius to the girl holding the tray. "You're Bill Stacy, huh?" *Sort of.* He paid her for the Coneys and watched her skate off.

Eating in the car was the new norm, the pair having little time for anything else. Stacy couldn't remember the last time he had a home-cooked meal. Or rewrote a story on the Underwood. Or sent out demo tapes. Work had consumed his life. Work and his obsession with the Texomaland Torch.

"Base to Mobil 6." They stared at the radio. *What more could Toole want today?* He'd already assigned a package on the AIDS scare in Texoma—not that there was one—another on drought losses for local farmers—talk about beating a dead horse—and a VO/SOT on drug seizures at Clarion High—not exactly a news flash.

"I'm starting to hate this damn radio as much as the scanner!" Stacy grabbed the handset. "Mobil 6 here."

"Stacy. Larry Toole. Where are you?"

"We're at the Sonic Drive-In in Clarion." He took a bite.

"A boat just exploded on Konawa Lake. It'll go nicely with the oilrig disaster we're covering in Bonham." Stacy shoved the dog back in its bag. "Call me when you get there."

The drive took minutes—they even beat some of the rescue workers. As Julius rolled to a stop, Stacy scribbled notes. *Small vessel listing in the waves. Hundred yards offshore. Bow engulfed in flames.* He glanced at Julius who was already shooting, then remembered Toole's instructions. "Mobil 6 to Base."

"Talk to me."

"It's bad, Larry." A Lake Patrol unit advanced on the craft, wind bringing the smell of burning gas to shore. Stacy could see two victims in the water, not sure if either was still alive. "It looks like…" A fire truck roared to a stop a few feet away, the men jumping down and splashing into the lake. "…at least two people are hurt." Lake Patrol officers plucked one from the whitecaps, then circled for the other, firefighters forming a human chain. "But there could be more. We've got a rescue boat involved and a handful of firemen in the lake."

"Any other news crews there?"

Stacy looked over his shoulder. "Not yet."

"Outstanding!" Rescuers pulled the other victim from the water, dodging smoke and flames. "I need you to wade out there and stand next to the firemen. I want it to look like you're helping."

Stacy stared at the handset. "Are you nuts?"

"Not even close. And make sure Julius shoots everything."

"But they don't need *me* out there. And besides, I'm wearing a suit!"

"I'll pay for your fucking dry cleaning!"

This was a new low. Someone's life was being destroyed. And all his boss could think of was the next Great 8 news promo. With the boat racing for shore, Stacy had to make a decision.

*Dammit!*

He tore out for the ramp, kicking off his shoes. The water was surprisingly warm, the concrete slope thick with algae. Navigating the muck, he signaled Julius, the stunned camera op turning his lens on the reporter-turned-rescuer. Stacy felt like a complete jerk when he joined the firefighters, none of them saying a word. As the boat slowed, the men on board barely looked his way. *Why should they?* They had *real* work to do.

186

They passed the first victim to a fireman, who sent him up the line, an ambulance waiting on shore. As Stacy reached out to 'help', he saw the man's skin, pink and bubbling. He wanted to run, to climb out of the water and drive straight home to his mother. But that wasn't an option anymore. His boss had given him an order. And, yes, he could've said no, could've told him to 'go jump in a lake'. But he didn't.

And that sickened him more than the scene before him.

The second victim, a woman, was clearly dead. A third victim, the couple's two-year-old son, was never found. Stacy went live from the scene at six, the last insult of the day coming when Toole asked him to wade back in the water moments before air.

He wanted his clothes to look wetter.

*** 

Stacy hurried through the kitchen, he and Julius running late. "Hey, Jul—" He opened the door, stopping cold. The man was putting his shirt on, a galaxy of scars, burns, and welts on his exposed back.

Stacy toppled into a vacuum, memories flashing like lightning. When he landed, he was back in Portland. On 78th Street, the band of thugs surrounding him in the alley. "Ain't got no momma to save you now, do you, white boy?" Indeed, he didn't. Helen Zwardowski had gone to the store and wouldn't be back for hours. "And you ain't never had no daddy!" Nothing hurt worse than references to his father. Not a punch in the gut, a jab to the eye, or a kick in the head—all of which he was about to receive.

"Why are you doing this?" he heard his eight-year-old voice beg.

"'Cause you ain't like us!" Dexter Monroe answered, his cronies closing in. The first blow buckled Stacy's knees. After that, it was a firestorm of fists and feet. Facedown on the asphalt, he thought he'd imagined his mother's voice. But when he wiped the blood from his eyes, he saw her. Hearing screams when she returned for her grocery list, Helen Zwardowski burst out the back door, grabbing Stacy's attackers and tossing them aside. All but Dexter Monroe, that is. He was considerably larger than the rest. It took all the strength she had to pull the bully off her son. In the process, she ripped his T-shirt, exposing his back. The other boys stopped and stared, as did Stacy's mother. The young man's back was covered with the same scars as Julius', some fresh, some dark with age. Stacy would never forget what happened next. The 78th Street bully, the kid who'd tortured him for more than a year, took out in a dead sprint, wailing at the top of his lungs, *"You ain't no better than me!"* His followers watched in silence, then filed away, their eyes conveying the same defiant pride as Julius Candelle's.

"Sorry..." Stacy watched as Julius pulled his shirt down, his mind still reeling. "...are you...ready?"

The cameraman nodded, turning away.

As Stacy backed off, he licked his lips, tasting blood again. He wanted to ask Julius about what he'd seen. Wanted to offer comfort. But he knew that was impossible. "I'll meet you at the car."

*Jesus, Jul!* They were bound to see each other without a shirt on once in a while. Why hadn't he told him? *Isn't that what friends were for?* Stacy frowned, making his way outside. *What did he know about friendship?* And what had he ever told Julius?

As he walked to the Escort, he did what he always did—buried the new image with the old. One day, he'd go looking for them. But not today.

188

He climbed in the car and waited, glancing at the house next door. A silhouette filled the window, their neighbor staring him down again. In the two months they'd lived next to Earl Reeves—they'd gotten his name from a misdelivered letter—he'd yet to wave or say "hello". But his gaze spoke volumes. Chief Allenbaugh said he had "lotsa eyes in this town". Maybe two belonged to 'Redneck Earl'.

As a police cruiser passed, Julius walked out to the car. Without a word, they fastened their seatbelts and drove to work.

***

As he rolled into Sulphur, he clicked on the radio, KAVN offering a New Age instrumental. The station was making every effort to distance itself from Nate Shefler, a format change—one emphasizing music over murderous DJs—the latest strategy.

Stacy was meeting Katie at the Chickasaw Motor Inn. Although he had serious doubts, he wanted to see if they could rekindle what they once had.

But there was something he needed to do first.

He stopped at Pearl's, rushing inside. Across the way, Marv Bridges waved from a booth, Stacy apologizing for being late.

"They actually give ya a day off, huh?" Stacy sat, the undersheriff removing his worn but 'lucky' fishing hat.

"Thanks for coming, Marv."

Doris dropped off menus and iced teas. "Your treat, Bill?" Stacy nodded. He ordered the deluxe chicken dinner. "An' add me some extra gravy, will ya, hun?"

Stacy chose the French Dip, then turned to the matter at hand. "I need to be straight with you." The lawman raised an eyebrow. "First off, my real name's

Stacy. Stacy Zwardowski. This whole 'Bill Stacy' thing wasn't my idea. And if you want to know the truth, it's worn itself pretty thin."

"'Magine it has. Pro'ly feels like you're lyin' ever' time ya open your mouth." *He didn't know the half of it.* "'Course, I'd bet dollars ta donuts ya ain't the only one."

"You'd win that bet." Doris delivered bread, Bridges grabbing a roll. "So have you had any luck with what I asked for?"

The man raised his other eyebrow. "Hell, I figgered we could have us a little lunch conversation—maybe even talk some football—'fore we got down ta business."

"Sorry." Stacy checked the clock. "I'm meeting someone at two."

"I'm guessin' she's prettier'n me?" Stacy blushed. "All right, let's get after it then." He reached in his pocket and pulled out a sheet of paper. "I didn't find much, Bill...er...Stacy. This here Toole fella ain't got no record ta speak of. Parkin' ticket here an' there. Speedin' violation. But nothin' criminal."

"Are you sure you looked everywhere?"

Bridges cocked his head to one side. "What exactly is it you're lookin' for?"

Stacy trusted the undersheriff. But he didn't want to say—not yet. "When I find it, you'll be the first to know."

"Son..." The man stared. "...are you all right?"

The question took Stacy aback. He thought he'd tucked everything away, the concern for his friend, the pain from his childhood—the guilt. "I'm fine."

There was a long silence before Bridges continued. Finally, "When ya become an adult, your juvenile records're sealed. Makes it a whole lot harder for anyone ta get 'hold of 'em. But I can tell ya someone who knows an awful lot 'bout Larry Toole, the boy."

Stacy leaned forward.

190

"Name's Russell Longdale. He was the Dexter County D.A. ten years ago. Lost his job. Got debarred. Even did some time. But don't let that fool ya. He's a damn good fella." He paused to sip tea. "Lives up in Coalgate now. Keeps to hisself mostly. I don't know if he'll talk ta ya, but if ya wanna learn more 'bout your boss, I'd start there."

As Doris brought their meals, Stacy closed his Steno. "Thanks. This helps a lot." He took a moment to unfold his napkin, placing it in his lap.

Bridges stared, a look of disquiet moving over his face.

"What is it, Marv?"

The undersheriff shook his head. "Nothin', Stacy." If Stacy didn't know better, he'd swear the man was fighting back tears. They ate their lunches in silence, Bridges, when finished, pulling out a pen. "I need ya ta promise me somethin'." He wrote his number on a business card. "If ya ever need me—for anythin'—you call me, okay?"

Stacy slipped the card in his pocket. "Count on it, Marv."

They stood, Bridges grabbing his hat as they moved for the door. "Well, good luck with your two o'clock meetin'."

Stacy glanced at his watch.

In ten minutes, he was going to need all the luck he could get.

\*\*\*

He stared at the ceiling. She lit a Virginia Slim. "That was great."

"Yeah, great."

Stacy coughed, wondering when his girlfriend took up smoking. "Missed you."

191

"Missed you, too."

They shifted and stirred, both trying to get comfortable.

"Isn't it great about the ratings?"

"What ratings?"

"You didn't hear?" Her smile lit the room. "Larry announced it yesterday. We finished second again, but only a point behind Channel 2!" He shook his head, wondering why no one had told him. Since moving to Clarion, he and Julius had been made to feel like a pair of Gilligan-esque castaways.

"Would've been nice to hear it from my boss."

"Oh...I'm sure Larry meant to tell you." She blew a white trail. "We've just been so busy. Seems like every day we're off to a mall opening, or a pep rally, or—"

"Gee, all that and he still has time to invent the news."

"What's that supposed to mean?"

He peered through the smoke. "You know what it means, Katie. Our newscast is a joke. And Toole's the punch line!"

"Where's this coming from?"

"Do you even listen to what you read on the prompter? Toole's orchestrating everything at Channel 8, the stories we do, the live shots—"

"That's his job, sweetie."

"Was it his job to send Julius to a Klan rally? Or have me jump in a lake and pretend to help rescuers? How about putting me on set an hour after I survived a tornado?" She tried to say something, but he kept going. "He's shot fake interviews, aired phony live shots, even dropped bogus tips on the competition. The man'll do anything for ratings, Katie!"

"Stacy." She flashed a condescending smile. "I think you're exaggerating."

192

"If there's no news, he *creates* news. You saw what he did last week. He set that cop up. Chip said he bragged all over the newsroom the next day."

"If Larry's guilty of anything, it's being a workaholic. I mean, the man never sleeps." *How would she know that?* "News is his life, Stacy. And regardless of how you feel about him, you can't argue with success."

"Is that all you care about?"

"Why shouldn't I care about it?" Her eyes looked duller than he remembered. "We finished a point behind Channel 2. We've never even come close to those numbers. And if you ask me, Larry's a hundred percent responsible." She snuffed out her cigarette. "Instead of knocking him, maybe you should give him credit. He's turned this station around single-handedly, and in the process, made each and every one of us a commodity. People look up to us now. They think we're something special."

"*Something special?*" he chuffed. "Because we B.S. our viewers? Hype every story? Because our 'award-winning' news director lies to his own employees?" Smoke curled from the ashtray like a sickle. "He wouldn't tell us why we were going to that motel, Katie, because he didn't want an argument. We were his pawns. And then, worst of all, he let us take the fall for him."

"'Take the fall'?"

"Do you know where we spent the next afternoon? At the Clarion Police station. Payback for Toole's little sting operation."

She stared—*had he finally gotten to her?* "Look...I'm not saying I agree with everything Larry does. But I know we're better off with him than without him."

"*Dammit*, Katie! The *ends* don't justify the *means*!"

She inched away. "You're scaring me."

193

"I'm scaring *you*?" His face reddened. "You know what scares me? The other stations in our coverage area are starting to imitate us. I'm seeing anchors look more like actors, reporters becoming the focus of their stories, news writers forgetting the word *news* is in their title. And it doesn't stop here! I guarantee it's happening in Tulsa and Oklahoma City. Everyone's trying to one-up each other. And where does it all end? Are we going to come to work one day and find out we're doing the six o'clock news naked?"

"Stacy..." She reached out as if petting a rabid dog. "...I know you've been through a lot, but you're way off base. No one ever said the news business was perfect. And if you're trying to blame it all on Larry, you're barking up the wrong tree."

"Am I?" He paused, ignoring Julius' warnings again. "I think Toole's the Texomaland Torch!"

"You *what*?"

"Hear me—"

"Jesus Christ, Stacy!" She tore back the covers, grabbing her clothes. "You've completely lost it! First, you accuse Phil, and now you're pointing the finger at Larry!"

He grabbed her wrist, feeling bones. "How come Channel 8's always the first crew to arrive? Because Larry tips us off before anyone else knows!"

"This is insane."

"Is it? Then, why do we beat these stories like a drum? Go live five times a day?" He looked deep in her eyes, deeper than when they kissed at Turner Falls, than when they made love for the first time. "How come the Torch never struck in Clarion till KEGT opened a bureau there?"

She stared for a long time. When she spoke, her voice was a little girl's. "Why in God's name would Larry start those fires?"

194

"You already know the answer, Katie." He eased his grip. "You said it yourself, we finished a 'point behind Channel 2'. And 'Larry's a hundred percent responsible'."

She ripped her arm away. "Do you know what you're saying? You're calling Larry Toole a murderer!"

"I'm aware of that."

"Then where's your proof?" He cut his eyes to the bed. "You remember the word. It's what we need to convict someone of a crime! What we need in the news business to report a story!"

"I don't have proof...*yet*."

"Honestly, Stacy..." She threw her clothes on. "...you need help! Maybe you're still spooked from the tornado. Or haven't dealt with your mother's death. Whatever it is, you need serious psychological help!"

"Oh, really?" She buttoned her blouse. "So you think no one in his right mind would accuse a Channel 8 employee of this?" Stepping into her pumps, she stomped to the door. "Then why are the Clarion Police calling Bill Stacy and Julius Candelle 'persons of interest' in this case?"

She hesitated, refusing to look at him. "Get help, Stacy. *Please.*"

As the door slammed, silence engulfed him.

It wasn't the first time a lovemaking session ended this way between them.

But it would be the last.

\*\*\*

"I know I shouldn't have, Jul." He emptied his stein. "But what's done is done."

Julius glanced over his shoulder, keeping tabs on the crowd.

195

"It just pisses me off how she defends him all the time." The barkeep brought two more beers. "I mean, is it me, or is something going on between those two?"

"Don't know, dude." Julius turned as the door opened, a pack of frat boys stumbling inside. The Lion's Den had gone from quiet dive to hopping hot spot. College students packed the dance floor, moving to Rick Astley's *Together Forever*, while cowboy-types lined the cinderblock walls, waiting for the next country segment. Stacy and Julius had come here often since their encounter with Trevor Carson, but they'd never seen it like this.

They'd never seen the eccentric lawyer again either.

"Let's get out of here," Stacy hollered over the music.

"You read my mind. Where to, dude?"

"The bridge."

On the way to the Clear Boggy, conversation drifted from Katie to Toole to Reg McNair's giant hair. Words came easy between the two, laughter easier. But the topic Stacy wanted to broach—needed to broach—was no laughing matter.

He'd been holding out hope that Julius would bring it up, but the stoic camera op had yet to do so. They'd been at the bridge for more than an hour when Stacy's patience waned. "Hey, Jul..." He opened another beer. "...what happened to your back?"

The man's gaze shifted from the darkness to Stacy, then back again. For a long time, he said nothing. Finally, "Ain't somethin' I like talkin' 'bout."

Stacy watched. Listened. Waited him out.

The man cleared his throat, listening to the river. "My father worked for the railroad...when he worked at all. And my mother...well, let's just say she did whatever he told her." A cricket chirped, the air smelling of summer wheat. "She got herself pregnant right after high school.

My father had no problem messin' around with her. Big problem marryin' her." A faint smile graced his lips. "Then grandpappy got 'hold of him. Threatened to gut him like a carp if he didn't buy her a ring. Needless to say, he did." He flipped a bottle cap, waiting for the plink of metal on water. It never came.

"They were married a year when he lost his job. That's when he started dealin'." He turned to Stacy. "He was a drug pusher, Stace. Nothin' glamorous. Just a smalltime hood in a smalltime neighborhood. But that's how he supported his family. Worst part was he got my mother hooked on the shit. And pretty soon, that's all they lived for. Us kids—there were three of us—we just got in the way." He set his empty beer down and opened another.

"I was three the first time he hit me. I wanted seconds at dinner. And my father, he was like a tickin' time bomb. Me bein' a kid, I didn't know when to shut up." He took a drink, adjusting his glasses. "He got angry, started talkin' 'bout how I'd cost him—how we'd *all* cost him. Then he backhanded me, knocked me right outta my chair. I was so scared I didn't even cry. But I can still remember how my cheek hurt, and how I felt...like I could never trust him again." He looked down. "As I got older, he started usin' cigars for punishment. That's what the scars are from. Most of 'em anyway."

Stacy felt sick to his stomach. He couldn't believe what his friend had endured.

"It was the drugs, man. I can't remember a time when they weren't high or tryin' to get high. I mostly just stayed away...you know, down in the basement with Cousteau. That was my safe place. I woulda stayed down there forever if it weren't for my brother and sister." He swallowed hard. "They didn't deserve what they got either."

Stacy was scared to ask, but he had to. "Why didn't you tell someone, Julius? Why didn't you go to the police?"

"I *did* go to the police!" His voice trembled with anger, Stacy regretting the question. "When I was fourteen, he hit me in the mouth, closed-fist. Knocked me out cold. When I came to, I jumped on my bicycle and pedaled all the way to the police station. You know what they said?"

Stacy shook his head.

"'Where'd you steal that bike, nigger?'" The words hung between them, foul and searing. "When I got home, he was waitin'. Grabbed me by the throat and hauled me into the kitchen. Started hittin' me again." For the first time, Stacy saw tears in his eyes, tears he was sure Julius hated more than the memories. "I couldn't take any more, Stace. I grabbed a knife and sliced him 'cross the chest. When he looked down at the blood, it gave me a chance to run. I ain't stopped runnin' since."

Stacy stared in disbelief. "You've been on your own since you were *fourteen*?" Julius nodded. "But how did you survive? How did you finish school?"

"It wasn't easy. I lived with my grandmother for a while—she was the one gave me the camera when I was little. Far as school goes, I just lied, said I was still livin' at home. Worked two or three jobs to get by."

"Didn't your parents come looking for you?"

He laughed, raising the bottle. "Pretty sure they were as glad to get rid of me as I was of them. Lookin' back, the only guilt I got's for my brother and..." His voice wavered. He drank to mask it.

"You've got nothing to be ashamed of, Jul."

"Maybe not. But I'll always wonder if I did the right thing."

Stacy peeled the label off his bottle. "I always figured being abandoned by your father was the worst thing that could happen." He let go, watching it float away in the darkness. "My dad left before I was two. Only thing I remember's the smell of his skin. When he came home from work, he smelled like fish." He shook his head. "That's all I've got, Jul—that's *it*. When I was older, the kids in the neighborhood would run out to greet their dads. I just walked inside. Alone." He wondered how far to take this. "After a while, they started teasing me. Asking where my dad was. I'd tell them he was a pro ballplayer or some big general in the army. I never had the guts to tell the real story—that he'd left us, moved to Alaska, and died in a fishing accident." He paused in thought. "Guess that's why I never had friends. If I didn't get close to anyone, I never had to tell the truth." He turned, guilt stinging his eyes. "All these years, I've felt sorry for myself for not having a father. But now—after hearing what you went through—I have to tell you, Julius, I'm ashamed."

"Two different kinds of hurt, that's all."

Stacy considered his words, the pair settling into silence.

After several minutes, Julius hopped up on the beam, the river flowing fifty feet below. "I love the sound of water."

"Be careful, Jul."

He stepped forward, arms out. "Know how Cousteau got into divin'?" Stacy didn't respond, paralyzed with worry. "Broke both his arms in a car accident, started swimmin' for therapy. He and I got more in common than our initials." He turned, walking the other way. "My father broke both *my* arms—one when I was six, the other when I was ten. I swam to get better, too. And to be free. Ain't no one can catch you in the water!"

"You need to get down, Julius."

"Relax, dude. Livin' on the edge makes life worth livin'. And long as I'm here, I'm gonna live mine to the fullest, just like my man, Jacques. Besides..." He leaped and spun, landing on the beam with a wobble. "...ain't got much to lose, do I?"

The circus act wasn't exactly out of character. Stacy had seen Julius perform all kinds of crazy stunts, most with a camera. Since arriving in December, he'd risked his life shooting fires, near-riots, and an F-5 tornado. But this was too much.

Stacy grabbed his arm and pulled him back down. He'd already lost a mother this year. He wasn't about to lose a friend.

As they left the bridge, Julius glanced over his shoulder. "Ever think 'bout what Shefler did out here?"

"Once in a while."

"Whatta you s'pose made him do it?"

"I don't know. People do bad things sometimes."

"People like Toole?"

A burst of wind sent the oak limbs rubbing together. "Toole's the Torch, Jul. I'm ninety-nine percent sure. And when we're through, I'll be a hundred percent."

"*We're* through?"

Stacy nodded. "I'm going to need your help."

"I was afraid you were gonna say that."

As they turned for the car, a whistle blew, the sound of a train chugging beneath the stars.

# CHAPTER 12
## *July 1988*

*(NEWSWIRE): BANKS RAISE PRIME LENDING RATE FROM 9 TO 9.5 PERCENT ... OLIVER NORTH ORDERED TO STAND TRIAL IN IRAN-CONTRA SCANDAL ... 166 OIL WORKERS DIE WHEN PLATFORM EXPLODES IN NORTH SEA*

"He knows we're coming, right?"

Chip took another hit of his joint. "'Course, he knows."

"Good." Stacy made his way to the porch, Julius skulking in the shadows.

"Toole's got the NBA Finals on tape." Chip flicked the roach away. "I just told 'im we wanted to watch 'em, is all." Seeing doubt in their eyes, he added, "I *think* that's what I told 'im," then cracked up, ringing the bell.

As the chimes sounded, Stacy and Julius looked at each other, Toole easing the door back. "What are *you* doing here?"

Stacy leered at Chip. "Sorry, Lar." He pushed his way inside. "Guess I forgot to mention we's comin' by to watch the game."

"*What* game?"

"Game seven of the Finals," Stacy answered, Toole's eyes settling on the Clarion duo. "We had to work that night...so we...didn't see how it ended."

*God, he was a bad actor!*

"Hey, Larry," Chip hollered from the kitchen. "Got any nachos?"

Toole held his stare on the men at the door. After what seemed like hours, he motioned them inside. Julius took refuge on the overstuffed couch, Stacy sitting next to him. "Nice place." It was more than nice—the room resembled a magazine shoot.

"Whatta ya expect on a news director's salary?" Chip yelled, foraging a bag of chips. "I'd have me a leather sofa and some sexy paintin's, too, if I's pullin' down fifty G's a year."

"It's not what you make, Chip. It's what you do with it." Toole walked to the TV and fired up the tape player, Kareem dropping a sky-hook over Bill Lambier. "Can I get you something, Julius?" The quiet cameraman shook his head. "How about you, Stacy?"

"No thanks." The reporter glanced at the pack of KOOLs on the table, 'Magic' firing a no-look pass to Kurt Rambis.

"Laker fans?" Stacy and Julius nodded, Toole lighting a cigarette. "Fifty bucks says they win it all."

Stacy attempted a smile, Julius staring at the wall. "How'd ya program that damn VCR in the first place?" Chip asked, tromping back into the room. "Every time I tape a stockcar race, I end up with six hours a' *Who's the Boss*!" He bummed a cigarette. "Don't get me wrong, I like

202

that Tony Danzer, but it'd sure be nice if I could record all m'shows on one tape an' speed through the commercials!"

"Those commercials pay your salary, Chip."

"In that case, somebody better sell more of 'em!" He cracked up again, searching the room for support. None came. "Got any beer, Larry?"

"I would've thought my uninvited guests would bring their own." Chip shrugged, walking back to the kitchen.

"Can I use your restroom?" Stacy stood, Toole eyeing him.

"First door on your left."

He excused himself, moving into the hall. Sure he wasn't followed, he ducked into the bedroom. A light burned on the nightstand, the room hotel neat. He peeked under the bed—nothing, not even lint. He opened the armoire—twenty suits, arranged by color. He attacked the dresser—T-shirts, socks, underwear, all folded to perfection. He knew Toole was anal, but this was ridiculous. *Dick Wilhelm would be proud!*

Stacy hoped to find something—anything—to link Toole to the fires. But the room was bare. Disappointed, he turned to go, spotting a photo on the shelf. Two minutes had passed since he left the living room. *Could he afford one more?* He picked it up.

"I see you've met my wife."

The frame nearly slipped from his hands. "Sorry..." He turned to see Toole in the doorway. "...I must've ...taken a wrong turn." Stacy replaced the frame. "You're married?"

"*Was* married." His eyes clung to the photo. "She died in August of '77. Three months after we said our vows."

Stacy looked for signs of deceit. There weren't any. "I'm sorry."

"So am I." He looked up. "I miss her every day."

203

An awkward moment passed, Stacy hesitating, then exiting the room. "I hope you don't mind me asking...but how did your wife die?"

"It was an accident." Stacy waited for him to elaborate. He didn't.

Stepping into the bathroom, he closed the door and stared at the mirror. *Could the accident have been a fire?*

By the time Stacy returned to the party, Chip had downed three Becks and eaten everything in the pantry. Julius looked miniature on the massive couch, doing his best to nurse a single beer. As the first half ended, Stacy found an excuse to leave.

"Thanks for stopping by—*I think.*"

As the door slammed, Stacy and Julius stared at Chip, the man producing a beer. "Got me a frostie to go!" he giggled, tossing the cap in the flowerbed.

"Jesus, Chip!" Stacy stormed away, Julius following.

"Dude had no idea we were comin'!"

"You guys worry too much." Chip sparked another joint as he caught up at the curb. "Ya'll hear that?" Stacy and Julius looked around. "That's the sound a' twenty-four Coors callin' our names. Got me a case on ice in the trunk!"

Stacy shook his head. "We've got a long drive."

"Yeah," Julius added. "And we'd like to do it sober."

"Since when?" *He had a point.* After a deep guzzle, he hopped in his '69 Chevelle. "Next time we get together, let's do it without the boss!"

"Drive careful, Chip."

"I'm always careful!" He raised the joint to his lips and roared away.

Stacy turned to his co-conspirator. "You ready?"

"Ready to get this over with." They moved up the sidewalk, then darted up the drive, disappearing behind a hedge. Kneeling in the shadows, Julius whispered, "What makes you think we're gonna find somethin' in his garage?"

"Reporter's hunch. Now stay low." They duck-walked across the yard, slipping through an unlocked door. "We're in."

"No shit!"

"*Shhhhhh.*" It was pitch black inside and smelled of fertilizer, Stacy powering up a flashlight. In the corner, he saw a stack of flowerpots, on the ground beside them, two bags of planting mix. He moved the light, revealing a case of Pennzoil.

"What the hell are we lookin' for?"

Stacy swept the beam over a folded tarp, a box of tools—and something that chilled his blood. "*That*, Julius!" He aimed the flashlight at a pyramid of gasoline—ten cans total. "We just found the smoking gun!"

The cameraman looked to his 'partner in crime', then back at the cans. "Gas in a dude's garage ain't no smokin' gun. People gotta mow their lawns, don't they?"

"Maybe. But *ten* containers?" He moved the light to the far corner, where it came to rest on a manual mower. "And when's the last time he needed gas for that?"

Julius tried to respond, but a noise outside stopped him. "Shit, dude!" They ducked in unison, extinguishing the light. "Let's get outta here!"

***

He sat at his desk, waiting for the day's assignments. Toole always called by nine. And there was nothing Stacy dreaded more.

"Mail call." Julius entered the room, carrying a stack of letters. "See if our checks came."

Stacy rifled through the pile. Ad. Catalog. Voter pamphlet. "Here you go, Jul. One for you..." He handed

Julius an envelope. "...and one for me. Three days late, just like clockwork."

"Thought we were s'posed to get a raise when the ratin's went up."

"So did I." The phone rang, Stacy bracing himself. "Clarion bureau."

"Hi, Bill. Rrrrrich Martin."

"Oh, hey, Rich." He looked at Julius and shrugged. "What's up?"

"Just handing out the assignments."

"Where's Toole?"

"Off this morning. He and Katie are the grand marshals at our Independence Day parade. They get to ride in a covered wagon and everything! Jerry's shooting the—"

"Jerry? Who's Jerry?"

"Jerry Feinbloom. The guy who took Bub's place."

"Bub DeSpain left?"

"Got a job in Wichita. He ate an entire pepperoni pizza at the going-away party!"

Bub wasn't the first employee to leave since Stacy and Julius moved to Clarion. Jennifer Riggs had fled to Albuquerque. Mike Bartell took a job in Shreveport. And Randy Tanner left to start his own production company. Small market news wasn't exactly a hub of employee stability. "Who's doing the newscast?"

"Reg, but we're cutting away live to Katie and Larry downtown. They're gonna be dressed in turn-of-the-century garb. Katie's wearing an old-fashioned bonnet, Larry a false mustache!"

"Sounds great, Rich." Stacy wasn't listening. He was seizing opportunity. "And don't worry about the assignments. We've already got something planned." He glanced at Julius. "We'll be covering the Fourth of July Picnic in Coalgate."

"Gee, I—"

"Trust me, it's a huge event. There'll be dignitaries, politicians. Word has it, the governor might even stop by." He was lying, but he'd learned from the master. "We'll cover the picnic as the main story. Throw something together on small-town economic growth. Maybe even get a bite or two on the legislature."

"But Larry said—"

Stacy hung up, turning to Julius.

"We're goin' to see Russell Longdale, ain't we?"

The reporter smiled, returning his attention to the mail—another ad, a special offer, and a plain white envelope addressed to *BILL STACY, BUREAU CHIEF*. He tore open the seal, a sheet of yellow paper inside. A *Herald* article on the hospital fire was taped to the top, the headline—*Texomaland Torch Strikes Again*. Below were four words, the mismatched letters cut from a magazine— *DON'T BE A HERO*.

\*\*\*

He couldn't go to the cops. Nor could he tell his boss. In the end, he showed the letter to Julius and stuffed it in a drawer.

"Just get me some B-roll. I'll be back in twenty minutes."

Julius nodded, shooting a three-legged race, then turning his lens on a pie-eating contest, the winner buried chin-deep in rhubarb.

Stacy hurried up the walk, the air ripe with cooking burgers. The fire station was empty, both engines moved to the bandstand for locals to admire. Stopping at the rollup door, he checked his Steno—*Meet Longdale, 10:30*. He looked left, right, the street deserted. Maybe the ex-prosecutor had changed his mind. Stacy could tell from their brief phone conversation that he hated news people.

*But who could blame him?*

The town clock chimed half-past-the-hour, Stacy checking his watch—10:30 on the nose. As he looked up, he saw a man in a straw hat round the corner, cigarette burned to the filter. "Mr. Longdale?"

He nodded, coming to a stop several feet away. "Wasn't sure I was coming." He dropped the butt. "But if Marv Bridges gave you my name, he must think highly of you."

"Yes, sir. And I of him." They stared at one another, the heart of the celebration beating several blocks away. "I appreciate you meeting me."

He nodded again, opening a fresh pack. In the distance, a high school band butchered Lee Greenwood's *Proud To Be An American.*

"What can you tell me about Larry Toole?"

He struck a match, eyes burning like a smelter. "What do you want to know?"

"I'm trying to find out what he was like as a kid. In particular, if he had any run-ins with the law."

The man took a prolonged drag, leaning against the wall. "I assume this is off the record?" Stacy assured him. "Toole had plenty of run-ins with the law. Every juvenile offense you can imagine, he and his derelict friends. Trespassing. Drugs. Vandalism."

Stacy moved closer. "Did you ever put him in jail?"

"A number of times. I just couldn't keep him there. He was smarter than the rest. And his parents had money. Mother was a lawyer and a damn good one. She was able to keep her son's nose clean. Most of the time."

"Most of the time?"

He tossed the match. "One night, Toole and his cronies jacked a car in Avalon. Took it down to Gainesville

208

and met up with some college girls. Cops popped them on the way back." He turned his head, blowing smoke. "Since they took the vehicle over state lines, I was able to push for grand theft auto instead of simple joyride. Could've made it stick, too, but in the plea bargain process, we agreed to drop all charges if he left the area. At the time, that was good enough for me."

He adjusted his hat, eyes still smoldering. "Unfortunately, he got the last laugh. When he came back as a reporter, he aired a story that got most of us fired, or in my case, worse. Some of it was bullshit. Some wasn't." He looked the reporter in the eye. "I've made mistakes. And I've paid for them."

Stacy knew all about the exposé. Billy Nemetz of the *Herald* had filled him in on the details, Diana Grimm of the *Gazette* providing the rest. "Mr. Longdale, did Larry Toole ever commit arson?"

The man smiled, smoke escaping his lips. "Not that I know of."

Stacy shot a glance at the faraway gala. As the mayor announced a raffle, someone lit a cherry bomb, causing momentary panic. "Is there anything else you can tell me?" Longdale shook his head. "All right. Well, thank you for your time."

Stacy turned to go, the man's voice stopping him. "Why arson?"

He looked in both directions, not wanting to show his hand.

*But a card or two couldn't hurt.*

"I have reason to believe Toole knows something about the Torch fires."

Longdale flicked his cigarette away. "So what's your next move?"

"I've got an associate at the newspaper looking into something for me. Toole was married once. Back when he worked at Channel 8 the first time. His wife died in some sort of accident. I'm hoping there's an obit."

"Not bad. For a reporter." The man pushed away from the wall. "But I can save you some time. She died in a house fire. They never determined the cause."

***

'Felon Friday', that was the name they'd given it. Twice a month, inmates were paraded over the courthouse lawn for hearings, appearances, and trials. As usual, all three news crews were there. So far, they'd captured a child molester covering his face and a drug dealer offering the middle finger. Nate Shefler was also scheduled to appear. And deputies had just arrested a rape suspect, the man being transported to town now.

"Hey, Candelle," Channel 2's camera op chirped, "where'd you get that Sony?"

"Got it from your *mama* last night!"

"Easy, Jul." Stacy pulled a folder from his briefcase, setting it on the courthouse steps. After a glance behind him, he surveyed the article, dated August 8, 1977. Billy had faxed it over that morning, the archival obit verifying Longdale's story. Melissa Toole, 21, had died in a *fire of questionable origin*, survived by *her husband, Lawrence, and parents, Lucinda and Caleb Wells of Massachusetts*. As far as Stacy was concerned, it was another huge strike against his boss. Not only had they discovered physical evidence in Toole's garage, he was now linked to an actual fire—*one that killed his wife!*

"'Comes another one, Stace." As the other cameramen took aim, Julius moved closer, deputies walking a hairy man in a jailhouse jumper past them. He was accused of stabbing someone on the wrong side of town, known in the news business as a 'misdemeanor murder'. Julius moved to within inches, the Neanderthal swearing at him.

"One of these days, you're going to get hurt, Jul."

"No way, dude." He continued to roll. "I can run faster'n I can swim." As the courthouse door shut, a black-and-white rolled up to the sheriff's station. "Just watch!"

He took out sprinting, arriving a full five seconds before the others. As they jockeyed for position, Stacy watched a deputy move to the door. Instead of the rape suspect, a young victim emerged, her frightened face covered in bruises.

Stacy made eye contact with the girl, a college student no more than eighteen. A few hours ago, she was planning her weekend. Now her whole life had changed. In the moment their eyes met, Stacy glimpsed all the pain, the helplessness, the utter shame she was feeling. It weakened his knees.

"Don't, Julius." The camera op looked over his shoulder, Stacy having joined him. "Stop rolling." Julius lowered the camera, the others tracking their subject to the station. Stacy shuddered—*that poor girl!*

She'd already been violated. Now she was being violated again.

Moments later, another sheriff's vehicle arrived. As the hungry journalists moved in, Julius looked to Stacy, his expression saying, 'Should I or shouldn't I?' After a long pause, Stacy nodded.

Two deputies pulled a man from the backseat, a stubby little man in filthy clothes. Thanks to Oklahoma's Cap Law, one forcing penal officials to thin populations when they neared capacity, Rocky Tumwater had been released from prison. Stacy watched him mug for the cameras as he entered the Hall of Justice, wanting badly to wipe the cocksure look off his little face.

This man had raped before. And now, because of a ridiculous mandate—one his victim had probably never even heard of—he'd raped again.

*What justice?*

***

Light pierced the window, the exploratory beam of a police car. Neither Stacy nor Julius flinched. They'd grown used to the harassment. It came at all hours. Searchlights. Sirens. Loudspeakers. Between the regular patrols, threatening letters, and stares from their neighbor, they weren't exactly feeling welcome in their new community.

"How come you never showed me how to play this thing?"

Stacy reached for the guitar.

"Never asked." Julius placed his roommate's fingers on the frets. "It ain't hard." He helped him with a *C*-chord. "Just hold the strings and strum."

Stacy's digits responded as if webbed. "My God, Jul... I'm horrible!" Julius smirked, showing him a *D* and *E-minor*. In the corner, the television flickered—a wrestling match of some sort.

"Maybe you should stick to the squeezebox."

The ex-accordion player frowned, continuing to mangle chords.

"Hey, I went to school with that dude!"

Stacy looked to the screen. A man in a tux stood next to a wrestler, who promised to snap his opponent's neck 'like a Pixie-Stick'. "Hope you didn't piss him off."

"Not *that* dude. The one with the mic." The camera panned to Danny Fox, the fearless interviewer braving threats and spittle. As the wrestler stormed off, Fox teased an upcoming 'cage match', tickets on sale now.

212

"How did he get *that* job?"

"Don't know. He graduated top of our class, Summa Cum somethin'. Got hired a week later as a reporter in Fort Smith."

"A reporter? How long ago?"

"Last May."

"He moved on after a year?"

"Dude moved on after a week!"

"A *week*?" Stacy wondered what it would be like to leave Channel 8.

"Went to work one mornin', found out there was a kid missin' at the mall. Spent the whole day coverin' the story." Another light flashed through the glass. "Come four o'clock, they find the kid locked in a bathroom at Radio Shack. He gets a shot of the mother-and-child reunion, then runs back to the station to edit. That's when the news director shut 'im down."

"Shut him down? Why?"

"Said it was a 'non-story'. 'Cause it didn't end badly."

"That's bullshit, Jul."

"That's what Fox said. Quit the next day and started sendin' tapes to the WWF. Said if he was gonna be part a' bullshit on TV, he wanted people to—"

A knock at the door cut him off, Julius urging Stacy to stay put. After a peek, he turned the knob, revealing a dark figure on the porch—the overhead light hadn't worked in weeks.

"Got the money?" Julius reached in his pocket for a wad of bills. "Almost didn't risk it. Neighborhood's crawlin' with cops."

"They ain't lookin' for you." Julius slipped him the cash, the man handing him a giant tube as he slunk into the night. The cameraman grinned, hauling his newfound booty into the room. "Been waitin' for this a long time!"

"What is it?"

213

"Sachtler tripod. Check out how light it is." He opened the tube and fished it out, Stacy feeling uncomfortable as he lifted the thing. It was light, all right—*it was also hot!* "Fifteen hundred in the catalog. Buck-fifty on the street."

Stacy grabbed the remote. "Ever feel guilty about this stuff?"

"Hell, no," Julius responded. "*I* didn't steal it."

Stacy clicked to Channel 8. "Fire claims another local landmark." A monitor rose over Toole's shoulder. "The old Dexter County Jail is in ruins tonight. Reporter Reg McNair joins us live. Reg, is this the work of the Texomaland Torch?"

Stacy had already heard about the fire, having spoken to Roy Maghee by phone. Off the record, the investigator had all but credited the Torch. Same M.O. Same burn patterns. And another Wilhelm building—the fifth 'officially'. Fortunately, there was no one inside this time, the jail having been abandoned for a modern structure next door.

"Larry, investigators are remaining tight-lipped at this hour. But all signs point to the elusive Torch, a dangerous serial arsonist who seems hell-bent on destruction. And shows no signs of letting up."

*No doubt who wrote that lead-in!*

"Dude's hair looks huge tonight!"

"*Shhhhhhhh.*" Stacy moved forward, listening to the man's package. There were no new details. Despite amazing video, the writing was pedestrian. Reg was a handsome man, but that was about it.

"Larry, one last bit of information. According to a credible source..." By now, Stacy knew that 'credible source' meant friend of a friend, wife's cousin's neighbor, or worse. "...a team from the ATF is flying in from Rockville, Maryland to assist in the investigation."

214

Stacy leaped to his feet. "The feds are coming, Jul!" The cameraman nodded, shoving the tripod back in place. "Toole's *really* going to have to watch his step now!"

"If you say so, dude."

Stacy flipped channels to see how the other stations covered the rape story. Channel 7, against all protocol, mentioned the victim's name—she was the daughter of a local doctor. Channel 2 withheld the name but aired a close-up of the woman being led from the car. Stacy flipped back to Channel 8, *his* package focusing only on the suspect.

In his eleven months on the job, he was never more proud of a finished piece.

That didn't stop the phone from ringing ten minutes later. Stacy thought about answering, thought about listening to Toole's lecture on 'reporting the news, no matter how unpleasant, especially during ratings month'.

Instead, he killed the lights and went to bed.

\*\*\*

"What do you mean, he didn't say?" Stacy braced himself as Julius steered.

"He rattled off an address and said, 'Go shoot it.'"

"Shoot what?"

"Somebody's house." They turned left. "Told me to get some exteriors, is all."

Stacy shook his head. "I don't like it, Jul."

"What's not to like?" They stopped at a traffic light. "It ain't even our story. Just a pick-up shot for someone in Avalon."

"You remember the last time Toole sent us somewhere without explanation?"

"'Course, I remember." The light turned green. "But what was I s'posed to do?" When the reporter didn't answer, Julius hit the gas.

Stacy sighed, opening his Steno. Ratings month was more than half over, and his boss was using every trick in his mawkish bag to nab the blue ribbon. There'd been solo and team coverage reports on murders and rapes. More features on pornography. And, of course, the Torch had struck again, hyperbole in scripts reaching an all-time high. Stacy had kept a log. The phrase "disturbing trend" was used 23 times, "epidemic" 31, "crisis situation" 40. But that wasn't the worst of it. Toole had managed to identify two Nielsen families in the area, sending crews to their homes for an exclusive— 'What's It Like To Be a Nielsen Family?' And if that wasn't enough, he gave viewers one more reason to tune in, a nightly spin-to-win game known as the 'Great 8 Giveaway', where one lucky fan could win up to a thousand dollars cash. Stacy couldn't believe his eyes when Katie spun the wheel, nor could he believe his ears when he heard the promos— "The Great 8 News Team. Paying the Bills When You Can't!"

The Escort squealed to a stop, Stacy looking up.

The house was nothing special—brick facade, attached garage. Stacy climbed out of the car, glancing at the windows. The shades were drawn. He looked to the driveway. No cars. For a moment, he thought he smelled roses, but the scent disappeared on the hot western wind.

Julius began shooting. A wide shot of the house. A pan from street to yard. A close-up of toys on the lawn. Somewhere in the distance, a meadowlark sang, the street otherwise quiet. Nothing seemed amiss, yet Stacy's gut twisted like a rope of tobacco. "Let's get out of here, Jul."

"Couple more shots."

Without warning, the front door opened, a man in rumpled clothes trudging out to meet them. His hair was

216

a tousled mess, his eyes two swollen orbs. It looked like he hadn't slept, eaten, or done anything else in days.

He had reason.

"Please go." He spoke softly but firmly.

"Public street, dude. We ain't—"

"Julius." Stacy peered into the man's eyes. He knew that look, knew it all too well. He'd seen it in Toole's eyes when he spoke of his wife, seen it in his own mirror after his mother died, could still see it if he looked hard enough. He reached down and killed the deck. "I'm sorry, sir. We didn't know."

Julius was confused but trusted his friend. By the time he loaded the gear, Stacy was already on the radio. "Mobil 6 to Base!"

Julius cranked the engine, the reporter slamming his fist against the dash.

"*Mobil 6 to Base!*" he repeated, his skin the color of blood.

As the Escort pulled away, the radio crackled. "Go ahead, Mobil 6."

"What the *hell* are you trying to pull, Larry?"

There was a lengthy pause, then, "I don't know what you're talking about. But if I were you, I'd calm down."

"Yeah, dude." Julius shot him a begging glance.

"You're *not* me, asshole!" The cameraman winced, Stacy barreling ahead. He could no longer listen to a man he didn't respect—*a man who'd committed murder!* "Why the hell did you send us to that house?"

"Perhaps you should remember who you're talking to."

"I know *exactly* who I'm talking to. Why did you do it?"

"Because we need the footage for a story."

Stacy keyed the handset, cars flying by like shrapnel. "*What* story?"

217

"Not that I'm obligated to tell you, but it's a story of family tragedy."

"What *kind* of tragedy?"

Another pause. "I think this conversation's better suited for a landline. Why don't you head back to the office and we'll finish it by phone."

"We'll finish it *now*!" He struck the dash again, Julius leaping in his seat.

"Fine..." Toole appeared to gather himself. "...it was a suicide. A nine-year-old boy locked himself in the garage and started his father's car. By the time they found him, it was too late."

"Jesus, Larry!" Stacy stared at Julius, hands shaking. *What kind of hell was that family going through? What kind of pain?* Imagine the mind-numbing shock of finding that child in the garage. *Imagine the guilt!* "For God's sake, we can't do this! That family's been through enough!" His mind raced out of control, lurching to a halt in a stuffy college classroom—Media Law, Junior year. "What about the rule on suicides?" *Toole couldn't fight the basic principles of journalism, could he?* "We only cover them if they happen in public, right?"

Stacy heard static, then, "There are no rules."

*No rules?* The hair on his neck stood.

"Then what about *reasons*? Give me one good reason why this story should air!"

"All right, for the sake of argument, I will. The boy in question learned about carbon monoxide poisoning on TV. From a Saturday morning cartoon, no less. I think we owe it to our viewers to raise awareness in the community. By covering a story like this, we might just save another family from similar tragedy."

"That's noble, Larry." He leaned forward, gritting his teeth. "It's also *bullshit*!" Julius made hand signals, Stacy ignoring them. "I'll tell you why we're doing this story.

We're doing it to exploit this family, to ogle at their pain! We're doing it so we can all sit back and thank our lucky stars it didn't happen to us. But how many people does it really affect? How many lives?" The words roared from his mouth like a speeding train. "And 'for the sake of argument', how many lives does a traffic fatality affect? Or a murder? Or even a fire that burns down an empty building? We air these stories because they're sensational. We do it for the same reason we slow down to look at a car wreck!"

"You better think long and hard about what you're saying. And I'm going to give you that opportunity." The reporter stared through the windshield, eyes wide open. "I want you to drive back to the station, feed me the footage, and take the rest of the day off. And I suggest you use every minute of that time to evaluate your future."

Stacy looked to the deck in his lap. "Good idea, Larry." He popped the carriage. "Just let me check video first."

Julius tried to stop him, but Stacy yanked the tape, unspooling ribbon till a brown mound lay at his feet.

"Looks like we had some 'technical difficulties'." With that, he killed the radio, shooting a satisfied glance at his cameraman.

"Dude, you're in serious shit now."

\*\*\*

"'Nother round?" the barkeep asked.

Stacy nodded. He had the right to drink. He'd just pissed away a career. Or at the very least damaged one, maybe beyond repair. *But how could he keep doing this?* Hurting people. Using them.

He shook his head, staring at his own reflection in the glass. He'd never expected such a quandary. He'd been

219

so excited when Meeks called, so hopeful when he climbed in the Celica and headed east.

It all seemed like a dream now.

"A child is dead. And a devastated family looks for answers." Stacy's eyes moved to the TV, the dial—like most dials these days—tuned to Channel 8. "I'm Larry Toole. The body of a nine-year-old boy is discovered in Clarion. The cause of death? Suicide."

Stacy searched the room. "Can somebody turn—?"

The bartender shushed him, pouring a beer as he watched the report.

"Great 8 anchor Katie Powers joins us with a closer look at this terrible tragedy."

Stacy's eyes shot back to the screen.

"Larry, tragedy doesn't begin to describe..." His ex-girlfriend showcased a bold new hairstyle, but Stacy didn't notice. Inside his head, a tempest raged. In his ears, a buzzsaw screamed. He leaped to his feet, knocking over the stool.

"Keep it down!" a patron shouted, eyes glued to the tube.

But Stacy didn't hear. He was already out the door.

***

"Wear something mauve tomorrow." Toole placed his scripts in a file, lighting a fresh KOOL. "I bought a new tie today, mauve with blue paisleys."

Katie smiled. "I don't have anything mauve."

He reached in his wallet, peeling off two hundred-dollar bills.

She took the money, helping herself to a cigarette. "Have you decided what to do with Stacy?"

He flicked his lighter for her. "Sleep on it, I guess. Make a decision tomorrow."

She blew a needle-thin trail. "Go easy on him, huh? He's had a hard time of it." Toole stared at his desk. "You ready?"

"I've got some work to do. I won't be long."

"Good." She leaned down and kissed him on the cheek. "You know how I hate cold sheets."

The walk from Toole's office to her car was delicious, the air smelling of zinnia. It was love this time, she was sure of it. Larry Toole was everything she wanted. He was powerful. Wealthy. And had scores of industry contacts. The total package.

As she reached the Mustang, someone stepped from the shadows. "Jesus!"

"How could you, Katie?"

She raised a hand to her chest. "My God, Stacy...you scared me half to death!" Smoke from her cigarette curled between them. "Why, if Thad sees—"

"How could you do that story?"

"What do you mean, how could I do that story?" She maintained her distance, smelling liquor. "It's my job to do that story. Just like it's your job to listen to Larry."

"Don't tell me what my job is."

"Well, somebody needs to. You're blowing it, Stacy. You've got all the talent in the world. But you're throwing it away. And for what? Because you don't want to hurt someone's feelings, someone you don't even know? Think how ridiculous that sounds."

"I don't think it sounds ridiculous."

"Of course, it does. In six months, you'll be in Tulsa, or Little Rock, or Colorado Springs. And the people of Texoma will all be a memory. Why in the world would you sabotage your future by worrying about someone in Clarion, Oklahoma?" She waited but got no answer. "We can't bring that little boy back. Or take his family's pain away. It's not our responsibility."

221

"What is our responsibility, Katie?"

"To 'give our viewers more'," she quoted her new boyfriend. "And, no, it won't always be pretty. Won't even be fair half the time. But that's the way it is."

"And you can live with that?"

"Yes, I can live with it." She moved forward, softening her tone. "When I chose this career, I knew there'd be difficult days. And there have been. But never once did I question my choices. Do you know why? Because I know in my heart that what I do for a living means something." A gust of hot air blew through the parking lot, her helmet-like hair refusing to budge. "And being on TV's a dream come true! What's wrong with living out our dreams?"

"Nothing, Katie. As long as we don't hurt people in the process. But that's what we're doing. And I'm not just talking about that family in Clarion. We hurt people every day. Scare them. Misrepresent them."

"Misrepresent them?" She surveyed the lot for support—it was empty. "How, Stacy? By letting them have valuable airtime to express their views?"

"You call an eight-second sound bite 'valuable airtime'? When they've spoken for twenty minutes on camera? We take one sentence from a judge, a cop...hell, even a man on the street, and let that one comment— sometimes pulled completely out of context—represent his entire viewpoint on the ten o'clock news. And then we go on to the next story, and the next, while the poor bastard's left to explain to his family and friends what he *really* meant."

"You're being melodramatic."

"Am I? We can make these people say whatever we want them to say."

She raised her cigarette and puffed, wishing she'd left an hour ago. "If what we do for a living's so bad, why don't you just quit?"

"You think I haven't thought of that? I think about it so much my head hurts!"

"Then stop thinking about it!" She flicked ash. "You're a reporter, Stacy. And a damn good one. And you'll be great if you just allow yourself to be." He cut his eyes to the ground. "I've been thinking a lot about you lately, ever since our little fight up in Sulphur." He looked up. "And frankly I'm worried. You've been through so much in the last few months. More than you can handle maybe." She reached out and touched his arm. "You lost your mom, sweetie—"

*"Don't talk about my mother!"* He jerked away. "You have no idea what it's like to lose someone!"

"No..." His reaction startled her. "...but I do know what it's like to care about someone." She dropped her cigarette, smashing it with a heel. "I care about you, Stacy. And I think your paranoia might—"

"Paranoia?"

"Your obsession with the Texomaland Torch isn't normal. It's self-destructive. And so's all this endless introspection you're putting yourself through."

"Oh, really?" He offered a crooked smile, the overhead lamp painting him green. "Well, what about you, 'Miss Quest-for-Perfection'?"

"What's *that* supposed to mean?"

"Tell me why you wanted to be a reporter in the first place."

"I *have* told you. It was my dream. And I wanted to help people."

"Great answer if you're competing in the 'Miss Texoma Pageant'. But I'm not buying it. You wanted to be on TV because you thought it would make you special.

223

People would look up to you, right?" He shook his head. "Not people. *One person.* You wanted to show your father that Katie Powers was worth something."

"*How dare you!*" she screamed, a chorus of crickets going silent. "You have *no idea* what you're talking about!"

"Don't I?" He hunkered down, ready to pounce. "You want to talk 'self-destructive' behavior? Let's do it. Everything you do in life is designed to get your father's attention. To make him notice you. That's why you're so obsessed with your appearance. Why you got a boob job. And why you run to the bathroom after every meal to make yourself throw up!"

A violent chill racked her body, her face going pale. She wanted desperately to speak, but no words came.

"Listen to me, Katie." He grabbed her by the arms. "You don't have to prove yourself to him. So he wasn't there for you growing up. *So what?* That's his loss—*his!* Can't you see that?"

"No, I can't!" She wiggled free. "But I'll tell you what I *can* see. You're no different than I am, Stacy Zwardowski. You think I chose this career to impress my father? Well, I've got news for you...*so did you!*"

"What are you talking about? My father died when I—"

"But he *abandoned* you first! And ever since, you've been trying to prove to yourself—and everyone else—that he made a mistake!"

When he didn't respond, she pushed him aside and jumped in the car, black tears streaming down her cheeks.

As she cranked the engine, he moved to the window—a move of helplessness, of desperation. "Are you sleeping with Larry Toole?"

She hit the gas, spraying him with gravel as she sped into the night.

# CHAPTER 13
## *August 1988*

*(NEWSWIRE): SEN. DAN QUAYLE CHOSEN AS PRESIDENTIAL RUNNING MATE; FIRST 'BABY BOOMER' NOMINATED FOR OFFICE ... U.S. AND SOVIET SCIENTISTS CONDUCT JOINT NUCLEAR TEST ... TV VIEWERS WATCH LIVE AS JET CRASHES INTO CROWD AT AIR SHOW*

Katie was right, of course. Stacy had become a reporter to prove something. Conscious or not, he wanted to prove to his father—perhaps equally important to himself—that he was someone worth sticking around for. It didn't make sense. William Zwardowski was dead. And the only thing his son had managed to prove was that he was a very confused young man.

He stared at the clock—9:15. *What was Toole waiting for?* He'd always called by now. *Why should today be any different?* Stacy took a breath. Today *was* different. He'd never disobeyed an order before. Never destroyed company property either. His actions, no matter how well-intentioned, deserved punishment.

"I'm gonna load the car, dude." Julius' face said it all—neither could imagine life at Channel 8 without the other.

He watched the cameraman leave, glancing at the Dan Rather photo, the men in the Polaroid—Dan and Bill—soldiers in some freakish well-dressed army. How had the network anchor made it through all the pitfalls of a journalist's career? *How did he live with himself now?* Stacy hated working at Channel 8. Yet when he thought of leaving, he felt only panic. He *could* leave, of course. With a year of experience, he could start sending out tapes again. *But what was the point?* His next stop would be no different than this one. Did it really matter *which* 'Channel 8' he worked for?

More importantly, his work here wasn't finished. He'd forgotten that yesterday, forgotten how vital his presence at KEGT was. He was the only person at the station—maybe the only person in Texomaland—who believed Toole was the Torch.

And the only one determined to prove it.

The phone rang, nailing him to the chair. After a labored breath, he grabbed the receiver. "Clarion bureau."

"Stacy. Larry Toole." The reporter bowed his head, sweat rendering him blind. "I've got Dick Wilhelm on the line with us."

"Hello, Stacy."

"Good morning, sir."

"We're going to make this short and sweet," Toole announced, Stacy listening. "Your insubordination yesterday calls for disciplinary action. Dick and I have discussed the situation, and we've decided on a one-week suspension. Given the circumstances, I'd say that's quite generous."

Stacy didn't know whether to kick up his heels or throw up his breakfast. In the end, he did neither. "Okay."

"*Okay?*" Wilhelm challenged. "Don't you mean, thank you very much?"

Stacy swallowed what little pride he had left, repeating the G.M.'s phrase.

"And by the way..." Toole had one final point. "...the only reason you still have a job is because I like you. Because I see something in you. Perhaps you remind me of myself ten years ago." Stacy retched. "If I were you, I'd use the next seven days to figure out what the fuck I was going to do with my life!"

\*\*\*

He couldn't sleep in. A construction crew at Long John Silver's made sure of that. They started banging, drilling, and sawing at 6:00 a.m. By 6:30, Stacy was staring at the ceiling, water stains staring back.

He threw off the sheets, head pounding to a symphony of hammers. It was already hot, the thermometer pushing 90. Stacy yawned, having no idea what he was going to do today. He hadn't had a day off—a real day off—in weeks. Not that this was a vacation. More like a humiliating public reprimand.

He yawned again, then walked to the Underwood, fingering the keys. The *H* and *Y* were still missing, Stacy having combed every antique shop in Clarion for substitutes. He hit the space bar, remembering all the scripts he'd written when he started at Channel 8. The stories he'd typed as a kid. The look on his mother's face when she surprised him with it.

His eyes moved to the photo of Helen Zwardowski. When he and Julius moved in, he'd set it on the windowsill, never bothering to move it when he unpacked the rest of the boxes. He stared at it now, then cut his eyes to the closet. He hadn't unpacked *all* the boxes. The one

227

from the hospital—the one with his mother's things—was still inside.

Waiting.

"Jesus, dude, put some clothes on!" Stacy turned to find Julius in the doorway, dressed in a shirt and tie. He'd even shaved. The week ahead wasn't going to be easy. Toole expected as much news from Clarion as he'd gotten the week before. Julius would have to write, report, even go live from the studio once or twice. He was heading in early to prepare.

"Anything I can do to help?" Stacy asked, throwing on a pair of shorts.

"Not 'less you can speed up time." The cameraman frowned. "Gonna be a long week, dude." Stacy nodded, his roommate turning for the door. "By the way..." He paused without looking back. "...I'm glad you're still here."

"Thanks, Jul."

As the door fell shut, Stacy felt the silence—the crew next door had apparently taken a break. His eyes strayed back to the closet. He'd spent the last few months dodging thoughts of his mother. Sidestepping memories. Burying emotions.

*How long could he keep it up?*

He went to the kitchen for a bowl of cereal. When he returned, the closet still beckoned. He took a bite, the sound of chewing stealing the silence. Unable to think of another stall tactic, he set the bowl down and walked over. The box was wedged in the corner, behind a mountain of shoes and a deflated basketball. He pulled it out, tearing open the seal. His mother's coat lay on top—the coat and all that went with it. He raised it to his face, smelling her again, seeing her.

A tear slipped down his cheek. He wiped it away, reaching for her purse. He started to go through it, but noticed the address book, the one with the note placed as a bookmark. For so many years, he'd taken those notes for granted.

Now he longed for them.

Opening the book, he stared at the scribbled text. He'd expected another *WORK HARD* or *FOLLOW YOUR HEART*, but this note was different. It was written in a shaky hand, maybe even her left hand. Stacy remembered what the doctor said—the "first event caused paralysis."

*Could his mother have written this after her first stroke?*

He read the word on the paper—*SEE*.

*See what?* He turned it over, finding nothing on the back. As he raised it to the light, he noticed the entry below—*Robert Zwardowski, Rural Route 7, Panna Maria, Texas*. His eyes moved to the margin, his mother having added *UNCLE* in the same shaky hand. *SEE. UNCLE*. She'd never mentioned an uncle before. Never mentioned any relatives on his father's side. The whole thing didn't make sense. And he didn't have time for it.

As he lowered the book, he saw the address again. *Panna Maria, Texas...how far could it be?* He hesitated, hearing his mother's voice— "You *do* have time, Stacy." She was right. For the next seven days, he had nothing but. He stared at the notes again. *Did she really want him to 'SEE' his 'UNCLE'?* And why? Whatever the reasons, she was determined to get her message across, so determined she used the last few moments of her life to write it down. He swallowed hard, hearing her voice again— "*Go!*"

Sighing, he tucked the book under his arm. *This was crazy!* he thought. But no crazier than sitting around all week, listening to construction noise. A siren blipped, the scanner sounding in response.

If nothing else, a trip to meet his uncle would get him out of Clarion.

And if his mother wanted this, he had no choice but to honor her wishes.

He grabbed his suitcase, walking to the dresser. As he started to pack, he thought about the journey. *How would he find the place? What would he say to the man?* If his uncle was anything like his father, he wanted nothing to do with him.

He tossed a shirt in the bag, thinking. *Texas*. There was something he'd been wanting to do there. And the drive to Panna Maria would give him the opportunity.

A smile moved over his face.

*Might not be such a bad trip after all.*

\*\*\*

Stacy looked to the giant spire, its Greek colonnades framing the sun. "Is that the Main Building?" he asked a kid on a skateboard.

The kid nodded, offering a 'Hook 'Em Horns' gesture as he skated off.

Stacy headed for the entrance, ditching the UT map he'd grabbed earlier. Once inside, he wiped a quart of sweat from his brow, following signs to the Records Office.

"Help ya?" a pretty clerk spoke in a syrupy twang.

Stacy smiled, making his way to her window. He'd seen Katie turn on the charm before. Now it was his turn. "I hope so." His smile grew as he pressed against the counter. "I'm thinking of hiring one of your grads and needed to verify some things." He'd researched Toole's life as a juvenile. Investigated him as an adult. Now it was time for 'Larry Toole: The College Years'.

"Ya'll *own* yer own business?" She was clearly impressed, Stacy shrugging. "We can give ya name, major, degrees, dates a' attendance, and awards." She rattled off

230

the list as if she did so in her sleep, her eyes never straying from Stacy's. "Just fill out the form and I'll pull the information for ya."

"Thanks...uh..." He looked for a nametag.

"Shari," she gushed. "Shari Browning."

"Thanks, Shari." He filled out the card and handed it over, the woman fanning herself as she walked away. Stacy wiped more sweat. He was nervous, but the hard part was over. He was sure she'd give him what he wanted. If he'd learned one thing in his twelve months on the job, it was how to identify a willing subject.

He walked to the cooler and poured himself some water, downing it in a gulp. As the air-conditioner blew, burnt orange streamers danced like flames. He couldn't help thinking he was just one clue away from nailing Toole. And though he had no idea what today's search would yield, he was sure he'd find something.

"Here ya go." The woman returned with a fresh coat of lip gloss. Stacy reached for the Xerox, scanning its text. *Major: Journalism. Degree: Bachelor of Arts. Awards: Dean's List, Magna Cum Laude, Student of Valor*. He flipped the page over, nothing on the back.

"Shari?" She smiled. "I thought this might include a disciplinary record."

"Oh, we can't give out that information." She unwrapped a stick of gum, placing it on her tongue. "But I doubt he had one. I mean, in four years, *I* never made the Dean's List. And this guy made it every semester. On top a' that, he was a hero."

"A hero?"

She worked her gum, moving closer. "UT doesn't give out many Valor awards. Whenever I come across one, I look it up." She spoke in a whisper, Stacy getting a hint of cinnamon. "Back in '76, yer little job applicant discovered a fire in one a' the dorms."

231

*Fire?* The word followed Toole like a shadow.

"Seems he alerted the authorities and saved hundreds a' lives."

Stacy nodded, eyes moving back to the printout. *Dean's List. Magna Cum Laude.* It didn't make sense. Toole was a full-fledged juvenile delinquent in Avalon. *How could he turn his life around so quickly?* Russell Longdale said he was smart. Maybe he was too smart for campus police. And maybe he hadn't just discovered the fire. Maybe he'd set it, then lost his nerve.

"Mind if I keep this?"

"Don't mind at all." She smiled, tucking a loose hair behind her ear. "Hope ya'll hire 'im. Can't go wrong with a Texas grad."

Stacy smiled back. "Thanks, Shari. Oh, and one more question." She leaned in, clearly expecting a date request. "Is there a payphone nearby?"

Visibly disappointed, she stepped back and pointed. "Up the hall to yer right."

He thanked her again, then hurried off, attacking his pockets for change. As he reached the phone, he checked his watch—4:30.

He hoped Roy Maghee hadn't gone home early.

Then again, when had *that* ever happened?

\*\*\*

He stared at the battered mailbox, the land flatter than a military sheet. On the horizon, the late-day sun hung like an ember, a hot breeze stirring the dead mesquite.

Stacy turned up the drive, half-expecting a nest of rattlesnakes to greet him, but the only life he saw was an eastern phoebe perched on a boulder. As he pulled to a stop, a cloud of dust devoured him. When it settled, he killed the engine and climbed outside.

232

The house was built on a low plateau, a stone cottage with a covered porch and steep-pitched roof. A barn loomed in the distance, the terrain treeless but for a clump of oaks on the faraway ridge.

He walked to the porch, running a hand through his hair. After a deep breath, he knocked, the heavy screen banging against the frame. No one came. He peered through the net, seeing an old rocker and twin bed. He knocked again. Still no one.

Making his way past the house, he surveyed the grounds, ears aching with the screech of insects. "Anyone home?" he hollered, scanning the distant fields. Corn. Alfalfa maybe. Too far away to tell. The farm was enormous, at least a thousand acres.

A big black dog trotted up, joined by a white one a moment later, the pair only mildly interested in the intruder. Stacy patted them on the head. "Where's your master, fellas?" They stared, then padded off to find shade, curling up against the cool round stones of the house.

He heard something—the faint sound of metal on rock. It came from behind the barn, a good distance away. Shading his eyes, he moved toward it, his tongue tasting like lye. Through the dust, he saw a figure, a man in worn overalls crouched to the ground. He was building a rock wall, held together with sweat, gravity, and sheer determination.

Stacy worked his way past a chicken coop, stopping a few feet from the wall. "Excuse me..." The man continued to hammer. "...are you Robert Zwardowski?"

He stopped what he was doing and stood—six feet, five inches of sunbaked work-hardened Texas farmer. "I am."

At 6' 3" himself, Stacy wasn't used to looking up at people. But that's what he was doing. The first thing he noticed was the eyes—identical to his father's. As the man stared back, those eyes seemed to focus.

"Mr. Zwardowski..." The reference felt awkward. "...I'm—"

"Stacy." His uncle spoke in a whisper, the Zwardowski eyes filling with tears. The resemblance was indeed remarkable, neither of them able to move. With the exception of old photos, Stacy had never seen anyone who looked like him before. He had no idea what to do...or say...or feel. He just stared. Finally, Robert Zwardowski extended a hand. "I'd have known you anywhere, young man." His palm was rough, his smile, like Stacy's, a bit crooked. "You look just like your father."

They broke eye-contact, both glancing at the wall of stone between them. "Quite a project you've got here." His uncle nodded, gripping the hammer. "I tried calling..." Stacy looked back. "...but the operator said your line was disconnected."

"Got rid a' my phone when I realized I had no one to call." They stared at one another again. "I can't get over it, Stacy. If I didn't know better, I'd swear I was looking at my brother, twenty years ago."

For the first time, Stacy considered his uncle's feelings in all this. Up to now, he'd only thought of himself. "I'm sorry, sir. I shouldn't have just shown up at your place like—"

"Nonsense. This place is as much yours as it is mine."

Stacy smiled. He hadn't expected to like this man, hadn't expected to feel anything. But the connection was unmistakable. "I guess this is strange for you, too... seeing me now, looking so much like *he* looked...you know, when he died."

The man's expression changed, his eyes moving to the fractured earth. "Stacy..." He looked back up. "Your father's as alive as we are."

"But...that's impossible..." He sat on the edge of the fireplace, clutching a glass of tea. "My mother...she never would've lied to me."

Robert Zwardowski straddled a chair, legs longer than a spider's. "She had her reasons. And if we're going to talk about this, I need you to listen. And to believe me."

"Believe *you*?" He set the glass down and stood, a tormented child in search of a target. "Why should I believe a total stranger over the woman who raised me, the woman who sacrificed her own happiness for mine?" His eyes sought escape from every object in the room. A roll-top desk. An old painting. "My mother was there for me." A worn fiddle. A set of wooden shoes. "She spent her whole..." He stopped, staring at a photo on the mantel. After a beat, he moved toward it. The man in the picture stood next to a boat, the name on the aft—*Saint Helen*. Stacy stared at the face. Same nose. Same crooked smile, a Zwardowski standard no doubt. His mind raced back to the photo his mother sent, the one of a father holding his one-year-old son.

This was the same man. Older. Grayer. *But the same man!*

"I think you better sit down." Stacy turned to his uncle. "Your mother never meant to hurt you. None of us did. But I'm afraid that's what we've done." He pointed to a chair. "She wants you to know the truth now. If she didn't, she wouldn't have sent you. So that's what I'm gonna give you—the truth. But damned if it's gonna be easy."

Stacy hesitated, then sat. "Look...Mr. Zwardowski—"

"I wish you'd stop calling me that. I'm your uncle. Uncle Robert." He paused. "I know I haven't been much of an uncle to you, but I'm hoping it's not too late to start."

Stacy stared, offering neither affirmation nor protest.

His uncle took a breath, then began. "When your father and I were kids, we used to play make-believe. I was always a big fancy king looking out over his kingdom. But your father liked to play the rogue. Cowboys. Knights. Even the occasional pirate."

Stacy stole another glance at the picture.

"When I was fifteen and Billy was eighteen, our dad died. Died at the reins of an old plow. Mom was devastated. We all were. Billy and I...we did our best to keep things going 'round here. But farming's a full-time job."

As Stacy listened, he felt every emotion imaginable. Anger. Hurt. *Curiosity.*

"A year after dad passed, we ran outta money. Lost half our crop to drought, the other half to grasshoppers. Back then, we didn't know our asses from two holes in the ground. Billy hated farming. And I was too young. Anyhow, he comes home all excited one day, says he knows how to save the farm. Shows us a newspaper article 'bout crab fishing in Alaska, kids our age making twenty grand a year working on crab boats."

He rubbed the back of his neck. "Mom was dead set against it, of course. And so was I if you want to know the truth. But when Billy gets an idea in his head, there's no prying it out. So two weeks later, we take off for Alaska, bumming rides, walking when we had to. Took us a month, but we rolled into Kodiak, tired, hungry, and freezing our butts off!"

"What did you do?" It was the first question Stacy felt like asking.

His uncle smiled. "We did what anyone would do—went to the local bar. Place was like something out of a movie. Loud. Raucous. Seemed like a fight broke out every few seconds." He leaned back in his chair. "We met up with a local who was shipping out the next morning. Told us we could stay in his cabin till we found work. That's how people are up there. Hard as nails but give you the shirts off their backs. Anyhow, we talked to every skipper on the island, but no one had an opening. When we were down to our last dime, we ran into a captain we'd met. He mistook us for someone else, told us to be at the docks at six a.m. to replace a couple hands he'd lost at sea. Said he had two half-share berths. We had no idea what that meant, but we showed up anyway."

He smiled again. "Your father took to it immediately. Me on the other hand..." He grabbed the pitcher, pouring himself a glass of tea. "...I was throwing up 'fore we left Chiniak Bay. Shaking like a leaf, too. Never could stand the cold or anything else in Alaska. And the work was brutal. We'd do fifty hours straight without sleep or a decent meal. But your dad thrived in those conditions. 'Fore long he was pitching crabs with the best of 'em!"

Stacy listened to every word, his expression wooden.

"Every week, we'd fill the boat, then empty the tank at Whale Pass. Cleared twenty-five grand apiece that winter. Sent most of it home to mom, then sailed to Newport, Oregon for repairs."

"Newport?" Stacy edged forward, his uncle nodding.

"Billy sliced up his hand one day, and the skipper sent him to the infirmary. Your mom was working there. And the rest, as they say, is history."

Stacy felt the need to add something. "It wasn't love at first sight."

"It was for Billy. Told me Helen O'Roarke was the prettiest girl he'd ever seen. And that he was gonna marry

237

her. 'Course, she didn't make it easy. Made him work for everything, especially that first date."

"He got her pregnant." It came out more accusation than fact.

"They loved each other, Stacy. It's important you know that." They traded stares before his uncle went on. "We shipped out in April. Billy got the call a few months later. News hit him like a falling crab pot. But he did the right thing, went back to Newport and married your mom immediately. In fact..." He grinned. "...I was the best man! First and last time I ever wore a tux." His grin disappeared. "After the wedding, I figured it was time to come clean. Your dad and I drained a bottle of whiskey, then I told him... 'I'm no fisherman, Billy. I'm a farmer.' He knew I hated the ocean, the ice, even the damn seagulls! I wanted to go home. The 'king' missed his 'kingdom'."

"Was he angry?"

"Disappointed's more like it. Looking back, it probably seemed like the whole world was crashing down on him. He was losing his brother, his newfound career, and his beloved Alaska."

"But he was gaining a family."

"That he was, Stacy. But I'm not sure he saw it that way...at least not then." He switched the glass to his other hand. "Your parents made a good go of it in Newport. Billy found work at one of the canneries. Provided for his family. And loved his boy." He moved forward. "He did love you, Stacy. He *does* love you."

Stacy looked away.

"Hard as he tried, the sea was too much for him. He had to look at it every day. Hear it. Smell it. When he couldn't take anymore, he convinced your mom to go back with him. But it was a huge mistake."

"My mother never told me we moved to Alaska."

238

"Doubt she would've. Those weren't the best of days. Your dad was gone all the time. And your mom couldn't stomach the weather. Six months in, they decided to move back to Oregon, but when push came to shove, Billy couldn't do it. He couldn't leave the place—the life—he loved so much." He sighed. "This is hard for me to say. And it's gonna be damn hard for you to hear. But I promised you the truth." He looked his nephew in the eye. "Your father loved you and your mom very much. But he loved the sea more."

Stacy stared at the man. It *was* hard to hear, but he needed to hear more. "Why did they tell me he died?"

"During those six months in Alaska, your mom got a good taste of what it's like to love a fisherman. The sea claims thousands of men, and makes thousands of widows in the process, the worry constant. She didn't want that for you. When your parents split, you were young enough to forget the few memories you had of your father. Your mom thought it was the best way— 'William Zwardowski died at sea.' She made Billy promise he'd never contact you. Made me promise the same thing. And after all that had happened, we didn't have the will to argue with her."

As the moon rose in the window, Stacy lowered his head. He'd come here to appease his mother, not learn his entire life was a lie. *How could she have done this to him? How could any of them?*

"I'm sorry, Stacy. You'll never know how sorry."

"Yeah, well..." Stacy stood, rubbing his eyes. "...I have to go."

His uncle rose from the chair, bones creaking. "I'd like you to stay. You can sleep on the porch tonight. More needs to be said. A lot more."

Stacy tried to argue, but his uncle wouldn't have it. An hour later, he found himself in the little bed, staring up at the stars.

They were so bright he wondered if they were real.

After today, he wasn't sure about anything.

\*\*\*

Stones of all sizes. Big ones for support. Flat ones for shims. Robert Zwardowski dumped the wheelbarrow, face glistening.

"What are you building this for?" Stacy probed, walking up with the dogs.

"Thought you were gonna sleep all day."

"Not in that sauna."

The man chuckled. "Your dad loved sleeping on that porch—but nothing else 'round here." He looked to the fields. "Billy hated this place as much as I loved it. Used to say he was gonna leave someday and never come back. I didn't believe him."

"He's never been back here?"

"Guess he's waiting for an invitation."

Stacy grabbed a rock. "Any method to this?"

"Trial and error is all." He pointed to a crevice, Stacy shoving it in place. "Half the time you gotta force 'em. Other half baby 'em."

"Seems simple enough."

They worked in silence for a time, Stacy making mistakes, his uncle correcting them. "Always wanted me a rock wall. Finally came up with a reason to build one. Got me a wily old fox getting into my chicken coop. Hoping this'll give the dogs a fighting chance to corner him."

Stacy stared at the hounds. One was asleep. The other scratched itself. It didn't look like either could corner anything. "Have you always lived here?"

"'Cept for my time in Alaska." He wiped sweat. "This is my home, Stacy. I couldn't imagine living anywhere else."

"And you own it?"

"*We* own it. Your father and I...and you."

"Me?"

He grabbed a rock. "Your mom ever tell you 'bout your heritage?"

"Well...I know I'm half-Polish."

"Silesian, actually. Ancestors came over from a place called Strzelce. Poverty's what drove 'em, along with taxes and cholera. Sometimes you just gotta pick up stakes and move on."

He shoved the rock in a gap. "First ones left in 1854. Sold everything they had and sailed to America. Spent two months on a cargo ship, eating what they could scrounge and throwing it back up." He shook his head. "*I* never woulda made it."

Stacy smiled, placing an L-shaped stone in an L-shaped crack.

"Things didn't get easier from there. When they landed, it took 'em weeks to get to Panna Maria. Some traveled by oxcart. Others walked—in wooden shoes, no less. They worked for the locals at first, sharecropping, sawing lumber, till they had enough money to buy land. Your great-great-grandfather bought this place for six hundred dollars. Built a house. Made it a profitable farm on guts and willpower alone."

Stacy looked over his shoulder. "Is that the same house?"

He nodded. "With a few key improvements. My father added indoor plumbing!" He laughed. "You would've liked my father. He was a writer, too."

Stacy's eyes widened. "But how—?"

"Your mom and I exchanged letters, not often, but enough. I never lost track of you, Stacy." He smiled, then went on. "Your grandfather wrote for a Polish-language newspaper, the *Nowiny Texaskie*, they called it. I've still got some copies. 'Course, my Polish isn't—"

"Wait a minute..." The puzzle was coming together. "...are you saying my grandfather was a reporter?"

"Along with a farmer, builder, and pretty good fiddler. But writing was his first love. He even penned a novel, in Polish." He paused. "He and your grandmother are buried up on that ridge, under the old oak."

Stacy looked to the horizon. He could smell the crops. Taste his own sweat. "Why do you say this place belongs to me?"

"When your great-great-grandfather bought this land, he vowed it would stay in the Zwardowski name forever. And it will." He climbed to his feet. "You know you're the first member of the family to earn a degree? That's what our forefathers came here for, a better life." He offered a crooked smile. "You're a Zwardowski, Stacy. We're family. And that means what's mine is yours. Forever."

Stacy stood, staring at a man who, before yesterday, was a complete stranger, yet now—unbelievably—was kin. But his uncle was right. They *were* family, regardless of the circumstances. And for now, that seemed like enough.

\*\*\*

He pushed the plate away, stuffed. Two rounds of pork sausage, corn on the cob, and watermelon would do that to a person. And now his uncle was serving cobbler.

"Are you trying to kill me?"

"Just feed you is all. You're too damn skinny." He added ice cream and sat, Stacy digging in. "Just like your father. He never could pass up dessert!"

Stacy wiped his mouth, looking back up. There was something he wanted to ask. "How did you know my mother died?"

"Billy wrote me." He glanced at the mantel. "When he sent that picture."

"How did *he* know?"

"Your mother and father stayed in close contact. A lot closer than she and I did. They traded letters five or six times a year. Phone calls. He even—"

"Wait a minute...they actually *called* one another?"

"Lotsa times. And Billy sent money. Your mom didn't always take it, but he sent it just the same. Gifts, too."

Stacy's mind was reeling.

"Speaking of gifts..." His uncle left the room. "I've hung onto this for years," he shouted up the hall. "Never had any use for it." He returned, carrying an Underwood No. 5—the exact twin of Stacy's. "My father gave this to me when I was ten years old. Gave Billy one, too." He set it down, Stacy eyeing the keys. They were *all* still intact. "He hoped we'd develop the same love of writing he had, but neither of us did. Guess it skipped a generation." He smiled. "Your grandfather would be so proud of you."

Stacy's chest ached, realizing for the first time the greatest gift he'd ever received—his beloved typewriter— had come not from his mother, but from his father. "I don't...think I can accept this."

"Of course, you can. You're the writer in the family. And you're lucky. Some folks spend their *whole lives* trying to find that one thing that makes them feel whole."

Stacy stared at the Underwood, thinking about *his* life. He'd dreamed of being a reporter for as long as he could remember. But as he'd come to find out, dreams and reality were *not* the same thing.

His uncle studied his face. Finally, "Your dad has a crease on his forehead. Right between his eyebrows. Gets real deep when something's weighing on him. You have it, too." Stacy looked up. "Billy would always tell me what was wrong—eventually. I'm hoping his son does the same."

Stacy swallowed. Something was wrong, all right— *everything* was wrong.

*But could he really expect his uncle to understand?*

"*SEE*," his mother urged.

"I've...uh..." He looked to the Underwood, then back to his uncle. "...seen some things...been a part of some things...that make it hard to go to work every day." There was no judgment in Robert Zwardowski's eyes, only concern. For the next hour, Stacy told him about Channel 8. About Toole and the Torch fires. His relationship with Katie. The Clarion Police. As he spoke, he felt the burden lighten. But the gnawing worry refused to go away. "I don't know what to do, Uncle Robert."

It was the first time he'd called him that, his uncle fighting a smile.

"The passion I had when I took this job is gone. I still love to write...to report even." He thought of Wilhelm's speech. "But 'the news business is changing'...into something I don't recognize. What we do isn't journalism. It's rhetoric on good days, out-and-out lying on bad. And worst of all, if my suspicions are right..." His voice trailed off, replaced by a howling dog.

244

His uncle walked to the desk, the other dog joining in—perhaps they'd finally cornered the fox. "My father wasn't much for advice, but he always got his point across." He opened a drawer, fishing out a newspaper. "This is the paper he wrote for. Read the words at the top."

Stacy stared at the fading text, all in Polish. He cleared his throat. "Powiedziec Prawde," he read, struggling with the pronunciations. "Zawsze."

His uncle smiled as if hearing music. "I'll translate it for you." He looked to the picture of his brother. To the fiddle his father played. To his great-grandfather's wooden shoes, the first in the family to touch U.S. soil. He turned to his nephew, a look of steel in his eyes. "It means, *Tell the Truth*."

If Stacy didn't know better, he'd swear the dogs quit howling.

And the earth froze on its axis.

"*Always*," the man added.

\*\*\*

The drive back to Clarion took hours. Along the way, Stacy's mind played scenes from the trip. So much had changed. When he drove to Panna Maria, he had no one. Now he had an uncle, a rich family history—and a father.

"You better write," Robert Zwardowski warned as he waved goodbye.

"You better hook up your phone," Stacy hollered from the road.

As he sailed up the interstate, he looked repeatedly at the newspaper, hearing his uncle's voice again and again— "*Tell the Truth. Always.*"

It was 1:00 a.m. when he rolled to the curb. He glanced at Long John Silver's, the place closed. So much for grabbing a bite before bed. Juggling his things, he

245

made his way to the house, noticing a sign in the neighbor's yard—*FOR SALE*.

*Hallelujah!* No more 'Redneck Earl'!

Clutching the Underwood, he pushed his way inside. The room was dark, the scanner humming softly in the corner. It was strange to be back here, to the place he'd called home for four months. But this wasn't home. The Zwardowskis had a home in Texas. A place of stability. Of permanence.

He closed the door and dropped his things. As he reached for the lamp, a knock came behind him. At this hour, it could only be one person, Julius' friend with another contraband delivery. Stacy hit the porch light—it still didn't work. When he cracked the door, a slump-shouldered man stared back, face in shadow. "Sorry ta bother ya. Truck died in the lot next door." His voice seemed vaguely familiar. "Wonder if I could make a phone call."

It was an odd request, but Stacy nodded anyway, turning for the phone. A violent pain shot through his head. He grabbed the chair on his way down, the room spinning like a carousel.

The man wielded the club again. "Ya stupid sum-bitch!" That voice. *Where did he know it from?* "I told ya we wasn't done, you an' me!"

Stacy stared at his attacker, blood marring his vision. "*Please...*"

"Beg all ya want, ya pile a' shit!" He cracked Stacy's outstretched hand, the pain mind-numbing. "Ain't nobody here ta help ya!" He hit him again, Stacy fighting to stay conscious. "Thought ya could make fools of us, huh?" He laughed, a disgusting little hog snort. "Oughta be more careful who ya go movin' next door ta. Like I said, we got brothers all over Texoma!"

It all fell into place. The voice. The elfin stature. 'Butch' Stark of the Ku Klux Klan. He laughed again, grabbing Stacy by the shirt and dragging him across the room.

"Never used m'nigger-knocker on a white man before!" He delivered another blow, kicking Julius' door open. "Guess it works on Polacks, too!"

Stacy wanted to fight back, but his limbs were unresponsive. Laughing like a sick clown, Stark hauled him into the room, hitting the light switch.

"I want ya lookin' at me when I gut ya!" Stacy focused on the razor in his hand, the world spiraling out of control. "I'm gonna enjoy this, ya nigger-lovin' bastard!"

As the man raised the blade, Julius leaped into view, bringing something big and orange down on his head. The accompanying thud was that of a pumpkin hitting concrete, Stark's eyes lolling as he slumped to the floor.

"Dude, are you all right?"

Stacy blinked, the room still spinning. "Where were...?"

"In the closet!" Julius helped him up, grabbing a towel to slow the bleeding. "I heard all the ruckus. Figured it was the cops comin' to bust us. So I hid."

Stacy sat on the bed. "But how...I mean...what did you hit him with?"

The cameraman smiled, holding a monitor wrapped in orange canvas. "My latest acquisition. Holds a charge up to four hours. Sweet, huh?"

Stacy nodded, still dizzy.

Julius glanced at the man on the floor. "Guess we should call 911."

"No..." Stacy pressed the towel to his head. "...that'll bring Clarion P.D." He pointed. "There's a card on the dresser in my room, with Marv Bridges' phone number. He'll know what to do."

"I'm on it, dude." As he turned, they heard Stark moan, the Klansman showing signs of life. Julius grabbed the monitor and clocked him again—no signs of life now. "Hey, Stace..." He checked his new gear for damage. "...you hungry? I got some pizza in the fridge."

# CHAPTER 14
## *September 1988*

*(NEWSWIRE):* *V.P. BUSH SHOCKS TV AUDIENCE BY CALLING SEPTEMBER 7$^{TH}$ PEARL HARBOR DAY ... FIRES CLAIM 4 MILLION ACRES OF U.S. FOREST ... ON SUCCESS OF MOVIE, 'BROADCAST NEWS', 'MURPHY BROWN' PREMIERES ON CBS*

It took thirty stitches to close the wounds. Stacy missed another three weeks of work, the first spent at Clarion Memorial, the next two at home. But his recovery, though slow and painful, gave him time to think. And plan.

There'd be no more rebellion at Channel 8. No disagreements with his boss. No insubordination of any kind. Not till he was ready.

"You did good today, dude."

Stacy's eyes moved from the darkness to the man behind the wheel. He never would've made it without Julius. Not only had the cameraman saved his life, he'd cooked his meals and swapped his bandages. He was a true friend. And so was Marv Bridges. When he got the call, the cagy undersheriff sent his cousin, Theo, a Quintoc County bailiff, to the house. The lawman called an ambulance, then dealt with Clarion P.D. himself. By morning, D.A. Ross Barton had charged the still-dizzy Klansman with attempted murder. Unable to post bond, Stark was moved to solitary confinement—apparently, he and his black cellmates weren't getting along.

"Mobil 1 to Mobil 6."

Stacy jerked to the voice. "Mobil 1?" Julius shrugged, his partner grabbing the handset. "Where are you, Larry?"

After a pause, "I'm taking care of a little business. But I wanted to tell you what a fine job you did today. I've seen a major change in you."

"Thanks, Larry." Stacy glanced at Julius. "The time off really helped."

"Glad to hear. You don't know how good it is to have you back on set. Healthy. Happy. The same old Bill Stacy."

"Thanks." He stared off into the night. "And thanks for talking to Thad for me. I'm glad we could finally bury the hatchet."

With the microwave down again, Stacy had been driving to Avalon every day, pushing the restraining order to its limits. After some closed-door negotiations—Stacy assumed cash was involved—Thad agreed to lift it. Since then, the reporter had filed his stories and appeared on set without incident, a model employee.

"That's what team leaders do. And that's why the Great 8 News Team is number one." Stacy nodded, having heard the news while he was out. KEGT had taken July Sweeps, finishing atop the heap for the first time in station history. "That reminds me, did you two get your bonuses?"

Stacy pictured his check. His name on top. Wilhelm's below. *Blood money.*

"Not yet."

"Didn't know how long you'd be out, so we mailed them to your house. You can expect more perks like this in the future." He paused again. "As long as you keep doing the right thing."

"Count on it, Larry. Mobil 6 out." He killed the two-way, easing back in his seat.

"Don't sound like the 'same Bill Stacy' to me."

"Just laying low, Julius." That's exactly what he was doing—a dog waiting for the fox. "How many fires while I was out?"

"Just one. Old Avalon High."

"Anyone hurt?"

"We been through this." They'd been through it, all right. In addition, Stacy had talked to Maghee. Made a trip to the site. And pulled footage from Channel 8's vault.

"First crew on scene?" Julius nodded, Stacy thinking. "That was almost a month ago, Jul. We're due for another. Winning the ratings is only going to make things worse. Toole doesn't want to lose his edge."

The cameraman sighed, turning up the radio. As Tracy Chapman sang *Fast Car*, he stomped on the gas, making it home in record time.

"See if our checks came, dude." Julius tossed Stacy the mail.

The reporter leafed through it, stopping at a plain white envelope. "Uh-oh."

Julius froze on his way to the scanner.

Stacy ripped the seal, pulling out a sheet of yellow paper. At the top was a photo from the *Gazette*—the dead janitor being wheeled from the elementary school blaze. Below was a row of pasted letters—*BACK OFF OR YOU'RE NEXT.*

"Jesus, dude...he knows where we live!"

251

"Of course, he knows where we live. It's *Toole*, Julius! And we can't afford to wait around for his next move anymore."

"What the hell are we s'posed to do?"

The phone rang, both men jumping. It rang again. "Go ahead, Jul."

He lifted the receiver, Stacy studying his face. "Uh-huh..." His eyes narrowed. His upper lip twitched. "...okay...got it." He hung up, hands shaking.

"Julius—?"

"It was him, dude...callin' from a payphone." Stacy was shaking, too. "Said he heard on the scanner...*fire*...at the trailer park south a' town."

\*\*\*

By the time they arrived, the blaze was contained. But unit twelve was a total loss, firefighters avoiding greater tragedy by dousing adjacent trailers.

As Julius skirted the caution tape, Stacy scribbled text. *Single unit. Two engines respond. Police cordon off scene.* "Hey, Jul, not too close."

The cameraman ignored him, rolling as he stepped through smoke.

"Fuckin' tape's there fer a reason!"

Stacy turned, meeting the baneful eye of Leonard Allenbaugh.

"You news folk"—he pronounced the words like 'pustules' or 'lesions'— "think you're above the law!" He glanced at the KPXZ news van, the cameraman assembling his gear. KYTF had yet to arrive. "Sure seems funny, Channel 8 always showin' up first. Almos' like ya know what's comin'." He spat tobacco, turning away. "Tell yer little sidekick he better watch it. Then again, maybe he'll get hisself killed, an' I'll only have ta arrest one a' ya!"

A half-hour passed, Julius taking unnecessary risks, Stacy worrying.

"Evening, Bill."

Stacy turned to see Gary Schnea in full turnout gear. Although he and his crew had extinguished the flames, smoke still billowed. "Looks like you've got this one under control."

"We do now. But it was pretty intense for a trailer fire."

"Any reason to think it's the work of the Torch?"

"I don't think so. The other buildings were old and much larger by comparison." He stared at the smoking trailer. "We see this sorta thing all the time. Guy gets drunk. Falls asleep with a lit cigarette. Next thing you know, he's shaking hands with St. Peter."

"Is that what happened here?"

"Looks like it. Neighbors say the guy's a real nut. No family. No job. Smokes like a chimney and stays drunk most of the time. My guess is, we'll find the body right where we expect to."

Julius slipped back under the tape. "The neighbors give you a name?"

"Not sure we—"

"Chief," his walkie-talkie crackled, "that's a ten-four on victim and location."

"Roger." The man lit a cigarette. "Coroner'll have to confirm this, of course, but we're assuming it's the owner. White male. Forty-six years old. Name on the park records..." He paused to blow smoke. "...is Trevor Carson."

Stacy and Julius locked eyes, guts smoldering like the charred tin in front of them.

***

253

The door flew open, Stacy rushing in. "How the hell do you open these things?" He grappled with a new CD. "Cellophane, cardboard, and now this damn—"

"Here, dude." Julius grabbed it, running a pick down the seal. "*Hearts and Bones*?" He stared at the cover, Paul Simon posing in front of a newsstand.

Stacy snatched it away, moving to the stereo. "There's a song on here we need to listen to." He loaded the disc and hit *PLAY*.

*"Oooh-oooh-oooh-oooh. Oooh-oooh-oooh.*
*Train in the Distance."*

"That the song dude played in the bar?"

Stacy nodded.

*"What is the point of this story?*
*What information pertains?"*

Julius grabbed his guitar and began to strum, Stacy straining to hear.

*"Everybody loves the sound of a train in*
*the distance.*
*Everybody thinks it's true."*

When the music faded, Stacy stared. "What do you think?"

"Good tune."

"I'm not asking for your *musical* opinion." He hit the *EJECT* button. "Carson said it was a metaphor. For 'finding the truth, no matter the cost'."

"Dude said lotsa things."

"And they're starting to ring true, aren't they?" He moved to the window, peering out on the tracks.

"Trevor Carson was crazy, Stace. His own neighbors said so. Ain't nobody knows what those lyrics mean but Paul Simon. And I doubt dude had any conversations with him. It's just a song, man."

Stacy turned, the light of a passing cruiser painting him in silhouette. "What if it's more than that?" He thought of the newspaper his grandfather wrote for. Of the words his uncle translated. "What if the train *is* truth? The thing we all lose sight of. Or worse yet ignore." His eyes widened in sudden realization. "Jesus, Jul, I haven't seen one train since I started working at Channel 8. *Not one*. And we live a hundred feet from the tracks!"

"Come on, dude. We've seen lotsa trains. You just ain't been lookin'."

"Maybe..." He stared at the CD, eyes burning. "...but the longer I keep writing these stories...keep feeding people trash...." He looked up, eyes full of resolve. "We *have* to tell the truth, Julius— 'no matter the cost'. And it starts with Larry Toole!"

"Okay, Stace..." He set his guitar down. "...but you've been lookin' for the truth on Toole for six months. And what have you got to show for it? A fire he reported in college. Some gas in his garage. Add it up and, yeah, it's somethin'. But it ain't enough. You need proof, dude. *Real* proof."

Stacy moved to the door, another police car cruising by. As light hit him again, he turned. "That's just what we're going to get."

***

"Might as well get comfortable." Stacy killed the engine.

"Tell me again why I agreed to this."

"Because it's going to work, Jul. That thing good to go?"

Julius raised the infrared. "Charged and ready."

"Good." Stacy hunkered down, staring through the windshield. "Now we wait."

Toole's house was the third on the left. From their oak-veiled vantage point, they could see his door, window, and driveway. If he decided to leave, they'd be on his tail in seconds.

"Dude, we could be sittin' here forever!"

"Not forever, Julius. Just till he makes his next move. And if my instincts are right, it won't be long."

"We've done some crazy things, but this here's the craziest."

"You mean the *smartest*! We're going to catch the Torch in the act, with video of him driving to the scene and setting the place on fire. You wanted proof. You got it!"

"Sounds too easy."

"It *is* easy. We've just got to stake him out every night."

"Every night?"

"It's the only way."

The camera op had heard enough. "If you mean it's the only way to get ourselves fired 'cause we're too tired to work, I agree. The only way to show people we're as crazy as Carson, you're right. I don't get it, dude! Why is this so important to you? Why are you so obsessed with the Torch that you're willin' to risk everything?"

Stacy was surprised by the outburst, but not the question. Julius had asked before. But providing the answer wouldn't be easy. He unhooked his seatbelt and stared at the darkness. There were pitfalls out there—huge pitfalls.

But he owed his friend an explanation.

"When I was little...I got picked on, Jul." He saw doubt in the man's eyes. "I wasn't always six-three. As a kid, I was the smallest one in class...and more often than not, the whitest." They traded stares. "We moved all the time, from one rental house to the next. I was always the 'new kid', moving into neighborhoods where everyone knew each other. And you know how kids are. If they already have friends, they don't want another, especially when it's a short white kid who's painfully shy. It made me an easy target, and without a father..." He paused. The phrase still hurt, despite his newfound knowledge that it wasn't true. "...there was no one around to help me protect myself."

He looked away, Julius waiting for him to go on.

"Worst place we ever lived was a little two-story on 78th. My mom and I lived downstairs. The landlady lived upstairs. Only time we ever spoke was when the rent was due, and believe me, the conversations weren't friendly. Anyway, there was this older kid—a black kid—named Dexter Monroe." Stacy paused again. He hadn't said the name in years, but it still produced the same results— sweaty palms, burning gut. "He liked to call me names, steal my books, hit me whenever he got the chance...he and his friends. I was the only white kid on the block. And he made sure I knew it."

Julius nodded, still listening.

"I don't blame them for what they did. Not anymore. They were just kids doing what kids do, lashing out at whoever's different."

"Don't make it right."

"No...but as you're about to hear, I'm in no position to judge." Stacy had never told this story before, at least not in its entirety.

"I heard one day that Dexter and his friends were looking to jump me. I spent two weeks tiptoeing around, hiding out in the house." He remembered the feeling of being trapped. "I was going crazy, Jul. So when my mother left for the store, I figured I could sneak out without anyone seeing me. I was wrong."

"How bad they get you, Stace?"

"Pretty bad. There were five of them. And they'd been saving it up for a long time. Not sure what would've happened if she hadn't come home." He paused to think. "Maybe it would've been better."

"What do you mean?"

"When she pulled Dexter off me, she ripped his shirt." He looked his friend in the eye. "His back was like yours, Julius—scars, welts. What he was going through at home was far worse than what he was putting me through."

"Ain't no excuse."

"Maybe not. But it changed the way I looked at him. Just how much, I was about to learn." He paused for a breath. "That night, I couldn't sleep. My body ached with all the blows I'd taken, but more than anything else, I couldn't shake the image. *That poor kid*, I kept thinking. There had to be something we could do, some way to help." Despite the heat, he shivered. "That's when I smelled smoke. I thought I was imagining it at first, but it got stronger...and then I saw it, curling into the room."

His mouth went dry. He licked his lips to continue. "I ran to the door, but there were already flames behind it. My only hope was the window. When I got there, I saw him, standing across the street with a gas can in his hand. Smiling and crying at the same time. I've never seen anyone more tortured, more at war with himself than that boy, that night. It made me go weak in the knees." It still did. "When he saw me looking at him, he turned and ran. It was the last time I ever saw him."

Julius shifted in his seat. "How'd you and your mother get out?"

"I crawled out the window and helped her out hers. We screamed for the woman upstairs, even tried to find a ladder...but it was no use. The fire devoured everything in its path."

"Jesus, dude."

"We sat on the curb...nothing but the clothes on our back and the few things we'd stored in a garage nearby ...watching the firemen. When the sun came up, they pulled the body out. It was just a bag with a zipper, but I knew what it was...knew what it meant."

"Ever tell anyone what you saw?"

A tear slid down Stacy's cheek. "I never did. I couldn't hurt that boy any more than he was already hurt...couldn't do what I know I should've. But somebody died, Julius ...somebody's mother...somebody's grandmother. And I did nothing!" He wiped the tears from his face. "I've had to live with that my entire life."

They stared into the night, Julius breaking the silence. "Right or wrong...ain't nothin' you can do 'bout it now."

"A few months ago, I would've agreed." His eyes moved to Toole's house. "But now I think maybe there is."

\*\*\*

Two weeks of surveillance passed without incident, Stacy and Julius surviving on Jolt Cola. Their efforts had yielded just one opportunity with the infrared. Toole left his house one night to buy a copy of the *Enquirer*. Still, the stakeouts weren't totally fruitless. Stacy had proven once and for all that Larry and Katie were sleeping together.

"How long've they been in there this time?"

Julius shrugged, surprisingly quiet tonight. Stacy assumed he was tired.

"Sure don't try to hide it, do they?"

"Doubt they know their coworkers are out here with a camera."

"You'd think they'd be a little more discreet, that's all."

"What *difference* does it make?" Julius barked. "So your old lady's screwin' the boss. Welcome to TV news!"

Stacy set the camera down. "Okay, what's eating you?"

"This is a *crapshoot*, Stace! You don't know who the Torch is. Nobody knows!" He removed his glasses, wiping sleep from his eyes. "Look...I understand why you're doin' this, even admire you for it. But if you ask me, Toole ain't even the best suspect."

"He's the *only* suspect!"

"You're forgettin' Maghee's theory, dude. 'Bout the other Channel 8 employees. Twitchell, Meeks, that Raul freak I shot poundin' his pud in the park." Stacy tried to respond, but Julius kept talking. "Maghee said the Torch was out for revenge. What if it's someone tryin' to *frame* Toole? Like that ex-con from Coalgate?"

"Russell Longdale?"

"Why not? Dude spent time in the joint 'cause a' what Toole did." He slipped his glasses back on. "And if it ain't him, how 'bout Carson. He sure had reason to frame someone at Channel 8. S'pose he set them fires, then off'd himself accidentally, just like Schnea said. Think about it, dude, there ain't been one fire since he checked out!"

"You don't believe that, Jul."

"I'm just sayin' the Torch could be someone else!"

"The Torch is *Larry Toole!*"

Julius frowned. "When you get an idea in your head, there ain't no pryin' it out."

Stacy smiled—his uncle had described William Zwardowski that way. "So are you going to tell me what's wrong, or do I have to 'pry it out' of you?"

Julius hesitated, then pulled a letter from his pocket.

Stacy stared at the Cousteau Society stationery. "Is this what I think it is?" Julius nodded, his upper lip twitching. They were offering him a job on the *Alcyone*, an ocean-going vessel with Cousteau's latest invention, 'Turbosails', designed to replace fuel. Julius was to join the crew in France for a yearlong documentary shoot, Cousteau signing the letter himself. "This is incredible, Jul. It's everything you ever—"

"I gotta leave in a week-and-a-half."

Stacy froze as the realization struck him. That's why Julius was acting so strange. He'd been sitting on this for days, not knowing how to bring it up. *He was leaving, for God's sake!* The thought was more than Stacy could bear, but he faked a smile. "It's all right, Jul. Hell, it's better than all right. It's fantastic!" Deep down, he meant it. "And don't worry about me. When Toole screws up, I'll be out of here, too. I might even hop the Atlantic and come visit. They have to give you shore leave, don't they?"

Julius grinned, clearly relieved. "Thanks, Stace." He stuffed the letter back in his pocket, then looked to the house. Several minutes passed before he spoke again. "How come you came over that night, back when we lived in Avalon?"

Stacy thought for a moment. "It wasn't easy, Jul. With what happened to me as a kid, I had some preconceived notions about black people. Notions I'm not proud of."

"I wasn't exactly keen on white folks either, dude."

Stacy smiled, the cameraman returning it. "If you want to know the truth, it came down to this. At the time, I thought you needed a friend." He studied the man in the passenger seat. "But now I know, it was the other way around."

\*\*\*

How they ended up at Wilhelm's ranch was a bit of a mystery, but beer was involved, as was Jim Beam. Stacy had insisted on cutting the stakeout short. After all, Toole wasn't going anywhere—not with Katie on top of him.

"I thought spyin' on Toole was the craziest thing we ever did!"

Stacy giggled, passing the bottle. "I can't let you go to France till we finish what we started six months ago—find a cow and tip iss ass over!" He powered up the infrared. "And we're gonna catch it all on video...for posterity!"

The pair laughed like winos, sharing the hooch as they crossed a moonlit field. Both reporter and cameraman needed a night to blow off steam. And cow tipping seemed like the answer.

"This time, we're going *nowhere near* the house!" Stacy pointed to the shadowy woods. "Thass where we're headed! You see anything on four feet, knock it down!"

"Dude..." They started laughing again. "...we get in those woods, I won't be able to see *four feet* in front a' me!"

"Sounds like good video to me!"

Still laughing, they shared one last drink.

"And remember, Jul—"

Before Stacy could finish, the man took off, his drunken partner scrambling to catch up. As they reached the woods, the sky darkened, Julius running like a blind man. Stacy followed, eyes moving from black landscape to green viewfinder.

"Shit, dude!" Julius caromed off a tree, Stacy laughing so hard he nearly dropped the camera. "I told you this was crazy!"

"Keep going, Jul!" They made their way down a culvert—no cows—then up an embankment—still no cows.

Julius tripped, Stacy howling as he struggled to keep him in frame. *NIGHTTIME FUN—Volume 3* was off to a great start! Before Julius left for Europe, Stacy would have to burn a copy.

"*Cows beware! Julius Candelle is coming!*"

The man scurried uphill, then roared down the other side.

As Stacy reached the crest, he heard a thud, then silence. "Julius?" He panned left to right. No sign of his friend.

"Down here, dude."

Stacy peered through the lens, seeing nothing but dense forest and heavy bramble. "Where are you?" They'd traveled half-a-mile, the trees growing thicker with every step. If there *were* any cows here, they were silent, the air ripe with rot.

"I'm stuck in a damn hole!"

Stacy tilted, seeing Julius' head covered in leaves. "Hold on," he snickered, zooming in for a closeup. Julius looked disgusted but unhurt. "You okay?"

"I think so." He fixed his glasses. "Help me outta here."

Stacy reached for his arm, stopping as he saw something in the viewfinder. Julius was in a hole, all right, but it was manmade. "Jul, can you see?"

"If I could see, would I be stuck in a fox nest?"

Stacy dropped to a knee. "This isn't a fox nest, Julius. Feel the edges." The man reached out and touched the boards, the hole a perfect square.

"What the—?"

"I don't know, but it wasn't put here by accident." Stacy leaned down, aiming the infrared—Julius was standing on a set of stairs. "There's something down there, Jul."

"Oh, yeah?" He struggled to move. "Then get me *off* it!"

"Will you relax!"

"Relax, my ass! You ain't the one stuck in a hole!"

Stacy zoomed past his feet, studying the hard-packed floor. "I'm going in."

"You're doin' *what*?"

The reporter muscled his friend out, then moved into the vacant space.

"Hold on, dude! You got no idea what's down there!"

"That's why I'm going in." He widened his shot.

"Think about it, Stace. If Wilhelm built this thing in the middle of nowhere, he don't want nobody in it!"

"And that's supposed to keep me out?"

Julius sighed, peering into the darkness. "Stacy?" He heard footsteps below. "Dammit, dude!" Swinging his legs back in the hole, he inched his way down. "Where the—?" He slammed into his friend's back, the effects of alcohol long gone for both.

Stacy moved forward, staring at the viewfinder. "It's some kind of equipment shed." He panned slowly. There was a wooden bench. A shelving unit. A two-drawer file cabinet. He ducked to clear the six-foot ceiling, Julius bumping his head.

"Ouch...gimme that thing!"

"Hold on." Stacy zoomed on a shelf to see paper bags, packing peanuts, a jar of paste. He checked to make sure he was still rolling—he was. The next shelf held a pry bar, some Styrofoam cups, and a roll of Saran Wrap. He swept the camera over a long thin pole, then focused on the bench. A pair of glasses fitted with miniature lights sat on a legal pad. Next to the pad were scissors, a pack of KOOLs, and a *People Magazine*, its pages littered with missing letters. "My God!"

"What, Stacy? *What?*"

He passed the infrared, Julius seizing it like a life preserver. As the cameraman zoomed, his heart began to drum. "Jesus, dude!"

"It's Wilhelm, Jul!"

"Jesus, dude!"

"Wilhelm's the Torch!"

"Jesus, dude!"

"Why didn't we see it? Why didn't we figure it out?"

"We gotta go!"

"No!" Stacy snatched the camera back.

"But he might already know we're here!" Stacy moved to the file cabinet, kicking a gas can. "The place could be wired! Or booby trapped!" He opened a drawer, rifling through files.

One was marked *MILL*, another *WAREHOUSE*, a third *HOSPITAL*. Each held blueprints, a red checkmark at the top. Stacy leafed through more folders, shooting close-ups of all of them. *ELEMENTARY SCHOOL. COUNTY JAIL. HIGH SCHOOL. TRAILER PARK.* "I *knew* it!"

"What, Stacy?"

"He killed Carson! There's a file on the trailer park. A file on all of them! And they're..." He paused, looking back over the tabs. "...*in order!*" He slammed the drawer, opening the one beneath it.

"Come on, dude!"

"Wait a minute."

"We might not *have* a minute!"

Stacy pulled the first file from the stack. If the top drawer was in order, why not the bottom. After all, Wilhelm was the most anal person he'd ever met. He zoomed in on the tab—*COURTHOUSE*. "I know what he's hitting next!"

"Please, Stace—"

"He's going to hit the courthouse! The Dexter County Courthouse!" Shutting the drawer, he moved the gas can back in place.

"But how—?"

"We just struck oil, Jul! But as good as this evidence is, it's all circumstantial. And it won't be enough. Not with the power Wilhelm wields in this town." He pushed his friend upstairs, Julius offering no resistance. "We need to catch him at the scene. Get a clear shot of Wilhelm torching the courthouse!" When they made it to the top, Stacy killed the camera. "Come on. Let's see if we can find our way out of here."

"First smart thing you said all night!" Julius bolted, Stacy one step behind him. When they reached the car, both were out of breath, neither one having seen a cow.

\*\*\*

The town square was quiet, same as it was the night before. Stacy sipped coffee, handing Julius the camera. They'd been sitting outside Flip's Deli for hours. So far, they'd seen three cats and a stumbling drunk. Not exactly headline material.

"Think he's onto us, Stace?"

"No, he's just waiting..." Stacy blew steam. "...for the right opportunity."

Stacy had missed *his* opportunity to talk to Roy Maghee. The investigator had flown to Atlanta for a two-week 'Cause & Origin' seminar and wasn't taking phone calls.

"This one won't be easy. Not with his target in the middle of town."

"Easy or not, he better hurry."

Stacy understood—the cameraman was leaving in three days!

They stared at the courthouse. It loomed like a castle on the moor. "Why do you think Wilhelm's doin' this?"

"Same reason we thought Toole was doing it." Stacy set his mug down, Julius checking the infrared. "Want to

266

hear something funny? First week on the job, he gave me his 'TV's a Visual Medium' speech, said 'pictures are everything', the 'more graphic, the better'. At one point, he actually told me viewers go crazy 'for fires'!" He shook his head. "Wish I'd listened."

"I got the same speech, dude." A car rumbled past, pausing at the *YIELD* sign. "Hard to look at this thing, huh?" Stacy's eyes moved from car to courthouse. "Knowin' we gotta sit by and watch it burn."

"We've got no choice, Jul."

They sat in silence for a time, tracking shadows.

"So...you packed and ready to go?"

The cameraman shrugged. "Gotta pawn my furniture ...but, yeah, I'm ready."

Stacy scanned the grounds. He and Julius had covered the Klan rally here, crossing paths with 'Butch' Stark for the first time. Stacy had come to Julius' aid that day. Months later, he'd return the favor a million-fold.

"Dude..." Julius stared at the viewfinder. "...was that car there before?"

Stacy squinted. There were three vehicles across the way—a custom van, a work truck, and a black sedan. "Which one?"

"The one on the left." He zoomed in, studying the image. "Tinted windows, nice rims. Looks like a new Mercury...maybe a Lincoln."

"*Wilhelm's* got a Lincoln!" Stacy seized the camera. It was a Lincoln, all right, but it was empty. And tired as he was, he couldn't remember if it was there before or not.

"Dude!" Julius pointed to something on the lawn. It looked like a shrub—except it was moving. "Gimme the camera!"

Stacy hit *RECORD*, handing it off. "What is it, Jul?"

The cameraman focused, watching the shape take form—it was a man, dressed in dungarees and a black

267

turtleneck. He held a paper bag in one hand, a pole in the other. Julius zoomed on the face. Beneath a stocking cap, a large forehead protruded, casting shadows over the eyes and mustache. "It's *him*, dude!"

Stacy's heart leaped in his chest. "Are you sure, Jul?"

"Hell, yes, I'm sure!"

"Zoom!" Stacy erupted. "*Zoom!*"

"I'm *already* zoomed!" He braced his arm against the door. "And if you'd stop movin', I might get some usable footage!" He followed Wilhelm up the walk, widening his shot to include the man's gait—the more points of I.D., the better.

"What's he doing?"

"Looks like he's casin' the joint." The man ducked under a willow, reaching in his pocket for the Kelly Tool. "He's got somethin', Stace." He moved to a service door, slipping the blade between the lock and jam. Seconds later, he disappeared inside. "*He's in!*" Julius started to power down, but Stacy stopped him.

"Let it run, Jul! We need this in 'real time'." He widened his shot to include the building, their hearts hammering in stereo. A minute passed, five minutes, the wait unbearable. It felt like everything—the cats, the distant traffic, the whole damn world—was waiting with them.

Then they smelled smoke.

"Julius—?"

"*I got him*, Stace!" He framed the arsonist as he ran for the Lincoln. When the car pulled away from the curb, Julius zoomed on the plate.

"Did you get the license? *Did you get it?*"

"Hell, *yes*, I got it! Clear as day!"

"*We did it, Jul!*" Stacy gushed. "Are you *sure* you got his face?"

268

"Like he was posin' for a portrait, dude!" Julius started to giggle, as did Stacy. But the sound of exploding glass stopped them. The stately structure was already ablaze, every window spitting hellfire. As alarms sounded, they thought of all the records inside, the irreplaceable photos. They felt guilty for their giddiness.

"Base to Mobil 6." They looked at each other, frozen. Toole couldn't know about the fire—not yet. "Come in, Mobil 6."

Stacy reached for the handset. "Mobil 6 here."

"Where the *hell* are you? I've been calling your house for half-an-hour!"

"The...news car broke down, Larry. We're on our way home now."

"Fuck *home*! I need you in Durl. They just busted a meth lab there." He rattled off directions. "Now move your asses before Channel 2 scoops us!"

"Ten-four."

Julius lowered the camera. "We can't go chasin' meth labbers, Stace! Not with the footage we're sittin' on."

Stacy peered into the fire, thinking. "Durl...that's Quintoc County. *Sheriff's* jurisdiction, not Clarion P.D." He turned to his friend. "Bridges knows those guys. More important, he trusts them. We'll shoot the bust, then hand the infrared footage over to them. Wilhelm'll be in jail by dawn!"

Julius grinned, flames dancing off his spectacles.

It was over. *Over!*

"Well, what the hell we waitin' for?"

\*\*\*

The scene was eerily similar to the one Stacy covered in January. Sheriff's cars and OBN vans lined the road, lights exposing a rickety old shack. "Mobil 6 to Base."

269

"Go ahead, Stacy."

"We're here, Larry. Are you going to send the live truck?"

"No, the Torch just struck again! Burned down the fucking courthouse! Can you believe it?" They could. "We're going live as soon as Brannuck gets the truck up. Just package the meth bust and hold it for noon."

"Will do." He replaced the handset. "He thinks *that's* a big story. Wait till he sees what we've got!" The cameraman nodded. "You ready?"

"Ready as ever, dude."

They left the Escort, meeting a throng of officers in the yard, the air thick with chemicals. "'Morning, gentlemen." Jim Peters of the Oklahoma Bureau of Narcotics stepped forward, hand out. Stacy took it, recognizing the man from their last meeting. "Nice to see you again...uh..."

The reporter hesitated, wondering if this was the last time he'd ever have to use his TV name. "Bill Stacy. Great 8 News."

"Yes, of course, *Bill*." The man's eyes shifted to Julius, the camera op grabbing a white balance from his shirt. "Shoot anything you want, boys. The people of Oklahoma need to know there are consequences for breaking the law, and that we at the Bureau are watching. This is the twelfth meth lab we've taken down this year."

As Julius headed off, Stacy opened his Steno, mind elsewhere. They'd solved the Torch crimes and were about to hand the evidence over to authorities. Evidence that would send Dick Wilhelm to prison—or worse. After all, two people were dead. And the G.M. was solely responsible. It was almost too fantastic to believe!

"We received a tip last night. A local farmer..."

Stacy looked past him, keeping an eye on Julius. He'd meant to tell his friend to be careful, remembering what

Bridges said about lab dangers. But Peters wouldn't stop talking. Julius was fifty feet away now, shooting through a split-rail fence.

"...that's when we moved in."

Stacy nodded, watching an officer separate glassware. "What did you...discover at the scene?"

"The usual. Listening devices, bear traps..." Stacy saw Julius near the porch, shooting a mountain of cans—chili, Spaghettios, refried beans. *Not too close, Jul.* "...no electricity or running water..." Stacy's mind strayed back to the courthouse, the images forever burned in his memory—the flames, the smoke, the Lincoln pulling away. "...of course, we're experts in this field."

Stacy forced himself to focus. "Can you tell me about the suspects?"

"We arrested four—"

"*Julius!*" He excused himself, bolting across the yard. "What are you doing?"

An agent was helping him into a HAZMAT suit. "What's it look like I'm doin'?"

"Exteriors only, Jul."

"Relax, dude." He flashed a radiant smile. "Ain't never got to wear one a' these. And this might be my last chance."

"We don't *need* to take chances." He lowered his voice. "Remember what we've got in the car."

"How could I forget, dude? But I'm still gettin' paid to get the best footage." He zipped his suit. "And right now, the best footage is in there!"

"Jul—"

"It's okay, Stace." He shouldered the Sony. "I live for this shit!" As the agent shoved a mask over his head, Julius winked through the plastic window. A moment later, he was gone.

Stacy's gut churned as he rejoined Peters.

271

"Where was I?" the man asked.

The reporter glanced at his notes. "The suspects?"

"Oh, yes. Four males. All wanted..." Stacy stared at the front door, hoping his partner was showing caution. *Just shoot the minimum!* "...Nolan Simms of Sapulpa..." Two agents made their way outside, carrying a vat of sludge. "...'Turk' Winterbrook of Tahlequah..." An officer paused near the window, adjusting his breathing apparatus. "...Cesar Jimenez of Weleetka..." Stacy glanced at his watch. *Come on, Jul!* "...and Percy McCarroll of Roff. All four were taken..."

There was movement on the porch, someone in a yellow suit backing through the doorway. Stacy held his breath. As the man turned, he offered a little wave, his lens reflecting the first light of dawn. Relief washed over the reporter, but as he raised his hand to respond, a brilliant flash came, followed by a sonic boom.

The explosion knocked Stacy to the ground, the world turning white around him.

"*Julius!*" he screamed, but the roar of the fire swallowed it. He staggered to his feet, horrified by the scene before him. The shack was gone, replaced by a wall of green-orange flames, smoke rising to the heavens.

As officers fled, some on fire, others purging their lungs, someone grabbed his arm. Stacy wheeled, hoping against hope it was Julius. *He'd survived everything, hadn't he?* The tornado. The abuse from his parents. The—

"We gotta get outta here!" Stacy focused on the face, begging it to be Julius'. But the man clutching his arm was Jim Peters, face black with soot.

"*No!*" Stacy broke free, storming the burning ruins. "*Julius!*" He peered into the flames, smoke stealing his breath. "*Juliuuuus!*" He had to be okay—*had to!* The fire thundered like an oncoming train. "*Juuuliuuuuuuuuus!*"

Two powerful hands grabbed him, a fireman dragging him to safety. The blaze had reached its apex, launching green pinwheels fifty feet in the air. Stacy watched in horror, tears drying as fast as they spilled.

He'd swear later, the fire had a face. With wicked eyes and an ugly mouth that offered no explanation—and no apology—for taking his friend.

# CHAPTER 15
## October 1988

*(NEWSWIRE): SPACE SHUTTLE 'DISCOVERY' COMPLETES FIRST MISSION AFTER 'CHALLENGER' EXPLOSION ... 'SHROUD OF TURIN', THOUGHT TO HAVE COVERED CHRIST, FOUND TO BE FRAUD ... KIRK GIBSON'S WORLD SERIES HOMER CARRIES DODGERS PAST A's*

The graveside service was the saddest thing he'd ever witnessed. A bargain-basement casket. Twelve empty chairs. And a single wreath, the same model Wilhelm sent for Helen Zwardowski—Avalon Floral was a long-time sponsor. Stacy was the lone representative from Channel 8. "It'll be easier that way," Toole said.

*Easier for who?* It was the hardest day of Stacy's life.

He shook hands with the pastor, the funeral home providing his services for an extra hundred bucks. Stacy felt compelled to pay it in case someone else showed up. No one did. No one from the Oklahoma Bureau of

Narcotics. No one from the Quintoc County Sheriff's Office. No one from Julius' family.

Stacy had called James Candelle personally. The man listened, asked if there was money left after expenses, and promised to attend his son's funeral. He didn't. Neither did Roy Maghee and Marv Bridges. Stacy was sure they would have, but Maghee was still in Georgia, and Bridges had driven to Branson, Missouri with his wife.

"Remember, son..." The clergyman glanced at his watch. "... 'the Lord is near the discouraged, and saves those who've lost all hope.' Psalms 34:18."

"Okay." It was the only response Stacy could muster.

After an awkward hug, the man walked off, Stacy's eyes glued to the grave site. The coffin had been lowered at the end of the service. Workers would return in an hour to cover it with dirt. He stood there, shivering, not knowing what to do next.

*What could he do?*

His best friend was gone.

After a beat, he stepped forward, clutching a bag to his chest. "I'm...sorry, Jul." He knelt, staring at the particle board coffin. "If I hadn't dragged you into this, hadn't been so stubborn, maybe you'd..." He choked on his words, bowing his head and crying. It wasn't the first time. He'd spent the last three days in a tear-filled stupor, blaming himself, playing the 'what if' game. He'd found no answers.

"You deserved better, Julius." He looked up, wind stirring the overhead leaves. "A better life." His eyes moved to the empty seats. "A better send-off." He looked back to the casket. "A better friend."

Another wave of sorrow struck—it came in unseen torrents, racking his body and strangling his heart. As the tears flowed, he shook his head in disgust. *What had*

276

*Julius died for?* A story. An insignificant piece of data stuffed between fire and rape on the evening news. In the grand scheme of things, who would remember it?

*Who would remember Julius Candelle?*

Stacy would. Forever.

He reached in the bag for the *Strong Persuader* album. Robert Cray looked up at him, grinning, full of life. Stacy wanted to remember Julius that way. He dropped it in the grave, then pulled out the 8 X 10 of Jacques Cousteau. The black-and-white photo was Julius' most prized possession. It seemed fitting that he take it with him.

Stacy held onto it for as long as he could. But as the wind picked up, the picture slipped from his hand, drifting like a feather to the coffin below. "Peace, Jul."

\*\*\*

The light on the answering machine flashed, a beacon in the fog. Stacy stared at it. *Did he really want to hear the messages?* Shaking his head, he turned for the bedroom, but something stopped him—Julius' guitar. He pictured his friend playing it, the image more real than he wanted to admit. As the Jul of his mind finished a riff, he looked up and smiled— "You need to listen, dude."

Stacy turned to the machine. After a breath, he walked over and hit *PLAY*.

*Beep.* "Stacy. Larry Toole. I know how close you and Julius were, so take as much time as you need. When you come back, I'll have a replacement—"

*Replacement?* Stacy hammered the *ERASE* button, another beep sounding. "Oh, sweetie..." He knew the voice, as did most of Texomaland. He killed Katie's message without listening.

*Beep.* "Just got back ta the office and heard the news." There was a long pause. When Bridges continued, his voice wavered. "I'm sorry, son. Julius was a good fella. A good friend." Tears welled in Stacy's eyes. "I know you're hurtin', but there's somethin' ya need ta know. We just got word from Clarion P.D. They've issued a warrant for your arrest. Three counts a' arson in connection with the Torch fires." Stacy's jaw dropped. "Allenbaugh says he can place ya at the scene a' the last fire. Says he's got surveillance photos ta prove it. Now I don't know what that bastard was doin' outside my courthouse, but I do know one thing. You ain't guilty! So if you're fixin' to do somethin'—anythin'—ya best do it quick!"

The unit beeped again, but Stacy didn't hear. He grabbed the machine and heaved it across the room. "*Has the world gone mad?*" The scanner came next, flying through the air and exploding against the wall. "*Why'd you have to die, Julius?*" He kicked the TV, tube shattering as it hit the floor. As the circuits sizzled, he raced to the window, searching for cruisers. "*Jesus, Jul! What am I—?*"

His eyes locked on the Escort, zeroing in on the Great 8 logo.

"We're going to give viewers more," Toole's speech echoed in his ear. "Entertain them, dazzle them, shock the hell out of them if we have to."

A faint smile crossed his lips, the answer hitting him like water from a fire hose.

Julius was *not* going to die in vain.

He moved to the phone and dialed. "Newsroom."

"I need you to do something for me, Larry."

"Stacy?"

"I need you to send Brannuck and a camera op to Clarion with the live truck." He glanced at the clock. "I've got an exclusive for noon."

278

"But you're not even—" Toole paused, his interest clearly piqued. "What kind of exclusive?"

Stacy smiled again. "One Texomaland will never forget. But I don't have time to explain." He reached for his coat. "Just send the truck. I'll be at the City Limit sign north of town."

The reporter hung up, knowing full well the truck would be there. Toole couldn't pass up an opportunity like this. The temptation was too great. After one last look at Julius' guitar, he bolted for the door.

\*\*\*

Chip Hale fired up a cigarette. He hadn't eaten since hearing about Julius. He preferred smoking his meals, then chasing them with alcohol.

"Two minutes," the floor director barked.

"You coming?" Amy Chow asked on her way to the booth.

Chip waved her on, pouring himself a cup of coffee. He was hungover again. In fact, he was still drunk.

"You get the changes?" Toole handed him a script. "You look awful."

"I *feel* awful." The disheveled T.D. puffed on his cig. "Place has a way a' doin' that to ya."

"I know people who'd give their right nut for your job." Chip walked off, Toole checking his makeup. Reg McNair, who now anchored at noon, was out on assignment this morning, his boss filling in. Perfect timing, as it turned out, for Stacy's exclusive.

At the Clarion City Limit sign, Don Brannuck feverishly swapped cables. His head was already on the block for failing to solve the microwave problem. One more screw-up and he'd be punching the clock at

Uniroyal. "I got it!" He poked his head out the door, patch cables everywhere. "One minute, Bill!"

Stacy stepped from the weeds, taking his place beneath the sign. When he arrived at Channel 8, he couldn't have imagined doing what he was about to. That Stacy and this Stacy were two different people.

"This is insane!" Rich Martin was shaking, having turned the color of his OU sweater. "I've got a career to think about. They're gonna fire me if—"

"They're not going to fire you, Rich. Just frame the sign and pull out when I give you the signal."

The cameraman refused to move. "I won't do it."

Stacy stepped forward. "Look, *Rrrrrrrich*, I've had a bad week." He lowered his voice. "Either you do this, or I'm going to kick your ass on live TV!"

The man looked up at him. "I think you're bluffing."

"Do I *look* like I'm bluffing?"

The flustered camera op looked away. "I...guess not."

"Thirty seconds!" Brannuck loaded a tape. "They need a sound check, fellas."

Stacy held out his hand.

After a gut-wrenching sigh, Rich passed him the microphone.

\*\*\*

"Okay, people," the director spoke into his headset. "We're going to bump the lead and go live after the intro." Chip sat to his left, head pounding, Amy to his right. Each stared at the overhead monitors. Number one held a wide shot of the set, number two a low angle of Thad, number three a medium shot of Toole, and number four a close-up of the Clarion sign. "Stand by, Larry."

The anchor shuffled scripts, working his eyebrows into the appropriate concerned position.

"Fifteen seconds."

Thad checked his teeth for chives.

"Ten."

The audio tech waited. "Stand by, live truck."

"Standin' by," Brannuck responded.

"Five...four...three..."

"Ready intro." The clock hit twelve. "And roll intro." Chip punched the *TAPE* button. *Whoosh.* Flying states. Synthesized beat. "Get ready, Texomaland!"

Stacy listened through his IFB. "Yeah...*get ready*," he whispered.

"...the news starts *now!*"

"And take three. Cue talent."

Toole leaned into camera. "One journalist is dead. Another flees from justice." It was the first time he'd ever read a Bill Stacy lead-in verbatim. "I'm Larry Toole. A shattered community looks for answers today. Answers in a senseless death. Answers to a devastating crime spree. Answers from the man allegedly responsible." A monitor rose over his shoulder, the Clarion sign filling it. "Reporter Bill Stacy joins us live from Quintoc County. Bill, I understand you've got those answers."

"Ready four." Chip reached for the switch. "And take four."

The Clarion sign went full screen, Rich cueing Stacy. "Larry, I'm standing just outside the city limits..."

"Son of a bitch!" Leonard Allenbaugh spilled coffee in his lap, then reached for the radio, legs on fire. "All units! Proceed north a' town immediately! Bill Stacy's on live TV, reportin' from the turnpike!"

"The sign behind me, as you can plainly see, includes the town motto— 'See Things Clearly in Clarion'." He signaled Rich, the reluctant camera op zooming out to include Stacy in the foreground, his face in extreme close-up.

"What's he doing?" The director stared at the monitor. "Pull out, Rich!"

No response.

"My hope is that every one of you will see things clearly after this report." He tossed his notepad aside. "When I came here last summer, I believed in the media. Believed in what we do. Believed in who we are. I believed in the truth."

The director turned to Amy. "Where's he going with this?" She shrugged.

"At one time, our credo at Channel 8 was 'News You Can Use'. And, true, our newscasts weren't flashy. Weren't full of glitz or scandal. Weren't even very interesting at times. But they informed the viewer. Provided him with the truth, no matter how mundane." He shook his head. "Unfortunately, that philosophy earned us a last-place finish in the ratings and got a good man fired."

"He's rambling, for God's sake! Ready camera three."

"No," Toole intervened. "Let him go."

"Today, our task is no longer to 'inform' the viewer, but to 'entertain' him. That's a direct quote from our illustrious G.M." Wilhelm sat bolt upright in his office. "TV's a 'visual medium', to further quote the man. And 'pictures', preferably graphic pictures—dead bodies, drug raids, fires— 'are everything'. I've been told people 'eat this crap up'."

The director swiveled. "Did he say *crap*?"

Chip raised a hand to cover his smirk.

"Our news director, the man at the anchor desk right now..." Toole straightened. "...thinks you, the viewer, want to be dazzled, bowled over, bullshitted!"

"We've gotta pull the plug—"

"No," Toole ordered.

"He thinks you want a newscast that resembles the *National Enquirer*. And the owner agrees. They think shows like *Entertainment Tonight*, *A Current Affair*, *Geraldo* are the signposts to the future."

"Goddammit!" Wilhelm stormed out of his office.

"So in the name of cutting-edge television, we've brought you conflict, hyperbole, melodrama. If stories were vanilla, we spiced them up. If they weren't controversial, we made them controversial. We've falsified interviews. Faked live shots. And when we ran out of news to air, we created news."

"Jesus Christ, Larry, let me kill this thing!"

Toole shook his head, refusing to turn from the monitor. This was great TV!

"And in the process, people have been hurt." Stacy looked to the ground. "People like Julius Candelle. My friend. He died for the ideals this station, and countless other stations across the country, are preaching. 'Shock TV'. Sensationalism. Winning at all costs." He looked deep into the camera. "He died for nothing."

Wilhelm sprinted down the hall.

"And now, the Clarion Police want to arrest me. They want to put me on trial for the Texomaland Torch fires." Employees rushed to monitors. Salespeople dropped their phones. "I'm not guilty of these crimes. But I am responsible. And so was Julius. Katie Powers. Thad Barton. And Larry Toole. So is everyone at Channel 8, everyone who bought into this dangerous muckraking philosophy. And didn't say anything. Didn't do anything."

Wilhelm reached the staircase, gasping for breath.

"And you're responsible, too, folks. You, the viewer. You may not have asked for this. But you're watching in record numbers. You're saying to the program directors of this country, 'Give us more!'" He pointed to Rich, the man zooming out again.

Stacy was wearing no coat. No tie. No shirt.

The director froze.

"And I'm warning you..." The shot continued to widen, Stacy wearing no pants, no underwear—*no anything!* He stood there, feet planted in the Oklahoma soil, naked as the day he was born.

Every crew member gasped, Brannuck dropping his Fresca.

"If you don't change your viewing habits, don't stand up to the people in power and tell them to stop feeding you garbage..." He paused, glancing down at his exposed body. "...then you're looking at the future of television in this country."

"That's enough!" Wilhelm raided the control room. "Cut him off, goddammit! *Cut him off!*"

"Take three!" the director screamed. "Cue talent!"

Chip punched up camera three, the shot a close-up of Toole looking dazed. "I...uh..." He shifted in his seat. Twisted a cufflink. Tightened his tie.

For the first time ever, the garrulous anchor had nothing to say.

\*\*\*

As the first squad car arrived, he climbed in the Celica. Fully clothed now, there was no cause for panic. He'd expected the police—they were a crucial part of his plan.

"Step out of the vehicle!" the loudspeaker boomed. Stacy ignored it, starting the engine and pulling away from the shoulder. As two more units arrived, he drove off, heading back to town with the urgency of a tractor. All three cars screeched *U*-ies behind him, sirens wailing, lights flashing. In seconds, they were on his bumper. "Stop the car!"

He checked his speedometer—45 in a 50-mph zone. Navigating his way through town, he passed the KEGT bureau, the Lion's Den, the Quintoc County Courthouse.

As he cruised past the Clarion Police station, five more units joined the chase. Stacy ignored them, obeying all traffic laws, respecting all road signs.

"He ain't stoppin', Chief."

"Whadda ya mean, he ain't stoppin'?" Allenbaugh raised the microphone, spittle flying everywhere. "Take 'im down, goddammit! *Take 'im down!*"

"We can't shoot 'im, Chief. He ain't even breakin' the speed limit. An' b'sides, there's people everywhere."

Crowds were indeed gathering. In an effort to save his job, Brannuck had called in the story, Toole announcing the chase to a still-riveted noontime audience. As Stacy puttered through Clarion, people were actually cheering!

"All right then..." Allenbaugh smoothed the FBI bulletin he'd just mangled. "...tell me which direction he's headin'?"

"West on 89er." The cop glanced in his rearview mirror. "We got eight 'r nine units in pursuit. Think he's headin' fer the interstate."

The chief grinned, exposing long skunk-like incisors. "Then that's where we'll nail 'im! Stick to 'im like glue, an' lemme know if he changes directions. I'm gonna arrange fer a nice little OHP welcome."

Katie threw a fifty-dollar bill down and ran for the Mustang, hair dripping wet. Everyone at the Marseille Salon was watching when Bill Stacy appeared 'au natural'. "Why'd you let *that one* get away?" one of the stylists trilled. She didn't have time to answer. She had to find him.

"What the hell were you *thinking?*" Wilhelm roared like a lion, six employees cowering like mice. Five-and-a-half actually—Chip looked bored. "I want to know who made the decision to stick with that feed!"

285

The director looked to his associates, the 'mice' silent.

"It was my decision, Dick."

Wilhelm wheeled to see Toole enter the control room, expression matter-of-fact. "*Your* decision?"

Toole handed the C.G. op a sheet of paper. "I need you to make these changes for the six o'clock."

"How can you think of the six o'clock news at a time like this?"

"Relax, Dick." Toole loosened his tie. "You know as well as I do there's no such thing as bad publicity." He looked around. "Can you people imagine the numbers we're going to pull tonight? Tomorrow?" He laughed like a kid who'd just solved the Rubik's Cube. "After Bill Stacy's little 'exposé', our number-one rating is set in stone!"

"The only thing set in stone is the fine the FCC's going to hit me with! That's if they don't yank my license altogether!"

"That's not going to happen, Dick. If it comes down to it, Texomaland'll revolt!" He smiled. "Bill Stacy was right about one thing. The people want more."

There were twelve cars in pursuit now—two Quintoc County Sheriff's vehicles had joined the chase, as had news vans from KYTF and KPXZ. Stacy continued his trek westward, passing an *I-35 1 MILE* sign. He saw lights up ahead, counting cars as he approached—one, two, three. A pair of OHP troopers blocked the road, another guarding the northbound ramp.

"Stop the vehicle!" a trooper demanded over the P.A.

Stacy slowed, a line of glistening spikes directly ahead. He looked behind him. KYTF had pulled into the oncoming lane for a better shot. KPXZ was pinned in. Stacy nodded to the trooper, then made a hard left, bypassing the spikes and veering up over the berm—he

286

knew what the Celica was capable of, having explored countless logging roads back in Oregon.

"He got past the roadblock, Chief."

"He *what*?"

"Swerved off the road and went over a sand bar. Drove 'at li'l car like a dune-buggy. Shoulda seen them troopers' faces!"

"*Son of a bitch!*" The chief's head looked like something for the bomb squad. "Where is he now?"

"Gettin' on 35 south. We're right on his tail. Troopers, too. Weird part is, he ain't doin' but fifty. Almos' like he wants us to catch 'im."

Allenbaugh glanced at the map. "I gotta pretty good idea where he's goin'. Keep 'im in your sights. If he pulls over and tries to run, shoot him!" He grabbed his keys and bolted for the door.

Katie screeched into the lot, hair a wind-blown mess. She'd called Stacy three times, her ex-boyfriend refusing to answer. "Chip!" she screamed, leaping out of the car. "What in the world's going on?"

The weary T.D. sparked a jay. "Hey, Katie," he rasped, looking the woman over. She wore sweatpants and a *Dallas Cowboys* T-shirt, her hair extremely un-helmet-like. "That's a new look."

"Where's Stacy?"

"Headin' down 35, with a dozen cops on his ass!" He cracked up, taking another hit. "Toole just sent a crew."

"He did *what*?" Chip nodded, holding smoke in his lungs. "Sweet Jesus!" She stormed the station, her stoned coworker basking in the autumn sun.

The chase, if one could call it that, went on for more than an hour. At no time did Stacy exceed the speed limit. Nor did he place another driver at risk. Six years later, the world would watch a white Bronco evade capture in similar manner on live TV.

Of course, by then, they were used to such things.

"Mobil 2 to Base."

Toole reached for the radio. "Go ahead, Reg."

"We found the motorcade, Larry. Fifteen cars, counting the news vans!"

"Then start rolling. And make sure you get better footage than 2 and 7. Break the law if you have to. Remember, they're after *him*, not you."

"What the hell are you doing?"

Toole turned to find Katie in the doorway. "Well, don't you look lovely."

She touched her hair self-consciously. "Why are you doing this?"

"It's a news story, Katie. Last I checked..." He reached for a cigarette. "...that's what we do here."

"This isn't a *news story*. He's one of us!"

Toole struck a match and inhaled. "He's never been one of us."

"Mobil 2 to Base."

"I'm here, Reg?"

"He turned off the highway. At the last Avalon exit." A burst of static followed. "He's heading straight for the station."

Toole and Katie looked at each other. "Then I guess we'll see you soon."

Stacy stared through the windshield, oilrigs pumping on both sides. As he headed east, he thought about Julius. Through the tragedy of his friend's death, he'd found strength. And in that strength, forgiveness. Forgiveness of his mother. His father. Maybe even himself.

"Stop the vehicle!" a pursuing officer ordered. Stacy wondered why the cops—two Avalon Police units had just joined the chase—still bothered. Surely, they'd figured out his plan by now.

Up ahead, satellite dishes loomed, each casting a shadow over the *Great 8* sign. It suddenly dawned on him—he'd worked at Channel 8 for fifteen months, a 'reporter's average stay in a beginning market'. Smiling at the irony, he pulled into the lot, eighteen vehicles following. As expected, he found two Dexter County Sheriff's cars waiting, along with three fire units and Billy Nemetz's beat-up Mazda.

Stacy rolled to a stop, staring at the impressive gathering. Roy Maghee was there, just back from Atlanta. So was Gary Schnea, Ross Barton, and Marv Bridges. They'd apparently all gotten his messages.

He climbed out of the car.

"Freeze, scumbag!" The cop who'd led the chase drew down on him, his fellow officers doing the same.

Stacy raised his hands, sweeping his eyes through the crowd. Larry Toole had joined the fray. As had Katie, Chip, Thad....

...and Dick Wilhelm.

"I want this bastard arrested!" The angry G.M. separated himself from the mob, pumping a finger at his soon-to-be-ex-employee. But before he got his wish, another car screeched into the lot.

Allenbaugh leaped from the driver's seat, drawing a snub-nosed .38. "Hit the dirt!" he ordered, pushing his way through the crowd. "I said, *hit the goddamn dirt!*"

Bridges stepped in front of him. "That's far enough, chief."

The lawman stumbled, leering up at the deputy. "Outa my way, 'Barney Fife'. I got me an arrest warrant, an' there ain't no way some two-bit local sheriff—"

"Actually, I'm the undersheriff. And this here's *my* backyard." He pointed. "See that telephone pole?" The man turned. "It marks the end a' Avalon city limits. Makes this station jurisdiction a' the Dexter County Sheriff's

Department." He looked to his friends from the local P.D. "Not Avalon Police." He winked at his brothers from up north. "Not Quintoc County Sheriff's." He glared at the man in front of him. "And sure as *hell* not Clarion P.D." He turned, walking to Stacy's side. "If there's gonna be an arrest made here today, it's damn sure gonna be me who makes it!"

Toole signaled Jerry Feinbloom. The nervous camera op stepped past the others and zoomed on his coworker, an engineer racing up with two hundred-foot cables—the news director had given instructions to go live the second they had a signal.

Bridges turned. "Ya got somethin' to say, Stacy...ya best say it." He stepped aside, his fellow officers waiting, guns drawn.

Stacy walked to the Celica and popped the trunk, a pair of troopers cocking their rifles. He pulled out the monitor, dented from 'Butch' Stark's head but still operational.

"Where did *that* come from?" Wilhelm clamored.

Stacy carried it to the center of the crowd.

"This man soiled my reputation!" Wilhelm screamed. "*Arrest him, goddammit!*"

Stacy walked back to the car and grabbed the infrared.

"What the...*that's* not station property!"

He set the camera next to the monitor, attaching cables. Task complete, he rose to his feet, staring at Bridges. "With all due respect, undersheriff...I'm through talking."

He reached down and hit *PLAY*.

Allenbaugh was the first to approach, eyeing the monitor with laggard interest. Barton joined him. Then Maghee, Schnea, and Bridges. The other lawmen followed, as did Nemetz, all three news crews, and Toole.

The video from Wilhelm's underground shed aired first, complete with damning images and descriptive dialogue. Schnea and Maghee watched intently, Barton stroking his chin. Wilhelm stood on the nearby walk, too far away to see. "What are you waiting for? *Lock him up, goddammit!*"

The tape transitioned to an exterior of the courthouse. A shadow moved through the frame, Julius zooming on Wilhelm's face. The assemblage moved closer. As the shot widened, they all looked to the guilty G.M.

"What the hell are *you* looking at?"

Bridges stepped forward, cuffing Wilhelm's wrists. "Ya got the right ta remain silent."

"What in *God's name* are you doing?"

"Arrestin' ya for the Texomaland Torch fires." He clutched Wilhelm's arm, finishing the Mirandas as the man struggled for freedom.

"*Take your hands off me!*" Six cops moved in, making sure it was a struggle he didn't win. "*Do you know who you're dealing with?*" They forced him down the sidewalk, hands soiling his expensive suit. "*My family built Texoma!*"

Stacy watched in silence, as did the rest of the Channel 8 crew.

"What the fuck are you doing?" Toole screamed. Jerry winced, having lowered the camera. "Roll on this. *Roll on this!*"

The image of Wilhelm being thrown in a sheriff's car and hauled off to jail went out live to three-hundred-thousand viewers.

It seemed like the perfect ending—but it wasn't.

"This's all been *real* dramatic." Stacy turned to see Allenbaugh slither forward, gun in one hand, slip of paper in the other. "But I still got me a warrant for this man's arrest!"

Bridges pushed through the crowd. "I thought I told ya—"

"I know what ya told me, *undersheriff*. But a warrant's a warrant. And this here paper don't say nothin' 'bout grandstand maneuvers, hidden cameras, or incriminatin' films. All it says is I got the right to take 'im in!" He looked over his shoulder. "Ain't that right, Barton?"

The D.A. fingered his mustache, Stacy cutting his eyes to Bridges. For the first time all day, the undersheriff looked unsure. Ross Barton strolled over the asphalt, eyes down. "I'd say the chief's right." He looked up, making eye contact with Stacy, the reporter imagining his stay in Allenbaugh's jail. "In nearly all cases...but not this one." Stacy exhaled. "Although I don't necessarily agree with Bill Stacy's methods, he did something no lawman in Texomaland..." He turned to Allenbaugh. "...and that includes *you*, chief, was able to do." He paused, letting the 'jury' digest his statement, then turned for the car. As he opened the door, he looked back. "The D.A.'s office will not seek prosecution of Mr. Stacy in this case."

"Goddammit, Ross!" Allenbaugh stormed over. "If we can't arrest 'im fer the fires, how 'bout fer indecent exposure? Evadin' arrest? Reckless endangerment, fer Christ's sake? He led my men on a wild damn goose chase all over the state!"

"To repeat..." He waited for Jerry to zoom. "...the D.A.'s office will *not* seek prosecution of Mr. Stacy in this case. Or any other case."

A few people in the crowd cheered. Allenbaugh looked like he'd swallowed a gerbil. After a loathsome pause, he leered at Stacy, his expression, which vaguely

292

resembled 'Butch' Stark's, saying, 'We better never cross paths again!'

Stacy could guarantee it. That chapter of his life was over.

As Barton drove off, the chief climbed in his car and followed. Ten minutes later, they were all gone—police, troopers, deputies, media. Only Stacy's coworkers remained. He walked to the Celica and pulled out his gear. The Ikegami 730. The 3/4" deck. The tripod, batteries, and mic. He piled everything up on the sidewalk, then turned to his boss. "Consider this my resignation, Larry."

Toole stepped forward, Katie peering over his shoulder. "Hold on a minute, Stacy." The man offered a wicked smile. "You don't have to leave. The board'll have a new G.M. in place tomorrow. We won't even skip a beat!" He glanced at his employees, then back at Stacy. "I wasn't sure, but after what I saw today, I think you still have the makings of a star reporter. In fact, I've never met anyone with the balls to do what you did—no pun intended." He laughed. Stacy didn't. "You're the hottest thing to hit Texoma since the Torch himself. You're on fire, kid! People'll be talking about you from Dallas to Oklahoma City! You're going to be more famous than I am!" He leaned in. "And that means we've gotta strike while the iron's hot! We can ride this thing, you and me. Ride it all the way to the top. I'm talking *Good Morning, America*! *60 Minutes*! *The Tonight Show*, for God's sake! There's no telling how far we could take this." He put his hand on Stacy's shoulder. "What do you say, kiddo?"

Stacy stared at the man, then looked past him. His coworkers waited for a reply, Thad frowning, Chip sparking another joint. Katie peered through the smoke, eyes unreadable. He looked at her for a moment, then back at his boss, considering a million responses. He chose the simplest. "No thanks."

293

As he turned for the car, Toole shadowed him. "You're making a mistake, Stacy! Opportunities like this don't come along every day!" Toole grabbed his arm as he reached for the door. "If you walk away from here, you'll never work in this business again! I'll make sure of it."

Stacy shook his head, feeling almost sorry for the man. Wrenching his arm free, he climbed in the car.

"You're *blowing it*, Stacy! Do you *hear me*?" He started the engine. "You're pissing away the best chance you'll ever have to *be somebody*!" He stared at Toole through the open window.

"I *am* somebody, Larry. I'm Stacy Zwardowski."

Dropping the shifter in gear, he punched it out of the lot, raising a cloud of dust behind him. As he disappeared up Main, his ex-coworkers filed back in the building. All but Katie, that is. For several minutes, she stood there. Watching. Waiting.

When he didn't return, she smoothed her hair and walked inside.

*\*\*\**

"Well, if it ain't the naked hero!" Marv Bridges and Roy Maghee made their way down the library steps, Stacy waiting on the sidewalk.

"Afternoon, gentlemen." The ex-reporter smiled, seeing his friends for the first time in a week. He'd been busy. While Bridges' cousin, Theo, stood guard outside the house, Stacy had cleaned, packed his things, and tuned up the Celica. It took some doing, but Clarion was finally a memory.

"*Gentlemen*?" Bridges looked to his fellow lawman. "Who's *he* talkin' ta?" The undersheriff cackled, Maghee thumbing through a book.

294

"Wouldn't have taken you for a Judith Krantz fan, Roy."

The man stared at the emasculate cover. "Checked it out for the wife. Got us an anniversary coming up. Figured since I was here—"

"—an' too damn cheap to *buy* 'er a copy!" Bridges reached in his pocket for a Winston, offering one to his friend.

Maghee shook his head. "Another gift for the wife. Told her I'd quit if she cut up her credit cards." He watched longingly as the undersheriff struck a match. "Damned if I thought she'd go through with it."

Bridges blew smoke, then turned to Stacy. "Thanks for meetin' us here. Couldn't let ya go without askin' ya somethin'." He leaned against a pillar, crossing his arms. "How'd ya do it? Figger it all out, I mean?"

"I didn't...not intentionally anyway. Julius and I..." He hesitated—the mere mention of his name still hurt. It would for a long time. "We stumbled onto the shed. Just a couple drunks out looking for trouble. Truth be told..." He looked at Maghee. "...I thought it was Toole. Would've bet my life on it. Guess my reporter's instincts weren't as sharp as I thought they were."

"I wouldn't say that." Maghee tucked the book under his arm. "Larry Toole was an excellent suspect. Fit the profile to a tee. Cunning. Attention-seeking. We looked at him long and hard." As a young couple passed, he lowered his voice. "ATF installed a tracking device on his car. Put his house under surveillance. Even tapped his phone. 'Course, you didn't hear that from me. We checked out every tip you gave us, Stacy. The gas in his garage? Turns out he was cheaper than I am. Didn't like paying the high price of fuel on Lake Texoma, so he stockpiled it for the boat."

"We never saw a boat."

"Time you were there, it was in for service."

"But what about the late-night phone calls? And the hours he kept? We watched him for weeks, Roy. He never slept a wink."

"When we tapped his line, we found out he was getting calls from your G.M. right before he got on the phone with you. That's what got *us* thinking about Wilhelm. That and the fact that Toole never left his house on the nights of the fires."

"He was too busy," Bridges jumped in. "Snortin' cocaine. Man's got a helluva drug habit, Stacy. Ain't no one could sleep with 'at much powder up his snout."

Stacy looked from one to the other. "Unbelievable."

"What's unbelievable is how we were able to connect the two."

"Toole and Wilhelm?"

Maghee nodded, glancing at Bridges. "Looks like that fire you told us about, the one that killed Toole's wife, was no accident. Wilhelm set it." Stacy's face went flush. "Seems she wanted to move closer to her parents back east. Wilhelm wasn't ready to lose his ace reporter, so he torched the place with her inside." Smoke curled from Bridges' cigarette. "We can't exactly prove that yet. But we're working on it."

Stacy felt sick to his stomach. "What about the dorm fire?"

"Looks like just a coincidence. Guess he deserved the 'Valor Award'."

"Maybe *then*..." He thought of all the sordid things his boss had done, the things he'd asked his employees to do. "...but never since."

"You were right on motive, too. At least partially. Wilhelm did set those fires for ratings. It was a formula he'd tested in other markets—Lubbock, Odessa, Corpus

Christi. ATF's got records of Torch-like crimes in all three cities, all while Wilhelm was acting as general manager."

"But I don't get it..." Stacy thought of Wilhelm & Son. "...why would he torch his own family's buildings?"

"That's where it gets complicated. Our criminal psychologist believes he had *two* motives in the Texoma fires—greed and revenge."

"Revenge?"

"You know about the wills, right?" Stacy nodded, remembering what Katie and Bub told him. "When his father and grandfather left their money to charity, Wilhelm felt slighted. So he decided to exact his own payment. And what better way—at least in *his* twisted mind—than to destroy everything his father and grandfather created."

"And fill his own pockets in the process," Bridges added.

Stacy stared at the library. The structure was a masterpiece of twentieth-century architecture—columns, scrolls, ornaments. If not for a failed fuse, he'd be staring at a vacant lot. "What's going to happen to him?"

Maghee fished for a cigarette, stopping himself. "Too early to tell. His lawyers are weighing the evidence right now, evidence we feel pretty strongly about. Not only do we have your videotape, we've got his prints on the timing device and threatening letters. My guess is, we'll see a plea to avoid the death penalty."

Stacy thought about Trevor Carson, of the horrible death sentence he'd received. "Doesn't seem fair."

"That's the system." Maghee glanced at a passing FTD van. "Think maybe I'll go pick up some flowers. You two got me thinking this book isn't enough." He extended a hand, Stacy taking it. "Keep in touch."

"Will do, Roy." He walked away, leaving Stacy and Bridges alone.

The undersheriff dropped his cigarette, looking down as he stepped on the butt. "Stacy...there's somethin'..." He looked up, clearing his throat. "I had me a son once." Stacy's eyes widened. "Jake was his name. Football player. *A* student. An' the best friend I ever had...other than the wife, a' course." He tried to smile but the effort fell short. "He...uh...passed away, see? An' there ain't been a minute since...that I don't think about 'im ...miss 'im...wish I could do things over." They stared at one another, the noise of the street fading away. "This may come as a shock...but you look like 'im. A *lot* like 'im, in fact. Even sound a little like 'im—minus the accent."

Stacy nodded—*so that's why Bridges was always looking out for him.*

"When I first saw ya on TV, I figgered God was either playin' a cruel joke...or givin' me a second chance...ya know, an opportunity ta right some wrongs." His eyes narrowed. "But now I know that wasn't the case. You ain't Jake, Stacy. I didn't realize that—*really* realize it—till that day at Pearl's, when ya spread that napkin in your lap." He chuckled. "In all m'years a' fatherin', I never could get Jake ta use a napkin. 'Why should I,' he used ta tell me, 'when I got two perfectly good sleeves?'" They traded smiles. "Anyhow, I'm tellin' ya this, 'cause I think ya were sent here for a reason. Ta make me realize Jake ain't never comin' back. An' ta make me see that that's okay. I still got me a lot ta do in life. An' someone damn special ta do it with." He swallowed hard, eyes moist but full of hope.

Stacy held out his hand. "Thanks for everything, Marv."

Bridges took it, the pair shaking for a long time. Finally, "I best be goin', too." The undersheriff looked up the street. "Me an' the wife're gonna clean out Jake's room ...take some stuff over to Goodwill. Then I reckon I'll start on that gazebo." He smiled, a sad but reposeful smile,

Stacy returning it. As they moved up the sidewalk, Bridges turned. "I b'lieve Jake woulda liked you."

Stacy nodded, eyes glistening. "I believe my mom would've liked you, Marv."

They shook hands again, much being left unsaid.

"Make sure ya write." Stacy promised, Bridges watching a gaggle of geese fly by. "So, where ya headin' anyhow?"

"I'm not sure."

It was a lie. For the first time ever, Stacy knew exactly where he was going.

***

"I will...I promise." He leaned against the payphone, staring at the Safeway sign. "Love you, too, Uncle Robert."

A gust of wind shook the plexiglass. He zipped his jacket and headed inside. Safeway had purchased the Super-K Market six months ago, the previous owners unable put the mass shooting behind them. The corporate giant hoped a new name and shiny makeover would help people forget. It seemed to be working.

Stacy grabbed a cart, filling it with junk food. "Is that the man on TV?" a toddler asked. His mother shielded his eyes and ushered him away.

Apparently, they'd seen his final report.

As shoppers stared, he reached for a bag of Bugles, Fleetwood Mac's *Go Your Own Way* playing over the Muzak. He couldn't wait to be 'invisible' again. Fame, even on a small scale, had its price. He knew that now.

"Y'all ready to go?" a checker spoke up.

He steered the cart to her register, noticing how cheery everything seemed. It was hard to imagine the scene he'd covered here just fifteen months before.

"Twenty-three-fifty."

Stacy reached for his wallet. "Oh...do you have maps?"

"Every state in the union." She pointed to the rack behind him. He grabbed one, handing it over. "Alrightee..." She punched a few more keys. "...twenty-four even."

He paid in cash, the checker thanking him. As he wheeled his cart to the Celica, he heard a siren, the noise growing louder as he loaded the groceries and climbed inside. A fire truck passed, followed by two police cars. For the first time in a long while, he didn't care where they were going.

"Good afternoon, Avalon. This is Nigel Henry with a KAVN news up—" Stacy killed the radio. As he drove out of the lot, he saw the Ferndale Apartments up ahead. He pulled over and stared. Same nondescript units. Same empty lots on both sides. Nothing had changed, yet everything had changed. He looked to the last unit on the left, the place he'd called home for nearly eight months. He'd watched himself on TV here. Made love to Katie. Drank beer with Julius.

He'd come of age in this place. And he'd never forget it.

After a long pause, he drove away, wanting to see the station one last time. Stacy slowed as he approached, the place looking as harmless as it always did—but he knew better now. He wondered who'd arrived to take his place.

*Good luck, kid. You're going to need it.*

He drove to the interstate and headed north. In no time at all, he was passing the Arbuckles. Katie and Bub were right. There *was* a certain beauty to the timeworn range, a quiet dignity. It was a dignity he'd take with him on the journey, one that would complement the memories —good and bad—of his life-altering experiences here.

As the road straightened, he glanced in the backseat. Both Underwoods were strapped down safely, Julius' guitar between them. He'd never part with any of these things. They were as much a part of him as the heart in his chest, the blood in his veins.

Turning back to the horizon, he heard something, indiscernible at first, then clear as the road ahead. In one ear, his mother's voice— "Follow your heart, Stacy"—in the other, his uncle's— "Tell the truth. Always."

He smiled, then reached for the map in the passenger seat, reading the lone word on the cover. *ALASKA*.

# Epilogue

He stared at the screen, needing an ending. The right words would come, he told himself, if he just stayed out of the way. And listened.

"Two minutes," he heard in his IFB. He glanced at the camera and nodded. He was used to multitasking—writing, researching, doing radio and television interviews. He'd devoted his life to such things.

A knock came at the door, a twelve-year-old boy invading his home office. "How much longer, Dad?"

Stacy smiled, his son's face a mirror image of Helen Zwardowski's. "Few more minutes, bud." The boy sighed and left. Billy Zwardowski was so much like his father, stubborn, persistent, his sister the polar opposite.

Stacy had waited a long time to start a family. Truth is, he wasn't sure he wanted one. Not with the job occupying so much of his time. Of course, he had no one to blame but himself. When he started the business in 1990, it was the only one of its kind.

'The Naked Truth' provided fact-checking services for media outlets all over the world. Based in Kodiak,

Alaska, Stacy—as an initial army of one—launched a Web site a year later, the precursor of companies like Snopes and Politifact. Since then, he and his employees had worked diligently to expose every distortion, fabrication, and falsehood out there, the company motto—*Tell the Truth. Always.*

"Last segment, Mr. Zwardowski," the voice came again.

Stacy cleared his throat, glancing at his mother's photo, the typewriters on the shelf, Julius' guitar against the wall. CNN's bumper music filled his ear, followed by the voice of a cheeky late-night anchor. "If you're just joining us, Stacy Zwardowski is here to discuss the state of journalism today."

On the monitor, a C.G. listed his titles—*Author & "Fact" Checker.*

"Before the break, you said you had a warning for us."

"That isn't—"

"I certainly hope you're not here to defend the *ex-*President."

Stacy smiled—a Fox News anchor had asked him the same thing when the *last* President took over.

"I'm here to defend the truth."

"Thirty seconds."

"I don't necessarily like the term 'fake news', but we in the media—"

"We?" the man interrupted again, sneering.

"—have certainly earned it. We've swapped objectivity for opinion." A ticker ran below his face—*APPEARED NUDE ON LIVE TV*. "Injected bias into our stories." It continued to roll—*ONCE ACCUSED OF ARSON*. "Taken sides on every issue. And if things don't change—"

"Out of time," the man cut him off. "Thank you for joining us, Mr. Zwardowski. And good luck with the new book."

"Clear."

Stacy shook his head. Another interview. Another 'journalist' trying to quash the message. Sometimes he wondered if it was worth it. He glanced at his watch—11:00 p.m. His family had waited long enough.

"Surprise!" Stacy froze as he left his office, the living room packed with friends and neighbors. He found his wife among them, hoisting two Molsons.

"I thought I said no surprises."

Celia Zwardowski passed him a bottle. "Since when do I listen to you?"

*She had a point.* "Despite all this..." He took a sip. "...I still love you."

And he did. They'd met in '89. A grad student at the University of Alaska, Celia was working on her thesis, 'Crab Fishing and the Environment', having pissed off every fisherman in the Aleutians. They didn't like her questions, but she was sure easy on the eyes. And she could hold her own in a drinking contest, too.

Stacy fell in love with her instantly.

At the time, he'd given up all hope of a news career. But Celia forced him to see things differently. She was the one who suggested a fact-checking service. "What better way to fight for truth?" she'd asked. Two years later, with the business flourishing, they married in a traditional Silesian ceremony.

"Happy Birthday, Daddy!" Ala Zwardowski hugged her father's leg, eyes as blue as the nearby Gulf. She wasn't used to staying up late.

"Why, thank you, Alie." He picked her up and held her, surveying the room. The Nielsens were there—not the ratings family, but his neighbors up the street. So were the

305

Kjensruds, Murphys, and Changs, the island a diverse collection of locals and transplants.

It was one of the things Stacy loved about it. His father was another.

"Happy Birthday, old man." Stacy stared at William Zwardowski, his hair a gray mop. Like his son, he was a survivor, having lived through arctic storms and financial busts. He'd even survived the return of a son, a son he'd lost but never forgotten. Their relationship was solid now, but putting it together took time. There were tough questions and difficult answers, their reunion unlike the ones on TV. But in the end, they came to a conclusion—the future was more important than the past.

"*Old man*?" Stacy shook his head. "You'll notice *I* don't have any gray hair."

The elder Zwardowski glanced at his grandchildren. "You will."

"Great party, Stace." Stacy flinched—he'd never get used to that voice. It was so much like Julius' it hurt. It also nourished his soul.

"Glad you could make it, Jaron." Julius Candelle's younger brother had come to Kodiak thirty years ago—and never left. Stacy had managed to get Jaron and Jessie away from their father, offering a fresh start in Alaska. Jaron went to work for Stacy's dad, eventually buying his own crab boat, the *Jewel*. He made a good living, owned a house, and was waiting for the right woman to come along. His sister ran the Sea Life Center in Seward, having earned a Marine Biology degree. She and her husband visited often.

"Where's the remote?" Irv Nielsen barked, staring at a wall of TVs. "I wanna watch Seacrest!"

Stacy hit the power button, all nine units leaping to life. For a guy who once smashed his only television, it was strange to own a medley. But it came with the job. Over

306

the years, he'd watched good and bad coverage of every news event, from the fall of Communism and 9/11 to the election of Donald Trump. Along the way, he'd witnessed such televised sludge as *Jerry Springer*, *Survivor*, and *Real Housewives*. While doing so, he thought of just one thing—Dick Wilhelm was right. He knew exactly where TV was headed.

"Time to open gifts!" Celia led her husband to the couch, Stacy having a pretty good idea what was coming. The first present was a bottle of Geritol, the next a pack of Depends, the last an aluminum walker with tennis balls for feet.

"Gee, thanks, everyone." Laughter caressed his ears, warmth from the fireplace filling the house. There was no place he'd rather be.

"I almost forgot, you got some cards." The first was addressed to *The Old Geezer in AK*. Marv Bridges had retired and moved to Missouri, where he lived on Table Rock Lake with his wife, Kaye, and two bird dogs. The next came from Roy Maghee, who still lived in Avalon, still worked as a fire investigator—and still smoked. The last card was straightforward and simple, just like the man who sent it—*Happy Birthday* on the cover, *Love, Uncle Robert* inside.

"Turn it up!" Jaron pointed to the stereo, Billy hiking the volume. As The Gap Band played *Party Train*, Celia danced with her daughter, Stacy watching in amusement.

Till an idea blossomed.

He slipped back in his office and closed the door. His other books had all been essays, ranging in topic from media ethics to not-so-hidden bias. But this one was different. When Trump took office, 'fake news' became part of the American lexicon. The term—often used but loosely defined—pointed to everything from Internet fluff to political attack. But where did it all begin?

307

Stacy knew.

It began in Avalon, Oklahoma. Biloxi, Mississippi. Rockford, Illinois. Like a Phoenix, it rose from the ashes of the Fairness Doctrine, growing on television, exploding on the Internet. Along the way, news agencies like MSNBC and Fox took clear positions on the left and right, while CNN and other networks followed suit. The result? Unbiased reporting was dead, or at least on life support. And worst of all, no one seemed to care.

Stacy leaned forward, reading the last few lines of text.

*In one ear, his mother's voice— 'Follow your heart, Stacy'—in the other, his uncle's— 'Tell the truth. Always.'*

*He smiled, then reached for the map in the passenger seat, reading the lone word on the cover. ALASKA.*

He paused, organizing his thoughts. This book *was* different. It was a memoir of sorts, a look back as a means of looking forward. And a caution to us all.

He took a breath, then began to type.

*As he looked up, he saw something. Smoke. From a freight train. Its engine chugging tirelessly for the sun. He thought about Trevor Carson. Of the train he sang about. And the* truth *it stood for.*

*He smiled, hitting the gas.*

*After all this time, Stacy had found the elusive train. And he was gaining on it.*

He reached for the mouse and hit *SAVE*, then hurried back to the party.

# ABOUT THE AUTHOR

S.W. Capps is a former TV news reporter. Since leaving the world of glitzy sets and pompous anchors, he's spent much of his time on two wheels, exploring the country via motorcycle and writing about it. His features have appeared in *Rider*, *RoadBike*, and *H.O.G.* magazines. He lives with his wife and 'investigative' dog in the Pacific Northwest, currently at work on a new novel.

## Other Exquisite Fiction from D. X. Varos, Ltd.

*Chad Bordes*
The Ruination of Dylan Forbes

*Therese Doucet*
The Prisoner of the Castle of Enlightenment

*Samuel Ebeid*
The Heiress of Egypt
The Queen of Egypt

*G. P. Gottlieb*
Battered
Smothered

*Jeanne Matthews*
Devil by the Tail

*Phillip Otts*
A Storm Before the War
The Soul of a Stranger
The Price of betrayal
*(coming Oct. 2021)*

*Erika Rummel*
The Inquisitor's Niece
The Road to Gesualdo